EVERYTHING
FADES
IN
TIME

Everything Fades in Time

Matthew McConkey

Broken Tribe Press

For Warren...
that typewriter meant the world to me.

CONTENTS

ALL THAT WAS LEFT BEHIND

THE ATTIC HAD NOT EVER BEEN a place where people went and stayed for a measurable amount of time. The most human activity the place upstairs ever saw was when someone, usually Jeb, the family patriarch, put something up in storage; which usually meant it was not ever going to see the light of day again. The attic had become a place where material things went to retire; things that were once bought and proudly displayed throughout the house or used until something better came along, ended up in the cemetery of those once *needful things*.

The attic was enormous, dusty, and old. It was like a place in the house that time had forgotten; a place for junk in other words; things that should've been taken to the landfill or given away decades ago. Old paintings sat helter-skelter, propped up on their ends leaning against small end tables along the walls. There were boxes upon boxes stacked floor to ceiling with writing scribbled on them to tell what the contents inside were. That was June's idea, the matriarch of the family. She was always full of them.

The dust inside the attic was measurable, to say the least. Brooklyn, standing there in the middle of the attic beside her brother, guessed it had been years, maybe even decades, since anyone had been up in the attic. She looked around the attic and all its relics of the past.

"When do you think the last time someone was up here?" Dan asked, looking in awe at all the stuff.

"I bet not since Pop died last year. You know Mom wasn't coming up here." Brooklyn walked over to the far end of the attic and pulled a sheet cover off what was a table and a lamp underneath it. She looked at the table and lamp and couldn't for the life of her remember seeing it in the house. Could have been something that was given to her parents as a wedding gift or something they bought when they first got married and needed furniture. Who knew for sure? Not Brooklyn.

"Probably right," Dan replied, waving dust from his face that flew in the air from the sheet. "Come to think of it, I don't think Mom ever came up here. She made Pop do all of that."

Brooklyn walked slowly around the sprawling attic, "Where's it at I wonder?" she asked, looking down at the floor.

"Where's what?" Dan looked around the attic and felt momentarily overwhelmed at all the junk; "organized chaos", their dad called it.

"The hole? You remember that Thanksgiving when Pop fell through the ceiling in the dining room?"

Dan smiled, "Yup, we were all eating dinner and he wanted to show Uncle Ernie something that was in the attic. So he gets up here and is fooling around and steps onto a weak spot and falls through the ceiling landing on the table. Classic." Dan and Brooklyn both laughed loudly. God, it had been a long time since the two of them had laughed together like that. It made Brooklyn feel all gooey inside, sending her back to a time when they used to play together as kids.

"He cussed for days about that, didn't he?" Brooklyn said absently as he kept walking around, looking for the patched hole. She found it. Although it was covered with dust, she could make out a piece of the attic floor that did not belong. The wood patch looked newer, not old like the rest of the attic floor. Brooklyn kneeled and swiped some of the dust away to give it a better look.

It was a piece of patched ceiling but as she touched it with her hand she could feel the connection with her father. He was here, years ago, holding and nailing this very piece of wood with his two bear-like hands. Brooklyn remembered the day that she helped him fix the hole in the ceiling/hole in the attic floor. She was his little helper that day, handing him nails when he needed them. That scene in her mind's eye caused her to smile and miss her dad at the same time.

"Hey sis, check this out!" Dan shouted as Brooklyn rose from her knees to see what her brother was wanting. "Here's where all our board games came to die."

Brooklyn walked over to her brother and the two of them started moving around all the games which by the looks of the boxes had seen their better days. "We've got Trouble...Monopoly...Battleship...Connect Four...Trivial Pursuit...Clue. God, remember when Pop would make you play Monopoly for hours until you or him was out of money?" Brooklyn said through her laughter.

"Yeah, I do. I remember a five-hour game once. You weren't home that night. I think you were spending the night someplace and Pop got bored because college basketball season was over and he asked if I wanted to play. I said 'sure'. Five..hours...later!"

"Oh cool...I wonder..." Brooklyn started as she pulled Yahtzee out of the game pile. She opened the Yahtzee lid and dug around the contents. She found an old score sheet that had their mom's name and the dates of the scores from the games on them.

"Yup, here's one of the last games we ever played. She beat me of course. Right here...1989. So long ago. I was, what? Ten on the night we played this game?" Brooklyn teared up at seeing her mother's name written elegantly in pencil on the upper right-hand side of the Yahtzee scorecard.

Seeing that his sister was about to cry, Dan leaned over and took her under his arm as he did most every time when his younger sibling was about to cry. He never knew why he did it. He had always seen their pop do it to their mom and Dan thought that was the way to operate when those you loved began to cry. He did this to his own family when the tears came.

"So much of our family is in here, you know?" Brooklyn said through the tears as the both of them looked at the board games.

"I know, sis. I know. But we'd better start getting an idea of where this stuff is going to go. By the looks of it, it's going to take the better part of a year to just clean this attic out, not to mention the rest of the house."

"Well," Brooklyn said sniffling and wiping her eyes, "I'll take the board games back home with me. Unless you want to split them."

Dan shook his head, "Nah, you take them. You, Mom, and Pop played them more together than we did."

Brooklyn looked around the attic and spied something standing up in the far corner. It looked like her old twin bed from when she was a teenager, "Is that my old bed?" she asked, knowing the answer, walking toward it. "I thought Pop threw this out?"

"Ah, you know pop. He'd never throw anything away. He always said, 'You might need it later'. This whole place up here is a whole 'you might need it later'".

Brooklyn studied the old, long two rails and white head and footboard. "I wonder..." Brooklyn asked herself as she wriggled the headboard out from under the mattress. She examined the wood and then turned the headboard over and saw what she had carved into the wood when she was thirteen or maybe it was fourteen. It read: Brooklyn Luvs Donnie. She remembered carving that when she was dating a boy in her class named Donnie Simms.

Of course, dating meant seeing him at school and talking to him on the phone back then. Pop would not allow Brooklyn to date so when she went to the movies, she would tell her mom that she was going to see it with Donnie but tell Pop that she was going with friends. As far as she knew Pop never had a clue and Mom never told. It was a secret just between the two of them.

"Oh hell! I found Pop's old golf clubs," Dan said as he pulled a five iron out of the bag and did a practice swing. "I'm for sure taking these. Can't believe Mom didn't tell me these were up here. I thought he had gotten rid of them because of his back. Wow."

"Don't throw it away because you might need it later," Brooklyn said, repeating the words of her mother as she leaned the headboard against the wall.

Brooklyn wandered away from the remains of her old bed and looked at the huge oak chifforobe. "Any idea what's in here?" she asked, not waiting for her brother's response. He was still pulling out golf clubs from their dad's bag and inspecting them.

As she opened the two, wooden double doors, hanging there in front of her was the wedding dress of her mother and the tuxedo of her pop; both nicely hanging in see-through plastic bags, preserved for all eternity. Brooklyn gasped because she had forgotten that these articles of wedding day dress had still existed. "What's wrong?" Dan asked, walking over there with a seven iron across his shoulder.

"It's their wedding clothes." More tears. Dan stood there looking at the clothes that had once been a part of two people's best day ever. It was a surreal moment shared between the brother and sister. A long time ago their parents once donned those clothes to get married and at some point later, started a family, he and his sister. Now, they were gone and what was left of them they were standing in. It was the Westerfield Family Museum.

———

For hours, which seemed to be nothing more than just mere minutes, Dan and Brooklyn milled about the attic uncovering things and finding themselves transported back to times that had been long gone; each item they found had a story, an origin. Sometimes it was a funny story or memory but most times it evoked sadness because their parents were not alive anymore and neither was their childhood. The things that were left behind were rediscovered by Dan and Brooklyn; things that were forgotten were now remembered, cherished as they once were, and recalled with a memory that brought them to the very first interaction with the lost artifact. The attic was a time capsule, locked away for decades with an inventory that had a story attached to the dusty items.

Brooklyn and Dan sat on the dusty floor of the attic looking through Christmas ornaments and other such tree decorations that were in a huge box marked, XMAS STUFF. It was all there: all the arts and crafts stuff they made from their years in grade school; the popcorn stringers; the ornaments with Brooklyn and Dan's pictures in them; the reindeer faces made of Popsicle sticks; the Santas that were made with red and white cotton balls on white construction paper. It was all there in a box long forgotten.

"When's the last time all this was on the tree?" Dan asked, sitting there holding a crudely made snowman that he had cut out of thick cardboard back in the fourth grade.

"The last year Pop was alive I believe. Mom didn't decorate a tree last year."

"Amazing that all this junk we made back when we were in school still held up."

"Amazing that they kept...everything," Brooklyn replied, looking around the attic.

"You want all of this?" Dan asked, referring to the Christmas stuff.

Brooklyn looked at the Christmas tree box where the family tree lay in state and then at the huge box of decorations, "Yeah I think I do. Split the decorations and you take the tree?"

Dan nodded, "Yeah. Pop always liked that tree. Hate to see it go out to the trash."

Brooklyn laughed, "Mom always hated the tree. Every year she and Pop would fight about the tree and how Mom wanted a new one. But Pop never gave in. How old is that thing?"

Dan considered and did the math in his head, "I think nearly forty years plus, maybe? They bought it before I was born."

"Never throw anything away because you might need it later," Brooklyn said, putting the decorations back into the big box.

"Is that?" Dan spoke seeing something hanging on the wall across the attic next to the dirty window where rain smacked against it from outside. "It's Big Wally!" Dan got up from the floor and walked over to where the record-setting bass hung. "Damn," he said, mouth gaped open, marveling at the mounted specimen on the wall. In gold under Big Wally was its weight, length, where he was caught, and the year. "You remember when pPop and I got this fish, sis?"

Brooklyn walked slowly over to Dan who looked like a kid in a candy store, "Oh yes. I remember Mom having a fit about it too because he was still alive in the bucket."

Dan brushed his fingers across the big fish's white belly, "Yeah. We like to have never gotten that fish into the boat. Still a state record large-mouth bass I believe. Man, Pop was proud of this fish. Big Wally. I remember me and dad taking this fish to the taxidermist. That guy was amazed."

"Mom wasn't a fan. Remember Pop hanging it up in the living room?"

"Yeah. Everyone that came over talked about it. Great conversation starter for sure. You care if I take it?" Dan asked, putting his fingers in the dead fish's mouth.

Brooklyn smiled, "I was going to fight you over it, but what the hell, you win."

———

As the day progressed and the rain outside came down in sheets, echoing through the attic, Dan and Brooklyn dug around some more into the time capsule. In a huge oak table hidden underneath another one of those dingy white sheets, the siblings found a cache of picture albums inside. The pictures, neither one of them ever saw before, were of their parents back in the day. In almost every picture, their mom and pop were arm in arm smiling, in love. It was in those pictures that Dan noticed a striking resemblance to his pop, and Brooklyn a carbon copy of June. It was like literally looking at themselves in those old color and black and white pictures.

Some of the pictures had people that they did not recognize at all. The brother and sister who sat on the floor going through the pictures guessed that they were family members long gone and friends that had come and gone. At any rate, the pictures had meant something to June and Jeb at some point. Brooklyn had meticulously separated the ones of their parents in one pile and the others were cast aside beside Dan on the floor.

Another hour had passed with ease and the brother and sister were standing at the window that overlooked the street where they used to play as kids. Rain was still coming down and every once in a while a loud boom of thunder would rattle the house and their bones. Visiting their old home and playing around up in the attic was the last order of business for the kids.

Both parents were now dead and they were tasked with what to do with everything. The attic yielded a lot of childhood items that they wanted to take back home with them so their own family could see them. It was clear to Brooklyn and Dan that the entire attic was sacred. But they could not take it all. After all, "The what to do about the house we grew up in" issue had to be dealt with.

"So what do we do?" Dan finally asked his sister.

Brooklyn watched out the attic window as the rain came down and seemed lost in her thoughts. Finally, she spoke. "I honestly don't know. I mean we can keep the house in state I guess. Maybe visit it sometimes. Maybe even have family get-togethers; gather for holidays maybe."

Dan walked about aimlessly in the attic looking at things, but not really *looking*; just merely gazing about absently. "I guess so. So you don't want to sell it and split the cash?"

Brooklyn turned to look at her brother, "Is that what you want?"

Dan, with his hands in his jean front pockets, twirled around like a little ballerina, "I don't know. Maybe. I mean," Dan stooped twirling around, and looked dead straight at his kid sister. "Don't you think it sucks coming back home and Mom and Pop not being here? It was hard enough coming into the house knowing Pop wasn't inside it anymore. Now with mom..." Dan trailed off.

Brooklyn dropped her head. She knew exactly what Dan was saying because she felt that way too. It was difficult to visit when Pop died. Now, it was nearly impossible to come to the house with their Mom gone. "The house just seems empty now. It's like a hollow Easter egg."

"Feels that way," Dan agreed.

"So...sell it?" Brooklyn asked, finally getting out of her head.

"Yeah, maybe. Hell, I don't know. I mean, it's hard coming back, but at the same time, I don't want to sell it and never be able to come back, you know? Because this house, all the years in it, is a part of us. I mean look at the maple in the front yard here," Dan said walking over to the window to look out.

"I remember when Pop planted that tree. It was only knee-high.

Mom said it'd never survive but look at it now. And out in the backyard is where we used to cook out and go for a swim afterward in the lake. You learned how to ride a bike on that old country road out there," Dan said, making the case that they should keep the place. "Face it, kiddo...this place is woven into the fabric of our lives."

Brooklyn stood, arms wrapped around herself, biting her lower lip and wrestling with the decision of what to do. "So we're keeping it?"

Dan stood there and considered things over in his head. He looked at his sister and then out the window again. "Well, there's not really anything to pay for because the place is paid off. We can just cut the water off at the main until we all come back for get-togethers and holidays like you suggested. And if Kimberly ever kicks me out on my ass, I'll have a place to stay," Dan said, making Brooklyn smile.

"We'll split the water, electricity, and taxes fifty/fifty?" Brooklyn asked.

"Hey, you're the attorney. You tell me what would be the best thing to do," Dan said, walking over to hug his sister. "Now...race you to the living room!" Dan pushed his sister away and made a mad dash to the stairwell. Brooklyn followed laughing, calling him names as they raced down the stairs just as they did when they were kids.

SLUMBER PARTY

COVERED IN BLOOD, Dave had no idea what had happened when he woke up lying beside his in-ground swimming pool that night. His eyes hurt and stung. He was cold even though it was midsummer and humid. His arms had smears of something dark on them. Dave did not know how or why he was lying on his back looking up at the stars, but there he was, feeling the echoing effects of a long-ago headache. From the faint thumping of his head, it must have been a bad one, although he could not recall having one. Matter of fact, lying there on his back, he could not recall much of anything at the moment.

What he did know was that he was scared out of his wits by finding himself outside in the dark. Dave rose and sat up, in his boxers and Braves tee, and looked about the strange environment that was his backyard. Everything looked in place: the patio, the chairs, the grill, and of course the six-foot privacy fence that he had installed himself two years ago. It was his backyard, but why was he out there? The last thing that he remembered, and it was vague at best, was that he told them good night and went upstairs to bed with Hannah. That was it. He did not remember going to sleep and certainly didn't recall coming outside to lay on the ground beside his swimming pool.

He looked down at his hands and arms and saw that they were covered in dark red smears. At first glance, Dave thought the stuff all over his hands was some sort of black substance. He looked at his t-shirt and saw the same dark color. With a little more inspection, he determined that it was blood, darkened by the moonlight. Where did it come from? Dave ran his hands frantically around his head; down his chest and stomach; underneath the shirt; and down his legs and back. No scrapes or deep wounds– nothing on him to suggest that the blood had come from him. Then if not from him, where?

Dave looked over to his side and saw a rather large hunting knife; jagged on one side, smooth and razor-sharp on the other. Just like Dave, it was covered with that same dark color that was on him. Looking at the knife caused him to tremble in fear. Even as fuzzy as his mind was right then, he could deduce that the knife had something to do with the blood that was all over him. It was that missing link, now found, that somehow connected him to whatever had happened earlier. But what happened? Dave could not remember.

Trembling and trying desperately to get his emotions under control, he began to slowly rise from the ground, feeling as if a panic attack was coming. Standing on legs that felt like jelly, Dave took a few steps over to the edge of the pool and picked up the knife. It was a hunting knife, all right, and one that could skin a deer with no problem. It was a gift from Hannah's dad a few years ago. Dave had no use for a knife like that and put it away, never using it. So why was it out there lying beside the pool covered in blood?

Dave stood there beside the pool under the serious moonlight and examined his arms, his legs, his boxers, and his shirt once again. He looked over at his house and saw that the back door was standing wide open. He would never leave the back door standing open like that. And what time is it, Dave wondered. He glanced down at his watch, and the face of it was smacked and smeared with dried blood. He put his fingers to his mouth, licked them, and wiped the face of the watch off. Tilting the watch face to the moonlight, the hands showed five minutes after midnight. He looked at the open back door and decided that the answers lie within. Not sure that he wanted to go in the house, Dave forced himself to do so anyway. Slowly, he walked across his yard and over to his house, with the knife in tow and lowered down to his side.

What did he remember? What did Dave recall before he woke up lying on his back, looking up at the starry night sky? Just telling them goodnight and going upstairs to bed. That was it. Nothing else. As far as he knew, he hit the bed and fell asleep. There were no dreams, no getting up to pee, and no late-night snacks.

Dave stood there at the threshold of the open back door and pondered numerous questions for a moment. From inside the house, from his vantage point, there was a flickering light– faint, but noticeable. He tried hard to rummage through his mind to find what it was that he had blocked out. The only thing his mind played for him was that he had told Emily and her friends goodnight before he and his wife went upstairs for bed. That part was pretty vivid, pretty memorable.

Then it came to him in a flash: his sixteen-year-old daughter and her two friends had a slumber party. Emily had begged and begged her parents for weeks for it; finally, they had given in. *Oh God, what has happened?!* Dave screamed inside his mind. He would have screamed this question out of his mouth, but his voice seemed to have up and left for the moment. His hands shook at that revelation of the slumber party. He dropped the knife absently on the ground. He looked once again down at his hands and arms. Dave's mind was starting to piece together that the knife, the blood, and the slumber party all had a sinister connection.

Dave took a step into the house, through the back door, and slowly stepped inside the dark kitchen. Things seemed quiet– almost too quiet. The light was off in the kitchen; that was strange and out of place. Dave and his wife, Hannah, always left the overhead light on above the sink because their daughter, Brooke, was afraid of the dark. Her bedroom was just off the side of the kitchen, and the light always made her feel comfortable even though she was "getting too old for a night light," he had often told her. The light in the kitchen being on was an every night thing even if Brooke was spending the night with her friends on the weekends.

Dave did not like the feel of the kitchen. There was heaviness in there. The air in the kitchen seemed to be pushing down on Dave's chest and clamping a hand over his mouth and nose, making it so he could not breathe. Also, the kitchen had a noticeable chill– a rattling chill in the air that was out of place on a hot and muggy night. He licked his dry lips and walked slowly through the kitchen toward the dining room. The flickering light that he had seen from the back door of the kitchen grew a little bit as he walked closer to the living room through the dining room. The light itself had thrown flashes of white and gray light– going from dark to bright in instant flashes. He thought it was the TV but was not sure, not entirely. Hell, Dave was not too sure of anything, creeping through his house.

Inside the dining room, the heaviness seemed to be more oppressive than inside the kitchen. The air was so heavy in there that it nearly stole what breath Dave had managed to keep. Dave had to stop and take deep breaths to get his breathing rhythm back. There was a much colder feeling in the dining room– a coldness that caused chicken skin to flash on his blood-stained arms. Through the white and gray light flickering on and off from the living room, Dave could see his breath before him, tumbling out of his mouth like he was outside on a January evening. He knew what awaited him in the living room. He was not sure exactly how he knew, but he just knew.

"Hannah?!" Dave called through the dining room to his wife. He stood, waiting for his wife's response for a few terrifying moments. Nothing.

"Emily?!" Dave called to his daughter. Nothing.

"Hannah?!" Dave called out again. "Emily?! Anybody?!" he yelled at the top of his lungs, seeing stars before his eyes immediately afterward from the force of the calls.

He knew what awaited him on the other side of the wall. All he had to do was walk through the archway that communicated from the dining room to the living room, and his questions would be answered. Dave's mind began to assemble the puzzle: the blood, the knife, the heaviness, the coldness of the house, the silence, and the slumber party; all of it added up to something horrific, and Dave knew it. He slowly began to shuffle his bare feet to the archway.

Dave closed his eyes and tears began to roll out of them. He felt as if he was going to throw up. He could taste it building up in his throat– the stinging bile bubbling slowly and creeping its way up his esophagus. He walked out of the dining room and through the archway. As he entered the living room on cat paws, the mystery of the flickering was solved; it was the TV with the sound turned off. The heaviness was at full tilt in that room, and the coldness was arctic which caused his teeth to chatter, and his breath was more visible in the air and thicker than in the dining room. He had reached the malevolent "ground zero."

There on the floor, Dave saw the final piece of the puzzle: his daughter and her two friends dead– soaked in blood. Over to his left, across the living room, he saw his wife. She was on the floor, lying on her back just off the final rung of the staircase.

Dave stood among the murdered and screamed.

-For Corky Derrick...
keep the lights on!

EXPECTATIONS AND PREDICTIONS

WE FANCIED ourselves as know-it-alls at sixteen. And who doesn't know everything there is to know at that age, right? We thought we did. Where will we be at thirty? That was a question first sprung on us by William, the philosopher of the group. He was the guy who asked all the deep questions: questions I never thought to ask, nor did any of the other two in our small, close-knit group. I guess every group has one of those guys.

The question came about on an unassuming Friday night. We were at William's house for our weekly campfire. His place was just right because he lived on the outskirts of the city limits, but not too far for us to pedal our bikes to. None of us had cars at sixteen—at least not yet, and especially not before that campfire conversation at William's house.

I sat around the roaring fire that Friday night in October with my three best friends in the entire world: Freddie, Buddy, and of course, William. We started doing those campfires every Friday night when we turned fourteen. We did them whether it was cold or hot; we didn't do them in the rain though. We found out the hard way on that one.

We sat around the fire in the darkness, talking and drinking Mountain Dews that Freddie had brought from home. It was always Dew for those campfires. Don't ask me why because I can't tell you. It just happened to be our drink of choice.

We were sitting around the campfire, talking back and forth in our chairs, enjoying the night and the company of our friends, when William asked the question that I still remember. It's like remembering where you were when 9/11 happened. Some things you never forget where you were when the particular event occurred. "Where do you guys think we'll be in fourteen years, you know, when we're thirty?"

We all looked at William and his thick glasses that kept sliding down the bridge of his nose. He was a nerd as well as a philosopher. I always liked him but most kids at our school didn't. They didn't pick on him because me, Freddie, and Buddy wouldn't allow it. If anyone was going to pick on William, it was going to be us. No outsiders.

"Who knows, man," Freddie said, turning up his can and swallowing the last of the Dew. "I'm just trying to get through school. Fuck the future."

"So you don't think about the future at all?" William pressed.

"Well, we know you do, four eyes. Where do you think you'll be at thirty?" Buddy teased.

William sat back and considered this. He clearly had been thinking about it for some time.

"Well...I'll graduate high school. Go to college and be a veterinarian. Probably have a nice house with a wife and kids. Maybe a dog," he said.

We all looked at William and laughed. How could anyone, especially a kid at sixteen know the future? But knowing William, we all knew that was probably what was going to happen. He was the smartest of the bunch; and if anyone was going to become a vet, he was.

"Okay, smart asses, where do you see yourselves?" William prodded, trying to goad us into predicting our futures.

I hated trying to predict the future then and still do now. One thing I've learned in this life is that nothing ever happens the way you think it will or the way you imagine. Life is full of curveballs. Some you can hit, and some you can't. You have to adapt to life because life doesn't adapt to you. Insert your own cliche here.

Freddie sat back and thought for a minute. "Well, let's see...thirty? Fourteen years from now...playing pro football."

We all nodded our heads to that because Freddie was a dynamite linebacker for our high school and had already made All-Regional twice.

He had offers from several colleges, and two of them were from the University of Tennessee and Auburn University. We all could see Freddie playing for some pro team. It wasn't out of the realm of possibility.

"What about you? You see your future with Heather?" William asked Buddy.

"Yeah, I think so. I mean we've been together ever since eighth grade, dude. We're already planning to spend our lives together."

William pressed Buddy again, "So in your future, it's you and Heather...and...what else?"

"Shit man, I don't know. Go to some sort of trade school. Maybe be an electrician or something. Maybe have some kids. A nice house."

"So the American Dream idea, huh?" William asked.

Buddy nodded. We all nodded to that one, too. We could see Buddy being the guy who comes out to wire our houses or even works for the power board in our town. He was capable.

"Nothing wrong with that," William said. "What about you, Perry?"

I sat there with the others looking at me. "What they said."

Everyone called bullshit on that, and rightly so. "Okay...okay...okay...settle down. I don't know. Get married. Have a few kids. Nice house. I guess like everyone else. I guess we all kind of want the same things out of life."

"And for work?" William asked.

I laughed and then got serious, "A famous writer."

Everyone nodded at this because they all knew I was always writing stories. Hell, they had even read some of them and said they weren't too terrible...in that special kind of best friend way. My friends always encouraged me to keep at it because I was good—damn good. Teachers used to say the same thing. I had even won several contests where my short stories had gotten some notoriety. It was little acclaim, but acclaim nevertheless.

"See, was that too hard?" William said. "So, fourteen years from nowm we're going to be doing what we want on our terms, right guys? But promise me something," William continued, "we all come back here, right here, and take stock of where we are when we're thirty. No matter what?" We all nodded and agreed, thinking that the predictions that we made that night were going to come to pass.

We were young. We were winning. We had all the momentum of youth so why not? Was it so impossible for us to go out there in the world and grab what we wanted or saw for ourselves? To us, fourteen years into the future might as well be as far as Jupiter. Plenty of time to get what we wanted. Being thirty? Forget about it. Thirty got here quicker than I thought it would. It came on cat paws.

Life fucks you up pretty quickly, doesn't it? One minute you're sitting around a campfire talking about the future, and then before you know it you're in the future you were just talking about. A few days ago, I found myself realizing that the night at the campfire was fourteen years ago. I had just turned thirty. God, had it been that long ago?

I looked in the mirror, and I still looked the same, I guess. I was a little heavier. My hair was still intact, but it was scaling back a bit—not too much to be alarmed about...yet. I did have some crow's feet around my eyes. When did those get there? Teeth still looked good. A few fillings, but who doesn't have them?

When I hit thirty, I swear to God I heard William's voice ask, "Where will you be in fourteen years?" And yes, I recalled what I said, along with everyone else's reluctant predictions for the future. I wished that I never opened my mouth that night at William's. I wondered if the other guys felt the same. Or were they doing exactly what they said they would be doing? I certainly wasn't, by any means.

Did I become a world-famous writer? Nope. Not even close. I quit writing when I hit twenty. I was in college and got those childish notions out of my head. I studied to become an English teacher instead. Did I marry? Of course I did. But it didn't last. Kids? Yup, but they live in another state with their mother. I get 'em during the summer, spring, and Christmas breaks. I got two-thirds of my prediction correct, but it didn't last.

I had lost track of the guys after high school. It happens. I wouldn't have believed that if it hadn't happened to us. I mean, the four of us were as close as brothers. So when the end came, no one fought it. It was just life. Everyone scattered to the four winds. I was all right with it. Looking back, I wondered if I used those guys as get-bys, meaning we were friends just to get through high school and our awkward teen years. I hate to admit it, but probably.

I hadn't seen or heard from the guys for the better part of maybe ten years, probably closer to twelve if I'm being honest. I had no idea where they might be. But thanks to the internet and social sites, I was able to track them down. Sure it was stalking to a degree, but I wanted to know if their predictions fourteen years ago at William's campfire came true. Mine didn't. Secretly, I wished that they suffered the same fate as I did. I wanted them to fall on their faces. I know that sounds like a terrible thing to say, but it's the truth. If I couldn't get what I wanted, why should they?

In my scouring of the internet, I found out some things here and there. I discovered that William had not become a vet after all. He became a vet of the military. As far as I could tell, he wasn't married and had no children. That was according to his Facebook profile I found. It was last updated three months ago. The picture on his page didn't match the one I had in my mind from when we were younger. The years have played tricks on us all. William, at some point during the years after the campfire predictions, had lost sight of becoming an animal doctor. I wonder when he decided to stop chasing that and join the military. Never picked him as a military man, that's for damn sure.

Next, I found Buddy Richman. He was in the carpet business down in Florence, Alabama. The girl beside him in his profile picture wasn't Heather Staples from high school. It was some Latin chick. He did have some children. I wonder what happened to him and Heather? I personally never saw them away from each other coming up through high school. I thought for sure that Buddy's prediction for his future was going to be right. It must've been something awful that busted them up. I wondered what it was. He never got to be an electrician– it didn't seem. Carpet was his business. Like with William, I wondered when he stopped thinking about being an electrician. Better yet, why the hell carpet?

Last, but certainly not least, was Freddie Trout. He said back then he'd be playing pro football. We all agreed that was probably going to happen just because he was that good– the best in the state. He did, according to what I could find online, play for Middle Tennessee State University. He was good for a while but a knee injury killed any chance of him playing pro football. His college football career and dream of hitting it big in the pros was over. According to his Facebook account, which had been updated by someone he entrusted to have his passwords and such some years ago, I discovered some news that hit me like a ton of bricks.

A few years back my friend of a long time ago was killed in a motorcycle accident. Apparently, from what I read about the fatality, Freddie was going at a high rate of speed and hit a rather large rock that was in the middle of the road that night. He wiped out, slamming his body into a tree. DOA. I sat back and felt weird about what I had just read. Not sad, but a strange mixture of shock and numbness. I remember Freddie as a kid, not a man. I guess my memory of him and what he looked like will always be him in his teen years. Sucks.

Fourteen years ago, we sat around a campfire and tried to guess what the future held for the four of us. We all had these high aspirations of where we were going to be at thirty years old. Predicting the future is for suckers. Nobody ends up where they think they will. Take it from me. Certainly take it from Freddie Trout, William Kessler, and Buddy Page.

HALLOWEEN NIGHT

1

"I LOST CONTROL THAT NIGHT," Abe Tanner said, looking stoically at the reporter from across the desk.

He paid no mind to the producer or the three cameramen that were standing behind the brunette, who was stationed behind him and off in the center of the room to capture them both. His eyes were fixed on her and had been ever since she came into the room. When she had mailed Abe asking if he would be game to talk about the events of thirty years ago, he had no idea what she even looked like, at first.

Then, with some rec time, he was granted supervised internet surfing. He Googled Jennifer Jones, host of Streamflix's, *It Happened Long Ago*, which was a crime series that focused on long-forgotten cases that stunned small towns. Abe did his homework, as he felt she did on him; he replied to her letter in kind, granting her permission for an interview. However, he did not think that the powers that be that ran the prison, where he was serving three life sentences, would allow it. To his surprise, they did, but only because of Jennifer's background as a seasoned pro in the world of journalism.

Abe had not spoken about the events of that Halloween night much since his incarceration. He was asked from time to time by newer inmates what he was in for. He'd tell them but not in-depth. "I murdered my family." That was it in a nutshell. There was no need to go into all the details and the recount of days gone by.

When he received the letter from Jennifer Jones, he was stunned that someone had reached out to him. It had been thirty years ago– a generation lost to time. After he was put into his cage for life, years went by. How many? Abe had lost count after the third year. Days and months seemed to jumble together. He remembered looking at the letter that Jennifer had mailed and was shocked to see that on the heading of it: the date was 8/1/2015. *2015?! God, where has the time gone*, he sat in his cell and wondered.

Someone wanted to bring up the past for a news program. Why? Because what he did a long time ago was heinous. Still is, even if time has blown the events out of the town's consciousness like dust in the wind. He was sure that there were people left behind who remembered his deadly acts. His in-laws for sure– if they were even still alive. Abe had no way of knowing that.

"I know. I saw the crime scene photos. I gotta say, some of the worst I've ever seen, and that's saying something because I've seen some pretty bad stuff," she replied as the cameras were recording.

Abe nodded in shame, "Yeah."

"Mr. Tanner, you savagely murdered your wife and two sons on Halloween night with a pair of oversized hedge clippers. I think you're a special kind of evil. But we're here to go over all that and to get your side of things...to get answers on why you did what you did that night on October 31st, 1985."

"I'm sure that you read the transcripts of the trial, Ms. Jones. What's talking to me going to do?"

"Maybe shed light on why you did it?"

"I just...things finally snapped, I guess you could say. The pressures of everything finally wore me down. Looking back...I guess I saw myself like a rough rock in a creek, you know? Over time, the water that runs over it starts to smooth it out, wears it down. I think I was wearing out."

"And that meant killing your family?"

Abe sat there in his orange jumpsuit, feet shackled to metal hooks on the floor, looking at her, "It appears. So, I guess I don't understand why talking to me is so interesting."

"Because I don't know how a man that was as mild-mannered as you appeared to have done what you did. I spoke with family, friends, coworkers, everyone...and they never saw what you did coming. Help me with that. That's why I'm here."

Abe sat across from her, hands folded on the table, unshackled, and considered going through the story. He had never told anyone about what had led up to the murders on Halloween night– not even his defense team at the trial. What was the point? He knew that he did it. An insanity plea, temporary as it was, would never fly to a jury, especially after what he did. Abe Tanner took his fate like a man and paid the price. He never felt as if he was wrongly convicted, just the opposite. He felt that he should rot away in prison and relive that night over and over. That was what Abe figured Hell was like: repetition.

Abe looked down at the table as the camera behind Jennifer focused on him and his reaction. He could still hear the words, "We the jury, find Abraham Jonathan Tanner...guilty on all counts of murder in the first degree." Abe shook his head a little bit, lost again as he so often did back in the days when he was still a young man in his thirties. He had so much going for him back then: family, career, a whole life to explore and live. But all of it was ruined by the events that unfolded on Halloween night back in 1985.

"So..." Jennifer situated herself in her seat, readying for the in-depth interview she had been waiting years to do, "let's start at the beginning. How did you and Mary Ann meet?"

The sound of her name put a smile on Abe's face. He had not heard anyone say his wife's name in three decades. Just the sound of it made all the times they had together come rushing back into his mind. Those were the best times of his life...

2

"We met in 1973 at a drive-in diner, pretty much like the ones from the 1950s. She was working there as a waitress. God, she looked good back then," Abe smiled, thinking back to when he first saw his future wife. "She was blonde, thick wavy hair, and man, when she would put it up... wow. She was a knockout. I remember the song "Runaway" was playing from Del Shannon on the speakers outside.

"I was sitting in my car with my best friends, Johnny Songer, Steve Kuntz, and Richie Rodriguez. We had been out most of the night bowling down at Classic Lanes for several hours with some of the other kids from high school. Nothing major...just having fun. We got tired after that and decided we wanted something to eat. Classic Lanes had food, but nachos and stale pizza got old, real quick. So, we decided to roll on over to Al's, the 50's place.

"I pulled into one of the stalls- might've been around ten that night. Man, they were busy as hell. It was Saturday, and they usually were. Let me tell you, they had the best milkshakes you'd ever tasted. Sometimes, I get a craving for one in here so bad that I can taste it in my mouth-something like that so long ago you can still taste it...crazy, ain't it?

"Anyways, we're all sitting there, just talking away, when Mary Ann came strolling out and over to my car, over to the driver's side window..."

"What can I get you boys tonight?" Mary Ann asked, chomping on a piece of gum, holding a notepad in one hand and an ink pen in the other.

Abe sat there and stared at the vision of beauty before him. He was certain that he had never seen her around school before. He would have remembered a girl like her. Mary Ann stood there looking at Abe who was looking back at her, dumbfounded from his driver's seat. Johnny looked at Abe and then into the backseat at Richie. Richie shrugged and smiled.

Johnny pushed Abe and he snapped out of his trance, "Oh...sorry," he stammered, "We'll have three cheeseburgers and three chocolate shakes...please." He sounded like such a kid that it made Johnny and Richie bust out with laughter.

Mary Ann smiled and wrote down the order, "We'll get you boys set up in a few. Anything else?" she asked, bending over a bit to look into the car. Her and Abe's eyes locked for a brief moment ,and the both of them knew right then and there they had met each other's destiny.

"That's it, I think," Abe said, feeling his face get hot as fire.

"Okay," Mary Ann replied. She straightened up and walked away but before she got too far back to the hub where the food was cooked and the waitresses came in and out, she turned and looked back at Abe.

"I think she likes you," Johnny remarked.

"And that's how you two met?" Jennifer asked, secretly wanting to smile but keeping that in check somehow. It was a sweet story of young love; two hearts meeting for the first time. It should have been the beginning of a Hallmark movie.

Abe nodded slowly in a state of fond remembrance, "Yeah," he slowly said, recalling that magical moment. "It happened just like that. Me and the boys ate and talked about what we were going to do tomorrow because this was Friday night, you see, but I wasn't really paying attention to what Richie and Johnny were saying. I was watching Mary Ann come back and forth to cars bringing them their food."

"So how did the two of you get together?" Jennifer asked.

Abe rubbed the stubble on his jaw, thinking back to a time that was so far away that it hurt his heart to recall it. But he could recall it. That memory with Mary Ann never went away. It was always there inside him. Every time he closed his eyes in his cell, he saw her– the love of his life– for the first time at Al's.

"I went back the next night, Saturday, to see if she was working. I left the guys at the bowling alley and took a drive out there. And just as I hoped, she was there waiting on cars.

"I pulled into a stall, and another girl came to my window and asked what she could do for me tonight. I asked her what the blonde's name was, and she told me Mary Ann. I then asked her if Mary Ann could take my order because I had something I wanted to ask her. She smiled this really cheesy smile and said, 'you bet', and walked off to get Mary Ann. Mary Ann comes over there to my car..."

3

"Where's your friends tonight?" Mary Ann asked, chomping on a piece of gum, holding her notepad in one hand and a pen in the other.

"I left them at the bowling alley. Just me tonight," Abe said.

"Same as last night for you?" Mary Ann inquired as the song, "This Magic Moment " played on the speakers at the drive-in diner.

"You remember that?" Abe asked with surprise.

"Sure do. I have a good memory. Plus, there're not many people in town who drive a yellow Ford truck. I think yours is the only one I've ever seen if I'm being honest."

"I believe it is. I've never seen one," Abe returned. "I've never seen you around school. Do you go to William Blount?"

Mary Ann smiled, "No, I go to Jefferson High. Junior class."

It was Abe's turn to smile, "Ah, I see. Our rivals."

"You go there, I guess?"

Abe nodded, "Yup, senior this year, thank the Lord."

"I can't wait to get out myself. School is such a drag."

"You ain't telling me nothing." Abe sat there after that reply, and it got silent between the two of them except for that song that was playing.

Abe was about to say something else when Mary Ann backed away from his driver's side window, "I better get going. Get your order in so you can eat."

"Thanks," was all Abe could manage to say.

4

Abe sat at the table across from Jennifer with a half smile on his face, recalling that special memory of that night at Al's. He never told anyone about that night, not even his parents when they asked where the two of them met. He told them, "I met her at school." Abe's father was a hard man with hard hands when he got to drinking, which was all the time, and he put off bringing Mary Ann over as long as he could.

They dated for a year and a half until Abe finally brought her by at the request and nagging of his mother. That visit lasted ten long minutes.

"When she came back with my food, we made some more small talk, and then I got brave enough to ask for her phone number. She wrote it down on a piece of paper from her notepad and gave it to me. And that was how we met."

"You and Mary Ann got married two years later in 1975. What was that like?"

Abe looked up at the ceiling and smiled, "God...it was magical. It wasn't a big wedding, you know. It was modest. All the families from both sides were there. My dad ended up making a scene– being drunk. He was always drunk...always got mean when he drank. He and Mary Ann's dad got into this big fistfight because he grabbed Mary Ann's ass when I wasn't looking. Her dad, Bobby, saw it and confronted my dad, and then it was on. It took five of us to get my dad off Bobby. Once Dad got going, it was hard to stop him...kind of like trying to stop a train, you know."

"Did you have a lot of problems with your dad growing up?" Jennifer asked, wanting to go down this road.

Abe looked from the ceiling and then into Jennifer's eyes absently. He hated talking about his dad and never liked the subject much. "Yeah... you could say that."

"Like what kind of problems?"

Abe was silent for a few moments. He didn't want to go down that road, but he did open the door for Jennifer to come on through. "He was not a bad man all the time. He turned into one. He was one of the hardest and most violent people I ever knew as a kid *and* as an adult. It's funny, but I was always afraid of him. Every day after he started drinking heavily. When he died, I remember telling Mary Ann that I was afraid that I would see his ghost, and he would haunt me forever. I swore that I'd never be like him. But I ended up doing something worse than he ever did."

"Did your dad abuse you?" Jennifer asked.

Abe bit the lower inside part of his lip and considered if he wanted to keep going down this road. After a few seconds that felt like long minutes, he answered without any thought, "Yeah...plenty of times."

"In what ways?"

5

One particular incident was when Abe was ten. He was outside playing in the front yard with his friend from down the block, Chucky Bradford. He and Chucky were playing a game they invented called, "Knights." They had taken two, four-foot-long lead pipes from Abe's dad's tool shed and used them as swords. The metal-on-metal sound rattled out loudly when they would smack them together, oftentimes stinging their small hands. But it didn't matter to them; they were laughing and having fun sword-fighting.

Abe's dad, Peter, already drunk on brown liquor, grew tired of the metal-on-metal sound out in the yard. He was inside the house on that hot July day, windows in the house raised, a baseball game on the radio. He got up from the kitchen table, staggered at best, and looked outside the kitchen window. He thought the sound was from Ernie West next door building something. To his surprise and anger, he saw his son and his friend swinging his pipes from out of the tool shed as swords. That pissed Peter off greatly.

Mad as fire, Peter walked out of the house and over to the boys and grabbed Abe's pipe away from him. He pushed Chucky to the ground and grabbed his pipe. "You want to make racket?! Let's make some racket!" Abe knew what was coming. He had been hit by his dad before but never by a lead pipe. Before he could turn and run, Peter swung like Babe Ruth and connected the lead pipe across Abe's ribs, breaking a few of them. Abe fell to the ground in acute pain with the wind knocked clear out of him.

Peter looked down at Chucky with wild eyes, "Get the hell home... NOW!" Chucky sprang up from the ground and ran as fast as he could back home. He never came back.

Abe, lying on the ground, struggling to breathe, feeling the pain of broken ribs, tears flowed heavily. Nothing came out of his mouth but a few gasps. He laid on his side trying to get up. "I didn't hit you that hard! Get up!" Peter said sternly.

By this time, Judy, Abe's mother came rushing out of the house and over to her fallen son, "What happened?!" she screamed as she went to her knees to gather her son in her arms.

"The bastard and his fat fucking friend were out here sword-fighting with my pipes causing all kinds of racket!"

"And you hit with that?!" Judy screamed.

"What's your point!"

"He's just a kid! You could have killed him!" Judy screamed.

Peter stood there holding his pipe in the front yard as some neighbors walked out of their homes to see what the commotion was at the Tanner house. Feeling eyes on him, he stepped over and grabbed Judy by her arm and pulled her away from Abe who was still on the ground, "Get in the fucking house...right now! You're causing a scene!" He took her and flung her off to the side.

She had seen that look before, that violent, wild look he had when he had been drinking. Judy knew that if she didn't comply with his order, that pipe would be used on her when he got inside. She knew this to be true because he had done much worse in the time they had been married.

6

"Things like that went on and on. I ended up going to the hospital the next day. Had three broken ribs. My dad told the doctors that I had fallen off my bike jumping a dirt pile. I guess they believed it. By then, Dad had sobered up and told a really great story that *I* nearly believed."

"Were there more instances of abuse before that and afterward?" Jennifer asked, horrified by the one story.

"Yeah," Abe replied, "Dad was mean as the Devil when he drank, which was often. I only remember him a few times when he wasn't lit. When he was sober, he was the greatest man. When he would get to drinking, you had to approach him like you were walking on a frozen lake: step where the ice wasn't hard enough– the ice would break, and you'd go under.

"I went under a lot; Mom did, too. I remember him throwing her out of the house through the front door once by her hair one night. They had been arguing about something, I don't know what, and Dad just got up from his recliner, grabbed Mom by her hair, dragged her across the living room, and out the front door she went. Mom could just look at Dad the wrong way, and there it went.

"I remember once, I brought home an F in math on my report card, and my dad beat me silly with a mop handle and locked me in a closet for a few hours. That house was hard to live in. But...he could be the nicest man you'd ever meet. I remember my dad like that. I remember times-- I was about six or seven-- when he got off from work, Dad and I would go outside in the backyard and have a catch with the baseball. I remember him teaching me how to ride a bicycle out on our street. I remember him letting me help when he would be working on the car. But when he drank...when he got that liquor in him– watch out– because he would get set off by the smallest thing.

"For a long time, the Dad I knew was gone. He was drinking more and more. It used to be just on the weekends after work. Then, over time, it got to where it was every day. The man who played catch with me out in the yard, the man who let me help him in the garage working on the car, had disappeared. What replaced him was an overbearing, abusive, son of a bitch."

"How did you get out of that house?" Jennifer asked.

Abe exhaled deeply at the question and the memory, "I moved out. I told my mom to come with me, but she was too afraid of him and what he might do to her if she ran off. I had just graduated high school, and I wasn't about to stay. Richie Rodriguez's parents had a loft apartment upstairs above the garage, and he and I lived there for a bit. He went to college, and I continued to live there until me and Mary Ann found a place before we got married. By then I had a good job down at the Dura-cell plant to afford us a bigger and better place to start our family."

"What happened to your father?" Jennifer asked.

"He ended up dying of stomach cancer," Abe replied, looking off in the distance at the floor, pondering the day the news came. "I was in the mill working when I got a call from Mary Ann. She told me the news. A son should cry when he hears that his dad has just passed, you know? But I didn't. I didn't care. After the situation at our wedding, I kicked him out of my life. Mom, too, because she got to the point where she made excuses for him and enabled him to be the bastard he turned out to be.

"He didn't respect her at all. He kept right on beating her and treating her like shit the whole time– right up until he died. I often hoped that he had a slow and painful death. I never asked Mom about it. Mostly because I was afraid that she would tell me he went peacefully. I didn't want that. I wanted that man to suffer for turning from the man I loved to the man I hated and feared."

"Did you ever find closure after his death?"

Abe smiled and nearly laughed, "Closure? There's no such thing, sweetheart. Closure is just a word that some well-educated person made up to make us think we can move on with life and the things that have happened to us. There wasn't any *closure* when that man died. I didn't feel good about it because the hurt and pain he caused didn't die with him. It lived inside of me and my mom.

"The scariest thing– I mean the thing that would wake me up in the middle of the night in a full-blown panic– was thinking that I was going to turn out just like him. I thought maybe it was genetic, you know? Turns out, I followed in my dad's footsteps. I had kept the violence out of my house until that Halloween night."

"You blame your dad for that?" Jennifer asked.

Abe looked around the room for a few moments; he looked into the cameras, at Jennifer, at the floor and ceiling before he answered. "I'd like to. Wish that I could say that I was influenced by living in a home where violence was just as natural as blinking your eyes. But I can't. What I did was on me. I got drunk– some hard liquor like good old Dad used to drink– the same brand, Wild Turkey, and went at my wife and kids. I guess I saved up all the violence for one night instead of distributing it all across my marriage and the kids' lives. Maybe I was like my dad, after all. Maybe things are genetic. He had a monster living inside him just as I did.

"Do you remember much about that night? You said to the police that you didn't have much of a recollection of what you had done. Was that true?"

Abe sat and thought about that night in question. His memory of that night over the years filled in mostly; but on the night it happened, there wasn't much in the way of coherent memories to tell the police what he had done. He knew that he murdered them all with a pair of oversized hedge clippers from his shed out back, but at the time he couldn't remember the play-by-play; just some of the highlights.

While in prison– where there's nothing but time to reflect– memories of that Halloween night came to him, seeping into his brain from the partition where those events were held and made him remember. Over the last thirty years, Abe Tanner was finally able to put all the pieces of the puzzle together that his mind had put away while on his violent murderous rampage.

"Yeah, I'll be honest…I don't remember how I ended up at the police station that night. It wasn't until I heard it at the trial that I kinda of remembered that. Over the years in here, everything has finally come back to me: what I did to my family; what led up to it; why I did what I did. I know the whole story now."

"And you're willing to tell that story now?" Jennifer questioned.

Abe sat for a few moments, as he was prone to do, and thought it over. He began to see Jennifer Jones as a therapy of sorts. There was nothing that could fix him nor was he searching for abolishment for his sins, but he wanted to tell someone about what he had done on that Halloween night back in 1985.

"Yeah, I think I do. It's not a good story, and there's no happy ending– as you already know. In the trial, they painted me as someone who was a monster. And maybe I was that night. I had a moment where I turned into one and in that moment, it cost me everything…my family. I accept that I'm in this prison for the rest of my life. I deserve that. I should be locked up for what I did. But there's a story that led up to that night…a story of that night, after all the years that have gone by, I finally remember. It's not easy living with this. Hard to look at myself in the mirror. I don't even know what I look like anymore. It's been so long since I caught myself in one."

"When does this story begin?"

"At the end of September 1985…"

7

September 27th, 1985

Abe Tanner had gotten fired recently from his job at the Duracell plant outside of town a month ago. He had been there going on twenty years and liked it okay. It wasn't the best job around, but it paid very well. He was raising a family with his salary, and his wife could stay at home and look after the kids and whatnot. It wasn't what she exactly wanted to do with her life, but she was okay with it until the kids got older. She made this point crystal clear to Abe when the kids came into their lives. They had no one close by to look after their children. Abe's parents were a no-go: his dad was dead (thank God) and his mother was about to hit seventy and could barely get out of bed.

Mary Ann's family had moved to Florida and would come to visit some around the holidays. Once a year, Abe would load up the family station wagon and drive down to Fort Myers to see her parents. Abe got along with them pretty well; never had any issues with them. Mary Ann's dad and Abe shared a love for baseball ,and that was usually the conversation between the two. So when kids came into the picture for Abe and Mary Ann's family, they discussed it, and it was decided– more decided by Abe– that Mary Ann was going to have to stay home. There weren't any good options until they got older to become latchkey kids.

The Duracell plant paid well, and Abe was okay with it for the most part. His job, the one he had since he had gotten there a year after finding out that college wasn't for him, was loading and unloading trucks. Those truck trailers, fifty-two feet long, were pure hell for him and his coworkers to load and unload for ten hours a day, sans a thirty-minute lunch and a fifteen-minute break.

What they were loading those trailers with were pallets and pallets of car batteries and regular batteries for household use. Often those pallets would weigh over two tons and sometimes the two electric pallet jacks would be on the fritz. The guys in the warehouse would have to push the pallets by hand with a manual pallet jack. Had it not been for that, Abe would have been okay with the job. The manual pushing and pulling up an incline and into the trailer eventually wore on Abe. His left knee at the age of twenty-six had to be repaired, and a slipped disk in his back fixed at thirty, all thanks to the electric pallet jack never being available and the plant being too cheap to have it fixed.

At age thirty, Abe put in for a job for the supervisor position on the second shift at the Duracell plant, overseeing the warehouse operations. After several interviews and qualified internal employees, Abe got the job. Most on the shift were happy about that promotion because Abe was "one of them". He was good at it, and he treated his staff with the utmost respect, which was totally different than when Mike Haymaker ran the ship.

He was a boss that everyone hated, and, deep down, Mike loved to be hated. Abe thought it served him right: Karma. Mike was fired for inappropriate behavior towards one of the newer females in the warehouse. Everyone was happy about that termination. Abe even bought pizza for everyone to eat for lunch: to celebrate the man being out of the company and out of their lives.

Things went well for Abe for about two years. Then they didn't. One night there was a mix-up on two of the trailers. The wrong battery pallets got loaded on the wrong trailers. One that was ticketed to St. Louis ended up in Gainesville, Florida, and the other was ticketed to Albany, New York, and ended up in Nashville. It was an honest mistake but the plant manager, a kid fresh out of college no less, saw the screwup and wanted heads to roll. The head-to-roll was Abe's.

The day that was the beginning of the end for Abe and eventually, his family. Abe Tanner was called into the plant manager's office up on the third floor. He figured at best he was going to get a stern talking to, which he deserved. But what came was something that Abe and his peers thought was too severe.

"He's just using you to make a point to the rest of us…fuck up and this will be you," Dale Cline, the first shift warehouse supervisor, told Abe over the phone.

Abe sat quietly in Justin Mainlander's office across from his boss's desk. He was going over some paperwork. The HR rep, Jenna Warlock, sat in a chair on the far side of the wall. Anytime there was a write-up in the plant, she had to be there. Abe had only spoken to her a few times in his career there. Once, when he was hired on, the other times when he went out on medical leave. She seemed personable, and Abe didn't hear any alarm bells going off inside his head with her being in the office for what he thought was going to be a standard write-up over him sending out the wrong trailers. Just a mix-up was all it was...at least that's how Abe saw it.

"That little mix-up cost us about ten grand the other night, Abe," Justin started, leaning back in his desk chair.

Abe cleared his throat, "Yes, sir, it did. And that squarely falls on me."

"How did that happen?"

"Well," Abe began, "I guess I forgot which trailer was in which bay, and I ticketed the trailer in bay three with the ticket that was supposed to go to bay four. I had so much going on that night...I just flubbed it. That's all I can really say."

"And you didn't think to go back and double-check to make sure everything was right? Isn't that standard operating procedure in your job?" Justin asked, speaking all high and mighty.

"Well, it is, yes."

"So you just decided not to do it then, I'm guessing?"

"It wasn't like that. Kurt Johnston ran over his foot with a pallet jack while pulling a battery pallet, and you know how much those things weigh...I was at the podium writing up the tickets for the trailers when I heard a bunch of screaming. Dana Maven runs across the warehouse hollering at me that Kurt had gotten hurt.

"I tell Wes Blevins to finish off writing those tickets, and I run over to where Kurt was down. By the time I got there Kurt was all taken care of. I went back to the podium, didn't really look at what Wes had done to see if it was right or not, and I went ahead and had them given to the drivers. It was my mistake...I should have double-checked all that. And I usually do. I think Kurt getting hurt like he did, which he ended up having to go to the hospital, just rattled me out of my routine. If those electric pallet jacks would have gotten fixed when I put the work order in months ago, Kurt wouldn't have gotten hurt."

Justin sat back in this chair and looked at Abe and then over to the plant's HR rep. "You know," Justin began, taking off his glasses and sitting them down on his desk, "we're running on a budget here. I don't have to tell you that, right? Razor thin. Corporate likes to keep us all on the thinnest budget they can. The tickets being switched, although a mistake, have to be accounted for. Someone has to be held accountable for that. I mean, I got to answer for that, and they want to know what I'm doing about it at the home office. If I don't fix it then they'll fix me, you what I mean?

"They don't think a simple reprimand will work this time. We're going to have to let you go because of this. To be clear, this wasn't my decision. Jenna will tell you that in the meeting we had with the bigwigs; I fought for your job. I thought you should only go to a level two write-up...not a full-on termination. But there ain't anything I can do."

Abe sat there quietly, and at first, he didn't know what to say. He had gone into that office thinking he'd only receive a write-up and a stern talking-to, which he felt was right. But fired? That, he thought, was too much.

"It was a mistake. What did you want me to do, let Kurt bleed out over there until I got the tickets filled out, and hand-delivered to the drivers myself, and then go see what was the matter with Kurt?"

"It's not about..." Justin started to say but was cut off.

"I've been with this company for a long time. Done a damn good job. And now you're telling me that I'm fired over a simple mistake? That's some bullshit right there."

"There's really..." Jenna spoke before being cut off by Abe.

"How many times has Mitchell Owens on days fucked things up? I can count on both hands and nothing has ever happened to him because he plays cards with you and Ben McCallister. Had I been in your boys' club, this ticket bullshit wouldn't even be a thing, would it? Did you know about Mitchell having inappropriate relationships with the girls on his team?" Abe asked Jenna.

"Probably not. How could you, Justin here makes sure that his friends are taken care of. But what about me? I've got a family to take care of, and now just because of a simple mistake, I'm getting kicked out of here. Fuck this and fuck you too!" Abe jumped out of the chair and for a moment, Justin felt as if Abe was going to leap across the desk and deck him. Jenna had that thought on her mind as well as she tensed up.

8

"You didn't hit him?" Jennifer asked from across the table, cameras on the two of them.

Abe smiled, "Nah, I wanted to though. It would've felt good to do it. But what would it have solved? Nothing. It would've just made me look unstable is all. So, after standing there for a few seconds, looking at him and at the HR lady, I turned and walked out of the office. I didn't even go to clean out my locker."

"What did you do after that?"

Abe sighed and recalled that night, "I remember walking out of the plant for the last time. I got to my car and sat in it trying to process every-thing, you know? Me getting fired was huge– life-changing. I was trying to figure out how I was going to go home and tell Mary Ann, thinking how are we going to make it now because I was making pretty good money there…I was thinking how me getting fired was political… a lot was going through my head all at once."

"Did you ever find another job?"

"No," Abe said. "It was the Reagan presidency. Things were not good in several parts of the country as far as work and finding a good salary to raise a family. Duracell was the best job I was going to find, and I got lucky getting it. But to find another job like that around where I lived at the time? Good luck. And I knew that. You know, that was the scariest part of being fired…it was knowing that job was the best that I was ever going to get. So, that sunk me into a depression right there."

"How did the conversation go with Mary Ann when you came home to tell her the bad news?" Jennifer quizzed.

"It went good. She was upset like I was. She wanted to call the plant boss," Abe said, laughing as he recalled how mad Mary Ann was that night. "God love her, she was madder about it than I think I was at the time. I was just stunned…but she was very angry. Then she calmed down later that night, and we sat at the kitchen table and talked about what we were going to do...about the future, the kids, all that. Because when something like this happens, you have to have some sort of plan on where you're going."

"What was the plan?"

"The plan was that I was going to start applying for jobs, and we would apply for food stamps to get by until I made more money– or at least found something close in pay to Duracell. She said her parents would help out, which they would, no problem because her parents had money. Her dad worked on the railroad, so he made great money. We didn't want that, but at the time we knew, especially with the holidays coming, we were going to need a little push. But the bills were paid up for the month, and I wouldn't really have to start worrying until the end of October about a job."

"But things didn't go so well during that time, am I right?"

"No, they did not. The plans that we made kinda evaporated in thin air. I got more depressed about the situation. Mary Ann and me started fighting a lot more. At one point a couple of weeks after I got fired, she and I had this huge fight, and she took the kids and stayed at her friend's house for a few days."

"What was the fight over?"

"I had started drinking...like good old Dad. And just like him, I was getting violent when I drank. I took my last check, bought six bottles of Wild Turkey, and hid them out in the shed so Mary Ann couldn't find them. I started spiraling out of control pretty bad, I remember. I was yelling at the kids and breaking stuff in the house when I got mad. It wasn't them I was mad at. It was the situation I was in.

"I'd start cussing the kids and Mary Ann. I nearly hit her one night. That's the night she and the kids left. I had come in from the toolshed drunk, and she had put spaghetti on the dinner table. It was the third day in a row we'd had that, and man, that flew all over me. I took the plates, threw them against the wall, and forced my kids to clean it up. I was getting out of control. I knew it when I was in that moment, but I didn't care. I liked the feeling of rage. I guess that's what Dad felt like. I couldn't control anything in my life at that point, but if I'm being honest with you, I loved the feeling of controlling their fear of me when I was like that."

"She must've come back home, right?"

Abe nodded, "She did, about the middle of the month. I had sobered up enough to talk to her on the phone, and I told her I was sorry about everything. I meant it, too. I saw what I was becoming. I was turning into my dad. You see, sometimes you become the thing you hate the most. My biggest fear was turning into him. Maybe it was genetic like I said earlier– I don't know. Maybe my destiny was to end up like him. You know, maybe the Tanner genes are predisposed to alcoholism and violence."

"So she comes back...did your drinking stop?" Jennifer asked.

"No. I thought that I could control it some. And I guess I did for a bit. Instead of drinking out in my toolshed or driving down the road, I would only take a few sips here and there– just to relax a bit. I was going around and putting in applications in places but never got any callbacks. Mary Ann said that I would eventually, but I didn't believe her. As October rolled along, I was getting more and more worried about the state of our family. Bills were coming due."

"When did things get really bad?"

"Around that last week of October...right before I killed them."

"What happened?" Jennifer pushed a little.

"Um...it started on that Halloween afternoon ...."

9

It was October 31st, 1985 when the end came.

Outside it was a bright and unusually warm late fall afternoon. Temps were going to reach nearly eighty-five that day. But a cold front was said to be coming later that night: bringing behind it much colder temperatures, rain, and some isolated thunderstorms. The here and now: things were sunny, bright, and warm.

"I'm going to go outside and wash the car," Abe told Mary Ann that mid-afternoon in the kitchen.

"You know it's going to rain tonight," she replied absently, washing up some dishes from the breakfast she cooked earlier.

Abe looked out the backdoor window across the lawn, "Yeah, but what else have I got to do? Nothing. We still taking the kids out trick or treating?"

"Yeah. I figure around six. Their costumes are finished. I put the finishing touches on them earlier. Hope we beat the rain."

Abe opened the back door and went out to the toolshed to gather his car washing equipment. Inside, he gathered his pail and oversized yellow sponge but stopped before he walked out. He needed a drink– just a swig. He placed the pail and sponge down on the countertop workbench and reached behind it on the floor to pull out his nearly-empty whiskey bottle. Taking the cap off, he put it to his lips, turned the bottle up, and took a mighty strong swig from it. It was smooth, like velvet, running down his throat. He took the bottle from his mouth and looked at it. "God, you're good," he told the bottle.

10

In the driveway, Abe hosed his 1981 Chevy Malibu Classic off and then started washing her with some Dawn dish soap with the oversized sponge. With a few swipes and circular motions on the passenger side of the car, Abe dipped the sponge back into the pail of sudsy water and noticed that the water was already dirty. He couldn't remember the last time he had washed his car– maybe it was back in July, perhaps later than that. By the time he reached the passenger side tail lights, he had to change his dirty, soapy water.

It had taken forty-five minutes to wash that car from top to bottom and it looked good; the light Machine Blue paint job was still holding up from when it rolled off the assembly line four years ago. His hope was to one day give it to Ricky, his oldest. The kids, Ricky nine, and Marty eight, walked off the school bus that pulled up to the Tanner home and went over to see about their dad.

They talked a little bit about the school day, nothing much had gone on, both had reported. Marty went inside to find something to snack on while Ricky stood outside with his dad. He took the water hose, and even though it didn't need it, he sprayed the car off again.

Abe stood back and watched. "Son, you get old enough, this will be your car."

"What will you drive?"

Abe smiled, "I'll figure something out."

It was a simple October afternoon. The family was back after a brief time away when he had lost control. He had curbed his drinking to just a few sips here and there throughout the day, nothing like he had been doing. The fact of the matter was that Abe was scared of himself when he drank. He hated that loss of control, that rage that filled his mind.

He had grown up with a dad like that, and he didn't want his sons to have to deal with that kind of burden. They already had, and he felt like garbage about it. He hoped that they had forgiven him, but he knew deep down they would never forget his violent outbursts inside the home a few weeks ago. He could tell that Ricky and Marty were handling him with care like he was a bomb that could explode at any moment; they were cautious of their dad. Standing and watching Ricky wash the car off, Abe wondered if the family would ever be the same.

11

"What was having kids like?" Jennifer asked.

Abe smiled, "You know, it wasn't bad at all. There was a big adjustment at first. But it was good. I loved being a dad. You got kids?"

"Career comes first," she replied.

"Probably for the best. Kids can um...consume you: your time, your sense of self, your marriage, everything. When Ricky came we were happy. Her parents chipped in and helped us for a bit to understand how to do certain things before they moved... It was like we were learning on the job, you know? Because in reality, we were. We had not planned on having any kids for a few years after Ricky...but then Marty came the next year. That's when it got tense around the house."

"Tense how?"

"Kids are one thing- a certain kind of stress in your life. Mary Ann started having depression shortly after Marty was born. I recognized what it was and told her that she needed to go get treated for it. But she refused and told me there was nothing wrong with her. But there was. We went through a lot of bad years together until she finally sought help. About two years before I killed them, she was mentally stable again, and things were going pretty good. Then I got fired and everything started to unravel.

"But the kids were great. I loved them. It was hard raising them for sure. Me and Mary Ann were young'uns as well, but they were my sons. I would've died for them. I never hated them. When I realized that I had murdered them...I can't even begin to describe the amount of pain that I felt when I figured out what I had done– done to Mary Ann. I mean, I was watching the whole thing happen that night, but I couldn't stop myself. My alcohol-fueled rage burned too bright...but the kids...I loved being a dad. It was the best job I ever had. And I know I'll never get to do it again."

"How much do you remember from that night?"

"All of it. That's the thing with being in here...you got nothing but time to think. And what I didn't remember from that night, slowly crept back in from wherever it was locked up. I used to not believe in the death penalty. But now, being in here with the memory of what I've done over all these years...I think living is cruel and inhumane."

"Everything happened that night, on Halloween...exactly what sparked it?"

"Well, it started with a broken window..."

12

After washing the car, Abe went inside and got a Pepsi out of the fridge. He popped the tab of the can and took a big swig from it. It tasted good, cool running down his throat but not as good as the whiskey. He downed the entire thing standing in the kitchen.

After crushing the can, Abe was about to toss it into the trash when he noticed that the trashcan was heaping over the lid. Grumbling about how the household had so much trash and why can't the kids at least do this one chore, he went over and took the bag out of it and tied it up. He took it outside to the big green trash can that sat on the side of the curb next to his driveway.

Abe noticed his kids passing baseball in the front yard. Nothing abnormal, but they were too close to the car he had washed. "Ricky? Why don't you guys move away from the car before you miss the ball, and it breaks a window," Abe instructed.

"Okay," Ricky replied, moving away from the car but not far enough away to Abe's liking.

"Have you seen the costume I'm wearing tonight?"

"No, what is it?" Abe asked.

"A mummy."

"And I'm a scarecrow!" Marty interjected.

"Man, I bet you two will look sharp tonight." He was going to tell them to move to the backyard but decided against it. Ricky was a good fielder, and he didn't miss many balls that came to him. Besides, Martin didn't have a great arm at his age.

"Go out a little further, Ricky. I don't want the car dented or a window busted out." Abe waved Ricky further out across their front yard. The boys did as their dad asked. Abe stood there and watched them play catch for a few minutes and envied them. God, how he wished his life was that simple. *Was it ever*, he wondered.

Abe went back into the house through the backdoor and got a new trash bag. He stretched it out and put it in the trash can that stood next to the counter where the microwave sat.

"Well, that just about tired me out," Abe said to no one but himself.

Mary Ann came walking down the stairs from the second floor when she spotted her husband making a beeline to his recliner. "Taking a nap?" she asked.

Just because I sit in the recliner doesn't mean I'm going to sleep," he replied.

"Name a time when you didn't?" Mary Ann said playfully.

The two of them were slowly getting that husband and wife back and forth they had before her taking the kids and leaving for a bit. It was nice to see her husband come back around.

Abe sat down in the recliner, reclined the footrest out, and eased the back a little ways. He was getting into his nap position.

"I can't." They both laughed.

"Where are the boys?" Mary Ann asked.

"Outside in the front yard passing baseball," Abe said while he closed his eyes. Maybe he was more tired than he thought.

"Okay. I'm going to re-run that lasagna again tonight if that's good with you?"

Abe nodded and replied without opening his eyes, "Yeah, that's fine by me."

"Remember Saturday...Mom and Dad want us to come over and bring the kids since they're up for the week."

Abe gave her a thumbs up and began to drift off to sleep. Mary Ann was still talking to him, but what about he had no idea. Her words were slipping further and further away from him. In no time, he was in dreamland.

13

"So you weren't outside when it happened?" Jennifer asked.

Abe shook his head, "No, I was sleeping there in the recliner. Pretty good, too."

"Did you hear it break or..."

"No...Marty came in yelling..."

14

"Mom! Momma! Ricky broke the car window!" Marty screamed as he opened the front door and ran inside.

Abe's eyes flew open, and he looked around– dazed and confused. He saw Marty running across the living room and through the dining room screaming for his mother. Abe turned and looked out through the open front door and saw sunlight shimmering off the ground in the driveway.

Right away Abe knew what it was. He slammed the ottoman part of the recliner down in place and got up quickly out of the chair. With eyes still heavy from the deep sleep he was in, he stepped out on the front porch and saw Ricky bent down trying to pick the broken pieces up in his hand. The front passenger side window had been busted out. Abe was instantly infuriated.

15

"What went through your mind at that point?" Jennifer asked.

Abe looked down at the table for a moment, keeping his stare on it. Jennifer was about to ask him the question again but he finally spoke, "I was madder than hell."

"Why didn't you make them go into the backyard or park the car in the garage?"

Abe's eyes raised and caught her stare. For a moment, Jennifer's heart skipped a beat because she could have sworn that was the stare he gave the members of his family on that fateful Halloween night.

He licked his lips and leaned back in his chair, "Maybe I should've. It's kinda like when you think you need to take the chicken out of the oven but you leave it in there five minutes too long and it's dry. You knew that it would happen, but there's something in the back of your head that tells you you're being stupid. That's how I felt."

16

Abe walked over to his car slowly while Ricky was crouched, carefully plucking the shards of glass from the concrete. His hands were shaking something awful, and he just knew that his dad was going to be out there any minute. Before he could turn to see if his dad was coming outside, he saw his dad's shadow appear in front of him, casting down onto the thousands of pieces of broken glass. "I fucking told you, didn't I?" Abe shouted.

In one swoop, he grabbed Ricky by the back of his shirt collar and pulled him straight back, flinging him to where the grass and the concrete driveway met. Ricky lay on his back, a piece of glass sticking out of his palm. The wind had been knocked out of him while Abe stood there examining the damage, cussing up a storm. Ricky sat up and felt the stinging in his hand. He held up his hand and saw blood streaming down and felt pain when he clenched his fist. The piece of window was deep in his flesh. He tried to pluck it out, but it hurt too badly for that. He was going to need his mother.

"You could've broken his neck," Jennifer remarked.

"Yeah, probably. In a funny way, it probably would've been for the best. Maybe I wouldn't have killed them."

17

Mary Ann came marching out through the front door, Marty close behind jabbering. She saw Abe standing there at the car and over at Ricky getting up from the grass. She saw the blood dripping from his hand immediately.

She rushed over to him, "Ricky! What happened?!" That's when the tears came. He told her what happened through heavy sobs, tears, and the pain that was getting worse in his hand. Marty hung back and looked at the spectacle while Abe was growing hotter by the second.

"Abe! What did you do?!" Mary Ann shouted ushering Ricky back towards the front porch and up the stairs.

Abe turned around biting his lower lip, watching his family walk into the house. "I should've stomped his fucking ass! Goddamn kids!"

Mary Ann gently guided Ricky into the house, and she stood on the front porch staring darts at her husband. Things between them had been somewhat smoothed over from when she came back home from her friend's house, but there were still some issues that remained with her. She was waiting for Abe to have a blow-up like before and this seemed to fit the bill. "You could've hurt him! Listen to yourself!"

"Don't come out here and tell me a fucking thing! Your kids shouldn't have been playing around the car! I told them to get across the yard and did they listen?! No! So now I've got to figure out how to fix a fucking window that we ain't got the money for!"

"You're more worried about the car window than your kid! Did you see the glass he's got in his hand?!" Mary Ann shouted back.

"I better not see him the rest of the fucking night; I tell you that goddamn much!" Abe turned his back to look inside the car at the glass that was lying in the passenger seat.

"I'm done! I...AM...DONE!" Mary Ann turned and went into the house, slamming the door. Of course, Abe didn't hear her proclamation that she was done. Done with him and the marriage is what she was done with. Abe was too busy trying to figure out what he was going to do and how he was going to fix the window.

18

"The end had already started, hadn't it?" Jennifer asked, already knowing that it had.

Abe nodded, "Yeah. I finished cleaning the glass out of the driveway with a broom and dustpan and cleaned the inside of the car. Then it clouded up and started to drizzle. I went back into the toolshed and found a black plastic bag and some Duck Tape and made me a window to keep the rain out."

"What was going on inside the house?"

"Mary Ann was doctoring Ricky's hand in the bathroom while Marty watched. I came in and hollered for them. Of course, no one answered. So, I went down the hall and saw them in the bathroom, and Mary Ann slammed the door shut and locked it. I tried to tell them I was sorry but...I had fucked up majorly this time with my temper. I needed a drink more than ever at that point."

"And you got one?"

"Yeah. I um...eventually went out to the toolshed and turned the light on and sat on my stool at the table in there. I had resisted the urge for a while at that point to take the entire bottle and down it. You know, I'd sip on it here and there, just to knock the edge off. But it was a fight every day not to go in there and do what I did that night. That night, I just went for it."

"Do you think Mary Ann and the kids were going to leave you that night and never come back?" Jennifer asked, knowing the answer already.

Abe nodded his head, "Oh yeah. I knew our marriage was done. After that night I figured she was going to go back to her friend's house and eventually to Florida with her parents. She had told me as much one night if things got out of control again. And that was it. Lawyers would get involved...custody battles...child support...total disintegration of the family unit. All because I couldn't keep my temper and alcohol in check that night."

"So that's why you killed them all?"

"No...I killed them because I started drinking out in the toolshed that night. The more I drank, the madder I got about that window...the madder I got about the way Mary Ann yelled at me...the madder I got that I lost my job...the madder I got that I was going to lose everything and it was all my fault.

"You see, I remember thinking all that while I was losing control. I didn't remember step by step what I had done that night when I was arrested, hell, not even months later. That night came to me in pieces at a time until I had the whole thing," Abe raised his hand and tapped his right temple with his index finger, "Up here. And now it haunts me every second of the day."

"As it should," Jennifer told him.

Abe half smiled and nodded, "As it should."

"Can you take me through that night? I've seen the crime scene photos...it's pretty gory, I got to say, and I've seen a lot in my time. This one...this one was rough."

"Yeah, I remember enough to talk about it. But you're not going to believe me when I tell you some of this stuff."

"Why is that?"

Abe hesitated before he spoke. He paused, his mouth hung open like a trout out of water, gasping for air. It was something that he had never told anyone before. "I had a visitor that night. My dad."

19

You're going to let them just walk all over you, ain't you? Peter Tanner said to his drunken son in the toolshed.

Abe's dad wasn't in the toolshed physically but inside his head. His voice booming just like he recalled all those years ago growing up.

"No...it's my fault...I got your temper," Abe slurred, nearly falling off the stool, trying to keep his eyes open.

Since you've been in here drinking, she's been in there plotting her great escape. I told you, didn't I? I fucking told you that you needed to watch her, but you didn't listen! First piece of ass you get, and you marry it! Thought I taught you better than that!

"Leave me alone!" Abe slurred, trying to raise his voice.

He busted your window out, and she doesn't even care! You know why?! Because you'll fix it! You're letting a woman tell you what to do! Why, I never let your mom tell me a fucking thing! I wore the pants in that damn family, yes sir I did!

Abe rubbed his red eyes and looked out the toolshed window at the rain. It was raining but not hard yet, and it was already getting dark. He got up, nearly fell, and steadied himself against the wall.

You need to go in there and let them know who's the boss.

"What I need to do is go in there and fix this between me and her," Abe slurred his speech again. He was drunk, full-on.

I'll tell you what you need to do...

That was it; the spark that ignited the fire where the violence inside Abe Tanner had laid dormant. He was tired of hearing his dad talk. He clenched his fists while listening to the man that he hated. His dad talked about going into the house and "show'em who's boss". That rage that took hold of Abe's mind started creeping around, pushing him, pulling him. He gritted his teeth and started throwing wild punches in the air, screaming for his dad to leave him alone.

He threw the now-empty bottle of whiskey against the far wall, and it shattered into a million pieces. Abe stood coldly, staring at really nothing at all–his mind running a million miles an hour– when his focus landed on a pair of oversized hedge clippers hanging on the wall where the bottle was thrown. Abe's mind was in full-blown berserker mode now; he was tense, breathing harder by the second. He took the clippers from the hanger and turned to walk out of the shed and into the darkness and rain. *Show'em who's boss!* his dad rang out in his head.

He was on a mission now...walking across that yard there was no turning back: he was the maddest he had ever been, perhaps the drunkest he had ever been, and all he could think about was how his children disobeyed him and how Mary Ann told him that she was done.

"Oh, you're done?! You're done, bitch?! Nah, I don't think so...we'll see about this...we'll see about it all...I'm going to show you...all of you...who's the boss," Abe said, walking across his backyard snapping his clippers open and closed with each step.

The Abe Tanner that had taken a nap in his recliner earlier that day was gone...long gone.

20

Jennifer shifted in her chair and flipped her hair. She had heard her share of oddities in the past while face to face with murderers, but Abe Tanner was a horse of a different color. There was something about it that made him telling this story unsettling to her. If she was honest, she was scared of how this story was going to end, even though she already knew. Abe telling her about the events of that Halloween night was old and nearly forgotten news, even to her, but she was still scared for Mary Ann and the kids inside that house. She knew their impending doom was fast approaching.

21

Abe walked up the back porch steps and flung open the storm door. He twisted the doorknob to the backdoor and pushed it open. There in the kitchen stood Mary Ann on the phone, leaning up against the wall. One look at Abe and she screamed; she screamed as if she knew what her husband was up to. The man she met at Al's– the man that she married and had two boys with– that man that was about to end her life.

"Help me!!" Mary Ann screamed into the phone.

Abe reached over and ripped the phone away from her hand and busted it up against the wall. Mary Ann tried to run, but Abe grabbed her hair and yanked her violently down to the floor.

"Done, huh?! I'll show you done! I'll show you who the boss is!" Abe opened the oversized hedge clippers up quickly, putting them around his wife's neck, and snapped them closed.

Blood squirted out from all angles from the blades. She screamed the best she could for the boys to run away quickly, but doing that only made Abe madder.

He opened the clippers again and snapped them closed around her neck once more, this time cutting deeper into the sides of her neck. She was still screaming for help and for her kids to run away, but her voice was becoming weaker by the second. A third and fourth time, Abe opened the clippers and snapped them with authority, finally cutting into the bones and cords of muscles of her neck.

Covered in blood, Abe opened the clippers a fifth time and snapped them together. Her head was nearly detached from her body as it dangled by a few strings. Abe heard the kids running down the stairs from the second floor and when he went in that direction from the kitchen, he slipped and fell on Mary Ann's widening pool of blood on the floor. He landed on his clippers. The bloodstained blades, both open at the time, caught him in the ribs on the left side. Laying on the floor, he found himself impaled on them, nearly down to the black rubber grips.

Ricky, who was already dressed as a mummy and Marty as a scarecrow, came into the kitchen. At first, they had no idea what they were seeing. Ricky's first thought that flashed in his mind was that the scene on the kitchen floor was some kind of Halloween prank and that nobody was hurt and that stuff that looked like blood was just ketchup. He also wondered how Mom's head was hanging like that.

In that same flash of thought, Ricky realized that it wasn't a Halloween prank at all; it was his mother lying on the kitchen floor covered in blood, her head nearly gone, hanging by mere muscle and ligaments and his dad trying to get to his feet, covered in blood, with hedge clippers sticking out from his side. Ricky screamed out wildly and turned to run back up the stairs dragging his younger brother by the hand the entire way.

Well, you sure as hell showed her...now go show them kids who's the boss, Abe's dad said.

"Shut the fuck up! You're not real! You're not real!" Abe screamed at the top of his lungs. "When I get done with them...I'm coming for you, old man! Show you who's the boss!"

"I need a second," Jennifer said to the cameramen. She got up, wiped her tears from her eyes, and walked out of the room. She walked into the hallway to compose herself. She wanted to break down right then and there but somehow held it together– got back her grip that she temporarily lost. This was by far the worst interview that she had ever done, and she wondered if she would ever do another one. She had seen the face of evil before– monsters wearing faces of normal-looking men.

Abe Tanner was a monster wearing a man's face. Jennifer leaned up against the cool concrete wall and took several deep breaths before Kirk, the cameraman who was filming from behind her, popped out into the hallway. "You good?"

Jennifer quickly wiped her tears because she didn't want to seem weak to Kirk whom she had worked with many times in the past. "I'm good...just needed a breather is all. Heavy shit in there."

"You sure? Because you don't look so hot. You want me to get you a water or something?"

Jennifer shook her head, "No, I'm fine. It's just...it's a lot to take in with this one."

"No kidding. Worst one I've ever been a part of; I can tell you that."

The two of them stood outside in the hallway for a few more minutes, quiet minutes, while Jennifer got a hold of herself. She finally calmed herself down by counting to fifty inside her head, inhaling and exhaling as she went. Kirk didn't interrupt; he let Jennifer do her thing. When she was finally ready, she cleared her throat and adjusted her blouse. She looked at Kirk squarely, "Let's finish this, huh?"

22

Abe pulled those clippers out from his side and felt the blood gush out of him. He crawled around on the kitchen floor until he reached a chair. He grabbed hold of it and raised himself. It was a monumental task in doing so.

He was feeling woozy and wasn't sure if that was from the rapid blood loss he had taken or the alcohol. At best, it was a mixture of the two. He ran his bloody left hand through his hair as his right held onto the clippers. He stood there on legs of jelly trying to steel himself for what he had to do next. He walked slowly, albeit in immense pain, across the kitchen floor and to the stairwell. His vision came in and out of focus and Abe's head was swimming. He felt the sudden urge to throw up, and that's exactly what he did, bracing himself against the wall and letting it all go.

"I'm coming for you, boys! I'm coming to get you...B...O...Y...S...!" Abe managed a shout, wiping vomit and blood from his mouth and nose.

Abe started to climb the stairs as blood from his side kept pouring, soaking his shirt, and trailing down to his pant leg. He was hurting, and had he been sober and not running on adrenaline, the pain would have rendered him perhaps unconscious. Nevertheless, Abe Tanner took it slow, step by step up those stairs, clutching the oversized hedge clippers in his right hand, his grip tightening with each rung.

After twenty-eight steps to the second floor where Ricky and Marty's bedrooms were, Abe felt lightheaded and went to his knees slowly. He was getting tired, sleepy, and the wound to his side was still bleeding. At one point, he was about to close his eyes, leaning to the side of the hallway wall. Just before he closed his eyes, he caught a glimpse of Marty peaking at him through his open door that was cracked just a little.

Abe grunted and his eyes grew wide with rage and fury. He used the clippers as a crutch and made himself stand up, but not straight up, but rather with a hunched-over look. The wound to his side was worse now.

"I see you!" Abe lurched down the hallway a piece and stood before Marty's closed bedroom door. Abe lifted his leg and bashed the door in with his work boot. He was surprised that it had only taken one violent kick. Even more surprised that he had the strength to do it.

Inside the bedroom, he didn't see the kid at first. Abe figured that he was in the closet. He staggered over there, reached for the doorknob and flung open the door. Nothing but hanging clothes and junk on the floor. He then looked at the bed. He walked over to the little twin bed and flipped it over with his free hand, and man alive did that hurt, but he saw Marty hiding under the bed, shaking and crying.

Marty tried to crawl away as he screamed, but it was no use. Abe came down on his back with the clippers closed. The force of the blow went right through Marty's little body and the tips of the two blades stuck into the carpet through his son's stomach. Abe pulled them out but Marty wasn't dead yet. He rolled around onto his back and looked up at his dad, who looked like the scariest Halloween monster he'd ever seen, and tried to scream. Nothing came out.

"You should've listened to me!" Abe raised the closed clippers high in the air, above his head, and drove them down into Marty's chest. Blood went everywhere– on the carpet, on the nearby mattress, the bed frame, and all over Abe's clothes, face, and hair. Abe stabbed his son more times but he lost track of exactly how many.

"Leave him alone!" Ricky yelled from the other bedroom. He had no idea that his brother was already dead.

Abe pulled the clippers out of Marty's young body and opened and closed them, snapping them together violently, as he lurched out of the bedroom of his youngest and towards his oldest. Walking down the hallway toward Ricky's bedroom, Abe fell again, nearly on his clippers. He lay there on his back in a heap, staring up at the ceiling, feeling his vision spiral, spinning around as if he were on the fastest carousel.

"Show 'em who's boss," Abe mouthed the words.

He rolled slowly over to his side, the one that had the deep puncture wound, and managed to get on his hands and knees. His body was trying to keep him on that floor, but the rage that was in his mind was stronger. Again, using the clippers as a crutch, Abe hoisted himself up and stood on his two feet, dazed and wobbly. He felt as if he could pass out at any moment. He shook his head, trying to stop things from spinning around.

He took steps towards Ricky's bedroom, clippers down by his side held by a hand that was red with blood.

He bashed the bedroom door open just as he did with Marty's, and he didn't have to look around for his oldest. Ricky was trying to get out the window. Abe rushed over with the help of adrenaline and caught Ricky by his right arm. His son was nearly out the window. Abe struggled to bring him back inside, but he was finally able to. He flung him to the floor as Ricky kicked and screamed and even landed a few punches to Abe's face once he got back to his feet. He fought hard but it was useless in the end.

Abe overpowered him, opened the clippers once he got Ricky pinned up against the wall, and slid the open blades of the clippers around his son's neck. And just as he did with his wife, he closed them as hard as he could. He watched as life drained from Ricky's eyes with each open and close motion.

Eventually, Ricky's head was cut off after several brutal snaps. His small head fell to the floor. His decapitated body slid limply down the side of his bedroom wall where his *Ghostbusters* movie poster hung. Abe stood back, woozy, and looked at his dead son. Out of exhaustion, drunkenness, and blood loss, Abe, too, fell to the carpet and lay there sprawled on his back, looking up at the ceiling.

23

"And that's all I remember from that night," Abe said looking at Jennifer who was still holding it together the best she could.

"You don't remember the police taking you into custody? Had it not been for your mother-in-law who was on the phone, there's no telling how long you and your family would've been in that house before your discovery."

Abe nodded, "Yeah. That actually saved my life because I nearly bled out there in Ricky's bedroom. I've still got the scar right here. It was deep. Sometimes I lay in my cell at night and wonder why I didn't die that night. Doctors told me that I should've died with the kind of wound I had and the amount of blood I had lost. I don't know."

"Too bad it didn't kill you," Jennifer said totally out of character.

Abe half smiled, "Yeah, I wished it would've, you know. God's punishment is for me to live a long life…live that night over and over."

"Perhaps it is. But you're right where you belong…in a cage for the rest of your days."

"The best place for me," Abe replied. "So, is this it? We done here?"

"I am if you are," Jennifer replied.

"Yeah, I don't think there's anything left for me to say. You know the rest after what happened when the police came. You know all there is about the trial. Anything else you want to know?"

Jennifer sat there contemplating what else she wanted to know about that night. But was there anything else? And if there was, did she want to hear it? The stuff he told her about that night would give her nightmares for months to come, if not years. She looked at Abe; their eyes locked, and she was about to ask one more question– one she had been wanting to ask since she sat down to talk with him.

"Mr. Tanner, are you…" Jennifer's mouth hung open, ready to ask the rest of the question.

"Never mind. I think we're done here. Thank you for your time, Mr. Tanner."

Jennifer got up from her chair when Abe spoke to her, "The answer is yes."

"What are you talking about?" she turned to ask Abe.

"What you were about to ask me…yes, I do." Jennifer looked the man over one final time and walked out of the room.

HISTORY OF BIRCH

THE TREE HAD BEEN a staple of the Portman's backyard for decades. It was a simple tree: a tall standing birch with limbs, thick and thin, sprawling every which way providing all kinds of shade in the summer. It was not a flashy tree. It was not a spectacular tree, especially given the circumstances of how it came to live in the backyard; but it was, over time, a tree that carried a special meaning to the man who watched it grow over the years.

When Lois Portman had brought it home many years ago, Abe looked at it and thought to himself, why in the blue Hell she'd even bought it?

"That tree dead?" Abe asked, when Lois carried the potted tree over to him in the backyard.

"I don't think so. I got a discount on it," she replied happily.

"How much of a discount? Free?"

"I got it for five bucks. Can you believe it?!" Lois was awfully proud of her purchase. Abe stood there, sweating from the heat of cutting the lawn, and inspected it while she held it like a prize she had won at the county fair.

"It looks like it's about to die, hon," Abe said, looking at the dead branches.

"I think it'll make it. You'll see," Lois replied.

Abe did not think so but didn't say anything else about it. He could tell that his wife was happy about the tree. "What kind of tree is it?" he asked, looking around the black planter it was in for an identifying label.

"The man at the store told me it was a birch."

Abe nodded, "Well, let's go plant this thing, I guess."

She was mighty proud of it. Maybe she was proud of it because it was the first thing that she had bought for the yard since they moved into their new home. She was twenty-two, full of life, not yet riddled with the cancer that would quickly eat her insides away chunks at a time. When Lois and Abe planted that tree in the backyard, everything in their life was in full bloom.

After Lois' passing, Abe looked at that tree daily and was reminded of his wife and how tickled she was when she bought it. The tree itself had become a totem of his dead wife. Even in death, it was as if she was still there through the tree. Abe did not talk much about what the birch signified to him. As long as the tree stood in his backyard, she was always there. To Abe, there was comfort in that.

Their backyard was bare, back then. No plants, no trees...nothing. Not even a back porch to sit on. When Abe and Lois bought the house, they knew what kind of condition it was inside and out. It was such a great deal that they could not pass it up, even if they wanted to. The house itself was old and dilapidated. 1917 was the date of the build on the deed when everything was signed, sealed, and delivered.

Inside the house, the interior was still trapped in the 1950s. Not much had been updated in terms of décor, but that was going to be Lois's job to usher everything into the present. She had a good eye for color schemes and furniture layouts. Abe never questioned her decorating ideas and how she wanted the inside of their home to look. She knew better than him what would work best. Abe knew that for sure.

Abe was the outside man. He tended to the yard work and made sure that their small little place in the world looked decent. He laid down a new walkway from the front door, erected a beautiful white picket fence around the front and sides of the lot, and enclosed the backyard with a privacy fence. Eventually, he built a back deck where the family had many cookouts and where he and Lois could sit on summer evenings and watch the kids play when they were little.

The inside of the house, aside from the décor, was a challenge. The electrical needed to be completely redone. That was what the electrician that Abe had consulted had told him. "It's still in good shape, but you'll need to get rid of these fuse boxes," the burly electrician told Abe.

The house did not have breakers, like the more modern homes he and Lois grew up in. The old fuse boxes were in every room of the house, and they took those old screw-in fuses. The previous owners– the ones that had built the house back in 1917– did not get electricity in the house until the late 1930s, and that was the way the old man, Delbert Rocking-ham, had it done.

When times changed and electrical engineering became better, Delbert never bothered having the fuse boxes converted into one huge breaker box. That was left for Abe and Lois to have done when they purchased the house two years after Delbert died of a stroke, and Emma died falling off the front porch. It was one month to the day her husband had passed.

The electrical eventually got redone in that old house. All the fuse boxes had been taken out of the rooms, and all the wires rerouted to one main breaker box in the bedroom where their daughter, June, took up. The electricity was now safe, and neither Abe nor Lois had to worry about something going haywire and catching the house on fire. The electrical was only the tip of the updates they had to make in the home. The roof would be next.

The roof was just a plain old shingle roof that had seen its better days. The roof, according to the realtor, was just under twenty years old; but when Abe went up there to inspect it himself after the purchase, he discovered that the roof was depressing in places, and the shingles were crumbling between his fingers when he knelt to inspect them. "How's the roof?" Lois asked when Abe came down from the ladder.

"No good. I'd say those shingles are going on more like thirty years. There's some rotting plywood under them, too. The whole thing is going to have to be redone. Going to cost us an arm and a leg, I bet," Abe said, tipping his blue Auburn Tigers hat up on his head a bit.

The whole roof was indeed redone. When the roofers started, they confirmed exactly what Abe had told his wife: the shingles were so old that they did not even make them like that anymore, and the actual plywood of the roof was rotting away. Abe was right in his assessment when it came to price. It was around eight grand to replace.

The roof, according to the main roofer who had done more roofs than he could remember, had to be at least fifty years old, and the shingles were not far behind. In the end, the roof was finished, and the shingles were replaced with a nice metal roof. Abe was happy that he would never have to climb up there and fix another shingle ever in his life. It was well worth the price that he and Lois had to finance– just another bill with another kid on the way. The family was growing, as was the home they had bought now six years ago.

Lois worked her magic inside the home. She repainted the walls and trim with a bluish-gray color with white trim. It brightened up the rooms and made them appear much larger. It was a complete change from the peach color that was all over the house; Lois said she was pretty sure it was lead based paint. That was the last time the walls in that house were painted– the fifties at the very least. The new coats of paint that freshened up the house and the arranging of the new-to-them furniture that did not match, made the house warm and inviting. Most of all, Lois made it feel like a home– not just a house, but a *home*– where they were raising their family. Life was rolling merrily along for the Portmans.

———

Abe took the post-hole diggers out of the small garden shed that day when Lois brought home the birch, and the couple walked around their yard. They were looking for a place to plant it. Lois carried that nearly dead tree around and placed it in the side yard facing the fence and street. The two of them walked back a distance and looked at it. It would look okay growing there but there was one thing; power lines that went from the power pole connecting to the side of the house.

"Tree grows big; then it'll get tangled into those lines; and then I'll have to call someone to cut it down. Let's try somewhere else," Abe said.

They tried the front yard, and yes, it did look good there, too, but Lois pointed something out this time.

"If it grows the way I think it will, then it'll block the front of the house. These birch trees can get pretty big and wide." Abe didn't think that the tree was going to grow, being in the state that it was currently in when she bought it and brought it home. However, there was that off chance that it might, which is why they did not put it in the side yard around the power lines. Lois walked over and picked up the potted tree, and off the married couple went again in the yard.

———

Abe and Lois found themselves in the backyard, which was large and most of all, bare. The grass was lush and green, and Abe knew that planting anything in the back would probably grow very well. Abe stood and leaned up on his post-hole diggers, watching his wife place the tree in numerous positions in the backyard. Five different places to be exact. After each one, she would walk back over to Abe, and the two of them would look from afar. Each time, they decided that the placement did not look right, so out went Lois again to reposition the tree.

Finally, Lois placed the tree right smack in the middle of the backyard. She came back and stood with her husband, and the two of them looked at it. "I think we have it, don't you?" Lois asked.

Abe looked around, assessing if the tree did fall, would it fall on the house? No, was the answer; and if it fell, it also wouldn't damage any of their neighbors' property, like the privacy fencing that boxed in the Portman's backyard. The placement of the birch seemed to work right there in the middle of the yard. "Yeah, it looks good right there, I think," Abe said.

"Our first tree!" Lois said with excitement in her voice.

Abe and Lois walked over to the tree, ready to plant it. She pulled the tree out of the pot and what Abe thought was a harbinger of the tree's life expectancy, some of the small branches broke off in her hand. Abe wanted to say, "See, I told you this tree ain't worth planting," but he refrained. He knew Lois loved the tree because it had the odds stacked against it living, and it was their first tree. Abe began to dig the hole.

The first year went by, and the birch barely grew. If it did, Abe could not tell. While sitting on their back porch, somehow Lois could tell the tree had grown some and would sometimes remark about it. "The tree seems taller," she claimed one day as they sat in their chairs. Abe doubted it. To him, it still looked the same, brittle branches and all. He honestly thought the tree was dead.

The second year, Lucas came into the world during the heatwave of that March. An eight-pound, three-ounce baby boy. The birch in the backyard did appear a little taller to Abe. He noticed while cutting the grass out back that it had grown some and even had very small buds on it that would eventually form leaves. *Nah*, Abe thought to himself, *it ain't going to grow*. Abe kept on mowing.

The third year, Ava came along. A seven-pound, ten-ounce baby girl. It was late August when she arrived, and by then, the birch had grown exponentially. It was nearly as tall as Abe. Leaves were in full maturity, and the tree even produced a very small shadow on the lawn. Abe stood there looking at the tree, and it was as healthy as any tree he had ever seen. "Well I'll be damned," he simply said one day, looking at it.

———

Family life came into full swing for the Portman family from then on: job promotions, first days of school for Lucas and Ava, heartbreaks from when Abe's father passed away, the fights between Lois and Abe over bills and how to raise and discipline the kids as they got older, the tears and laughs, the cookouts, the holiday get-togethers, the planting of flowers in the yard, and everything that made life, life. In all that living, the birch grew and grew over the years.

Before anyone knew it, the birch had grown to its maximum height of thirty-plus feet and was a good fifteen feet wide. The shade it provided was a comfort to be under during the summer sun as the birch's millions of leaves protected those who sat underneath it.

"Can you believe that it got this big?" Lois asked Abe one evening on their back porch, marveling over her tree.

Abe chuckled in disbelief, "No, I can't. I remember back twenty years ago when you first brought that thing home."

"You didn't think it was going to make it."

Abe nodded his head, "Yup, I remember. I was surely wrong on that. You got a good tree. God, has it really been twenty years since we put that there?"

"Yeah, hard to imagine, ain't it? Kids weren't even here yet when I bought that tree. And now look at everything. Kids are planning their futures and will be out of the house soon."

"Yeah, it's like that tree has been a marker for our family growing, right? As we went, so did the birch," Abe remarked.

Lois nodded, "Yeah because it grew as we all grew. And like that tree, me and you have reached our full maturity."

Abe sat there beside his wife in his chair, holding her hand and looking out across the backyard at the tree. "That we have, my dear...that we have."

As the seasons changed, one right after another, the birch stood sentry-like over the Portman's backyard and could be seen all the way down the block. The birch witnessed the kids growing up, moving out, and visiting the house less and less. It also watched as Lois and Abe's hair turned gray, and their bodies seemingly became unlike what they used to be when they were younger. The birch was still magnificent and glorious in its thirty-year age, but that could not be said of the two who planted the tree.

Abe once said, sitting on the back porch with his wife one fall evening, looking at the tree, "That birch will outlive us all."

"Not bad for five bucks," Lois laughed, remembering that time nearly thirty years ago when she first brought it home and how terrible it looked.

"I didn't think it was worth even planting. But I never really said anything because you loved it so much."

"Oh, I know you thought it, though," Lois said, looking at the tree in the cool fall evening as the stars were beginning to hang in the October sky. That was the last time that Abe and Lois would sit out on the back porch together. Soon after that, Lois got sick. Stomach cancer was the cause. She was dead before the spring would come the following year.

———

It was summer—his first summer without Lois. Abe, an old man, tried the best he could to manage along without her; something that he thought he would never have to do. They had agreed a long time ago that he would die first because he was a year and a half older than she was. The cancer inside Lois had spread quickly, attacking her every cell. By the time the doctors caught it, it was already too late. Lois was going to lose a war before she knew a battle had started.

During that first summer–the first without the matriarch—Abe, his kids, and their families, had a get-together out in the backyard. It was a cookout that hot July evening, much like they had had every year since God-knows-when. Passing the family grill over to Lucas to cook the food on, Abe sat there amongst his family and thought silently about how he wished that Lois was there, like she was just a few months ago. Oh God, how he missed his wife.

Abe was drinking iced tea and sitting in a chair under the shade of the birch while his grandkids played out in the yard. Ava came over to her dad and sat in the chair next to him. "You okay?" his daughter asked.

"Yeah, I reckon I will be. Have to be, I guess. I really should be asking you that."

Ava looked around the yard trying to catch a floating thought, "I'm okay. Good days and bad ones."

"I know," Abe replied. "I have them myself."

Ava looked at her kids playing with her brother's kids on the swing set and smiled. Then she looked up at the birch and marveled at how tall it was and how wide the branches spread out.

"How old is this tree?" Ava asked, changing the subject.

Abe looked up briefly, "Oh, I think it's thirty years old. At least that's how long ago me and your mom planted it."

"You and Mom planted this tree?"

"Yeah, I thought that we told you that?"

Ava shook her head, "No, I never knew that. I just thought it was always here."

Abe laughed, recalling that day she brought it home, "Yeah, she brought it home, and man, did it look like it was already dead. Thing was about knee-high back then. She paid five dollars for it, if I remember correctly, from the bargain area at the store. It was so brittle that you could snap the thin branches off with ease. I didn't tell her that I didn't think the tree was going to live and that it would be a waste of time to plant. She was so proud of that tree because it was the first thing that she had bought to put out in the yard. God how she smiled when she got it into the ground. When we got married, there were no trees, flowers, or nothing around here. It was all bare. So, I kept my mouth shut, dug a hole for her, and she planted it."

"And here it is thirty years later," Ava said looking at the tree, appreciating it even more so than she did, even two minutes ago. "You know, it's kinda like she's here with us, in a way, with the tree."

Abe looked around the tree and saw the green leaves slightly dancing on the branches from the wind. A cool breeze kissed them both. He smiled, thinking back when Lois walked across the yard carrying the potted tree three decades ago– back when she was young and healthy and with her whole life ahead of her.

"Yeah, I think you're right, kiddo," Abe said, putting his hand on Ava's shoulder and giving it a light squeeze. "I think you're right."

DEATH ON A PARK BENCH

DEATH SAT on a park bench at the community park, doing nothing but wasting time. *What did it matter*, he mused. *It's my time to waste. Besides, I've never taken a sick day before or even a fifteen-minute break. It'll be okay.*

In his line of work, sick days were not an option. He had to come in every day and was on-call twenty-four seven, three sixty-five. There was no time to rest. So did Death feel badly about taking a knee for a little bit? A quick timeout to watch Life instead of taking it? Not at all. That rest was long overdue, in his mind. His body was constantly on the go, and it was nice to just...sit for a spell.

What did it matter if he was AWOL for a little bit? It's not like people would not be dying when he returned, right? A fifteen-minute break, just to stop for a little bit– to rest. Everyone has their time. Death knew that. He had so many hundreds of thousands of places and people to see around the world that just thinking about it tired him out. Was this what he wanted out of his life? He grinned a little when he applied the word *life* to himself. "I'm Death...do I even live?"

He had never been this tired before– this completely exhausted. Sitting on a park bench was something that Death had never done. In fact, this was the first time Death ever sat down and took a break. It was...kind of nice. He didn't know how tired he was until he rested his old bones there on the bench on that fine fall afternoon watching the world go by. There was a peacefulness to it.

The world he saw, from underneath his black hood, was a world without Death– without him and without a natural order of things. He was a built-in piece of the necessary fabric of God's Divine Design ever since the beginning. He was the most important part of God's plan. Death was the final destiny of man's being. It was a job he took seriously, but over time he had become less and less thrilled with the tasks at hand. It never stopped. People never stopped dying. There was no let-up. It was man, woman, and child over and over and over again; different places, different people but the same thing– death. How many people had he escorted from the Land of the Living to the Halls of the Dead? There was no way to quantify the true number.

As he watched ducks paddle slowly along in the pond across from him, a man, balding, carrying a folded-up newspaper under his arm, came to sit beside Death. The man was not frightened away by Death's black cloak, hood, and huge scythe. Death could change the person's perception of how they saw him. The man with the newspaper, who sat on the other side of the bench, saw a normal-looking fella with a tropical buttoned-up shirt, green cargo shorts, and green New Balance running shoes. All in all, a normal-looking middle-aged unassuming man.

"Afternoon," the man with the newspaper spoke politely.

Death looked at the guy. It was the first time someone had ever spoken to him who was not in the midst of dying, begging for a chance to live, or screaming and crying about how it was not their turn. Death was in uncharted territory. "Hello. I'm Ernest."

"Sam." The two smiled at each other. Sam opened the paper and crossed his legs to read the latest. "Good Lord, I can't believe all the people that have died in that earthquake in South America."

"Yeah, I was just there," Death replied, not thinking about how his comment came across to Sam.

"Excuse me?"

Death smiled nervously, "Nothing, sorry."

"I just hate to hear about all those dead kids. Damn shame."

Yeah it is, Death thought.

That was the toughest part of his job– taking the kids. Just because he was Death didn't mean that he was void of feelings. He hated taking those good people, and he could always tell the wicked from the good in death. He hated to see the good of the world die. If he could ever find God, he would ask him what the purpose was to take the good. It seemed, to him at least, that taking the good was counterproductive. But hey, who was he? He wasn't God.

Death sat watching the world go about its day. He watched the ducks swim from one end of the pond to the other– at a quick pace and then a slow one.

He watched clouds float on by in the sky. Looking up, it dawned on him that this was the first time that he had ever just watched the clouds move since he was a boy. It was fascinating to him– something so simple but yet so profound. He remembered being a small boy a long, long time ago. This was before he was given the eternal job of Death itself by God.

However, those memories of his time as a mortal human were nearly gone. What replaced those memories that were forgotten was nothing but a void. There were a few memories still around inside his head: his mother and father. He thought he had a sister, but he couldn't make her face out in his mind. Death remembered that he had a puppy who used to follow him to the creek when he would go fishing. The longer Death lived, the further back those memories got. He worried that one day he wouldn't even be able to remember those few, scant memories he still had.

Death turned his eyes, eyes that had seen it all ever since creation, to a couple hand-in-hand who walked on the paved path that wound its way throughout the park. Death never knew love or compassion in his Death form. Maybe he did as a young boy, but that time had been erased when God had put His hand on his shoulder and turned him into Death. He had no memories of feeling love.

He had seen love before– saw the exercise of it when he came to take the ones that had just passed from the Land of the Living. He had heard the cries and smelled the salty tears of those who held the hands of their loved ones as they died. He knew about love but never felt it in his Death form and wished that he could.

Sam, the newspaper-reading man, folded up his paper properly and placed it on his lap. He looked about the park with Death.

Clearing his throat, Sam spoke to his acquaintance on the bench, "What do you do, pal? For a living."

Death did not turn his eyes away from the couple that were walking further and further down the paved path, to answer Sam's question. "Reclamation."

Sam sat there and nodded to himself. "Sounds like a good industry, I guess. How long you been doing it?"

Death watched a Blue Jay perched upon the dirty, white birdbath in the middle of the park. "Forever. What about you?"

"Ah, I just retired yesterday. I worked at a factory, making socks. Spent the last forty years of my life there. I'm ready to just gear down and smell the roses, you know?"

Death watched as a Jay played and flapped in the water of the birdbath. And then, just as suddenly as it had landed there, it flew away in a gust toward a tree where Death lost track of it.

"Retirement," Death said absently. "I think I'd like to do that one day. Maybe soon."

"You look too young to retire, son. What are you, about thirty-eight, forty years old?"

Death smiled. He wanted to laugh out loud. Sitting there, another thought sprang on him: when was the last time he laughed? Certainly not since he took the job given to him by God.

"Don't be thinking about retiring just yet, son. You've got a long ways to go yet. Just enjoy life."

"Maybe. When did you decide that enough was enough?" Death asked.

"I guess when my body couldn't get going anymore. It was getting harder and harder to get out of bed in the morning. Plus, I felt like I was missing out on life. Hell, to be honest, I missed out on everything because I was working all the time. Always had something I had to do or someplace I had to be. I wish that I could have that time back now. Maybe by being retired, I can do some of the things that I had missed when I was young."

There were a few minutes of silence between the two on the bench before Death spoke. "I'm taking a break right now. My first one since I took the job. It's just nice to sit down and not have to be everywhere for a few minutes."

"Well," Sam began. "It's okay to take a break. I sure as hell wished I did. But no. I had to be the guy with the perfect attendance, never going to break. Sick or not, I was there. I remember one time that I came to work with a broken leg. And let me tell you, it's hard working on an assembly line when you're on crutches. This was back before rules and regulations made it to where you couldn't do stuff like that." Sam laughed at that memory.

"I just don't want to do it anymore. I hate my job," Death reflected, after soaking in what Sam had just said. It was the first time that Death spoke the words that he had been thinking for thousands of years. The words just seemed to roll out of his mouth.

"Welcome to the club, son. I don't know many people who like their job. I certainly hated mine and the people I had to work around to get it done."

"I didn't hate mine at first. But over time, I got to where I hated it. I wish that I could change jobs or just stop doing it. When I took the job, I was just so excited that He picked me out of everyone. I mean, He could have picked anyone else, but there was just something about me that He liked. I guess I keep going because I don't want to let Him down."

"Well," Sam said, looking around the park as the sun bathed the landscape. "What is it that you want to do besides reclamation?"

Death sat there and had no idea. "I don't know. But I know that I don't want to do this anymore."

"Some advice son…get out while you're young because the older you get; the harder it is to change careers. That's just fact."

"I don't know if I can do that actually," Death said. "I never had a say. I was asked one day by the Big Man if I wanted this job. I was young and didn't know any better. So I took it. I couldn't refuse Him."

"I think he would understand if you needed a change. I don't think humans are supposed to do the same thing over and over forever," Sam replied.

Death shrugged his shoulders, "I don't know about that. His wrath is terrible. Anyone that goes against Him is never the same."

"Are you saying that you're too afraid to go into his office and say you quit?"

Death sat for a moment and considered things. Yeah, maybe that was it. Or maybe the job had become a part of his being– like a second soul. How do you stop doing something that you've done your entire life? That was indeed the question.

"Not really afraid. Maybe. I don't know what I am. I'm just tired of the job. I have no direction for my existence even if I did just up and quit. Where would I go? What would I do? I have no skill set other than what it is I do. And I can't go back to what it was like before. I don't even remember what I was like before I took this job. The job has become my identity."

Sam nodded and smiled, "Yup, all the reasons why I never quit my job. What else was I going to do? Where else was there to go? I always wanted to be a barber. You know, just have a quiet shop where old men would come in and talk about the weather, women, and sports. Like a shop you'd see on TV.

"That's what I wanted to do– just cut hair. But I could never do it because I was too afraid to make a change. I had a family to raise that depended on me. Now that I'm retired, and the kids have families of their own; I'm too tired and old to start something new."

"As I sit here talking to you, work is just piling up by the split second all over the place."

"Ah," Sam dismissed. "Let the others deal with it for a while."

"That's just it, there's no others that do what I do. I'm the only one that can deal with what has to be done. I've never had help."

"Maybe that's your problem. Maybe you need more of a staff to help you handle the job. Could be why you're so burned out at such a young age."

Death wanted to laugh at having help. But then again, it would make sense. Maybe have a network of others that could be in all the other places where Death was to be. He dismissed it, feeling that God would never go for anything like that. He just had to face facts: he was

Death, the one and only– black robe, skull face, and scythe-toting…Death.

"Is this what it's like to have no deadlines or places to be, Sam?" Death asked, looking around at the park that seemed to be going about its daily business.

Sam sat there and exhaled deeply, "I don't know. This is all new to me. But I'm dying to find out."

Death sat there and watched the clouds, the birds, the people, and the squirrel casually jumping around the green grass.

Death wanted to just stop. And he did while he sat there on the park bench with Sam. As he sat there, thousands of people who were supposed to die did not; all around the world death was on pause. Accidents that would have claimed their lives had Death been on the job, were just accidents, nothing fatal. The fates of so many were now altered because Death wanted to take a fifteen-minute break. He would have to answer for that later; he was sure of that. His not being there to escort the dead went against God's Great Design.

Death wanted a new career. In the end, talking to Sam, he knew that there probably was not anything for him. There's always an excuse for people to stay where they're at, Death supposed. And what was his excuse? Fearing God's wrath? The fear of the unknown about what he would do with his life after he gave up the mantle of Death?

He was no different than the man who sat next to him that had apparent regret on his breath about the past. Death surmised that the problems that plague man are the same as the ones that eat away at supreme beings such as himself. In the end, there was no fundamental difference between Death and Sam.

Contemplating there in silence, dark clouds came across the sky, blotting out the sun. The beautiful park landscape was darkened by the swarming clouds above. The wind got up a little, and Death could feel the rain coming. Off in the distance, thunder rolled.

"Well, son. That's it for me. Looks like a storm is coming on pretty strong. You take care now. And think about what I said. I hope you figure it out before I did. I'm going to enjoy the rest of my retirement." Sam got up and began to walk away from the bench.

Death sat there and felt the breeze blow about him, cooling him a bit. This sudden coming storm was God. Death did not doubt it. It was a sign– a sign to get up and do his job. His fifteen-minute break was over. Death sat for just a few more minutes longer and thought about things as Sam walked further and further away, but not out of sight.

Death knew that Sam was right. He knew that if he did not get out while he was young, then he would never get out. But what was young? Death never aged. There was no young or old; only a distinct weariness that bore inside his semi-hollow soul. Sitting there on that bench was a great feeling. It was a feeling of letting go, if only for about fifteen minutes.

Death felt the wind get stronger and the thunder rumble more. He knew God was letting him know that his fifteen-minute break was over. Death took a deep breath and blew out mightily. He rose from the wooden bench. His ancient bones creaked and popped, begging to sit down for only a few more minutes; he couldn't. He had work to do– work only *he* could do.

Death began to march toward Sam who had not gotten out of his sight, not yet. Sam stopped as the storm began to drop rain, and he looked up. His right arm shot out from his side and then quickly to his chest. Then, like a load of bricks, the newly retired man fell onto the green grass of the park. By the time Death got to him, Sam's soul was standing beside his corpse, glowing radiantly and looking at the approaching man in black, who carried the long scythe.

Death took Sam's soul by the hand...his break was over.

EVENING DRIVE

AS THEY SKIDDED—FISHTAILING as she had heard her dad call it in the past– Brenda watched the dark, cold world from outside the SUV spin. Her mom's screams from the front passenger seat seemed to be a hundred miles away. Brenda, "Brenda" to those in her family and "Bren" to all her friends at school, did not scream like her mother. She was too enthralled by the spinning scene out her window. She did not know if her father was screaming or not; probably not because her dad never got himself worked up over much. It would not have mattered much though; Brenda wouldn't have heard him anyway. She was too captivated by the spinning of the SUV and the big white puffy clumps of snow that were coming down like huge cotton balls falling from the sky.

Twenty minutes earlier, Brenda was in her bedroom, safe, watching the snow from her window. It was not as if she had not seen snow before, but it was the beauty that captivated the fourteen-year-old freshman. The snow to her was pure– magical even– as it fell, hitting the ground in a quiet way that only snow can. Outside it was dark, and the streetlights illuminated the millions of snowflakes that poured down and lay on the cold ground below. It was a thing of beauty each time it snowed. Brenda always sat at her window each time and watched as it came down. To her, it was better than anything on TV.

In her town, snow did not come their way often. When it did come on those sparse times, it was always enough for the schools to shut down for the day. If the temps did not get over the freezing mark on the next day, schools would be canceled again due to the hazardous back roads the school buses would have to travel. When it snowed, it was an event to behold. In the next town over in Claxton, when snow came it signaled something more sinister; the return of a serial killer that stalked the college campus there. But in Brenda's town, away from the killer's hunting grounds, the snow was pretty and peaceful.

Brenda's first real big snow came in the form of a blizzard years ago. It was October 26th of that year Brenda saw her first real snow; a true anomaly. A snowstorm came through right before Halloween of that year. The weather elements happened to hit just right that day. A very strong cold front was coming down from the north, bringing with it single-digit temperatures. From the south, in the Gulf of Mexico, moisture was being pulled up into the southeast, causing a clash between the cold front and moisture. When they eventually did collide, snow came down in bunches around the upper states of the south. Kentucky, North Carolina, and Tennessee were the hardest hit, especially the higher elevations. Where Brenda lived, in Cahill, Tennessee, the town got eight inches of snow.

Brenda sat outside on the night of the blizzard on the back deck, bundled up in her thickest jacket and toboggan, holding a piping hot cup of hot chocolate and watched the snow come down with a fury. There were no small flakes that night– no build-up to the big show. The snow came in like a lion, dropping flakes so big that Brenda could hear the snow pelting the ground, the roof of her house, and the porch she sat on. Across the yard, all she saw was white stuff coming down, like feathers out of a pillow when she and her friends used to pillow fight back when she was younger. Before she knew it, there were already three inches on the ground. It was magical. The green, dying grass from fall's grip had been covered by a white, soft blanket of snow. Across the landscape, the white blanket lay undisturbed, and nothing stirred about. All was quiet except for the snow falling.

Getting up from her chair, she started to walk about her yard. The snow crunched underneath her shoes. When she looked back a few yards, she saw the tracks that she had made. This thrilled her. She had seen that sort of thing in the movies but not in real life. So, she walked a little more about her snow-covered backyard and then to the front. Soon, she retraced her steps making sure to step into the footprints she had already made. She did not want to disturb the white, beautiful blanket nature was creating. That was a good memory from years ago and one that she recalled with happiness each time it crossed her mind.

———

The SUV spinning out of control; she could have done without that. It was crazy to her that something like this was happening only five minutes from Brenda's house. Twenty minutes ago she was up in her room watching the snow come down and texting her friends about there not being any school tomorrow…YAY! Now, she was in the back seat of her dad's SUV on some back road they had driven down a thousand times, spinning to their impending doom.

Twenty minutes ago her dad had called up to Brenda's bedroom and requested her presence down in the living room. When Brenda walked down the stairs she saw her mom and dad getting their winter dress on. She asked them, "What's going on?" as she stepped off the last rung of the stairs.

"We're going out to drive in the snow. Want to come?" Brenda's mother replied.

"Awesome!" Brenda shouted, running back upstairs to gather her jacket and shoes.

Twenty minutes ago seemed like a lifetime ago now. Brenda pulled her eyes away from her window there in the backseat and watched her dad fight the steering wheel and heard her mom scream in terror. The road they were spinning out on was CO RD 500, a road that eventually led to Brenda's high school. The county road was a side road off the main highway that people took just so they could drive slower through the countryside. It was a road that her mother had taken often to drop Brenda off at school. If she was running late, which was not often, they would take the highway that ran parallel to the back road.

Twenty minutes ago, the three of them were driving slowly down the small streets that were like a spider's web throughout the town. The streets were already covered up, and she could feel the SUV slide sometimes. Her dad was in four-wheel drive and had both hands on the wheel and a foot poised over the brake. He did not go past ten miles per hour at any time. Her dad was one of the safest drivers she knew. Even her mom had said so.

After driving throughout their small community, up and down nearly every neighborhood, Brenda's father wanted to journey out a little further. Shirley, Brenda's mom, told Jack that she thought that they should just go on home. Jack wanted to see what CO RD 500 looked like. Shirley did not press the issue. It was only a few minutes from their home; what's the worst that could happen? Brenda settled in the backseat and watched the snow come down in earnest as the SUV trudged along at a pleasing ten miles per hour.

CO RD 500 was just your garden variety back road; nothing special about it at all, except that steep winding hill that you had to come down at the beginning. Other than that, it was nothing but flat, and for the most part, straight. As the SUV began to descend the hill, that's where the SUV began to skid. Jack got nervous, and so did Shirley. At that point, Brenda was still watching the snow, which was more difficult now because of the darkness. There were no streetlights down CO RD 500. It was pitch black.

The hill began to take the SUV's speed and sped them up coming down. Jack tried to lightly, very lightly, press the brake, but something caught that was not supposed to–the brakes locked down. Jack did not go into full-blown panic, but his wife did after she saw Jack starting to fight with the steering wheel. That was when she screamed because the SUV began to fishtail. Instead of a safe ten miles an hour, the SUV was coming down the hill at twenty, much too fast on snow and ice. Brenda turned her attention away from her window in the backseat and watched out the windshield at what was happening. That's when she got a little scared.

The SUV gained some speed, and the headlights caught two huge oak trees off the side of the road. None of the family members inside the SUV had ever recalled those trees being there before. But what did it matter now? They were heading right for them, closing in on twenty-five miles an hour with no way of stopping. "Hang on!" Jack screamed before the loud thud.

Then everything went dark, darker than it already was beforehand. The airbags, which should have been deployed, did not. A few months before the accident on CO RD 500, Jack had received a letter about a manufacturing recall on that particular SUV. It seemed that the SUV's airbags had a history of not deploying in some instances. He was asked to bring his SUV into his local dealership so this matter could be taken care of. Of course, Jack had no idea of the recall because he tossed the unopened envelope into the paper shredder, thinking it was nothing but junk as usual.

––––––

Brenda sits up in what used to be her bedroom and watches out her window. It's always snowing, just like it was that night of the fatal crash that killed her, her dad, and her mom. Everything is pretty much the same as it was right before her dad had called her down to the living room. Each time, Brenda comes down the stairs and asks what's going on. Then she's told about them going on a drive out in the snow. She says, "Awesome!" and runs back up to her room to get her winter stuff on.

They all retrace the exact roads they took that deadly night in the snow.

They go down CO RD 500, but each time, there's something about it that makes Brenda a little uneasy. It's like something is telling her that going down this road is a bad idea. Like something is trying to warn her about it. She sits back and watches out the window there in the warm backseat at the snow coming down. Then it gets dark. She takes her eyes off the window, there in the backseat, to see through the windshield at what's going on. There in front of them are two oak trees. She hears her mom scream and then a loud bang! Lights out.

Brenda finds herself once again sitting at her bedroom window, watching the snow fall. And then her dad calls for her from downstairs. Brenda hesitates, citing a strong sense of déjà vu. She stops walking across her bedroom and racks her brain, trying to figure out why this all seems familiar to her. It's like she had been here before. Standing there, she shakes it off and dismisses it. She walks down the stairs to find her parents getting their winter gear on. She asks what's going on, "We're going out to drive in the snow. Want to come?"

Brenda shouts, "Awesome!" and runs back up the stairs to get her cold weather gear on. And then, she stops for a second. Something about her doing everything she just did seemed familiar. And then it leaves her. Brenda gets her thick jacket and shoes on and rushes down the stairs and walks out the door with her parents.

Inside the house, a man and a woman sit in the living room. Mr. Watts is reading a newspaper and Mrs. Watts is playing Candy Crush on her phone. "Did you hear that?" Mr. Watts asks his wife, folding his newspaper down to look over at her. She was sitting on the other end of the couch.

"Oh you mean the running up and down the stairs and the front door thing again? Yes, I did."

"How long has that been going on now?" Mr. Watts asks, nearly passive.

Mrs. Watts takes her eyes off the phone and looks around the house. She considers her husband's question for a few moments. "Well," she begins, "We bought the house fifteen years ago when Matty was five...I think ever since then."

Mr. Watts pulls his newspaper back up to his face and disappears into the print. "Well, at least it only happens when it snows. Sometimes it's crazy to me that we live in a haunted house."

HUSH

1

HE WAS TIRED AND MUDDY. He hated driving on dark, wet roads. His eyes were not the best in the world, but driving at night– especially in the rain– was the worst for him. As a bonus, his wipers were shot, dry-rotted, and did nothing but smear the rain on his windshield. Will gripped the steering wheel and kept his eyes on the darting black road, minding the green digital clock on his dashboard. He was running late to get home for dinner. Jessica would want answers, and all that he was going to give her were going to be lies. He would never speak the truth of what happened out there in a field off of Brock Hollow Road. Never. It would be a secret that he would take to his grave.

It was a nasty business– the murders– but in order for him to keep living the life he was; it was a necessary evil. It had to be done. Had John never gotten mixed up with Becky in the first place, none of what went down out in a remote field would have had to happen. All of it was John's fault; Will concluded that before and after the deeds were done. Had he not gotten in deep with someone who could finish the both of them, everything would have turned out much better– a much happier ending perhaps. *I should've picked better friends*, Will considered as he drove in the rain. You can't pick your parents, and you can't pick your neighbors. But your friends? Of course you can.

Will Erickson had presided over Claxton Elementary School for a decade as the principal. It was a good job and one that he enjoyed very much. After all the years of teaching, networking. and ass-kissing, Will was finally given the job when crotchety old Mr.Wain retired... finally. Life could not get any better, and it seemed all that Will had to do was just live life and enjoy it as much as any man could. Driving on the dark, wet, and winding back roads with mud caked underneath his nails and his clothes soaked and muddied, Will thought about when this night took a turn. It was in his office– just when he was set to leave and actually be on time for home– when a friend came a-calling...

2

EARLIER...

Will was gathering his things to head home for the evening when Dr. John Henderson– the superintendent of the school district and his oldest friend– came into his office disheveled and wide-eyed. He shut the door behind him. Right away Will knew something was wrong. Usually, John was a cool customer, and Will had only seen him stressed a few times throughout their twenty-five-year friendship. But in his office, the man who came in was the opposite of the man he had known all those years.

"Can I talk to you?" John asked, pacing about the office, running his fingers through his thinning dark hair.

"Of course," Will said, putting his folders back down on his desk and easing into his chair. "What's wrong with you?"

It took John pacing about the office a few times before he spoke nervously to his friend, "We got a problem. HUGE."

"What kind of problem?"

Finally, John stopped pacing and plopped down in the chair that sat in front of Will's desk where many a frightened child had sat before. "One that could end up bad. Maybe worse; who knows?"

Will could see his hands trembling a bit, and this made him a little nervous. He had never seen John like this...ever.

"You going to fill me in?"

John ran his fingers through his hair again, a nervous thing he did, and leaned over his chair to give Will a closer look, "We've got a sex scandal brewing here in your school." After he spoke the words, a weight seemed to be lifted off of John's shoulders as he leaned back. He thought it was about the money they had been stealing over the years. What a relief that was that it was just a sex scandal.

A sex scandal he could deal with, maybe, but not if the secret about the money was uncovered. A sex scandal was not that big of a deal…or was it?

"A sex scandal? Involving?"

John looked around the room and then up at the ceiling before he answered, "Ms. Foyer and a certain junior student."

Will sat silently processing the news before he spoke. "Oh my God. This ain't good. This could be…catastrophic."

"Yeah this is bad, Willy," John replied, seemingly to have calmed down a touch from when he first entered the office.

"Was there a formal complaint filed?" Will asked, leaning back in his chair, considering what he had just been told.

John nodded and licked his lips to get them wet. With all the commotion that had been going on with him in his office, the drive to the school, and sitting there telling Will what was about to go down, John noticed his lips were dry as hell. He reached into his front pants pocket and pulled out his ChapStick, making several swipes on his lips

"Well, it all started like these things do. Some kid went around bragging about fucking Ms. Foyer at her house after the Central High School football game last week. Before you know it, it was all over the school and the town. It got out of control before I could even get out in front of it. Now, it's got a life of its own."

"This is the first I'm hearing about it. This happened last Friday? Like a few days ago? And I'm just now hearing about this?! Everyone else knows this is going on and I'm the last to know?!" Will spoke with anger with each rhetorical question.

"Yeah."

"Why didn't you tell me about this earlier?!" Will shouted.

"I just got made aware of it *yesterday*. Anyways, I got apprised of the situation by a concerned parent, and from there it just snowballed into what we've got now. It's growing by the minute. Maybe if I had known about this earlier, I might have been able…"

"You've talked to Becky I'm guessing?" Will asked, growing more agitated by the second.

John nodded, "Of course."

Will looked pissed about this, "Why didn't you tell me that one of my teachers had this rumor going on…"

"You were out of town yesterday when I found out, and I didn't want to bother you because I knew that you had a lot going on! Looking back now, I should have told you as soon as I heard about it. But let's be honest, what was a day really going to do for us?"

"Does Spec know?" Will asked, trailing off into thoughts about his vice principal.

"She got involved pretty quickly because she was the first point of contact with this kid's parent. I was sent the info afterwards. Spec wants your job and now she's all over painting you as disconnected and non-interested in this issue. She's basically sinking your battleship."

"I was gone for three days, hundreds of miles away and the person in charge didn't tell…"

"Doesn't matter," John interrupted, "she wants your job. She thinks that you are incompetent. We should've never made her vice. She's making it out like I've known about this for a week or something, and I've got parents gunning for my job every minute because Spec is out there spinning lies and making things worse than they really are. Instead of keeping shit in-house, this stupid bitch goes out there and drags me and you. Maybe I should've pushed harder for her to get that principal position at Mars Hill. That's what this is really about, you know? She's still mad that I didn't push her hard enough. She wants your job and I'm just collateral damage at this point."

Will leaned back in his chair and slammed his hand down on his desk hard. "You know I called her and checked in to make sure everything was going smoothly on my way back last night, and she said everything was great. And she knew about this the whole fucking time!

What does Becky say?" Will asked about the teacher in question, Ms. Foyer.

John shook his head, "She denies it of course. I believe her...I do. She said that Bobby Painter had been making sexual comments to her in the halls and in the classroom. And when he met her out in the parking lot last week at her car, he tried to grab her and she smacked him. That's when he told her she'd regret that."

"According to her."

"According to her, yeah," John replied.

"The parking lot? That's good! There's..." Will began and was cut off quickly.

"Camera wasn't angled out that way. I already checked, Bucko," John said, dashing Will's hope of some evidence to put the situation down.

Will sat and looked out his office window trying to corral all his wandering thoughts into one space. "So have the police gotten involved yet?"

John shook his head, "No, not yet. I spoke with the boy's parents today, and they want her job. Apparently, there's an audio recording of Bobby and Becky having sex. They're planning on getting a lawyer, and I've already advised them that we'd be investigating the matter– just a matter of time though before your school is a three-ring circus—my office included before it's over."

"But you never heard the tape?" Will asked, still lost down the twisting and turning roads of thought within his mind.

John shook his head, "No. But Bobby's mom has. Or claims she has. She seemed pretty intense when I spoke to her on the phone earlier. She wants to find Becky and kill her. She said she's got the tape and heard it with her own ears."

"So they may have a tape of the sexual encounter, and Becky denies anything happened. Even if they do have a tape, you can't really prove that's Becky's voice on that tape unless she's actually talking. Hell, it could be any female as far as they know."

Will stared up at the ceiling, still lost on the back roads of his mind, trying to find the main road of coherent thought. This was a major mess that John wanted him to clean up. But why? This was Becky's problem, not theirs...not really. If anything, the worst-case scenario was that one of his teachers would be fired, and that would be the end of the story.

He and John had too much going on with all the stuff they were into together– all the hiding and nefarious transgressions over the years. So the question that got Will back onto the main road was: what was John's *real* issue? Will started to fish because John was the type that if he was hiding something, he would never come out and tell you unless you started fishing for him by throwing him good bait; bait that he had to take. Will cast his line and began cranking...click...click...click...click

"Then she needs to take a few days off until this can get straightened out, John," Will told his friend. "I can't have her here at school. Hopefully, she'll understand. Get Brad to start doing his lawyer magic because if you don't do something, then we're going to look like we're trying to hide something or not even care. Now, I like Becky, but I don't think it would be in her or our best interests to have her at school with this still going on." Will was reeling his line hoping that would get John going.

John looked around the office nervously for a few seconds while Will watched him with curious eyes. John was about to speak and then laughed out loud causing Will to know in that instant that John had just taken the bait; he had him on the hook. This fish was going to be a whopper, one that you would mount on the wall in your den.

"This is a fucking mess," John said in total submission. He was about to spill the beans on everything. The way he sounded to Will was that he sounded...desperate, defeated.

Will looked at his friend and said, "Yes it is. But we'll make it through." Will sat still watching his friend fidget with his hands and look out the window. "What are you not telling me about this? Because this really ain't that bad for us. We just let the investigation run its course and go from there."

Nothing from John.

Will kept looking at John who finally turned his eyes to Will. "What is it?" Will again with some heat in his voice.

"Becky and I have had a relationship for the last six months," John said lowly, looking at his friend.

Both men sat there in silence looking at each other for what seemed to Will to be an eternity. Then Will asked, "Does Mandy know?"

John looked up at the ceiling and chuckled, "Yeah, right. And Becky told me that if I can't get her off the hook somehow, then she's going to tell my wife. It'll kill her. Destroy my family in the process. This bitch is in scorched-earth mode right now. I don't know what to do– partly why I'm here. I get the investigation going where it leads and all; but if she goes down, she pulls me down with her. That could be bad for me and you."

Will was stunned. He struggled for a few minutes to locate the words he could use to articulate how disturbing this meeting was. "You and Foyer? Are you out of your fucking mind here, John?! How could you allow this to happen?!" Will barked.

John sat in the chair and had the look of a desperate man trying to figure out how he was going to evade the electric chair that was moments away from taking his life.

"I honestly don't know. We went out for drinks after a PTA meeting at the district office, and one thing led to another. Before I knew it...six months had passed by. I didn't mean for it to go any further than just a one-time thing, but, goddamn, she was so..."

"I don't want to know anymore, John," Will held his hand up to shut him up. "I think the less I know the better off I am in this situation."

"She's going to tell Mandy, Willy. I know she will. I can't fix this where she comes out clean. I don't think that she did anything with Bobby Painter though; but if that tape does exist and it can be proven that it's her on it, then that's all she wrote, ain't it? I didn't mean for this all to happen," John said with tears forming in his eyes.

Will knew that his friend was broken in ways he had never seen before. Will wanted to help but had no idea how to even begin. The situation that John had brought before him was a situation that Will saw no way out of where Becky Foyer came out clean.

The accusations were already made public. As far as Will felt, she was probably done at that school– most likely the school district as well and perhaps even jail time– depending on how the investigation would go. But there was another issue: that issue was that this was now Will's problem. How? One thing that Will knew about his best friend was that John would fold under pressure like a cheap suit. It was not his fault, it was genetic. His parents were probably rats.

"She may not even tell Mandy," Will tried to assure John. "Becky may just be threatening you so you can get her out of this jam. Are you sure, one hundred percent, that nothing was going on with her and Bobby Painter?"

John sat there and considered Will's question for some time and shook his head no. "I don't think they've had anything in the way of a relationship, no."

"We got to work on the assumption that Bobby did record them having sex. That's the worst-case scenario. If he did it in secret, then Becky would never know about it. If she did fuck him, then she'd lie to you about it to get her into the clear. That's the size of it."

"Sounds about right, I guess," John said nervously, trying to manage his emotions.

"Then why is she going whole hog on you? I mean, if there's nothing there, then she won't go to jail and lose her job. She may be reassigned to another school or school district, right, just because of the accusations alone. You got enough juice to make that happen."

"Most likely."

"But on the B-side of this issue, I'm concerned that she knows Bobby might have something on her, and the two of them did have sex– which means she needs you to get her out of it using your marriage as leverage. I mean, if there's nothing there, then why is she threatening you? That doesn't make sense to me."

"If it did happen, and he did record them, there's no way we can get that tape. That genie's out of the bottle. Hell, it might be already turned over to the police for all I know."

"Too bad we can't get to Bobby himself and see what he has. But then again– it's an audio tape. It ain't a video. Brad can argue the point that it can be anyone on that tape. He's pretty good at what he does." Will mused looking out the window, trying to figure this one out.

"I wish that I never got with her," John resigned, looking down at his shoes. He wanted to cry but he had done too much of that on his way to see Will.

There was silence in the office. Both men were lost in their own thoughts.

Then John said, "We've got to shut Foyer up. I think it's the only way out now. Bobby has that tape, then she'll kill my marriage and my career in the process. I can't get her off the hook."

To Will, John was conceding to the fact that Becky had sex with Bobby Painter and that the audio tape in play of the encounter really had her on it.

Will looked at John from across the desk, "And how you going to do that exactly?"

There was a cold, long pause before John answered. And when he did, Will at first thought it was a joke, a tasteless joke at best. But the more he looked at the expression on John's face he knew that his friend, desperate as he had become, was deadly serious. "Kill her," he said softly as if he didn't want to say it.

Will sat there and gazed at his friend. They were not killers, thieves maybe, but not murderers.

"Get real, John. That's not an option. Don't even say stupid shit like that." It was the only thing he could think of saying.

"We've got nothing else here, Willy. Foyer isn't going to go quietly into the night. I can't get her out of this if Bobby has a tape and it's her on it. Like you said, we've got to assume that he has it, right? Why else come after my marriage? This will ruin her life, and she's playing for keeps because if she goes down I'll go down with her...my marriage and career...poof!"

Will considered their options in silent length. There were not many, not any good ones at all. "I don't know how to handle this one. I guess you'll just have to fucking deal with the consequences, John. Grown-up decisions often have grown-up consequences."

John got up from his chair and paced about the room like a caged lion, "This is us, Bucko! Me and you here!" He was in survival mode now. Will could see that in his body movements and hear it in his tone.

"I didn't fuck Becky! You did! I'm not the one that's going to lose my family and career over this!" Will lashed out.

"You're going to lose your job!" John stopped and pointed to Will. "Spec will bury you! Good luck finding a job in educational administration with this kind of bullshit on you! You think any system out there is going to take a principal that is painted like they knew what was going on but did nothing?! That's how Spec's coloring this, man!"

John stood there looking at his friend of decades. "We got no choice here," he said, lowering his voice. "We got no choice. Our livelihoods are being threatened over two bitches that want nothing more than to watch us burn. We've both worked too damn hard to get where we're at in life. And do you want to start over completely at forty-one? I don't. Foyer goes away– so do our problems. Spec won't have any power, and later you can get her out of your school. We'll figure that out. I can push her somewhere else later on. But Becky has got to go."

After minutes of careful consideration, Will finally spoke. "I'm not going to kill anyone. I'll roll the dice and deal with Spec trying to get my job. But you're on your own, Johnny. I'm sorry. There's nothing that I can do. I can't get you out of this one." Will was sincere. He wanted to get John out of the jam because he was afraid of what John would do if and when it all came crashing down. What came out of John's mouth next sealed the deal. Will was now the fish that John was reeling in.

John stood there with his hands on his hips in total disbelief. He was nearly speechless, but then his mind turned red with rage. He was going to have to pull out the big guns here. He anticipated Will would not help him out of this, especially when the mention of murder came up. That is why he came up with a backup plan– some insurance. He hoped that he could have appealed to his friend, but just in case he could not, he had this last trump card.

"That's fine. But be advised, that when I leave here, I'm going straight to Doug German at the paper and tell him about all the fucking money you've been stealing out of the school's kitty."

"That was both of us!" Will snapped as his eyes grew wide.

"Not anymore. I've got everything pointing to you. I'll be in the clear on this. But you?" John shook his head with a shark-like grin. "You? I've got all the missing money aimed right at you. I've got all the ledgers, remember? How much did we fleece this place for? Thousands a year, right? Split right down the middle– our retirement plan. I take half the money, and I doctor the account books, right? I've got two books: the cooked books and the real ones. Did you think that I'd just implicate myself, Willy? I've got it where it's all on you. And by the time that I turn over all the paperwork and books and show the investigators what's what, Spec will be the last of your worries. Please, don't make me do this to you. Help me get in the clear."

"You son of a bitch! How could you?! We're supposed to be friends!" Will shouted.

"We still are, Willy!" John shouted back, "But we got to get through this...together. And once we are I'll burn everything I've collected on the stolen money. I promise you that. But I need you here, man. We got to kill Becky. We don't have much of a choice. I wish we did. Like you said, assume that there is a tape; too much of a gamble now that you think about it not to."

3

Killing Becky Foyer was planned out in Will's office as night began to fall over the town. It was a gruesome plan. John went into detail on how it needed to go down, and Will nodded and agreed on everything. It sounded good to him even though he had never killed anyone before.

Sure, he'd seen a ton of true crime shows on TV, but by the sound of it, so did John. Will figured that John had been thinking about this end game for a while by the sound of it. As John told him the step-by-step plan to lure Becky to Brock Hollow Road, Will was coming up with a plan of his own. He was not going to be under John's thumb as it concerned the stolen money– money that they had stolen together back when they were friends. Will would go along with this plan, and then what? John gets into another jam and would lord the money over him again? Will could not take that chance. John had to go, too.

As John rambled on and laid out the plan for Becky's murder, Will thought about how he got sitting in his office listening to a man planning the murder of one of his teachers in the first place. It started years ago by stealing money out of the school's treasury, which was all donated by the big wheels in town and various school fundraisers. All that money that was raised and donated was supposed to go to things for the school. It never made it, not all of it, to its intended purposes.

Will would tally up the money at the end of the year, cut his and John's slice out, and announce to the school exactly how much they raised for the year. It was always around ten to fifteen thousand dollars lighter than what they hauled in. No one knew, and if anyone ever questioned, (which no one ever did) John had cooked the books to make it look honest. All that extra money went into John and Will's bank account under a bogus company name.

The plan was that the next summer they were going to meet a man who was going to launder the money for them in real estate deals. Had Will ever known that this day would come, he would have never brought up the idea of how they could steal money and save for a bigger retirement. At least John would not have any power over him. That was Will's biggest mistake: he trusted John. He never had any reason not to...until that night in his office.

After the plan was discussed, mostly by John– because at the end of the day, it was his plan, not Will's– John left the office and told Will that he would contact him shortly when things were ready. Will told him to just not even bother calling– just that they would meet at Brock Hollow Road out in the field around seven when it was good and dark. Will was about to help his friend murder someone, a co-worker, a person that he had seen and talked to for nearly ten years. The idea of killing her made him physically sick, much to the point where he threw up in the garbage can that sat beside his desk after John left.

The plan to get Becky out of the house was a good one, one that Will did not see any holes in. Not that he was listening too terribly hard. His mind wandered often as John went over what they were going to do. Will's thoughts wandered to his family and what would happen to them all if he got caught up in the stolen money. What would happen to his wife and kids, their good name in the town? Then he thought about how Spec had betrayed him and how he wanted to deal with her. Honestly,

Will had only caught about half of John's plan but enough to paint himself a mental picture of how it was going to go down.

John had called Becky on a payphone outside of Hammer's Diner on his way to her house and spun her a great lie– one that she took hook, line, and sinker. He told her that he had a friend, a very influential friend, that could make Bobby Painter and his parents go away. But this friend of John's wanted to meet with the three of them in his office there in town for a bit.

Becky, who wanted to clear her name and keep her job because teaching meant the world to her and avoid jail, asked John if this friend could get her out of this mess. John's reply was, "ABSOLUTELY". Plus, he oversold this fictional friend and what he could do and what he would want in return for the favor.

It would not be easy, John reminded her, but his friend, whom he only called Jordan, had the clout to make everything go away and put things back to the way they were. "You won't have to worry about Bobby or his parents," John said.

As night took a stronger hold and the rest of the streetlights throughout the town of Claxton clicked on in unison, John pulled up to Becky's modest two-story home on Juniper Lane. She was waiting on the front porch steps. She got up and walked over to John's car and got in. A light mist began to fall as the two of them pulled away from her home for the final time.

With the wipers on intermittently, John drove and did not say much. Becky was mostly doing the talking. It did not matter at all to John because in about an hour or so, Becky would not be a problem anymore. She would be dead, and her leverage on him would be buried with her in that shallow grave out in a field on Brock Hollow Road. Tuning Becky's yammering in and out, pretty much driving on automatic, John wondered how upset he had made Will. He knew that blackmailing him on the money that they had stolen over the years was a bitch thing to do, but he had no choice. Once he saw that Will was going to let him twist in the wind, it was the only card he had left to play. It was a terrible card to throw down, but he had to nevertheless. He hoped that after all this mess they could move past this night and forget the murder of Becky Foyer.

John was not sure if Will would. *That might be a problem*, John thought, hearing Becky talk in the passenger seat.

As John took Highway 411 out of Claxton, John broke Becky's one-sided conversation, "Did you fuck Bobby Painter?"

Becky looked at him, "What's it matter now? Your friend is getting me out of this, right?"

"It just makes it hard trying to get you out of this if I don't have all the information," John returned.

"It doesn't matter now. He gets me out of it, then you can reassign me somewhere else where I can start over. I know that I fucked up. I do. And I know that I lied to you. But we get out of this we all win. Just know," Becky said as heartfelt as she could, "that I never wanted to bring your family into this. It's just…I had to have some sort of cards to play here in case you didn't want to help me."

"You ever think that's how your reputation is going to be after he gets you out of this?" John asked.

"That's why I got you, Johnny," Becky said, looking out the windows and not at him.

John knew that even if there was a guy named Jordan that could get her out of this jam, she may never really let him go. There was no telling what she really had on him. *Did she tape us having sex*, he wondered. Probably so. She would never allow John off the hook. Any time she wanted something or wanted a promotion or anything, she would threaten him through his family and career. It would never end, and John knew that.

Getting mixed up with Becky Foyer was the worst thing that he had ever done in his life—worse than ripping off the school.

Knowing that she would never stop even if there was an actual way to get her out of this, which was fucking impossible because like Will said, "assume there is a tape." This seemed a real possibility because John thought Bobby's mother really had it the more Becky talked in his car. On top of that, Becky did not deny sex with Bobby Painter when he point blank asked her in the car. Driving to Brock Hollow Road to kill the woman who was sitting just feet away from him seemed more and more like the right thing to do. It was the only way out.

4

As John drove down the highway and away from the city and out into the country, Becky asked, "I thought we were going to his office in town?"

Without even turning to look at her, John replied, "He called and changed his mind. He wanted us to come to his house. Said just in case someone saw my car or us getting out to meet with him at his office– too many eyes. This guy is good, but paranoid," John laughed, trying to sell the lie. Becky, of course, bought it. She had no reason not to trust John because he had a stake in her getting off the hook as well.

"Where's his house at?"

"Brock Hollow Road," John replied. The closer that they got to their destination, the more tense John became. The moment of the killing was approaching.

Will walked about his empty school. It was quiet there. Always was when there was no one around. It was times like those when Will would walk around in the lonely school building and listen to the echoes of his footfalls. It was peaceful. Sometimes when he did this after hours, the quietness allowed him to think a bit. Many a significant decision was made when he ambulated around the hallways. That night was no differ- ent; for he knew when he left the school and got into that car of his, he would come back to school the next day a changed man: a murderer.

It was a tough pill to swallow but he knew that he had placed himself in the jam. He could blame John all he wanted and should deserve plenty, but had he been honest, he would have never gotten in this mess to begin with. He could have walked away not having John throw the money he helped steal in his face. At least he would not have a woman's murder on his conscience.

As he came down the metal stairwell from the second floor, Will began to think of how he was going to get himself out of this mess. He had an idea there in the lonely school, but it was a long shot. He did not like the idea that he was going to be a co-murderer in a co-worker's death. That just gave John even more power over him for the future. It was like another piece of leverage

John would have. The money was already too much leverage.

The question was: would John use it to cash in when he got in trouble later on? Will thought so, and what would his "friend" call on him to do then? Burn an orphanage? As the stairs spilled out into the enormous lunchroom, Will stepped off the last rung and looked around at his kingdom. All this was going to be gone if he did not do something to get out from underneath Spec's and John's thumbs. In the stillness of the school where his best ideas came to him, Will had an idea: a good one– one that had been brewing up in his office while John was going over the details of how to get rid of Becky.

Will had framed his plan in his office, but walking around the school, he was able to finish the house– finish the idea. The emptiness of the school provided him with the rest of the formula for how the rest of the night was going to go.

5

Meanwhile, John and Becky pulled down the long and lonely stretch of road that was known as Brock Hollow Road. The road had an ominous reputation of being haunted. Most of the drivers that came down the road were teens hoping to see the ghost of the man who was hanged from a huge branch of an oak tree sometime in the early 1920s. The tree in question was still there; at least the legend said it was, but no one was sure because all the trees on both sides of the road looked the same to various degrees.

Of course, the tales varied from not seeing anything to seeing something hanging on one of the limbs. These accounts were from kids that were either drunk, high, or just wanted attention. Regardless, kids always drove slowly down the road at night wanting and wishing to have an experience that they could report later on.

John knew that they were getting close to where he was going to pull the car off the old country road. On the left-hand side of the road, there was a trail that led about a quarter of the way into the woods. That was where the most adventurous high schoolers parked to have sex or do whatever kids did those days. John knew the road and fields well along with the woods because he used to hunt deer there. His dad had taken him once he was old enough to hold a rifle, and then after his dad passed, John always hunted in the woods and fields down Brock Hollow Road. He knew that when the time came to kill Becky and bury her body; nobody would find her there—not where he was going to put her.

The only snag that could trip John's plan up was if there was another car parked there. That would be bad. But as luck would have it, there was not when John pulled his car down the muddy trail. Becky was oblivious to what was happening or was about to happen. She thought that this was the driveway to Jordan's home. She was dead wrong.

John got on the trail, and halfway up, he stopped the car and put it into park. He and Becky sat there on the muddy dirt road that led to parts unknown. The mist had turned into a light rain, and the sound could be heard coming down on the roof of the car. John cut the lights off and the engine, and the two of them sat in darkness. Becky then knew that things were going to go bad in a hurry if she did not get out of that car.

It was then she realized there was no Jordan, and the only way she was getting off the hook for having sex with a student– who swore he would never tell a soul– was to get out of the car quickly and run for her life. Almost reflexive, Becky grabbed for the door handle, but John had already locked it. "We need to talk, Becky."

———

Will sat in the parking lot of the elementary school as the rain came down lightly in the night. He had an idea of how to fix all of this. They had agreed to meet at Brock Hollow Road at seven and the hour was growing closer. Will watched the streaks of rain slowly trickle down the windshield and wondered if he could go through with any of what was to come. *What choice do I really have*, he thought to himself. Passing this point of no return was going to be life-changing if it ever got out. Will was going to make sure that it never did. A secret stops being a secret when another one knows about it. This secret he was going to take to his grave.

6

Will knew Brock Hollow Road very well. His church had taken kids through there on creepy hayrides every Halloween. Even when he was a kid, Brock Hollow Road was a thing of legend. Many Friday nights Will and his friends would ride their bikes down the road at night in hopes of seeing something ghostly. They never did. They did, however, get scared a few times, mostly by their overactive imaginations. He knew where the side dirt road was where the kids parked and made out, had sex, or got high or drunk– sometimes all in one night. It was the only one on the long stretch of country road.

"Do you know where it's at?" John asked him in his office while laying the plan out.

"Yeah. Been down that road a thousand times," Will replied, still framing his own plan inside his mind.

The rain had picked up some and smacked angrily against his windshield as Will drove down the road in a calm state. He knew that his part was coming up. and he had to do his part of the deal to make this all go away. But Will had other ideas on how to make things disappear. He should have seen John turning on him coming a mile away. But he trusted his oldest friend too much. When you get greedy, you watch the money more than the people around you. He had no clue that John was building a firewall between them. That wall was going to come down and come down hard.

7

When Will pulled into the muddy dirt road and drove a cool five miles an hour down it, his car lights shone on John who stood there in the rain awaiting his arrival. The sight of him standing there like that made it seem to Will like he was in a bad horror movie. John leaned casually against his trunk with his arms folded. Will stopped the car, killed the lights, and got out.

"Took you long enough?"

"Yeah, well, I can't see very well at night...especially in the rain." Will walked over to John. "We set?"

"Yeah. I think so. I've got the shovel and flashlight in the backseat," John said, walking around the car to open the passenger-side back door to retrieve his tools.

"She dead?" Will asked, standing in the same spot. He assumed she was.

"No," John said as he brought out the shovel and flashlight. "I gave her one last chance but she refused. And you know what that bitch did to me? She clawed my fucking face trying to get out. I think she might've even broken my nose. Hurts like a bitch. I just took my stun gun and zapped her. She's limp in the front seat. Probably be out until we get her up to the hill out there. I don't know. Fuck it," John said, pointing ahead of them into the darkness.

Will could faintly see dried blood on his face and fingernail marks in a straight-down pattern from his forehead down to his cheeks.

"We're going to bury her alive?!" Will asked not expecting this. Honestly, he fully expected Becky to be already dead. But this...this was a curveball that he did not expect. *He's full of surprises tonight*, Will thought.

John handed Will the shovel and flashlight, "No, we're going to shoot her dead and then bury her body. I'm not a fucking savage, for Christ's sake."

"Shoot her?"

"Exactly how did you think this was going to go down, Willy?" John asked as he opened the passenger side door. "Now, you going to help me here, or do I need to wrench my back?"

Will walked over to where John was and put the shovel and light down on the ground as two of them reached inside the car and pulled the unconscious Becky Foyer out of the front seat and onto the muddy ground. It was during this transfer that things got real for Will. They were doing this. They were actually going to kill Becky and for what? All because John had been cheating on his wife with her and when Becky got into a jam she used that against him. He hated his friend for what he was making him do. But it had to be done.

John grabbed Becky by her two arms and started dragging her while Will picked up the shovel and light, "We're in this together, remember? I'll drag her for a while, and then we'll switch. It's about a mile up the trail here. Not much in the way of trees and such– pretty much an easy, straight shot," he said with labor in his breath.

8

Will's mind was whirling a mile a second as he followed slowly behind Becky's shoes. Ahead, John was having a devil of a time pulling the woman– who wasn't heavy at all– across the terrain, slipping and sliding and falling on his ass a few times. The rain stopped for a few minutes and then returned with a downpour and then turned to a drizzle. Will did not pay any attention to that at all. He kept his light trained on Becky's shoes as John dragged her. There was something hypnotic about it.

"You really think this is a good idea?" Will asked as they began walking through what seemed to be a very saturated area covered with pine needles, dead leaves, and small various shrubs.

"She didn't give us a choice, now did she?" John said panting. "You can't deal with crazy, remember that, Willy. Here, let's switch up a little bit. I don't think I can go any further. I'm already beat. And we got to hurry. I don't know how long she'll be out."

Will handed his shovel and flashlight to John and walked around to Becky's limp arms and picked them both up. She did not look heavy but dead weight made the thinnest-looking person forty, fifty pounds heavier.

John walked behind inhaling and exhaling deeply. He was tired but, most of all, out of shape. Dragging bodies across the forest was for the birds. While he walked slowly behind Becky's shoes, John got to thinking about how things had gotten way out of control. There was probably a better way to handle all this, but for the life of him, he did not know how. He came to Will for help but his friend, who was great with plans and knew how to get out of jams, came up with basically nothing. Killing Becky Foyer was not ideal, but in the end, it was the only way. At least, that was what John thought. Who knew what Will was really thinking. That notion frightened John a little. Who knew what a man was capable of when faced with choice-less choices?

The rain began to come down a little harder, hitting the leaves above and the deadfall around them. It sounded like small firecrackers popping all around. Their ears had gotten used to it.

"Right here's far enough," John said.

Will dropped the arms of the woman and stood there breathing hard with his hands on his hips looking around at the darkness, taking advantage of the quick rest. Like his ears had gotten used to the rain, his eyes had gotten used to the small light of the flashlight there in the dark. "I'll start digging. Maybe we can wrap this up quickly."

John walked around Becky's body with the shovel, placing the flashlight on the ground.

He took the shovel and stabbed it into the wet ground as if he were a pirate staking his claim. That was the place where they were going to bury their problems. As John began to dig into the ground, Will looked at his watch and could barely make out the faint light green hour and minute hands. He was going to be late, and Jessica was going to play "Twenty Questions" with him, especially with him being muddy and wet. How was he going to explain that one? *I'll figure something out*, he thought to himself.

9

John had dug around 3 feet, (but who was measuring) and Will dug the last 2 or so. However many feet it really was, it was deep enough for Will to have help to get out. John took the flashlight and shone it into the empty grave as rain fell, dropping in flickers through the flashlight's cone of light. Both men were tired and muddy and wanted this night to be over with. Especially Will as he looked at his watch again. He was for sure late now for home. Maybe he could slip into the washroom out in the garage and clean up without being hassled by his wife– more things to think about– Jessica would keep on and on until she got to the truth. She was like that sometimes.

"All right," John said, turning his attention to Becky's body lying on the ground. "Let's do this."

He pulled a small snub-nosed gun from his back waistband, a .38 Special. Neither man had ever killed a person before. Hell, neither man had dragged a body across a field and through a forest and dug a makeshift grave before, but here they were– putting down someone that could end it all for them. If they did not kill Becky, their lives would be ruined. She would destroy John's life, John would rat out Will, and the entire empire that they built on a foundation of sand would come down in a loud and everlasting crash. John hated that it had to end this way, he really did.

Will did not fancy himself a murderer by any means. He did not think that John was either. But there they were– ready to stop the breath of a woman who could bring down their lives piece by piece. It had taken both of the men a long time to reach personal success that was measured by wages, status, possessions, and family.

Becky was a threat to all of that. Had John been able to keep his dick in his pants, none of this would have had to happen. Will figured if it wasn't John being with Becky, it would've been something else John had gotten into like he had a few times in the past. Will always covered his friend's back and always came up with a plan to get him out of trouble. The last time was with the DUI a year back. That incident had taken his last favor with Det. Jones.

Will held onto the shovel tightly as his plan that he had finalized back in the empty school began to come into focus. John cocked the hammer back on the gun, aimed it towards Becky's body, and fired two shots—hitting her in the chest and head. The report was loud and caused both men, who knew the shots were coming, to jump in fright.

Before he could turn around to look at Will, Will swung the shovel like Babe Ruth and connected the metal spade against John's head, causing him to wildly fire off another round before falling onto the ground. The gun fell out of his hand and blended into the muddy ground. Will would never forget the feeling of the vibration in the wooden handle when he hit John's head. His hands stung. A handful of bees, baseball players would say when you caught the baseball in the palm of the glove instead of the webbing.

Will acted quickly as he swung again on John, who was already on his back, catching him on the side of the head where the first blow caught him. John tried to get up, but it was useless. Again, Will hit John in the head, and with that, his friend finally laid on his back, arms and legs sprawled murmuring something incoherent as the rain fell. John was pretty much out of it right then and there. He was dying slowly. Blunt force trauma to the head will do that.

Will grabbed John by his legs and pulled his friend to the grave, rolling him into it. John was barely talking, something Will did not understand nor care to. Then he walked over to Becky, dragged her corpse, and rolled it into the grave with John. Will stood there for a moment and thought about trying to find the gun, which he did later with the help of the flashlight.

He wiped the gun down from prints and tossed it into the grave, just in case someone ever did find them. Then he began shoveling the muddy earth on top of the two bodies. The two of them were buried after about forty minutes of non-stop shoveling.

With both of them gone, Will had no more worries aside from Mrs. Spec wanting his job. Good luck with that. His life would keep on going as it had with no interruptions. Of course, he did not like murdering his friend, no, not at all. But what choice did he give him?

John was setting up a frame job to get his help on killing Becky. *Fuck him*, Will thought as he walked slowly back through the woods and field to where his car was parked. End of story.

10

When a weary and soaked Will made it back to where he parked his car, he had forgotten about John's car. Looking around the darkness of the countryside, Will walked over to John's car, the driver's side to be exact, in hopes that he would see them. Eureka!

Inside, the keys hung from the ignition like an earring from a socialite. Will opened the door, slid into the driver's seat, and started the car up. He backed out around his car and headed to the only place he knew where no one would ever find the car.

It was about a three-mile walk back on curvy, dark back roads from the big rock quarry. Will had pushed the car off the side of the quarry and watched it fall straight down into the water. It made a loud splash and sank slowly. Another problem solved. Had John taken the keys out of his ignition, then Will had no idea what he would've done. Thankfully, that wasn't the case.

It was okay having to walk back to Brock Hollow Road. The rain, well, that was okay, too. It was not as if he could not get any wetter. Walking gave Will time to reflect on what had gone down tonight. He processed it the best he could– rationalizing what he had done. And one question that stuck out to him: was he a bad guy? Will did not think so. The way Will saw it, he saved everyone a ton of grief, especially himself. John would have eventually ratted him out. He knew that for sure. After all, John did come to him for help, right?

Will had finally made it back to the road where his car was stashed on the muddy trail. He started it up, backed out onto the small country road, and drove away from the crime scene to never return.

Will got home around eleven that night, muddy and wet. He was met out in the driveway by his wife. She was madder than hell, but fuck it, he had come up with so many good plans tonight, what's a few more? When Jessica asked why he was "coming home so late;" "why are you muddy;" the classic, "why didn't you call;" and let's not forget the tried and true, "you had me and the kids so worried;" Will stood in the rain in his driveway and let her cycle through all the nagging wife troupes. It was fine, all that nagging gave him time to build upon the lie that he was going to sell Jessica.

"It was John, honey. His car slid off the side of the road out on five hundred right out past Kirby's Farm. He called me from a guy's house and I went there to try to help him get it out."

"Where were you before that?" Jessica asked in the rain, still fuming.

"I stayed late at school. I had some paperwork to finish up. I know that I should've called, but I'm sorry I didn't. I was about to leave when my office phone rang, and it was John. I came as quickly as I could. I know that you're mad, and you have every right to be. This is on me. I'm sorry."

That seemed to quiet Jessica down some. Sometimes a woman just wants the man to admit his mistake and say sorry. As they walked into the house together from the driveway, she was still giving him the business. He was okay with that. If that was the worst thing that was ever going to come out of this night, he was okay with that.

11

In the ensuing days, the sex scandal heated up. Turns out that Bobby Painter did record Becky and him having sex at her house. Bobby wanted more from Becky, and Becky told him that it was a serious mistake on her part and that it would never happen again. Which caused Bobby to get mad and want revenge. He had taped the two of them and planned to blackmail her with the said tape. The only way she could get out of it was to have sex with him a few more times and then Bobby, true to his word as any sixteen going on seventeen kid can be held to, was going to give her the tape.

The problem was that Bobby's mother found the tape in his bedroom lying on his desk while she cleaned it. On the tape, Bobby had written, BECKY on a white label. Being a very nosey woman, especially when it came to her children, she popped the tape into her son's stereo and the sounds of Becky moaning and screaming with her son doing the same, her blood pressure nearly killed her right then and there as she ejected the tape. With rage hanging in her mind, she waited for her son to come home from school that day. She wanted to know what the explicit tape was and if, indeed, that was her son on it.

When the tape was presented to the town's newspaper and local police, nothing could really be made about it. There was not anything on the tape that implicated Becky. No names were used. As far as the lawyers on both sides were concerned, the tape could have been recorded off a porno. There was zero proof that it was Bobby and Becky. Will never heard the tape but was told by the school district's lawyer that there was no way to tell if that was Becky or not. She was safe.

Now the question was where was she, and for that matter, where was John Henderson?

That's where Will came in. He had one more good plan up his sleeve. On the days where the two of them went missing, Mandy had called Will and asked very worried where her husband was. Will said that he had to tell her something about John but it needed to be done face to face. She invited him over and Will told her what happened that night.

In the Henderson living room, where Will had been a thousand times over the years, Will told Mandy that John had called him because he had run off the road in the rain the other night out on County Road 500. John went out there to help him get out of the ditch, and he noticed that Becky was in the passenger seat.

"I didn't think much of it at the time but it did seem odd though. Like why would they be together on that road at that time of night?" Will said.

He added that John had gotten out of his car and between the two of them he said, "Me and Becky are leaving together. We're in love." Will paused for dramatic purposes for Mandy who he could tell had hooked with his lie.

"Mandy, John was having an affair with Becky. Six months. I didn't know until that night. I'm sorry." That part was the truth. He did not know until John told him about it in his office that night.

Mandy wanted to cry, but the tears would not come. She was too shocked to do anything but sit on the end of her chair and think back on some of the weird things that had gone on during the last six months. The late-night phone calls that he took in his office downstairs; the going to get milk at the store and being gone for an hour; the golf trips when the man hated golf. It all started adding up in her mind that was going a mile a second.

Will could see this and knew that he was going to be in the clear. There would be no missing person search, because as far as Mandy and Becky's parents were concerned after hearing Will's story, the two lovers fled town to start a life together. Everyone bought the story Will told, and it was backed up by Jessica because the night in question, Will did come home muddy and soaked. When asked at the lodge and church about

John and Becky, he told the same story. He never added to nor took away. He kept it simple. Only dummies got caught in their lies.

12

Mrs. Spec finally got out of Claxton but not in the way that she would have wanted. Later that year, in December, right before school dismissed for Christmas break, an ice storm hit the region producing two inches of ice. It was a record-breaking storm that roared through the state of Tennessee. Stepping out to see the ice, Marcy Spec walked out of her house, where she lived alone except for her six cats, and instantly slipped on a patch of ice on her front porch, breaking her hip and leg.

She tried to scream out for help but nothing ever came out. Even if it did, living out in the country, there was no one around to hear her screams and pleas for help for miles. She laid out there and froze to death before her daughter came to check on her when the ice thawed on the roads days later.

As for Will, he kept on keeping on. The night of the murders was well behind him. He kept stealing that money from the school figuring out how John was cooking the books to make everything look legit. Eventually, he was able to retire with his pension and the money he had stolen from the school over the years. Not having to split the money with John anymore, it meant a bigger take for him. He took the money and gave it to a guy who tied it all up in land and houses. Will made off like a bandit, and no one was ever the wiser about his past deeds.

How did he sleep at night knowing that he did what he did?

With a fan on...

JIMBO

JERRY JAKEWITCH WAS a farmer by trade. He was born into the family business. He did not know much, if anything else, outside of farming but man, oh man, could he grow just about anything. Jerry did not just have a green thumb– he had green hands and knew everything about every type of grass, flower, and crop. He also knew about weather patterns, when to plant, and when to sow. To those who knew him in town, he was a walking, talking farmer's almanac. When Jerry spoke about farming and raising crops, people listened.

Jerry and his family, the entire lineage of the Jakewitch name, were known throughout town as straight shooters, honest, and salt of the earth people. The day in question when it came out of the sky was October 26th, 1985. Jerry was on his tractor, brush-hogging one of his enormous sprawling fields. It had gotten nearly waist-high and had begun dying. He usually did not allow it to grow that high, but there had been other things on his hundred-plus acre property that needed to be tended to, to keep an eye on.

It was 1985, and the plight of the American farmer was in full swing. They had even done benefit concerts, these musicians, to help the farming communities. It did little in terms of money to dole out, but it did put the demise of the American farmer into the lexicon of the country. The actors and musicians throwing benefit concerts didn't matter to Jerry none. He was keeping on keeping on, a term that his long-dead daddy used to say.

It was cold that day in October when the alien crashed down on his farm. A cold front had lurched through earlier that morning, bringing with it rain and some heavy storms; it was nothing too serious, though. It was nothing like the year before when a tornado touched down about five miles from his farm. He did catch some of the wind off the F3 tornado on the northern part of his property. There wasn't much on the northern part except for an old shed and a barn that was over a hundred years old that was rarely used. The wind of the tornado had obliterated the small shed, sending pieces of wood and tin every which way. The barn didn't fare much better against the wind. Half of it had fallen while the other half was ready to go at any minute. Jerry ended up tearing the rest of it down.

The tornado was a year ago, nearly to the exact day that Jerry was getting ready to go on his tractor. He remembered the day of the bad storms and the F3 tornado with clarity. It was nearly eighty-five degrees, much like it had been yesterday. He was half expecting a round of bad storms that would produce some tornadoes, but nothing really happened– just a lot of thunder, lightning, and some of the hardest rain he had ever heard or seen in his life. Then, like last year, the temps fell and late October finally felt like fall.

2

Wearing his three-decade-old brown work jacket and his green John Deere hat, Jerry hopped on his tractor and was ready to get the day underway. The tractor was an old 1960s International that had been his dad's. The tractor was old and had sometimes been more trouble than it was worth, but it was his dad's. Jerry always felt his dad's spirit on that tractor when out on it. He was not about to give it up for one of those newfangled ones he had seen at the John Deere place in town. "No sir,"

Jerry would always reply when asked if he was ever going to get a new one. "This 'un does me right good."

With the bush hog attached back at the huge red barn where the International was parked every day, Jerry turned the key to the tractor. The engine stalled, then sputtered, and fell silent. Again, Jerry twisted the key in the ignition, and the tractor coughed and belched until it finally came to life. He let it sit there and idle for a bit, so it could warm up for the long day ahead. "Take as much time as you need," Jerry said to the machine.

When he got to the field, he began to cut it. It was wet, and at first, he thought he might want to wait until it dried up a few days before he went any further. Sitting there on the tractor, his boot on the brake and thinking for a few moments, he decided to keep cutting. He had too much to do the next few days; this day, after the heavy rains and such, was really the only day he could fit the bush hogging in. A cold, stiff wind battered his old, tired face, and again he wondered if he should maybe do it later on in the week when it dried up some. Then he thought about all the other chores he had to do day after day. "Might as well just power through and get this over with."

———

About halfway through the field, two hours in, his face was numb from the cold wind that howled from the west. The sun tried to peek through the dark clouds from the backend of the cold front that had passed earlier. The sun felt good, but there was not enough of it uncovered to warm him. His coat was zipped up, but his ears and face were still cold because they took the brunt of the wind. The gloves on his hands protected his fingers where the arthritis claimed him in his late forties. Jerry looked out across the field and saw that he still had a long way to go. The huge single oak tree that stood in the middle of the field was a landmark that noted the field was three-quarters of the way finished; Jerry was a long way away from the oak.

3

Another hour had passed by, and the tractor was at half full on the gas gauge. He was still nowhere close to the oak tree– still had a long way to go. The dark clouds had begun to scatter. and the sun that was playing peek-a-boo, was starting to come out for longer bouts. The rays of the UV felt good, and the wind had even died down some. He could feel it warming up a little and warmth, as little as it was, was a welcomed relief.

As Jerry was making the turn to cut the next row of waist-high grasses, he saw something streak across the partly cloudy sky. It was on fire as it streaked across the sky in an orange glow, and it looked close-like right there in his own field, off to the east. He could hear the whirling of whatever this thing was. Then BOOM…a crash. Jerry could feel the vibration of it on his tractor and could hear the dirt moving from the impact, way off. *That's got to be loud if I'm hearing it over this thing*, Jerry thought to himself.

He shut his tractor off, which getting it started again was iffy at best, and tried to gather his breath. He was scared to death by what he had just seen, felt, and heard. Off in the distance, right past the oak tree as far as he could tell– something was smoking– black/gray smoke, flowing up into the sky with the jet stream that was carrying it off to the west.

Jerry sat on his tractor in silence for a minute, trying to make sense of it all. Was it a comet? Was it a small plane? What the hell was it? He had heard of comets falling to earth before but never saw one in person. This was a first for him. *My God wasn't it loud when it was coming down*, Jerry thought to himself. It happened so fast that the logical side of his brain said that it had to be a small plane because he did hear a mechanical, whirling sound. At least that was what he thought it sounded like.

It was not unusual for planes to fly overhead, sometimes low, because of the small airport nearby. The low hum of the engines way up high was just part of the environment he had gotten used to over the years. Jerry had never been around when a plane had fallen from the sky, so he could only guess that's the kind of sound it would make: that whirling, mechanical sound and then a loud BOOM...nothing after that but silence.

Jerry turned the key to his International, and it hesitated as usual after a long continuous run, like the one he had been on. The tractor eventually roared to life, shaking and coughing white smoke. Jerry took his boot off the brake and drove the tractor towards the crash, off in the distance– all the while keeping the stream of smoke as his guidepost. He had no idea how much his life was going to change when he found what came out of the sky.

4

The closer that Jerry and his tractor got to the crash site, the heavier the smell of something burning was. The winds had changed direction, and now the smoke was moving to the east in plumes, almost in a lateral direction. It was so thick from the wreckage that Jerry's eyes watered. He stopped the tractor by putting his boot on the brake. He unzipped his jacket and pulled the right side of it over his face like Dracula would his cape, hoping for some relief. He got some relief but only for a second or two.

The smoke did not let up one bit. The tractor started to idle rough, and Jerry knew exactly what that meant: it was about to die. It had happened to him several times over the last few weeks, and he knew that the tractor was not going to make it much longer. Jerry uncovered his face and looked as best he could through the smoke and saw the oak tree and the outline of an object that looked like a disc, wedged into the ground. *It's not a plane*, the farmer thought to himself.

Jerry sat on the tractor and was about to lift his boot off the brake when the International finally gave up and shut off in the uncut field. He did not even try to start it again. "Damn it," he said, smacking the steering wheel with his gloved hands. With the smoke still pouring from the crash site, Jerry jumped off the tractor and walked towards the wreckage and through the smoke with his jacket pulled up over his face. The heavy smell of what he thought might be fuel made his eyes water and caused him to cough.

Jerry found it tough to traverse the nearly waist-high field through the smoke. He was halfway away from his International and halfway to the smoking whatever-it-was. A couple of times, Jerry stopped and had to turn away from the smoke with his back to it, and just breathe the best he could. There was no telling what kind of toxic chemicals he was inhaling, but he was too invested now to walk in the other direction. Besides, it was a long way back to the farm since his tractor decided to quit.

Jerry kept walking, holding his jacket to his face. He peered out for as long as he could before he covered his eyes to allow them to blink the smoke out. He walked in small steps. It was the best he could do before he reached the oak tree. Just on the other side of the oak tree was the wreckage, the disc that was wedged into the ground. It kind of looked like a Frisbee to Jerry– a huge silver metallic Frisbee with a few windows in the front that was wedged into the earth.

Jerry had made it to the oak tree. The wind shifted again and took the smoke back in the other direction. It was a sweet relief for the farmer, who lowered his jacket from his face. His eyes stung from the smoke, and he still coughed some– but the air was somewhat better, breathable. However, the smell of burnt metal and exhaust still filled the landscape. Jerry doubled over, hands on his knees, and he coughed and hacked for some time; so much, in fact, that he thought he was going to throw up.

"I never heard coughing like that before," a voice said coming from the crash site.

Jerry raised his head and saw a figure emerging from the wreckage and smoke. What Jerry saw made his eyes grow wide in terror. His blood pressure spiked exponentially, and his body trembled. His knees wanted to give out but luckily for Jerry, he grabbed onto a low-hanging limb from the tree as he fell against the trunk. He was speechless at the spectacle that was approaching him.

"But then again, I don't know any humans. Coughing like that might be normal for all I know," the little gray alien said jovially.

5

Jerry could not believe his eyes. He thought that maybe he was having a hallucination from the toxins of the smoke. That had to be it. It was a trick of the mind. Maybe he was having a stroke because he did feel his left arm go numb. Or was that for heart attacks? Jerry didn't remember while leaning up against the trunk of the oak tree, still coughing and still trying to maintain his steady breath. His voice had up and left for the time being. *What are you?* Jerry thought in his mind.

What am I? Oh, the alien smacked his forehead with his elongated hand and spoke inside Jerry's mind, as if the two of them were talking verbally. *That's right, your species aren't accustomed to beings like me. Sorry.* The alien laughed comically at Jerry's fright.

My name is James. Jimbo to my friends. I live out on the outer banks of Galagar. Way out there. Or maybe there, Jimbo said telepathically, pointing into the sky in one direction and then another in confusion. Truth was, even he did not have an idea what direction his home planet was at the moment.

I've gotta be dying or something, Jerry thought to himself, feeling his heart race and thumping against his chest wall.

I don't think so. But then again I'm no doctor; especially a human doctor. So you might be right. But don't die just yet, okay? I need your help to get back up and running, Jimbo said into Jerry's mind, inching closer to the panic-stricken farmer.

Jerry tried to speak again but could not. *Okay, just calm down. Jerry is it? Yeah? You're a farmer around here, huh? We got farmers on my planet, too. Critical job, you know?*

Jerry could hear and most of all *feel* Jimbo inside his head, and it was a horrible feeling to have. His knees finally gave out and he slid with his back against the oak to the ground looking at Jimbo, the alien. Jimbo stood unassuming before him, looking precisely like any alien Jerry had seen on TV.

How did you know my name? He asked Jimbo, inside his mind.

You do this enough– you learn a few tricks over the light-years. Don't worry, this is just until you can actually talk, and then I won't have to be inside your mind. I'm just trying to calm you down right now, Jimbo replied.

Well, this ain't doing it.

Jimbo the alien nodded his alien head unemotionally, *I know, Jerry, I know. And I'm sorry for that. I had no intention of crashing. I was just flying by and wasn't watching after my fuel measurements. I ran out and landed here. Dad's going to be so pissed. This ain't even mine. I don't know if I can buff that all out,* Jimbo gestured towards the crashed disc.

I can't believe this is happening, Jerry thought.

Believe it, farmer. So listen, I need your help getting me some fuel– at least enough to get me back up, outta here, and on my way.

Fuel? Jerry's asked from his mind to Jimbo's.

I've heard a tale while camping one night back home when I was younger that your planet is the only one in the entire Section 10 galaxy with a certain component that makes these ships of ours go. It's why some alien races continue to visit this planet.

What kind of fuel? Jerry asked, still terrified of Jimbo.

Qusator.

6

Jerry sat against the oak, trying mightily to calm down but getting the odd sense that Jimbo was a friendly alien. The odd sense was Jimbo relaxing his mind through his alien telepathy. It was working, much to Jimbo's relief. It'd been a while since he had to do that, and he was a little rusty. The last time he had to do his telepathic speak was when he visited the planet Somewhere, some twenty Earth years ago.

"I don't reckon we have anything like that here. Do we?" Jerry was surprised when the words came from his mouth. He smiled and reached up with his gloved hands and touched his lips to make sure they were still there.

"You might know it by its common earth name. Borax. I believe that's what I've heard it called."

"The washing stuff?" Jerry asked.

"I don't know what you Earthlings use it for, but I know what we Galagarains use it for. Fuel."

"Borax is fuel for your spaceships? Borax?" Jerry asked, dumbfounded.

"We don't call them 'spaceships,'" Jimbo raised his hands and used his three elongated fingers in quotations. "We call them Intergalactic Crusader Vehicles. ICV, for short."

"Borax?" Jerry repeated once again, in total disbelief.

"Yeah, it's not changed since the last time you said it." Jimbo said in his funny, sarcastic tone. "Now, you know where I can get some?"

"Clara has some in the washroom I think. But how much do you need for that thing over there?"

Jimbo turned and looked at the smoldering ICV. "About three penncilons should be enough."

"What's a penn..penncil...," Jerry tried to repeat.

Jimbo shook his alien head, "Just stop before you hurt yourself there, farmer. That would translate to what, in Earth measurements?" Jimbo started to calculate out the conversion tables in his alien brain. "I really wished I would have paid more attention in Galactic Time and Measurements class."

Jimbo stood looking up at the sky calculating in his head the measurements of conversion from penncilons to what exactly? "Gallons? Gallons! That's it! Three gallons of water, mixed with Borax."

"Three gallons of water mixed with Borax?" Jerry asked.

"Yeah, that should do it," Jimbo replied. Jerry sat there and looked in awe, still dumbfounded by the sight of an alien that crash-landed in his field.

"Okay, we just going to sit there and stare into each other's eyes lovingly, or we going to find the Borax and get me fixed up and out of here?" Jimbo asked.

Jerry, on legs that were initially like jelly, was helped up by Jimbo there by the oak tree. Standing up and looking at the alien closer, seeing his reflection in the blackness of Jimbo's unblinking eyes, Jerry was astounded beyond belief by what he was looking at.

Jimbo said, "I know."

"You know what?" Jerry asked, standing there face to face with the space traveler.

"It's crazy, I know. Me being here. What your planet calls aliens. Believe me, I am not like one of those crazy Lapperzoids monsters from the Cold Galaxy. Those are some real lunatics. If they ever come here, there will not be anything left– I can assure you of that. They love murder and mayhem."

Jerry's eyes got wide and Jimbo could read the thoughts of the human that were going in a million different directions at what he just told the farmer. "Oh, but don't worry… your planet is so primitive– they would not waste their time. They checked your planet out already, I bet."

"Well that's something, I guess," Jerry said, not feeling any relief in that. "Your spaceship…your cruiser…is still smoking. I think you're going to need more than Borax to get back up and running." Jerry pointed in the direction of the crashed ICV.

Jimbo turned around and looked, "Yeah, probably so. But I don't think the damage is that bad. Most of the smoke was from the sheer speed of the descent. It caught on fire, and the mechanical workings started to smoke because I was trying to pull it up by the yoke– but I was already out of fuel. I'm more worried about the scratches the ICV sustained. Structurally, it's sound and nearly impossible to smash. Although, it's not the *newer* model ICV because dad wouldn't spring the extra money for it."

"What do you use as money where you're from?" Jerry asked, from out of nowhere.

"Polymetal…or what you call wing nuts."

"Wing nuts? Holy cow." Jerry couldn't believe it. "I'd be a rich man on your planet because I've got boxes full of them in the barn."

"Good, I might need to borrow a few bucks to get the ICV washed and waxed when I get it back home. The Borax?"

"Oh yeah, let's go to the house. Got what you need there, I think."

"We won't have to walk. I'll transport us there," Jimbo said, not showing humor at all on his emotionless gray alien face.

"Really? Will it hurt?"

Jimbo shrugged his small shoulders, "Tickles a little. Just close your eyes and I'll take us to your house."

Jerry closed his eyes, there under the oak tree, and stood like an idiot. Jimbo laughed and clapped his elongated alien hands, "Come on man–I'm just playing with you!"

Jerry opened his eyes, "I thought you could do stuff like that?"

"I'm an alien. Not a magician. Now let's go get the fuel, so I can get out of here."

7

Jimbo and Jerry walked side-by-side from the smoldering ICV and towards the tractor that was out in the middle of the field. The grass and weeds were high and wet, making it more difficult for Jimbo to walk, given his five-foot-nothing stature. Jerry was still trying to get his mind under control and make sense of what was going on out in his field. He had never thought much about what lay beyond the skies and up in the stars. Jerry wasn't a thinker like that and never had the need to be. He would have bet his farm that things like Jimbo did not exist, not in a million years.

"I know," Jimbo said, falling behind Jerry in the field.

"You know what?" Jerry asked, walking slower to not leave Jimbo behind.

"You would have bet your farm that things like me didn't exist."

"You really got to get out of my head," Jerry said.

"Sorry."

"I just never believed in stuff like you before," Jerry said.

"It's okay. I'm not offended."

"So all the sightings and stuff. Aliens...like you?"

"Not really. You see, there are a lot of different types of aliens out there. Some are peaceful like me. Others? Not so much. Those that visit your planet here are just in search of penncilon...Borax. Your planet is right in the middle of the galaxy. A literal, last stop for fuel, to make it the rest of the way home. Those fuel-seeking aliens are mostly from my galaxy. But there are some alien species that I've heard of that come here to take humans and keep them on their planets as slaves or take them to their doctors to experiment on.

"I'd say some of what your planet sees in terms of spacecraft are fly-bys, you know, just being curious, I guess– just going on vacation and passing by or coming back from vacation. I did hear one time, in this bar over at the Romulus Galaxy, that an ICV went down a long time ago, and your military captured it. Even took the traveler."

"Roswell?" Jerry asked, referencing the famous supposed crash-landing in Roswell, New Mexico.

Jimbo shrugged his thin shoulders, "I don't know. All I heard was that the traveler was given back in return that the humans, your people, could keep the ICV for research. Mostly legend stuff used to scare us young 'uns about traveling where we're not supposed to. It's a spook story."

"Wow. Maybe that's why we have all the fancy electronic stuff we've got now."

"Maybe," Jimbo replied. "If your scientists have it, then it will be light-years until they figure out all the stuff they can pull out of it. Those ICVs aren't super complicated, but to your species, they are."

8

Jerry and Jimbo walked across the field and made it to the tractor that shut off earlier. Jerry stood there and looked at it, tipping his hat up on his forehead and rubbing his jaw. He was lost in thought, wondering if it would start or not since it had time to cool off.

"So this is...what is this?" Jimbo asked, standing beside his new human friend.

"It's a tractor. I use it on my farm. Been in the family for a long time, but it's seen its better days, I reckon. Maybe it'll start."

Jerry walked over and hopped on the old International and got himself comfortable on the hard seat that, much like the tractor, had seen its better days. Jerry twisted the key into the ignition, and the tractor sputtered, coughed, and blew out some gray and black smoke. It did come to life, but barely.

"This machine sounds sick," Jimbo said over the engine rattling and spitting.

"Ah, it always sounds like that," Jerry laughed. "Come over here and hop on. We'll drive this thing over to the farm. Hopefully, we can make it there."

Jimbo walked and stood beside the tractor, not knowing exactly how to even begin to get up to where Jerry was. Jerry offered his hand, and Jimbo reached for and took it. His human friend took his alien hand and pulled him up to where he sat on the wheel well. Jimbo's legs dangled off the huge well of the tractor's wheel, and his right hand clenched tightly on Jerry's coat.

"I'll take it slow. But hang on to me." Jimbo held onto Jerry's shoulder tightly as Jerry got the International into gear, and off they went across the field to his farm at a slow, comfortable speed. It was so comfortable that Jimbo loosened his grip on Jerry's shoulder.

On the ride across the field. Jimbo looked around at the landscape and thought how pretty it was here on this planet, at least this part of the planet, anyways. He felt the wind against his gray skin and what would have chilled a person– it did not faze him. Jimbo did not mind the temperature at all; did not even know that it was supposed to be cold. Jimbo just looked around the landscape with unblinking black eyes and watched birds fly by in the sky; the clouds moving; the trees, standing sentry-like off in the distance. If he could smile, he would have. It was truly a work of art, what he was seeing.

9

Jerry's farm came into view, and he stopped the tractor. He looked around and did not see his wife's car. That was good because the last thing he wanted to do was explain to her what Jimbo was and where he came from. Hell, he still did not truly believe it himself, and he was right there with him.

"Why did we stop?" Jimbo asked.

"Clara ain't home so that's a good thing. I ain't gotta explain you."

"Well if you had to, let's say, I could always wipe her mind with my ray gun."

Jerry slowly turned to look at Jimbo. "Ray gun?"

"It's a joke. I don't have a ray gun. Wow, your species does not get comedy on this planet."

Jerry sat there and set his jaw, looked at his alien visitor, and shook his head in a what-am-I-going-to-do-with-you? kind of way.

10

At the time that Jimbo's Intergalactic Cruiser Vehicle crashed in Jerry's field, the Pentagon had been monitoring the ICV's descent into Earth's airspace. Radar had picked it up instantly because Jimbo had forgotten a very important lesson his father had told him a long time ago when teaching him how to drive the vehicle: always turn on your invisibility shield when passing through a planet's air-space.

Jimbo had done that precise thing his father told him time and again, but had forgotten all about pressing the big red button marked INVISI-BILITY SHIELD when passing close to Earth. He was too busy drinking what Earthlings would call a milkshake that he had gotten some time ago twelve light-years from the sun in the Nano-12 Galaxy. They usually had the best shakes. Most aliens, far and wide, agreed that it was totally worth the drive out there to get a milkshake.

Inside General Shakes' office, a knock came rapping at his heavy wooden door that had the general's name in all caps on a black nameplate.

"Come in," a voice gruffly called.

The door swung open– and in walked a soldier– holding a manila file folder. He walked to General Shake's oak desk where he was sitting hunched over, reading another important TOP SECRET file.

"Sir, this just came for you," the soldier said, handing the general his file. He saluted him, then turned on his bootheels and marched out of the office before shutting the door behind him.

General Shakes opened the file and scanned through it; his eyes grew wide. Inside the file were aerial photos taken about thirty minutes ago of a craft that looked as if it was on fire, crashing down somewhere. There was a note that was attached with a paperclip on the side of the photo that read: WE THINK THIS CRAFT CRASH-LANDED. GETTING THE POSSIBLE COORDINATES ASAP.

General Martin Shakes leaned back in his desk chair and considered what he had just seen and read. *Could be just another Russian job*, the good general proposed. *We are in the middle of a Cold War. But then again...* the general trailed off, lost in thought. Eventually, he snapped out of his trance and back into reality. He leaned back over his desk and reached for his phone to page his secretary.

"Doris...get me a secure line to Larry Linkletter right now, please." His secretary obeyed his commands with a "right away sir" and began to patch him through.

General Shakes put the call on speaker and placed the phone back into its cradle. He leaned back and waited for Linkletter to greet him. He wanted to know what the director of the CIA knew about this. Stuff like this was seen nearly on a daily basis but an actual crash? That had only happened a few times. A crash, maybe from a spaceship, would be the first on his watch. Linkletter would know what was going on. He knew everything.

11

The International sputtered the rest of the way to the farm where it finally died this time around because it ran out of gas right in the middle of the farm, nowhere close to Jerry's farmhouse.

"Yeah, just park it anywhere I guess, right?" Jimbo said in his snarky alien voice.

"Anybody ever told you, you have a smart mouth?" Jerry said, getting off the tractor.

"Maybe a few times. Part of my charming personality. It's not really a mouth though. More like a slit."

"It's out of gas."

"Is there Borax in there?" Jimbo asked, pointing to the farmhouse.

"What was it you said you needed? Three gallons? Or three gallons of water mixed with Borax?"

"Yeah, three gallons of Borax mixed with water. Now what the ratio is —I have no clue. I guess we'll just mess with it and see."

Jerry stood there with his hands on his hips looking at the emotionless alien in disbelief. Come to think of it– he disbelieved the entire situation. "I'm going to go into the house and get what you need…I hope. Maybe there is enough inside. You stay here. Anyone shows up, hide over there, behind the woodshed. But I doubt anybody will be coming for a visit."

Jimbo just stood there looking at Jerry with his emotionless face and nodded, "Will do, chief."

12

"We must for sure have something that went down in the state of Tennessee not long ago," Linkletter told the general over the phone.

"Them?" General Shakes asked, knowing that Linkletter would know what he was referring to, just in case the secure line was somehow tapped by another agency. It wouldn't be a first.

"Fits the bill. An air traffic tower caught it on their radar, and we scrambled an F-16 within the area as fast as we could. Nothing on the targeting systems, but that was because it was probably already downed."

"No way it could've been Russian jets?" General Shakes asked.

"No way. Not coming from the direction it came from."

"Where in Tennessee do you think it crashed?"

"A town called Claxton. We've got top men en route as we speak. Our F-16 has pinpointed an estimated location within a mile radius. We're just following the smoke because the pilot reported smoke, and lots of it, coming from the crash site."

General Shakes rocked slowly in his desk chair, and a smile slowly etched across his face. He was happy that he was going to be the one on the watchtower to snag an actual honest-to-God alien. He had heard stories about Roswell when he was a kid, living in New Mexico. Oh, how he marveled over the notion that there might be actual little green men that were visiting from another planet.

General Shakes knew, thanks to his high-level security clearance, that the aliens were not just a notion, but an actual matter of fact. He had never seen one, but he knew through top-secret files that a few had landed on Earth by mistake, and we took their ships to reverse-engineer them. The good general figured that accounted for all of the huge leaps in technological advancement the world has seen over the years. "Still more to go," he had once said.

"Find the crash site, and if it's what we think, secure the perimeter. How long does it take to set up a containment field?"

"About twelve hours until we could get something better to secure it. My hope is that it's out in some remote field on some farm or something. Satellite photos look like it is. That would be the best-case scenario," Linkletter replied.

"Hopefully. Would you keep me posted? If you confirm it, I want a call. I want to see this thing for myself."

"Once we get confirmation either way, I'll let you know," Linkletter replied and hung up the phone. General Shakes sat there and smiled wide. He was as giddy as a kid on Christmas morning.

13

Inside his house, Jerry walked to the laundry room. He left Jimbo behind outside next to the tractor and told him not to move, and if he saw some-one, to hide behind the woodshed that was close by. Jimbo, never listening to those who gave him instructions, another part of his charming personality, saw the huge barn and decided to go have a look inside it. He was curious. Curiosity was another component of his charming personality.

Jerry walked into Clara's laundry room and saw not one but two boxes of Borax. Both boxes were unopened and full. This was a good sign. Now, he needed something else...*oh what else do I need*, Jerry was thinking to himself. *The washtub!* He spied it leaning up against the wall on the other side of the laundry room. It was stainless steel with two metal handles. Jerry thought that he could fill the tub up with water, mix in both boxes of Borax, and then take it to the crashed ICV. Surely there was enough for three gallons. He didn't know what the ratio of Borax to water was, but they would figure it out. Three gallons is what Jerry kept in his mind.

Just as he took the washtub, Jerry thought about something: *I can't do that. All the water will splash out, and I don't want to carry this heavy thing that's full of water across that damn field. Can't put it on the tractor because with every bump, it'll slosh all the water out. There has to be another way.* Jerry stood there in the laundry holding the two boxes of Borax and scanning the room, trying to come up with a Plan B. Then it hit him. Gallons. Jugs! He remembered having saved some gallon milk jugs and putting them under the sink. Brilliant!

14

The FBI and CIA were en route in black cars with black tinted windows to the town of Claxton. Of course they were black– what else would government covert agencies drive that were in search of aliens and their spaceships? They would be there in less than twenty minutes while looking for signs of smoke in the sky. The F-16 was still patrolling as the pilot would send verbal reports of the crash site back to his superiors. On their way back to the farm, Jimbo had looked up and seen the jet scream across the skyline several times but thought nothing of it. Jerry never heard the jet because of the tractor that was screaming in pain the whole way there, and his hearing was going bad; something he needed to get checked but kept putting off.

15

Jimbo slowly creaked open the barn door and peered inside. It was nothing extravagant, just an ordinary barn with ordinary farm stuff inside such as: hay, various hand tools like shovels, rakes, and the like, standing in corners. There was a strong musty smell, probably from all the hay that was everywhere. Also mixed with that musty odor were gasoline and oil. Jimbo walked in and looked about, not impressed with the place. They had similar places like Jerry's barn where he was from. Except they did not call them barns; they were called exo-coverings.

Jimbo walked around and examined some old tractor wheels that were lying off to the side of the barn; nothing interesting there. He walked over to the ladder that led up to the hay loft and looked up. He thought about climbing it but thought better of it. Climbing was not his thing. Then something caught his big, alien eyes. That something was over on the right side of the barn wall. A ray of sunlight coming through a knot-hole struck a box of something that was metal, and Jimbo thought he knew what that metal was.

Back inside the house, Jerry went into the kitchen and opened the doors underneath the cabinet. The empty jugs sat right next to the mouse traps that had not caught anything just yet, but the season for mice trying to get inside was closing in. Jerry hunkered down, got the three yellow milk jugs out, and twisted the red lids off them.

Turning on the faucet at the kitchen sink, Jerry put the first jug under the running water and filled up the jug halfway. He took the box of Borax, opened it by tearing the cardboard perforated opening, poured half of the contents into the jug, and screwed the lid back on. He shook it so it would mix. The farmer did this process with the next two jugs before turning to exit the farmhouse. *I hope this works.*

16

The FBI, CIA, and even the NSA, which had joined in the hunt last minute, were closing in on the exact coordinates of the crash. The cars, six of them in all, came into the town of Claxton– not minding the town's strict speed limits, nor stop signs, and not even the town's only traffic light. They had special clearance for a special top-secret mission. Ray's Barbershop, where the old men sat inside and talked about every-thing and anything, watched from the huge glass store window as the black cars rolled through downtown. None of the four old men in there, including Ray the barber, had ever seen anything like that before in their town. "What the hell is all that business, reckon?" Delbert asked out loud.

"Ain't no telling. Looks important though," Bobby replied.

———

"I'm rich! I can't wait for the girls to see me now!" Jimbo shouted from within the barn. He grabbed two boxes of wing nuts off the shelf on the wall and turned to walk out. Before he got to the barn door, he heard Jerry calling to him.

Jerry stood outside looking for Jimbo and did not see him. Panic rushed over him. He looked everywhere for his alien friend, and for a very brief moment, he wondered if all of this was some sort of dream or maybe something worse. He wondered briefly, standing there holding the three jugs of water and Borax, if an alien had even crash-landed to begin with. Then the barn door opened, and out came Jimbo, carrying two small cardboard boxes about the size of shoeboxes over to Jerry.

"I hope you don't mind, but I'm taking these. I'm going to buy the biggest home on my planet," Jimbo said.

Jerry felt relief rush over him, and panic vacated as Jimbo the alien came walking over to him. "Got your fuel."

Jimbo nodded, "Then let's go! Your machine good to go?"

Jerry shrugged, "I don't know. Let's try it. If not, then we're walking."

Jerry laid down the three jugs of fuel and climbed the tractor. He gave the key in the ignition a twist. The big International turned over several times to no avail. Jimbo stood there looking on and holding his cash. Jerry looked around for a few seconds and again turned the key. Nothing.

"Um...Jerry."

"Yeah?" the farmer said in frustration.

"Didn't you say that you needed gas?"

Jerry lowered his head and wondered how he could have forgotten that already. In his defense, it had been a crazy day. He was lucky that he remembered how to even get home at this point.

"Yeah, I've got a can back in the barn. Stay here, I'll be right back." Jerry got off the tractor and walked briskly towards the barn.

"Where would I go?" Jimbo remarked sarcastically, holding his fortune in those two boxes.

The line of black government cars drove outside the town on old County Road 145. They were ten minutes out from where the ICV crashed. The lead man in black in the last car sat in the passenger seat and kept his boss informed of their time.

"We're getting closer. Ten minutes out, maybe fifteen," he said on his car phone, which was better known at the time as "the brick". The black cars, all of them, drove at top-speed down those winding and turning county roads towards Jerry and Jimbo.

The men in those cars had taken the job of men in black to clean up messes and secure the areas before private citizens' eyes could see the incidents. Most of them had seen several incidents that could have turned into national news– but luckily for the FBI, CIA, NSA, and even the White House– the men in black had contained them all with a success rate of one hundred percent.

17

Jerry filled up the gas tank to the International and tossed the empty gas can to the side. He put the three jugs of fuel into a small basket that was attached to the right side of his back seat. He hopped back up on the tractor and twisted the key. It roared to life, shuttering and sputtering per usual, but the tractor came to life, nonetheless. Jerry grinned and helped Jimbo up by taking his boxes first and then reaching for his gray alien hand. Jimbo took a seat on the big fender of the tractor well like before, legs dangling off, holding his boxes.

"Hang on," Jerry said, putting the tractor in motion, and off they went back towards the crash site.

The black cars were now five minutes away...

Jerry and Jimbo raced across the field not having any idea that the men in black from various government agencies were coming to the field. Had they known what was coming, perhaps, Jerry would have been hitting the gas a little harder.

The black cars were now two minutes away from the farm...

The International drove past the oak tree and to the crash site. It was only smoldering now, not thick smoke as before. That was a good sign. Jerry stopped the tractor and shut the engine off.

"Here we are."

"Nothing gets past you, huh?" Jimbo said as he slid carefully off the tractor with his boxes.

"You know, I'm not going to miss you one bit. Listen, I mixed it with half water and half Borax. I don't know if it's right or anything." the farmer said, jumping off the tractor.

"I guess we're about to see," Jimbo replied.

"Where do you put the fuel?"

"There's a portal opening on the inside of the ICV next to the captain's chair." Jimbo walked over to the ICV, carrying his boxes of wing nuts and entered through the small open door.

Jimbo disappeared inside the ship as the door slowly came down shut behind him.

It opened again, and out poked Jimbo's big alien head, "Now hand me the fuel so I can get this thing outta here and back home." Jerry walked over to the ship and handed Jimbo the three jugs. Jerry was looking at the ship and was dumbfounded by the design of it all. *Nobody is going to believe me about this one,* he thought. *Would I even tell anyone?*

"You can but no one will believe you!" Jimbo yelled from inside the ship's open door. "Sorry, I'll get out of your head. Habit."

Inside the ship, Jimbo twisted the lids off the jugs and walked over to the captain's chair and over to where the dash panels of flashing lights of every color and shape were. Those buttons all seemed to have a purpose. Jimbo flipped open a metal flap that read FUEL and poured the contents of the jug down the hatch. The first gallon was drained in no time.

The men in black suits in their black cars rumbled into the Jakewitch farm, skidding to a halt. Men in black suits leaped out of the cars and ran in all directions: the barn, the sheds, and the farmhouse. They were on a seek-and-contain mission.

18

Jerry stood outside and looked over the ICV some more. Inside, Jimbo drained the second jug and the third went down like the other two. Jimbo tossed the empty jug onto the floor, closing the metal lid to the fuel portal. He then placed his hand on a small screen big enough for the alien's hand.

Outside, the ICV shook violently, causing Jerry to back away. The ship was coming to life, and the mechanical workings that made the ICV work began to whirl and whine. "I guess I mixed it right," Jerry said.

On the farm, the men in black suits all gathered in the middle, looking around, "Nothing," Agent 1 said.

The ship was shaking and moving, whirling, and rumbling as it slowly started to pull itself out of the crevice it made when crashing into the ground. Just then, the door opened, and out poked Jimbo's alien head, "Hey. Thanks for the fuel and the money. I'll remember it always. And when you think of me...think of me fondly."

Jerry tipped his cap back on his head and honestly did not know what to say. His mind was all over the place, watching the ICV hover just a few feet from the ground.

"Yeah." Was all that the simple farmer could manage to say.

"Wow," Jimbo said. "With that vocabulary, you should consider writing a novel. Take it easy, huh?"

Jimbo waved and ducked his head back inside, and the metal door slowly came down. The ICV raised itself a little more off the ground and in one quick shot, zoomed away across the field and high in the sky until it was completely out of sight. The whole thing took about three seconds and Jimbo was gone. The only thing that was left of him was the huge hole that his ICV had made when it crashed.

19

Back at the farm, one of the men in black saw something off in the distance, across the field out by a tree. It looked like a ship or something. He pointed it out, and then it was gone. The men stood for a moment all trying to figure out what it was. Some of them did not see it. A few did.

Agent 1 saw something but did not know what he had seen– it happened so fast. It was a blue streak to him. Nevertheless, they all retreated into their cars quickly, peeling out of the farm and out across the field towards the oak tree.

When they arrived there, they saw a man standing beside his tractor still looking up at the sky. The men in black all got out of their cars and made a beeline over to where Jerry was and the large crater the ship had made when Jimbo crash-landed.

"What happened here?" Agent 1 asked the farmer while the others walked over to the large crater.

"Something came out of the sky," Jerry replied.

"Well, what was it?" Agent 1 asked.

"You'd never believe me."

"Sir, we'll need to speak further with you about this incident. Can you come with me?" Agent 1 asked, not giving Jerry a chance to refuse as he gently grabbed him by the arm and guided him to his car.

"Sure," Jerry replied, still looking up at the sky. The two men walked over to Agent 1's black, four-door sedan.

"What came out of the sky, sir? What made that large hole over there?"

Jerry took his eyes from the sky and looked at the man in black. He could see his reflection in his black sunglasses looking back at him. Those glasses reminded him of looking into Jimbo's large, black eyes.

"Jimbo's ICV," Jerry replied, looking back up at the sky.

"Sir, we need to know exactly what happened here. It's a matter of national security. Your reluctance to recount accurately what occurred could land you under arrest until such time that the facts can be verified and documented."

Jerry paid the man in black no mind. He was still looking up at the sky...looking for signs of Jimbo.

WHAT EVER HAPPENED TO EDDIE MILLER

1998

IT WAS DRY THAT SUMMER–THE driest on record. When the tree caught fire, it was no wonder the entire forest burned out of control. It was quick, the fire, and spread to nearly all the homes that flanked the outer ridges before it was put out. It had taken firefighters two whole days to keep it from spreading, and to put it out. Had it not been for the town's firefighters, along with those from several other nearby towns within Brook County, the fire would have surely claimed the houses that dotted those ridges. It was the biggest fire in history, not only in the town of Claxton, but the entire county of Brook.

He never meant for the forest to go up; it wasn't his plan at all. When he saw the utter devastation that he had caused, he cried for days. It was all his fault, that fire, and no one would ever know it was him. It would be a secret he would take to his grave. No one could ever know. Why would they suspect a kid of thirteen, anyway? The fire chief certainly didn't, and neither did the state arson guys, even though they pinpointed where the fire had started. It was in the middle of the woods–Hudson's Woods. As to who or what started the roaring blaze, that was a mystery. Always would be; most people guessed. But ground zero was that oak tree in the middle.

As the fire blackened the countryside of Claxton, another mystery was being handled by the local police department: the disappearance of Eddie Miller. He was a kid of fourteen, in and out of trouble, and a kid that the police knew all too well. They were on a first-name basis with Eddie's family, too. When Eddie hadn't come home the day of the big fire over at Hudson's Woods, a call was made by Eddie's mother, Linda, to the police. Her boy had not come for supper. "It's not like him," she said to the police.

As the fire was finally put down and under control, the police focused on the whereabouts of their local teen troublemaker. The cops checked all the usual places for Eddie: the pool hall, the arcade where he stayed most times until too late, and the basketball court that was behind the First National Bank in the middle of town. Nothing. No one had seen Eddie Miller. It struck Officer Lowe as odd because that kid was everywhere in town all the time–always up to something. Surely, someone must have seen him?

When the hours turned to days, and the days turned to weeks with still no sign of Eddie, police began to wonder if their young teenage delinquent had been down at Hudson's Woods playing when the fire started. That became a topic of discussion as the lawmen began to search the charred and blackened woods for any of the kid's remains that may have survived the fire. It certainly made sense to the local newspaper reporter who covered the fire and the missing boy. Both occurrences had to be tied together, the reporter asserted. Eventually, people around town began to put two and two together and made their assumptions.

After a month and a half of canvassing the neighborhoods and the rest of the town, talking to scores of people who knew or had seen Eddie Miller on the day he never came home, Detective Purkey put Eddie's case and the fire at Hudon's Woods in the cold case file. Investigators assumed with reason that Eddie Miller was in the woods when they went up. Nothing else made sense at the time. "No matter what we all think," Det. Purkey went on record saying, "we'll have to keep both investigations open."

There still was no evidence– no remains of the kid left behind in the fire when investigators walked the charred remains of the woods in the weeks and months after the fire was put out. Det. Purkey typed up his final report, filed it, and that was that. Unless there was a break in the case on Eddie's whereabouts, then the case would turn colder and be left as such. Later on that year, Det. Purkey retired from the Brook County Sheriff's Department and headed West to Nevada– never solving the arson of the woods or finding Eddie Miller.

Before Det. Purkey called it quits, he called the Miller family into his office and told the mother and father that their son had probably been in the woods on the evening of the fire. "Was there a possibility that he liked playing with fire?" the lawman asked the parents.

"What kid doesn't," Rich Miller answered as if he was dumbfounded by the detective's question.

Det. Purkey asked, "Was it possible that Eddie had gotten a cigarette lighter or a book of matches and was fooling around down at Hudson's Woods, catching them on fire?"

Linda Miller, teary-eyed and sobbing, nodded her head saying, "Yeah, that sounded like something Eddie would do." And there it was…

With no evidence whatsoever, Det. Purkey concluded in his final report that the forest fire that burned over fifty acres before it was put down might have been caused by Eddie. His disappearance coincided with the fire–and like everyone else in town–the detective said that there was the notion that maybe Eddie was down in the woods playing around, caught some wood on fire, and didn't make it out before the whole thing caught.

"But we can't be one hundred percent sure," Det. Purkey would keep saying to the public when asked about the woods and Eddie. Det. Purkey thought about closing the case altogether before he left so people could move on, but he left it open.

Or there was another possibility. One where Eddie caught Hudson's Woods on fire and fled the scene, not wanting to be in trouble.

He assured the Miller family that he, along with other local law enforcement, would keep combing the entire forest for any indication that Eddie was in there. Even Eddie's family would join in the search down at what used to be Hudson's Woods. Nothing was found before Det. Purkey retired. With all the manpower that was used looking for Eddie, he was in there, not found until decades later. It was crazy how many people walked right by his charred remains, which at the time were covered by thick blackened wood that had fallen onto his skeleton.

There was something about the two events that did not make sense to the reporter who was on the case for the newspaper, *The Brook County Register*. "If Eddie had set the woods on fire, how come he did not make it out alive?" asked Nelson Hudson, the great-grandson of Charlie Hudson, owner of Hudson's Woods.

"What if Eddie was down there, saw who did it, and they killed him, leaving the body to burn? No more witness." That was a salacious accusation and one that many in the town of Claxton did not cotton to, especially the Miller family. But that was Nelson's style: he always asserted something more dramatic than what was on the face of it. Det. Purkey gave his thoughts to the reporter when asked what his opinion was, which happened to be the same opinion that was in his report.

"We may never know what really happened down at Hudson's Woods that day," Det. Purkey told Nelson during an interview, "but I strongly believe that Eddie Miller was down there when it caught and ended up dying. Until we find Eddie Miller, we won't ever know the particulars, I'm afraid. The disappearance of the kid and the Hudson Wood's burning will remain open investigations until we receive some breaks in the cases, which I believe are tied together."

That was the last comment the detective had ever made about the fire and disappearance. That was until twenty years later in 2018 when the cold cases of the Hudson's Woods arson and Eddie Miller's whereabouts thawed.

———

In 2018, twenty years later, a couple of quail hunters were walking through Hudson's Woods, which in the last twenty years had recovered from the massive fire that destroyed the entire forest. It was nowhere near what it used to be decades prior, but it was getting there. Trees were growing again; thick walls of vegetation were sprawling about; and wild bushes and grasses were dotting the floor of the woods. It would take another several decades to see what Hudson's Woods would grow to become, but the place was good enough for two quail hunters to hide in, looking for quail out in the nearby field that had managed to come back over the years.

Walking through the young growth of the woods, one of the hunters stopped to pee while his friend kept walking. Unbeknownst to the hunter, he was standing in the exact spot where the fire twenty years ago started. Although the oak tree was long gone, burnt to a crisp, and blown away to nothing but ashes by the winds of long ago, the hunter happened to look down and see that his urine had cleaned off something peculiar in the ground. He zipped his pants and knelt to give it a further inspection. To his shock, it looked like a skull. Filled with fright, he stood up and called for his hunting buddy to come over there.

His friend rushed over to where James McTyson was standing, "What's wrong?"

"I found a skull, dude," James pointed.

Arlo Gunner knelt down just as James had and looked at it closer, "Son of a bitch...it is a skull."

"We got to call the cops down here," James pulled out his phone and called 9-1-1.

Sure enough, it was a skull. When the Brook County Sheriff's Department and the Tennessee Bureau of Investigation investigated the scene, they uncovered more human remains that went along with that skull. The remains were eventually unearthed and shipped off to get an idea of the sex, the estimated age, and most importantly– who the bones were.

After months of testing, and with DNA provided by the Miller parents, the bones that were not enough to form an entire skeleton found in Hudson's Woods, were identified to be Eddie Miller. Eddie Miller had broken his shoulder when he was ten years old trying to perform a bike trick, his mother said. The break, although repaired, was still noticeable on the bone. Also, his right wrist was broken the next year– another bike trick. That hand was found and gave more evidence that it was indeed Eddie Miller's remains.

Nelson Hudson published in *The Brook County Register* the medical examiner's remarks that Eddie had sustained a broken ankle, and part of his skull was broken in the forehead area. When new detectives with Brooke County asked the medical examiner's opinion of how this kid died, the M.E. hazarded a guess by saying, "It looks to me that he might have died from the trauma to the head before he was burned up. This injury was pretty massive when it first occurred. In my medical opinion, he died from this injury."

"Could he have been running, broken his ankle, and then smashed his head on something?" Det. White asked.

The medical examiner stood over the skeletal remains that were on the table, looking down at them and thinking over what the detective asked, "I mean, it's possible. But the break here was from something heavy. I don't think trees or fallen logs could have done this here to his skull. Let's say he was running, breaks his ankle, and falls, striking a fallen log. It's not going to produce this kind of damage to the skull here."

"What about if he was running, breaks his ankle, and falls, hitting a rock?" Det. Dooley asked.

The medical examiner stood there and stroked his fine, gray beard, "That's plausible, yes. A log– if he fell on it– would have some give to it, but a rock? Now, that's worth looking into. Were there any rocks around where these remains were recovered?"

"I don't know, but we can go back and look at photos; then go to the actual scene and see," Det. White replied.

"You find the rock– you might solve the mystery of what happened to his forehead," the medical examiner said.

Det. White and Det. Dooley returned to Hudson's Woods– the scene where Eddie Miller was found. Det. Dooley was looking at photos of the scene and standing where the skeletal remains of Eddie were discovered, and his partner was roaming about the area, looking down at the ground for a big rock.

"You know, if it was a rock that caused that injury on his forehead, then we're looking at our arsonist," Det. Dooley said, going through the photos.

"Yeah, I know. My theory is that he was down here, fucking around with matches, and caught the woods on fire. I'm sticking with Purkey's case notes on this one," Det. White said, still looking around for a rock of some kind.

"Yeah, me too. I think it's pretty open and shut. He was fooling around down here with matches or a lighter, caught the woods on fire, tried to make a run for it, tripped and fell, hit his head, and got burned up in the process."

"Yeah, I agree, but where in the hell is the rock? I mean, it should be close to where the bones were found, right?" Det. White asked.

"You'd think so. And they found no rock when they did the digging?"

Det. White shook his head, "Nope. At least I don't think so, anyway."

"And according to these pictures here, the head was pointed in that direction. So that tells me that the rock should have been close to the skull, right? Which is right where I'm standing."

"Should be," Det. White said, standing there and looking around. "But what if he tripped and broke his ankle somewhere else; hit his head when he fell back yonder; and just ran out of gas right where you're standing?"

"Well, that's a strong possibility, too. That means we'll have to try to find a rock laying on the ground from twenty years ago, hoping that it ain't sunk into the ground since then. I'd think it'd have to be a pretty good-sized rock we're looking for, not a piece of gravel."

"Yeah, I think something pretty good sized," Det. White said.

"Why in the hell are we even looking for the rock? I mean, the kid was found– probably did the fire; case closed. We solved a cold case." Det. Dooley said.

"We didn't solve anything. It was handed to us. Besides, Nelson mentioned that maybe something else happened twenty years ago to Eddie. Maybe he was down here and saw who set the fire, and they killed him...leaving him in here to burn."

"Well, that's a leap," Det. Dooley said, closing the file folder with the photos of Eddie Miller's remains. "I think Purkey had it right back then.

We have the remains. Positive I.D. that it's Eddie Miller. The M.E. looked the skull over, and said it had to be a rock of some kind that did that to his forehead. I think the kid set the fire, probably accidentally, tried to run, broke his ankle, fell and hit a rock with his forehead, and that's that...burned up in the woods."

Det. White stood there wanting to go deeper into this cold case but also knew that they had a win when the hunters found the skull of a missing kid from twenty years back. He knew that most times, detectives do not catch breaks like this one in Hudson's Woods, especially when the incident happened twenty years ago when the two of them were fifteen and in separate counties.

"Maybe you're right. Eddie Miller was found. And he was probably the one that set the woods on fire. Pukey had it right, looks like. Maybe I'll give him a buzz and tell him."

"You do that," Det. Dooley said, walking over to his partner. "Let's go back, write this up, and be done with it. It's a win– no matter how it came. We got some closure here. You know how rare that is in today's time?"

Det. White stood and looked around at the woods that early October afternoon. Part of him wanted to find the rock Eddie fell on with his head, but where was it? *A needle in a haystack,* came to his mind. And would finding the rock really change anything? Doubtful.

"Yeah, let's go."

1998

On a bright and sunny late May afternoon in 1998, Buddy Green, a freshman of thirteen at Central High School—the same school that Eddie Miller attended—coasted his bicycle down the gravel service road that would eventually lead him to the burnt Hudson's Woods. Or at least what was left of them. Nothing was standing anymore but blackened hollowed trees here and there. Nearly 95% of the woods were nothing but charred remains. It would be years before the area would come back. Seeing Hudson's Woods in that state shocked Buddy. He had a lump in his throat because he knew he was responsible for what happened. It would be his secret, one that he would carry to his grave, never telling a soul.

School had been decent for Buddy lately. *Actually*, Buddy thought, *it's been really good since* he *went away*. Buddy didn't dread getting up when his alarm clock sounded off for school. Buddy didn't have to take three tablespoons of the white chalky medicine to calm his stomach down. Most importantly, Buddy didn't have to mentally prepare for the horrible day at school that was surely to come. All that was over now because Eddie Miller– the bully that picked on Buddy so much– was dead and would never be found; at least that was what Buddy figured.

Buddy reached the bottom of the hill and past the curve in the gravel service road. He nearly lost control of his bicycle on the loose small rock. There, standing in ruin, were the blackened remains of what used to be Hudson's Woods. Buddy came to a stop and stared at what used to be. Across the forest, a sagging yellow police tape, twisting ever so slightly in the warm breeze, stretched on for what seemed like miles.

When the woods were full of life, you could never see through them. But now, with nothing but scorched earth and trees that stood black with no branches, Buddy could see clear across to the other side. It was something, all right. Buddy began to feel a sense of macabre accomplishment. A sense of self, you might say. He never intended for the woods to go up in flames, not at all. But it happened, and there was nothing he could do about it. *At least they stopped it before it reached those houses*, he thought to himself, looking way out across the fields.

Looking around to make sure no one saw him, Buddy got off his bike and walked it over to the tall grass on the other side of the gravel road. He laid it down gently. He walked across the small service road and stood before what used to be. Buddy walked toward the former woods. First underneath the police tape, and then into what used to be Hudson's Woods.

He walked slowly, shoes crunching on burned twigs and thin branches as he looked around at the blackened wonderland he had created. He walked alongside the winding path that snaked throughout the forest in complete shock. He had not been down there since the incident. This was the first day he had returned to the scene of the crime.

But don't they always return to the scene of the crime? At least that's what Buddy remembered hearing a detective say on TV one time.

Buddy was not a bad kid. At least he didn't think that he was. Sure, he felt bad for what had happened to the woods but not for what happened to Eddie Miller– the tormentor of Buddy's days at school and about town. Buddy felt no remorse as the flames licked Eddie's flesh while he stood by and watched. He gained immense satisfaction watching him burn, watching the life go away from his eyes.

Buddy had reached a breaking point in his mind. He decided– shortly after Eddie had taken the book he was reading in study hall and ripped all the pages out of it while laughing– that Eddie was going to die. Not just beat his ass, which he couldn't do because Buddy was no fighter, but actually kill him. Torture him first– his mind told him– and then watch him die; watch as the life slipped out of him, leaving behind an empty shell. And who would care?

Certainly not the teachers. They all hated the black leather jacket-wearing prick that had greasy black hair, yellow teeth, and a complexion that would be suited for radio. No one would ever miss Eddie Miller, not really.

Nobody would miss hearing his work boots click and clack down the hallways of the school. Those boots would often find the shins and asses of most kids in school, but especially Buddy's. No one would miss looking at that yellow-decayed smile he flashed as he enjoyed what he was doing while hurting kids. Nobody would miss that. Certainly not Buddy.

If anything, Buddy saw himself as a hero. He saw himself as a knight back in the days of old, setting a course to vanquish the village of the terrible dragon. The only problem was that no one in this town would know it was Buddy who killed the dragon. But that was okay. He didn't plan on going to jail and spending the rest of his life there. He had executed his plan so well that once it started; everything fell right into place...well, pretty much. He was even able to hit the curveballs that came down the pipe when certain things didn't go exactly as planned. But it was okay. Eddie was dead and could never hurt him or anyone else again.

That day of the book ripping, Buddy came home from school and headed straight for his bedroom. He fumbled through his desk drawer and pulled out a pen and a piece of paper. He sat down and began to devise a sinister plan on how he was going to kill Eddie. It was something he had fantasies about oftentimes when trying to sleep.

He thought about just taking his dad's gun to school, walking up to Eddie, and shooting him in the head. That plan he had given serious thought to for weeks and had nearly convinced himself that was the route to go. Buddy had even swiped the gun from his dad's gun safe one day and put it in his backpack for school. He was committed to killing the bully. All he had to do was walk up behind him, pull the gun out, stick the barrel to Eddie's greasy head, and pull the trigger. Done and done.

He went all day with that Colt .45 in his bag, just waiting for the moment to end Eddie's life. The moment presented itself after school when all the kids were leaving and going to their cars and buses. Buddy stalked a safe distance behind Eddie as they walked towards the buses. He pulled his backpack off, unzipped it, and put his hand on the grip of the gun. He was about to bring it out when Glenn Guzman, Buddy's lab partner in chemistry, ran into him and playfully tackled him, sending the two of them onto the ground. Thank God Buddy had not pulled the hammer back on the Colt. It was at that point Eddie disappeared onto his bus and out of sight. Eddie never realized had it not been for Glenn; he would have been killed right there in front of God and everybody.

Then there was the idea of confronting him with a set of brass knuckles somewhere in the school hallway. The problem with that was: A) he didn't have any brass knuckles and B) Eddie would beat his ass for sure; if not then, maybe later on somewhere out in town or at school. With Eddie, the venue never mattered. He didn't care if he got a three-day vacation or was arrested.

Eddie was one of those kids that would eventually turn into one of *those guys*. Buddy felt as if taking Eddie out of this world was doing everyone a huge favor, not only in the present, but in the future. Who knew how much more pain and chaos Eddie Miller would inflict on those he crossed paths with? Buddy could see the future in his mind's eye. Eddie would drop out of high school, get with a girl– probably a girl that was very malleable– and beat on her; make her scared; control her. Then he would get her pregnant, and the world would have a little Eddie running around. Eddie would drift from job to job, never working in one place for very long. He would abuse drugs and alcohol and be in and out of jail for various things. Killing Eddie seemed like a just thing to do for anyone that he would encounter in the future.

Buddy knew that if he could kill this monster now– kill him before he could spread his sickness to everyone he came across– he was doing everyone a huge favor. That thought, along with finally having enough of being picked on, made murdering Eddie Miller more and more logical.

As Buddy sat at his desk in his bedroom, a flood of Eddie occurrences came to him like lightning. He remembered Eddie stealing his lunch in the cafeteria; there was the time that Eddie walked beside him and flicked his ears so bad that they stung for days; then there was the incident at the school dance. Buddy was slow dancing with his girlfriend in the dimly lit gym and out of nowhere– Eddie appeared, black leather jacket clad et al– and pulled his pants down right there in front of everyone. Everyone in the gym, including the teachers and especially his girlfriend, turned and looked at what happened.. They all laughed. Eddie stood there laughing right in Buddy's face.

Every day was a festival of pain when Buddy went to school. It had gotten so bad that his stomach would turn flips over and over, causing him to vomit before he got onto the school bus. Eventually, his mom and dad had to take him to the doctor and get a prescription for his stomach problems. It did help some, and then it stopped. The Eddie problem was always going to be there, never stopping. And then there was the book-ripping incident. That was the final straw—sitting in his desk chair while everyone laughed and looked on as Eddie ripped out all 800 pages of the book he was reading, flinging the pages into the air.

And as Buddy sat there, watching Eddie smile that nasty yellow grin as pages slowly fluttered to the floor like plucked feathers of a bird, Buddy knew right then and there that Eddie had to go. But how?

Call it fate, call it whatever you want, but Buddy was struck with an idea that he never saw coming. His hand began to map it out before his conscious mind could see what was going on. Before he knew it, Buddy had written down some items: rope, a book of matches, and a brick.

He leaned back in his chair and looked at what he had written down. *Now what in the world could I use these for*, he wondered. A vision of Hudson's Woods came into his mind, as did the oak tree that stood just a shade from where the UFO clearing in the middle of the woods was.

Now, Buddy had never even thought about what he was going to do to Eddie, not in this manner. So the idea, the notion, of Eddie being tied to that tree and set on fire wasn't something that Buddy contemplated. It just came to him. Ain't that how some of the best ideas come? They come to you on cat paws and are setting up shop in your mind before you are aware of it.

That night up in his bedroom, Buddy laid out the plan that would eventually rid the world of Eddie Miller. It was a good plan, an evil and sadistic one, but the question was...would it work? That was the trick, wasn't it? How in the hell was Buddy going to lure Eddie down to Hudson's Woods, and most importantly, how was he going to get him tied to the tree? Looking at the word BRICK down on his paper, Buddy figured that the brick had something to do with it. All the other details he was going to have to wing it, he guessed.

Before bedtime, Buddy had gone out to his dad's tool shed and looked around for the items he was going to need to kill Eddie. The rope– he couldn't find. He could have sworn that he saw a rope looped around a nail on the shed wall at one point. If he did, it wasn't there anymore. But off to the side, on the other side of the wall to be exact, Buddy found something that would be better and not burn away as fast. Duct tape. Six rolls of it. Perfect. The brick– he took from his mom's flower garden, and the book of matches– he lifted from the mantle in the living room. He was all set. Buddy couldn't sleep that night. He was too jazzed about what he was going to do the next day.

———

The next day, Saturday, was when the plan was put into action. Buddy got up around ten, went downstairs to eat breakfast with his parents, and then back up to his room to get ready for the day. When he came back down the stairs sometime later carrying his backpack, his mother asked what his plans today were. "Not much. Maybe go on a hike with my friends or something. Nothing special," Buddy replied, keeping his cool. Buddy's mother smiled and asked with whom? "Janey and Ty." She nodded in acceptance. She had met his friends a few times and liked them. With a wave, Buddy was out the front door, and his mom was none the wiser at what her son was about to do on that idle Saturday.

He rode his bike to Hudson's Woods and went inside to set up everything. All he had to do was place his backpack near the oak tree, and have it unzipped and at the ready for when Eddie showed. And how exactly was that going to happen? That part had come to him in a dream the night before.

In town on most days, especially on Saturdays, Eddie could be found in one of several places: the pool hall that Buddy was forbidden to enter by his parents; the basketball court in the middle of town behind the bank; or outside the drugstore sitting on a park bench, yelling obscenities at people when they walked or drove by. Sometimes you could see Eddie walking the sidewalks of the town, making dogs mad by clanging sticks against the fences that kept the dogs inside their yards.

Buddy steeled his nerves and went looking for Eddie out in town after he hid his backpack in the woods. He drove down all the streets where he had seen Eddie walking before; no sign of him. He peddled by the drugstore and saw nothing but an empty park bench. Then, Buddy went into a place he had never been before...the pool hall.

Inside, it was kind of empty with only a few old men shooting pool, listening to some honky-tonk on the stereo. Buddy walked up to the man who sat at a desk with a cash register off to the side and asked if he had seen Eddie. Buddy described him in detail before the fat man waved his hand at him, "Kid, I threw his ass out the other night for breakin' pool cues. You see him– you tell him I've already called the cops and made a report. Punk is all he is. You'd best stay away from white trash like that." Buddy nodded and left the pool hall. *So where could he be*, Buddy wondered.

After riding around town once again, down the streets looking for the bully in black, Buddy was almost to the point where he was going to ride by Eddie's house down on Tripper Street. He had heard where Eddie lived, and that part of town was no place for a nice kid like Buddy. Sure, Claxton was a small town, but even small towns have bad spots…and Tripper Street was bad, or so said the adults in Buddy's life.

But before Buddy resigned to take the excursion to Tripper Street, he thought he'd ride through town once more, just to see if he would run into Eddie by chance. As he rode past the post office, he heard the sound of rubber bouncing off concrete. It was a basketball echoing behind the bank. Knowing that this had to be Eddie, Buddy turned his bike in the direction of the bank and rode past it slowly. It led him to the back parking lot where he saw Eddie shooting basketball alone. Buddy nearly threw up. He was so nervous about what he was about to do. Fate had given Eddie to him all wrapped up with a bow– it seemed– with no witnesses around.

Buddy parked his bike there, and stood with his feet on the ground and the bike between his legs. He trembled with fear. He could hear his heart thumping in his ears. Eddie paid Buddy no mind as he kept shooting the ball at the goal, never sinking it one time. He would throw up the ball, it'd bounce off the rim, and Eddie would run and fetch it, boots scraping the concrete. He did this several times before he noticed his personal punching bag.

"What are you starin' at, bitch?" Eddie asked, getting the basketball and putting it in the crook of his arm.

"You…bitch," Buddy said sheepishly, cussing for the very first time in his life. *Such an adult thing to say*, he thought.

Eddie stood there, shocked at first, and then he laughed. He had never heard Buddy say anything back to him before. He knew better, for God's sake.

"I know you ain't talkin' to me."

"Look around stupid. You see anybody else?" Such bravery coming from this timid kid.

"You want your fuckin' ass whopped, don't you?" Eddie said, beginning to walk slowly toward the kid on the bike.

"If you think you can do it, you pimple-faced pussy, you come on and try it," Buddy said, as he saw Eddie rear back and throw the basketball towards him. It landed on the side of Buddy's face before he could duck out of the way. *God, that was fast,* Buddy thought, as the click-clack sound of Eddie's work boots struck against the concrete. Dazed, Buddy saw that Eddie was almost to him. He got up on his bike and started to pedal as fast as he could down the small side street with Eddie trailing behind. To be wearing work boots, Eddie was quick.

Eddie was running at top speed toward Buddy, but Buddy was a safe distance from him. To make sure that Eddie would continue to follow him, Buddy looked back and cussed him loud and proud. He called him every name in the book, mostly those he had heard in movies and TV and even around the school. Some of them, he didn't know exactly what they meant, but who cared? It was working. Eddie would slow down and walk, then pick up to a jog, and then to a full-out run. But he never could catch up to Buddy. The longer he followed Buddy, the madder he became.

"I ever catch you—I'm going to break your fucking face!" Eddie shouted, trying to keep his wind.

The entire way to the woods, Eddie was cussing at Buddy and swearing to God that he was going to kill him. Although he didn't see it, Eddie was so mad that tears were coming from his eyes. He had never been punked out like that before; he was going to make sure that when Buddy went back to school, he was going to show everyone on his face what happened to those who went up against Eddie.

It took about fifteen minutes of running, walking, and bike-pedaling for the boys to reach the top of the gravel service road that ran alongside the town's park. From there, all Buddy had to do was coast down the incline, make sure to keep his bike from sliding out from underneath him on the loose gravel, and make it inside the woods. Buddy's plan was nearly complete. Just a few more things, but those few more things were the hardest parts.

Buddy sat at the top of the service road on his bike, watching as Eddie jogged up the road still cussing him. Buddy could tell Eddie was winded by his words. The bully was worn out but was carried this far on pure adrenaline. His plan to tire Eddie out seemed to be working. Buddy felt that he was losing him a few minutes back before they reached the park, so he slowed down and started talking about Eddie's mother and how sex with her was really good—called her a doorknob because everyone in town got a turn. That seemed to hurry Eddie along.

He was seeing red by this point, screaming at Buddy, "You better hide good because when I get you, it's over!"

Buddy was feeling good so far, but there was a little bit of fear that still hung around in his mind. Just enough to give him butterflies in his stomach.

When Eddie finally got into good view of Buddy standing there with his bike at the top of the gravel service road, Buddy flipped him the bird and said, "Come on, you son of a bitch! Come and get me! Come whip my ass, you fucking pussy!" Buddy took his bike down the hill and coasted slowly as Eddie stopped, doubled over at the top, hands on his knees. He was trying to catch his breath.

Buddy slowly came to a stop on the gravel road and turned around to yell, "Come on! Come on pussy! Come and beat my ass! Come on, cock-sucker! Come and get me!"

Eddie stayed in that doubled-over position for a few minutes and then began to run full sprint down the gravel road. Suddenly, his boots slipped on some loose gravel; and down he went, scraping his elbows and hands. Blood came from the dirty wounds. Buddy laughed and laughed. Eddie got slowly to his feet and picked the tiny bits of gravel out of the palms of his hands. Blood was dripping from them. Once again, Eddie made a mad dash toward Buddy. That was his cue to turn and pedal further down the service road, leading Eddie the entire time to his death.

Buddy made it past the curve in the road, ditched his bike in the tall grass, and went into the woods to hide. He stood there in the thicket, watching and waiting for Eddie to appear. After a few long minutes—the kid appeared—huffing and puffing like a train tearing down the train tracks. Buddy could tell that his plan of tiring him out was working. Eddie looked worn out. He was staggering a bit; sweat glistened off his acne-riddled face. His hair, which was usually combed back, was a greasy, straggling mess.

Buddy came out of hiding from within the woods and waved to

Eddie, "Here I am, pussssssssy! Come and get me. Come on chicken shit! Come whip my ass! Stupid motherfucker!"

As Eddie walked closer and closer, Buddy inched deeper and deeper into the woods. As a visibly exhausted Eddie reached the spot where Buddy had been standing, Buddy had already run deeper into the woods, keeping his eyes on Eddie. All he had to do now was lead him, as he had through town and down the streets, to the oak tree just a shade from the clearing where it looked as if a UFO had landed (for sure landed). From there it should be easy.

Buddy stayed a good distance ahead of Eddie, like always, during the plan. No surprises, no slip-ups. He knew Eddie was fast and could catch up to him quickly now since he wasn't on his bike. Staying ahead of him was now the name of the game. All he had to do was lead the bully to where he wanted him to go.

Buddy stood on the path in the forest he had walked time and again, waiting for Eddie to appear through the thicket of bushes and trees; after a few minutes ticked away, there was still no Eddie. Then a thought came over Buddy: *What if he's already in here, coming in some different way, like from the left or right side of me?*

Frightened by this notion, Buddy looked both ways—first quickly, and then more surgical. The last thing that he wanted was to be jumped. If that happened, Buddy knew no matter how tired Eddie was from running and walking through town after him, he would beat the hell out of him or maybe worse, kill him.

A few more minutes ticked off and still no Eddie. Buddy was beginning to worry because this had not been in the planning. The plan was to get Eddie to follow him throughout the forest to the oak tree. From there he would hide and then jump him, clobbering Eddie's head with a brick to incapacitate him so he could tape him to the tree. Now, standing there on the path hearing his heartbeat through his ears, Buddy wondered what to do next. His hands began to shake.

On the outside of Hudson's Woods, Eddie was at the edge of the tree line where Buddy had appeared earlier. He was tired, bent over with his hands on his knees, drawing breath after breath; he was trying mightily to bring back the strength he had ten minutes ago when he was chasing

Buddy through town. Every thought that entered the greasy thug's mind was about Buddy.

Oh God, how he was going to beat the fuck out of that kid. Maybe even kill him and ditch his body somewhere there in the woods. The more he thought about killing Buddy—the more he convinced himself what he was going to do. He had killed animals before, cats and dogs from the neighborhood, but never a person. There was a time or two that Eddie Miller fantasized about what it would be like to kill someone, just to see what it would feel like watching them die. He had not gotten up the nerve to do it, but Eddie knew that it was going to eventually happen. The curiosity of it all was driving him mad that year. Buddy was going to be his first kill; that he was sure of.

Back inside the woods, Buddy began to think he had better find an exit strategy because Eddie had flipped the script. Now, the wild card was in play, and Buddy's plan didn't have a Plan B for that. Honestly, he thought that punking Eddie out would drive him to follow Buddy all the way through the woods. It had worked getting to the woods, so why not now? Then it hit Buddy: because he can't see me. And just as fast as that thought had struck him, so did another with the same speed. He would have to get Eddie to see him, so he could get the troublemaker inside the woods. But was he brave enough to walk back up the path and out of the woods to see where Eddie was? As he slowly walked up the path from where he had come ten minutes ago, the answer was a reluctant yes.

———

Buddy walked slowly, scanning the left and right side of the dense woods, making sure that he didn't see Eddie lurking in the overgrowth. With every step, Buddy held his breath, hoping it would increase his hearing. It was quiet in the woods that day. Eerily quiet. Sure, he had heard a few birds in the trees, but that was about it. It was as if all the woodland creatures stopped and settled in to watch the battle between Buddy and Eddie. The death match, as it was. Good vs. Evil.

As the tree line to the front edge of Hudson's Woods grew closer for Buddy, he wondered: if he saw Eddie storm in, would he be able to outrun him? No, was the loud answer to that. Buddy had been run down by Eddie before in town and at school. Back then, he had a huge head start and was still brought down by Eddie, who ran like a cheetah. This concerned Buddy a lot because he knew that he had pissed Eddie off, really pissed him off, this time around. Buddy began to think Eddie had it in him to kill him. With that thought, Buddy began to wonder if he should leave the woods and take a beating later on at school or out in town.

While Buddy was slowly coming to the tree line that separated the forest from the gravel service road, Eddie on the outside began to get his strength back a little. He began to walk around in a tight circle, pumping himself up for what he was going to do to Buddy, that little twerp from school that had the balls to call him pussy and chicken shit.

"Just who the fuck does he think he is, huh?!" Eddie asked, feeling that bully rage wash over him.

He was ready to go in there and track the little shit down and beat his ass...and then murder him. Eddie had decided earlier that he was going to commit his first murder there in the woods. In his mind, there was no going back.

What if you get caught, Eddie's mind asked.

"Fuck'em," he replied.

Ready to spring into action, Eddie walked toward the place where he watched Buddy disappear. The time was now to get this over with. Two worlds were about to collide...

What happened when Buddy nearly reached the tree line happened so fast that years after the deed went down, he still could not recall much of it. It's like being in a car accident. You're involved, but everything is spinning so quickly that you can only manage to grab and hang onto certain things. Eddie appeared in front of him, like Jason in a *Friday the 13th* movie, completely out of nowhere. Buddy definitely remembered that part with a chill for decades, especially when he closed his eyes to try to sleep.

Buddy had kept a sharp eye out ahead of him, to the left, and right, not knowing that Eddie had regained some of his strength and was coming into the woods after him. Buddy had taken his eyes off the tree line just for a second, one damn second—it was probably less if someone in there was counting—and in Eddie came. Turning his head, he saw Eddie, and he froze like a deer in the headlights. Across from him, Eddie did the same. Both were shocked by the unexpected happenstance.

Buddy can recall the feeling in his stomach. It was like he was about to throw up from fear of seeing the guy that he had taunted to the woods. *I'm dead*, Buddy instantly thought, as he turned quickly to run back down the path he had slowly and cautiously walked up. Then there was a hand that clamped down on his arm. It was a strong hand—a hand that Buddy had felt many times as a fist. But when Eddie grabbed a hold of Buddy as he tried to flee, he felt from Eddie's grip that this time things were different. Things felt...final. Somehow though, he managed to slip free of Eddie's hold—must have been the sweat on Buddy's arm.

The next thing that Buddy remembered from that particular moment in the woods, is running full throttle down the path and hearing Eddie behind him. Buddy recollects running so fast that for a minute, he didn't think his shoes were hitting the ground...

He remembered looking back and seeing Eddie running closely behind with his arm stretched out—fingers reaching for the collar of his shirt or his hair—something to reach and pull him down to his doom...

Buddy remembered his heart feeling that it was about to burst inside his chest...

Buddy remembered that he wanted to cry and scream for help at the top of his lungs...

Buddy remembered seeing the UFO clearing and the oak tree just feet away...

Then, Buddy remembered hearing a very loud CRUNCH. He turned to look and saw something he would never forget: Eddie rolling around on the ground clutching his ankle and screaming. Buddy kept running a bit further until he was once again a safe distance from Eddie. He was nearly to the oak tree. Yet another curve ball to Buddy's well-laid plan, but this one was okay. It worked out in his favor.

Watching Eddie cry—crying for God's sake—rolling around on the ground screaming at the top of his lungs that his ankle was broken. Buddy quickly seized on the opportunity. Instead of having to jump him with the brick in hand, Buddy now saw a different way this was going to go down. He walked rather casually over to where he hid his backpack of death and pulled the red unassuming brick out, holding it in his left hand.

Buddy knew that Eddie was in too much pain to fight, and he now held the upper hand that he dreamed about for so long. Now it was time for him to play the bully. God, if only the kids at school could see him now. Oh, how they would cheer him on. Buddy smiled a bit as Eddie lay on his back crying and cussing at his injury; God, how Buddy loved this recent turn of events.

"Get away from me, motherfucker!" Eddie shouted, as he tried to get up and take a stand.

Didn't work. Just as Eddie tried to use a nearby tree as a cane to help himself up, Buddy reared back and threw the brick at Eddie's head with deadly aim. The brick thumped off Eddie's head, and down he went without a whimper. The brick cracked open Eddie's forehead, causing blood to gush everywhere.

Buddy had no idea how long Eddie was going to be out, but hell, even if he did come, what could he really do? He had a busted ankle and a gaping gash on his forehead that had perhaps altered his reality. What was there to be afraid of now for Buddy? Nothing. *Fuck him*, Buddy thought. Buddy walked over to the kid and picked his legs up and dragged him the rest of the way to the oak tree.

Eddie was sitting down on the ground, back against the oak tree as Buddy wrapped him against it with all six rolls of duck tape. A tangle of sticks and dead leaves were piled up around Eddie's legs.

Eddie eventually came to, but only barely, and was mumbling something that Buddy couldn't understand. Plus, he was crying, sniffling like a child who just lost his kickball. Before he set him on fire, Buddy didn't think that his tormentor really knew where he was—total disorientation- didn't matter any. Buddy's plan, with a few unexpected things along the way, was almost ready to play the rest of the way out.

Buddy stood in front of Eddie and looked at him as blood from his forehead dripped slowly off the tip of his nose. He was still mumbling-something about his mom and dad. Who knew, really? He was probably hit so hard by the brick that it sent the boy into a state of dream-like images where he was talking to his parents. In a brief moment, Buddy kinda felt sorry for Eddie, sitting there on his ass tied to an oak tree. He crouched down in front of Eddie and leaned into his right ear, "Burn in hell motherfucker...this is for all the shit you've put me through."

Eddie didn't even raise his head from the mumblings to his mom and dad. Buddy struck the match head, and the flame flickered brightly. He slowly lowered it down into the mess of tangled sticks and leaves that lie about Eddie's boots and jeans.

First came the smoke, a slow gray smoke that snaked throughout the air. Then came the spark of fire that had finally caught...after a few minutes and a few more matches. Eddie was still mumbling about his mom and dad, never raising his head as the flames began to lick his body more promisingly.

When Buddy first devised this plan, he didn't truly think that he could watch someone fry, especially in real life. But standing there recalling all the shit that Eddie had done to him and to others, he didn't turn his eyes away as the flames began to burn through his black work boots and dirty blue jeans.

It was like watching it in slow motion; the flames overtaking the boy in time. Buddy thought he would hear Eddie scream in agony and beg him to have mercy. Nothing came from Eddie's crooked mouth but that damn mumbling. Buddy watched as the flames went higher and higher up the tree. In what seemed minutes, Eddie's body was burning away–nothing more than a shadowy image within the fire. The heat that it put off was so intense that Buddy had to step back. Plus, there was that smell. A smell that would take residence inside Buddy's nose for the rest of his life.

The final curveball came when the fire quickly crawled up the oak tree, catching the long sprawling branches on fire. With the woods being as dry as they were, the woods were nothing more than a tinderbox, readymade for a wildfire. Buddy didn't calculate the notion that setting his bully on fire was going to set the tree he was taped to ablaze. And that blaze begot a bigger blaze with other nearby trees. A huge oversight on Buddy's part, for sure. Also not in Buddy's calculus, was the drought that had gripped the region that summer.

Buddy grabbed his backpack, strapped it on, and ran out of Hudson's Woods. The fire behind him was licking the trees that had been there for no-telling how many decades. The plan was to burn Eddie alive and listen to him scream, but that went to hell. His plan never involved burning down the entire woods.

THE HOWLERS

1

CARLY HAD THE DREAM. It was a dream unlike some of the other
dreams. There was something about this one that hit home with her. You
see, Carly was what in the parapsychology world would call a clairvoy-
ant: a second sight into the unseen world. Now, this sense was not something that she realized she had until around twelve years old. Back then,
she could dream of things, and later they would happen. The problem
was that those dreams were not a play-by-play of what was going to
happen.

The dreams were simply a broad stroke of an event that was to take
place later on down the road. Sometimes the places and people were not
the same as those in real life, but the event itself did happen without fail.
The people in those dreams wore masks, hiding their true identities.
That was the frustrating part for Carly: the masks the people wore in her
dreams.

Carly never told anyone about her power of precognition while she
was a kid. It was her secret; something that she held deep inside her. As
she grew older, she began to hate the power that she had. The second
sight was not an every night event. Sometimes, she could go months and
months and not have a dream where she was in total control: seeing

things that were to happen to her or a loved one in real life. When she was in those types of dreams, she knew that it was what she called a "howler."

The howlers were the scariest of all dreams because when she awoke from them, she usually was scared beyond belief, screaming from her bed. Her mom and dad thought their kid had night terrors– if they only knew. Carly never told them about the howlers. Mostly because she knew they would never believe her. She went along with what they called her "night terrors."

The howlers, during a stretch from when she started getting her period, were intense.

Those dreams, those looks beyond the veil, provided her with some of the most frightening dreams in her life. Even as a forty-year-old married woman, she still remembered those dreams from long ago. They left lasting scars on her brain. The howlers were the singular reason that she did not have children of her own. She could not bear to lose them or see them die in one of those dreams. Falling in love was scary too because there was that potential of seeing them go in a howler.

One of those dreams that she would never forget was of her grandpa dying. It happened when she was fifteen years old. In the howler, Carly found herself at night time in an empty parking lot. There were no cars around. She turned around and saw that the parking lot belonged to a grocery store, one that she had never seen before. When she turned around to look about the streetlights that lit up the empty lot, she saw a man lying face down. Quickly, panic struck her, and she ran as fast as she could to the fallen man.

She did not roll him over to see who he was. She already knew. She had a feeling within the dream that it was her grandpa. Picking up the man that was twice her size, as you only can in dreams, she rushed him to the hospital, running the entire ten blocks. She looked down and saw blood streaming down from his busted-up face and down her hands. She could feel the warmth of his life and the coldness of his body through his clothes on her bare arms.

She made it to a hospital where she entered through automatic doors. The doctors and nurses were waiting on her, it seemed, and they took him out of her arms. In no time flat, the head ER doc came back to her and said that he was sorry, "He's dead."

Carly woke up screaming from her bed; another "night terror" as her mom rushed into her room, flipping on the light behind her. Carly was soaked in sweat and looked at her arms and nightgown, just knowing that she was going to find the blood of her grandpa. She pleaded with her mom to call her grandpa and see if he was okay. Reluctantly, she did after she calmed Carly down a bit. It was three thirty in the morning, and everything was fine at her grandpa's house.

"Of course I'm fine," Grandpa said. "You scared the hell out of me calling me this late."

A week later Carly got picked up from school by her Aunt Melaine. Aunt Melaine never picked her up from school. Carly then knew something bad had happened, probably to her grandpa. She was getting her nerves ready for the news that she knew was going to come eventually. Taking her from the office and outside into the sunlight, Aunt Melaine walked Carly to the outside of the school's fence and broke the news to her as gently as she could; her dad was dead. He was walking across a grocery store parking lot to get something for lunch when he collapsed face-first into the pavement. It would be later on that Carly would find out that there was a lot of blood.

She cried of course because of the death of her dad; but she cried also because just like in regular howler fashion, the dream showed her something that was going to happen but jumbled all the people– people wearing masks. Instead of it being her dad in the dream, it was her grandpa. It was like she was getting a message, but the important part was always left out. This howler was one of many that streaked across her teenage years. Those years were marked with death; death that she thought she could prevent, but the howlers were always mixed up with a certain code she could not break.

Eventually, her grandpa died. In a howler, Carly awoke to find herself at her Grandpa's farm on the outskirts of Claxton, the town that she lived in. She used to visit her Grandpa Wilson a lot during the fall. He would always let her sit on his lap on the tractor when she was young as they brush-hogged the fields, getting it ready for bales of hay later on that week. Those were good times and sweet memories. In the howler about her grandpa's farm, Carly was met by a scruffy man: he had a bushy black beard, shaggy hair, and was dressed in jeans, a white tee shirt, with a green army jacket.

He came up to Carly, who was standing at the front of the barn where her grandpa's tractor rested and said, "I'm the man from Texas. And I need a sandwich."

Confused, Carly asked the man that she was not afraid of, "How did you get here from Texas?"

"I was sent here. I walked all this way to tell you about the sandwich."

"Wait right here and I'll go make you one," Carly said.

She turned and went into the barn and somehow– the only way dreams can do– the barn inside was her grandpa's kitchen. She opened the fridge and got out the ham, the cheese, and the mayo. On the counter, she placed these items and opened the cupboards to get a loaf of bread out. Quickly, she made the sandwich for the man from Texas.

Carly walked out of the barn, and the man from Texas was still standing there, waiting. She handed him the sandwich, and he started eating right away. "Why were you sent here?"

With his mouth full, "To tell you about the sandwich. It'll be the last thing he eats," the mysterious man nodded to Carly and walked away, leaving her to watch him disappear into the fog that had begun to roll in that evening.

Carly woke up in a panic and looked around her bedroom. All was quiet. Her breathing was hard as if she had been running a full-blown sprint. She could feel her heart thumping against her chest. Carly looked at her hands and they were shaking. This was a strong howler, the strongest one yet.

Two days later Carly's grandpa was found dead in his kitchen at the table. He had a heart attack while eating his ham and cheese sandwich. He fell out of his chair that mid-afternoon and onto the floor; a half-eaten sandwich sat on the plate on the table. Carly cried a lot during the funeral and afterward. Most of the tears were about the howler she had and how she wished that she could have done something to save her grandpa. In the end, she could not say anything about what she experienced because no one would believe her. The howlers were a secret that she thought she would have to take to her grave.

Carly had another howler about another death. The star of this particular howler was her Uncle Lewis, a man that she did not see all that much nor care for. There was a vibe that he had given off that warned Carly to stay away. In this howler, she and Uncle Lewis were standing next to a wrecked car. She did not recognize the mangled pearl blue car at all– never had seen it before in her life. The other car that it hit was out of sight for Carly. She tried very hard to see the other car in the accident but it was blurry, like it did not want to be seen.

Uncle Lewis just kept saying over and over again in this howler, "Out of nowhere. Out of nowhere. Out of nowhere." Carly woke up from her bed drenched in sweat and wanted to scream.

A few days later, her mother was killed in an automobile accident. It was like the howlers had played another cruel joke on the dreamer; giving her scant few pieces to work with and yet nothing at all to work with all the same. When she saw the scene, there were two cars on the road. Both of them had been heavily mangled.

The pearl blue car had seemingly swerved into the lane of oncoming traffic, which was her mom's car: a gray SUV. It was at that moment in time that Carly realized that the car she could not see in her howler was her mom's. She could see the pearl blue car that was the cause of the deadly accident, but she was not allowed to see the other blurry car. It was then she knew why. She hated the howlers. She hated the gift of this peek behind the curtain of the unseen world. She hated that she could not do anything with the knowledge, no matter how limited it was.

2

Around eighteen, Carly fell into the pit of depression over all that she had lost. That depression saw her try to kill herself three times: twice with pills that she had swiped from her aunt's medicine cabinet and once with trying to hang herself out in her Uncle Ray's barn. The rope was frayed and could not hold her body as she stepped off the bale of hay. She hung by her neck for a mere three short seconds and then crashed to the ground. She might not have managed to kill herself but she did receive a sprained ankle from the fall.

Afterward, Carly's aunt and uncle had her taken to a place where she could get the help that she desperately needed. It was a retreat of sorts called Lake Hope. It was a place full of people who had lost their way and their will to live as the icy hands of depression squeezed their fragile minds. Carly did not put up a fight with her aunt and uncle, who had taken her in after the deaths of her parents, about going. She knew that she was in bad shape. The howlers had let her be during this time of depression and attempted suicide.

There was a doctor at Lake Hope who had taken a liking to her. Dr. Suzie Katz had befriended Carly one day at the dock of the lake. The sun was starting to bow out for the day while Dr. Katz was on her evening stroll on the grounds, trying to decompress from the grueling day of talking to people like Carly.

By the end of daily sessions, which ran ten to fifteen patients a day, six days a week, Dr. Katz was mentally exhausted. She had worked at the clinic for five years and had seen several very troubled teens and adults come through. Some she was able to help and reach. Some she could not. Carly– she thought she could help because Carly's problem was unique: the type of thing she read about in books and papers written about the subject.

Dr. Katz was sort of an oddball in her field. She fused psychology with parapsychology, and most times, that got her laughed at and not even taken seriously by her peers. She was brilliant beyond compare to those other doctors of the mind. But her reputation had followed her around as being a quack even though she carried with her the prestigious distinction of being a Harvard grad: top in her class. Why did they call her a quack? Was it because she believed in things that we could not see? Was it because she believed in things that went bump in the night? Could it be that she believed in little green men, Bigfoot, the Loch Ness Monster, ghosts, witches, and the theory of Atlantis? More than likely. Dr. Katz had gotten used to all the people talking about her and her beliefs. That never overrode the pure truth that she was head and shoulders above any of her so-called peers in the field of psychology.

Dr. Katz read the file on Carly and was intrigued. She was not the doctor in charge of her therapy, but she appealed to Dr. Russ Strope who was Lake Hope's chief administrator, to hand her Carly from Dr. Wilkenson. She thought she could help better than the other doctor. Dr. Strope liked Suzie and found her methods of helping people beyond anything that he had seen in the field of psychotherapy.

She was a great doctor, perhaps the most brilliant mind he had ever come across. He did not care about her reputation. He viewed Dr. Katz being the best in her field. Her papers on the human mind were published in countless journals across the world, and yet she came to Lake Hope because of her reputation of being different.

On the day he brought Suzie to Lake Hope, he toured her around the grounds, the facility, and introduced his staff. He needed someone that could make a difference in people's lives. Not that the staff of highly trained medical personnel, but having Dr. Suzie Katz working on your staff was a big deal. Having her would bring Russ Strope's Lake Hope to the forefront.

"Being different is what I need, Suzie," Russ told her when Suzie said that people knew about her reputation for having worked there. "Will you do it? Give me a year of your time. If you don't like it here, then you're free to go."

Of course, Suzie liked it from day one, and it was hard to tell her long-time friend no.

Dr. Katz walked on the outstretched dock that went sixty feet or so into Lake Hope. Carly sat there by herself, bare feet skimming the cool water below her. Suzie sat down beside her and struck up a conversation. Carly did not think much of her at first, but when Dr. Katz told her about herself and how she might be able to help with the howlers– a word she had read from her file– Carly looked at her and for the first time, she felt that maybe someone could actually help her. Maybe it was possible to get rid of the howlers or harness what they were and use the messages to help. Carly was excited that someone believed her about the howlers.

For two solid months, two-hour sessions in Dr. Katz's office every other day, she and Carly discussed her life before the howlers and after her parents' death. They talked at length about her suicide attempts.

"I just wanted the dreams to stop," Carly told her during one of those sessions. "Why dream about these things if I can't do anything about it?"

Dr. Katz sat there at her desk and listened to Carly. The more Carly talked, the more comfortable she became. Eventually, Carly stopped seeing Dr. Katz as a doctor but as a friend– a friend that she could be completely open and honest with– a friend that understood her.

Dr. Katz asked Carly during one of the first sessions why she called these dreams the howlers. Carly sat back in her chair and replied, "I remember when I was a kid, and there was a bad storm one day. My dad called it a howler. After that, I called every bad storm a howler."

"And I'm guessing that these dreams you have, the bad ones that you've talked about where you can glimpse into the future a little, you call them the howlers because they're very bad?"

Carly nodded, "Right." It was the first time Carly had opened up about the dreams and the origin of the name of the howlers.

"How often do these howlers come to you?" Dr. Katz asked.

The one thing that Carly picked up on right away was that the doctor, who wanted to be called Suzie, never wrote anything on a pad. She just listened and asked questions to get a better understanding of what Carly was going through. Suzie did not just ask the standard shrink questions like "How does that make you feel" or "Tell me more about that situation."

Suzie knew what Carly was talking about. Dr. Katz had written several papers about precognitive dreaming. Her questions were substantial in understanding what it was Carly was going through. Carly knew it; felt it. She felt Suzie knew what she was talking about.

3

As the sessions continued, the more open Carly became. Suzie, during the fourth session, revealed to her young patient about her life and her parapsychology pursuits as they were and what those pursuits had done to her reputation. The good doctor gave intensive background to Carly about who she was and why she was interested in the unseen world. Carly had a friend in Dr. Katz…"Suzie," Dr. Katz told Carly. "You call me Suzie."

It was during the sixth session in her office that Carly asked the doctor a question. "How far into the future do you think the mind can go?"

Dr. Katz leaned back in her chair and considered her question for a few seconds.

"I don't exactly know," she replied. "Think about this for a minute, Carly. In Alzheimer's patients, their minds slowly revert back to a time when they were young, like decades ago. The visions are so real to them that it gives them the sense that they are back in time without knowing they aren't in their body back in the past. However, their mind is.

"So, if the mind can go backward, then it stands to reason that the mind can go forward, yeah? How far into the future? Maybe days, weeks? Maybe months, I don't know. There's not enough data. I mean, there are prophecies and claims to foresee the future throughout the historical record: Nostradamus, John the Revelator in the Bible, Edgar Cayce."

"My howlers are real. Just the people in them– I guess the victims– are never the right ones that die. It's like the people that are dying or whatever are wearing a mask. Why do these dreams come to me? I mean, like, why me?" Carly asked from her chair. She looked as if she was about to cry.

Suzie looked at her from behind her black-rimmed glasses and shrugged, "Kid, I don't know. I wish that I did. I do. But you're not alone. I've interviewed dozens of kids and adults just like you that have these, what you call, howlers. They ask the same question. I wish I had something better for you as to why you. I've got nothing to offer but just interviews and case studies. But, at the end of the day, I still don't know why. Maybe God said here you go– try this one on for size."

Carly sat there and thought about that for a bit. "So you think I was just chosen to have these damn dreams that make no sense and where I can't help anyone who's going to die?"

"The gift of glimpsing into the future but not being able to do a fucking thing about it? Yes."

"Then what good is it?"

Dr. Katz, Suzie to Carly, shook her head, "It's not."

The sessions came and went and after two months and no more howlers, Carly did feel better about that part of her life. She still felt a profound amount of grief from not having her parents around. On the day of her leaving Lake Hope and back to her aunt and uncle's home, she and Suzie stood together at the end of the dock and looked out across the lake that shimmered in the sun. It was a perfect fall morning; not too cool, just right.

"What if I have them again?" Carly asked.

"Remember what I told you. What you've been practicing. When these howlers come– and they still may one day– never let your guard down, okay? You control your dreams. Once you recognize what's happening, you seize control, tear the masks away, and then you'll see who's really in danger. It's the only way that I know. And what's that called?"

"Lucid dreaming. Controlling the dreamscape," Carly said, turning her head to look at Suzie.

Suzie smiled looking across the lake. "Good girl. It's the only ammunition that you have, kiddo." Carly looked back out at the lake and the white caps that splashed here and there. She was glad that she came to Lake Hope and met Suzie. She was the only one who would ever understand the howlers.

4

Carly went back to live with her aunt and uncle. She graduated high school, and not one time did she have a howler. Not once. She had dreams and was learning with each dream how to control them. Each dream was a practice run for the eventual howlers that were sure to come one day.

Carly held onto a piece of knowledge throughout her life that Dr. Katz had given her years ago– something that she wanted her young patient to realize: in life, everything's eventual.

Carly grew up, went to college, and became a teacher, a respected

English teacher of the incoming freshmen in the high school where she taught. She was good at her calling. She never called it a job. She called it a calling.

The other teachers, the burned-to-the-crisp ones that had been toiling within the walls of the high school years before her arrival, called what they did a job. She loved her job, loved her life, and loved the peace of mind of not being afraid of falling asleep and having a howler. The girl who dreamed the bizarre and macabre– the girl who tried to kill herself– the girl who lost her parents at a young age had grown into a fully aware and resilient woman. All thanks to Suzie, who she kept in touch with over the years.

Carly had no howlers. In every dream Carly had, she walked through them in that lucid state where she could make decisions and use her brain. She had gotten so good at controlling the dreamscapes that she had trained herself to dream certain things. To turn that trick, she had to think really hard about it before going to sleep, taking control of her dreams. She was becoming a master of the art. Carly waited on the howlers; waited to rip those masks off and see who it was underneath them.

In her late twenties, she watched her marriage and friends grow and kept a diligent eye on her dreams. She was ready for the howlers more than ever. There were people in Carly's life that she did not want to lose if she could help it, especially her husband, Richard.

In Carly's late thirties, the howlers did not show. She began to wonder if they were gone for good; that whatever put the second sight into her had taken it out. It had been twenty-plus years since the last howler and even though two decades had passed, she could still remember it like it had just happened. Sometimes Suzie would call to check in on Carly to see how she was mentally.

"I've been good for a really long time. Maybe the howlers are finally gone," Carly told her once over the phone.

"Maybe, maybe not. Don't allow yourself to be lulled to sleep by inactivity. Just because you've not had a howler in a spell, doesn't mean they're not waiting for that perfect moment. Are you still controlling your dreams?"

"Yeah, I've become really good at it. I can dream whatever I want. But I keep my guard up."

"Good girl," Suzie told her.

Carly's forties came and saw her hair turn gray and her husband get that middle age spread around his midsection. Life was good, great even. Everyone close to her was healthy and in good spirits. Carly wondered some nights, while lying in bed, if the howlers were a manifestation of her going through puberty and if that singular event was the spark that started the howlers.

Maybe the death of her parents was the end of them. It made sense. Suzie agreed, although she was not completely sold on the howlers being gone. She had noted to Carly on their phone conversations over the years to always keep her guard up– that the howlers could be lurking in those dark recesses, waiting for that spark to reignite their presence. And just like when puberty came, so did menopause. That was the spark the howlers needed to come back.

The howlers eventually came back alive and loud. Those dreams, those nightmares, came without warning, much like they had back when she was young. The howlers came on a night that was just like any other night: a simple night, a night in which she and Richard had gone to bed for the evening, just like any other night in the middle of the week for the last twenty-something years.

Richard kissed his wife goodnight and turned to face the wall, pulling the covers up to his mouth– a move that he had probably started back when he was a kid. She lay there in bed, her back against the headboard reading a book called, *The Big Break* by Jerry Matthews. It was not a particularly interesting book, but she, being an English teacher, tried to keep her mind sharp by reading books– no matter how uninteresting they were. Her goal was to have read a thousand books by the time she was sixty. She was three hundred from that goal with eleven years more to go, God willing.

5

At some point during chapter fourteen, Carly closed her eyes, just to rest them for a second, and drifted. Her hands relaxed from the book's front and back covers, and they gently slid down to her stomach. With the cadence of Richard's snoring, there was a gentle and familiar yet soothing sound that was lulling her to sleep. In ten minutes, she went from drifting to full-blown sleep: her head tilted to the side, the book free from her hands, her body limp. Carly was in dreamland, and the howler was ready. It was going to be a bad one; it had a lot of time to make up for.

Carly was not up for the challenge in that particular howler. She had gone against Suzie's warning of not lowering guard. She had done so well for so long that over the last few weeks, she just got tired of controlling her dreams. What was the point? The howlers were gone. Or so she thought. Carly could control those dreams whenever she wanted. To Carly, she looked at controlling her dreams like flipping on a switch in the kitchen to turn the lights on; it was easy. In the last several weeks, Carly had gotten lax, a term that Suzie would have used and did on those phone calls when she warned her about keeping her guard up and her eyes and mind sharp. The first howler in a very long time came to Carly that night. It lived up to its name; it was indeed a howler.

———

Carly's dream/nightmare began with her being inside a creepy, huge mansion at night. All around her, she could hear the thump, thump, thump of what she thought was a heartbeat. It was as if the house itself had a heart.

"That's not right," Carly told herself standing in the middle of a room that was before a huge winding staircase, like she had seen in those old 1950s haunted house movies with Vincent Price.

Lightning flashed outside, and the windows that lined the rooms flickered with fright, bathing the inside of the home in an eerie silver-gray exposure. The heartbeat, or what Carly perceived to be a heartbeat, stayed steady and calm.

"Okay, a heartbeat. So there's that," Carly told herself, feeling her mind begin to feel the dream, something she had not done in a few weeks.

"Don't let your guard down, Carly," It was Suzie's voice inside Carly's head.

"I think I'm good. It's like flipping on a light switch. I got this," Carly spoke out loud in the old spooky mansion. Was it haunted? Her mind told her yes.

Carly walked with the softness of a cat, trying not to make a sound, towards the staircase. Another silver-gray flash of lightning sprayed about, and this time, looking out one of the windows from where she was standing, she could see the skeletal outlines of tree branches from outside against the house. The heartbeat sound was still inside the mansion and was giving Carly the willies with its monotoned rhythm.

"That's important somehow," Carly spoke, trying to get control of this dream, this howler.

"Is this a howler?" Carly asked, looking around the creepy old mansion. "Yup," she answered her own question.

She felt pulled to the staircase, but why? Carly placed her hand on the handrail of the staircase and in doing so, she felt a charge go through her. Something she had never felt before, and she equated it to a very low hum of electricity flowing through her. It tickled her more than anything. She took her hand off, and the sensation ceased. She looked up at the staircase. It was dark up there on the second floor where the stairs ended. What was up there? "Nothing good, I'm sure," Carly remarked, knowing that the creepy old house was not really a house at all but something else.

Taking in a deep breath, Carly placed her hand once again on the railing of the staircase, and the low hum of electricity tickled her. She began to slowly walk up the stairs one rung at a time. As she made her ascent up the staircase, the banister that she glided her hand on had gone from a tickle of electricity to a more noticeable electrical sensation.

The further up the staircase Carly climbed, the more intense the wooden railing had become with electricity.

"This means something," Carly remarked." But what?" She stood there on the staircase, a quarter of the way up, and another flash of silver-gray lightning flashed, causing everything around her to turn that silver-gray for a fraction of a second. It hurt her eyes.

Carly stood in the middle of the winding staircase, hand no longer on the railing and tried to grab hold of this dream that she knew was a howler beginning to prowl. At that revelation that it was indeed a howler, it scared her immensely because now she knew what they were. She had more to lose now with her husband, so figuring out this howler was paramount. His life just may depend on it– that she knew for sure. Carly scolded herself there on the staircase for not being diligent enough lately in her dreams. She allowed herself to lower her guard, a warning that Suzie had given her, but Carly felt that she had everything under control: just like flipping on a switch in the kitchen.

The lightning flashed with urgent frequency the more steps she climbed. What was waiting for her up on the landing when she reached the top? The thump, thump, thump, of that loud heartbeat echoed throughout the mansion the closer she came to the last rung of steps before the landing spilled into the second floor. With that last step, she was off the stairs and standing at the beginning of a long corridor, with rooms on either side that stretched all the way just like any old creepy haunted mansion would have. The lightning flashed brilliantly, and the heartbeat thumped.

Carly, feeling that her control was coming back to her slowly, took off and walked down the hall. The first door on her left was closed. On the door was a nameplate that read COLLEGE. Carly turned and looked to her right at another door that was closed across from the COLLEGE one. This one had a nameplate as well: THE GOOD DOCTOR. Carly walked over to that door and twisted the door knob. It was locked. She kept twisting the knob as much as she could, hoping that it would break the lock, and she could go inside: nothing. Carly stood back and looked at the nameplate on the old heavy wooden door in frustration.

She walked away from THE GOOD DOCTOR and passed a row of

three windows on the right side. Lightning flashed, bathing her and the corridor in silver-gray, but only for a fraction of a second. When her eyes adjusted back to the dimly lit hallway, she happened upon two more doors to the left and right of her. The left one was HIGH SCHOOL and the right one was STEVE COSWELL. The STEVE door was unlike the others. This one was cracked open and once Carly realized it, she heard the gentle sobbing of a girl.

Carly stepped over to STEVE COSWELL and peeked inside through the ajar door. Inside it was a bright and colorful girl's bedroom: boy band wall posters hung on the walls; a red polka-dotted comforter on the bed; a small desk with papers and books. And at that desk was a girl, probably no more than fourteen, with her head down on that desk weeping.

The little girl was crying over a broken heart, her first one. She could feel it. Carly's heart broke for her, and she wanted to rush in and console her. But something told her not to dare. This was a memory: someone's memory. Carly drew back from the door not to be heard and eased towards the middle of the hall. "Whose memory?" she whispered the question to only herself.

Carly looked down the dimly lit hall and saw more doors that seemingly went on forever. She walked away from STEVE COSWELL. Carly looked at the nameplates on the doors she passed by: FISHING WITH DAD, COOKING WITH MOM, HANGING WITH MY FRIENDS, MY FIRST DRINK, SEX, FEARS, DREAMS, MY GRANDPARENTS, ETC. At the end of the hall was a door in front of her. Carly's stomach filled with butterflies because she knew that this was the door she came up here for and what that pull was from downstairs in the main room.

The heartbeat inside the mansion thumped faster, like someone was running, now. Carly was tense and nervous as she approached the door at the end of the hallway. The nameplate came into focus better with each step. Carly stopped in front of the door and curiously looked at the nameplate: CARLY. Carly, with sweaty hands, reached for the doorknob to give it a hearty twist, but before she could do so, the door slowly yawned open a little way, giving a creepy creaking sound that only doors in haunted mansions can make.

Something was not right about this door and this room. Carly knew that, and it started with the nameplate. Something with the nameplate was not right. She was getting control of the dream a little better. Carly reached up and pulled the nameplate off the door. Underneath the CARLY was SUZIE. The heartbeat inside the mansion ricocheted about the walls of the mansion, growing louder by the second. Inside the room, Carly could hear a conversation between her and Dr. Katz.

Carly pushed open the door the rest of the way, and inside was Dr. Katz's office back during her time at Lake Hope. Carly saw herself as a teen sitting in a chair and talking to Dr. Katz who was at her desk. Carly walked in slowly, and neither of them acknowledged the grown-up Carly. Her younger self and Suzie were discussing the howlers and how to dream in lucidity: to take control of the dream. Suzie began talking about Carly's condition and how rare it is, and she theorized that it started because of her first menstrual cycle. Grown-up Carly stood there against a bookshelf off to the side of the room, watching her teen self and her doctor at the time talk. To her, it was like watching a movie.

Dr. Katz and young Carly stopped talking and both turned to older Carly. "You know what this is about?" young Carly asked her older self. "I think you do. You've gotten relaxed, and the howlers are here now." Her younger self said. "It's too late to take control now. They're been waiting on you to get lazy, and now they're here."

While her younger self was talking, Suzie calmly got up from her desk and walked over to the office window which was three stories up in the old renovated plantation home at Lake Hope. Older Carly watched terrified as Dr. Katz opened the window, crawled out of it, and jumped to what Carly figured was her death.

With eyes wide in terror, Carly looked down at her younger self who was still looking at her with piercing eyes of fire, "You don't have time. She's a goner. You took too long," younger Carly got up from her chair and walked over to her older self with those red eyes that glowed like a demon. Older Carly had nowhere to retreat to because she was backed up against the bookshelf. She was paralyzed with fear.

"This mansion…I'm inside Suzie's mind, aren't I? The doors… they're memories. Hers."

Younger Carly, the one that was still dealing with all the death and pain, grinned with teeth that were sharp and pointy covered in blood, "SEY, tub oot etal!"

Even though she spoke backward in a demonic guttural voice, older Carly's mind made sense of it. She was in total control of this howler now. Young Carly had just told her, "Yes, but too late!"

Carly jumped from her safe bed in her nice and secure home, screaming with panic. She screamed so loudly that her usual dead-to-the-world husband sprang into action, dazed and confused and coming out of a dream of his own. Carly was standing up in the dark bedroom, running her hands through her hair and screaming as if she had been shot. Richard rushed to her and tried to comfort his wife, asking her what was wrong, shaking himself from fear.

The only thing that Carly could do was scream, "The howlers are back!!" Carly kept screaming. Richard had no idea what she was talking about. They had never discussed the howlers before.

6

"She's dead," Carly said quietly, sitting at the table in the kitchen in a trance-like state while her husband sat across from her.

Richard had taken Carly to the kitchen from their bedroom in the wee hours of the morning where darkness still held guard. He walked her to the kitchen table and sat her down. He was still shaking himself from the scare in the bedroom. He had never heard his wife scream like she had before. He walked over to the wall and flipped the switch on. The overhead lights scared away the darkness.

"Who's dead?" Richard asked, sitting across from his wife.

"Dr. Katz. Suzie."

Richard asked who this "Dr. Katz" was because he had never heard of her before, not that he remembered anyway. His memory was terrible.

"There's some things that you don't know about me, Rich. Things that I never told you. You probably won't even believe me when I do tell you," Carly said, as she looked up from the table, and to her husband, seemed to wrap her arms around herself for comfort.

Richard was not quite sure how to respond to that. They had been married for over twenty years, and he thought there were no secrets between them. He was about to find out that people can bury secrets as deep as the deepest ocean.

It took about an hour for Carly to finish with her story, about the howlers and what they showed her. She talked about the death that ensued with the dreams. She talked about her suicidal tendencies. Spoke about Lake Hope back when she was a teen. She told her husband about how Dr. Katz, Suzie, had helped her feel not alone and how to take control of the dreams, but the last few weeks she had gotten relaxed "because I thought they were long gone."

"And these howlers are back?" Richard asked, after taking a few moments of reflective thinking on what his wife had just revealed to him.

She nodded slowly. "It would appear."

"Can you get a hold of Dr. Katz?"

She looked at him strangely, "For what?"

Richard looked stunned, "To see if she's okay? Maybe this dream was just..."

"The howlers aren't wrong. God, didn't you hear a word that I said? I was able to figure out that it was Suzie. Something that I couldn't do back then when it came to my parents. She's already gone. This howler wasn't wearing a mask. It was Suzie that jumped out that window."

Richard wanted to believe his wife, but the story was way too far fetched; he did not dare tell his wife that. He believed that she believed. But these...howlers? Richard just did not know what to think of them.

"What do you think caused this dream?"

"The howlers?" Carly insisted. "Menopause. Just like when I started my period way back when. Dr. Katz narrowed it down to the chemistry inside my body being was the spark. A working theory that seems to be right."

"I still think that we should reach out to her and see," Richard said, after some more thinking about his wife's tale.

"Go ahead. Number is in my address book in the kneehole on the desk. You call it. Then come tell me that you don't believe me afterward," Carly said, not caring if her husband believed her or not. Thinking on it for a bit, Carly sometimes did not believe it. The only person that did believe her was Suzie.

Another one of Dr. Katz's working theories, and one that Carly believed in, was that she could see these howlers because of the emotional connections she forged with those that were masked in the dreams.

"People die every day, Carly," Dr. Katz said in the sixth session in her office at Lake Hope, "but you don't dream of them. The howlers come to you because of the emotional connections that you have with those people in your life. It's like they come to warn you about something, but they wear these masks that keep you from seeing who's really in trouble."

"Do you think the howlers are a bad thing?" young Carly asked.

Suzie leaned back in her chair and pondered for a moment or two, "I don't think so. I think they are coming to you as a warning. Part of the precognitive dreaming package you seem to have that was started by your body changing: your first period."

"But they're really scary," young Carly replied.

Dr. Katz nodded, "Yeah, I'm sure they are. And they need to be to get your attention. But you have to learn how to control the howlers, to see who it is under the masks."

While she was thinking about the past in Dr. Katz's office, Richard got up from the table and went into the study where Carly went to grade papers in quiet, rooted around in her desk, and fetched the green address book. He flipped the pages and first went to the D's for doctor. Dr. Katz was not written down. He flipped a few more pages and found the S heading.

There it was in blue ink, Suzie Katz, and there was a number where she could be reached.

Richard sat down in her chair behind the desk and picked up the phone. He punched the ten-digit number on the number pad. It rang. And rang. And rang. And rang. After a few more rings, Richard just put the phone into its cradle.

He sat there and did not want to believe his wife because what she told him was crazy. Then the rational side of Richard took over. The reason she didn't answer is that it was way early in the morning, like three to be exact. But still, there was that shred of doubt in Richard's mind.

Back in the kitchen, Carly sat at the table, shoulders slumped, hair a mess, thinking about Suzie and about how much help and comfort she provided during her time at Lake Hope, even on those phone calls throughout her life. She was the only one who believed her story about the howlers and what they foretold. She was not like Richard who was skeptical.

Carly wanted to lash out at him, but she held back, knowing how ludicrous the story about the howlers was. She understood that he did not believe her. It was fine; it had to be. She did accomplish something this time around in that howler; she was able to unmask who it was that the howler was trying to show her. The howler had come to her too late for her to be able to do anything about anything. Hopefully, the next howler would come a few days earlier so she might have a chance to prevent something.

In the light of the ensuing day, Carly found out what she already knew: Dr. Suzie Katz was dead– died in her sleep. Probably a heart attack or stroke were the best guesses. She was seventy-three. Carly kept calling the number every hour, and eventually someone on the other end answered. It was Suzie's sister, Katrina. Carly introduced herself, and they talked for a few minutes. Carly asked about Suzie. That's when Katrina broke the sad news.

It was sudden, and it was in her sleep. Katrina said that they were supposed to go down to the park for their morning walk; but when Suzie did not answer the phone or her door, she knew something was up. Using a front door key to let herself in, Katrina called out to her sister, and when no answer came, she just knew something bad had happened– could feel it in the pit of her stomach. She walked to Suzie's bedroom and found her unresponsive, lying in bed. Carly had tears in her eyes, but she knew. She already knew.

7

Months passed by since the last howler that foretold the death of Dr. Katz, Suzie to her friends. Carly did not forget the dream at all nor the dreams that came afterward. She was hyper-vigilant: controlling the dreams and turning the potentially bad ones into good ones, making the dreams what she wanted instead of what the dreams wanted. It took her no time to get back into fighting shape. She was ready for the next howler. Carly just hoped that she would get enough lead time to do something about the next death that was foretold, where maybe she could actually do something about it. That would be nice.

Carly tried something that she had been thinking of doing during those months: she tried to call the howlers in her dreams and make them show up long before they wanted to. She hypothesized that maybe if she could bring about the howlers earlier before the death of a loved one, she would have time to prevent it. She never had a chance to bounce this idea off Dr. Katz, but she knew deep down that Suzie would have considered her idea worth a shot at the very least.

Every night, Carly tried to bring about the howlers. Nothing, not a peep, for two long years.

When the next howler came, it was a doozy. Carly found herself inside her dad's old Ford F150, with him behind the wheel listening to Johnny Cash lowly on the radio. Carly was in the passenger seat, and she felt herself being around twelve years old. A glance in the mirror that was underneath the sun visor confirmed it. Although her body was that of her twelve-year-old self, her mind was that of her older self. She looked at her dad, who was humming the Cash tune, and he looked younger too: back like she remembered him when she was twelve and long before he died.

Carly looked out the windows. It was night, but she knew what road they were going down. It was County Road 500– a road that she and her dad had taken many times leaving Claxton. Instead of being shocked and thrown by this dream, this howler, Carly managed herself rather quickly and took control of the dream, like all the dreams she had in the past that led up to this one. She knew it was a howler, and she was ready.

"Who are you really?" she asked her dad.

He turned to his daughter, "What?"

"You're not my dad. He's been dead for a long time. Now... who are you?" Carly asked again.

Her dad grinned and turned his attention back to the road.

"I ain't got time for games, Carls." That is what he called his daughter: a cute nickname that she enjoyed, but not at the moment. At the moment, she was all business and not all soft and mushy from seeing her dad sitting beside her.

"So...I'm guessing my husband is going to die soon. Be easier if you just tell me. Because I'm going to find out soon enough. Maybe give me a chance to stop it."

Carly's dad just kept his eyes on the road without saying a word. The Johnny Cash song ended and replayed in what was a forever loop.

"Try to stop it?" he asked.

Her dad laughed, driving on that country road, "You can't stop it! Just consider yourself lucky that you can even see us, Carls! We don't come to people very often."

"Then why do I even get that much?!" Carly shouted. "What's the use of having these howlers if there's nothing I can do?"

Her dad shook his head, "I don't know. We don't get to pick who we come to. Just happens. Too bad we don't give out lotto numbers, huh? At least that would be something useful."

Carly continued to look out the windshield at the darkness they were driving in while Cash played the same song on the radio. "Why my dad?"

He turned and looked at her, "Why is the sky blue and the grass green? I don't know, Carls. It's your dream. You're the one that can see past the curtain. You see us, and we see you. When you see us, you best believe something bad is coming down the pipe for you."

Carly sat there in her twelve-year-old body and tried to figure out what driving down a country road with her dad in his old truck and listening to Johnny Cash meant. Or was this a red herring altogether? Was the meaning something different like in times past? The last howler was not. The last howler was pretty straightforward even if it did take Carly some time to figure it out.

"Richard is probably going to die while driving somewhere. Probably going to be a ring of fire when it happens." Carly remarked, pointing out the significance of the Cash song that was playing over and over.

Silence covered the two passengers in the truck. Carly was in deep thought, trying to piece together what this howler meant. Her mind was working as hard as it ever had in this dream.

"You're not supposed to see behind the curtain, bitch!" the deep guttural demonic voice that came from her dad told her.

"Get out of here! Go back home and forget about us!" Her dad's eyes turned fire-red as he turned to look at Carly. His face began to transform into that of a demonic being, teeth growing long and pointy; its hands on the steering wheel turned into green claws.

"Get out while you still can!" her demon dad shouted in his guttural voice.

Carly bolted upright from her bed screaming, just like she had in times past. Richard jumped from his dead sleep with her, heart flying a mile a second, shaking just as before.

"What's wrong, honey? What's wrong? Another one of those dreams?"

Carly tried to gather herself there in the bed and looked around; her reality started coming back to her view. She was out of her dad's old truck and back into her PJs and bed. Her hair was sweaty, and her stomach was all twisted in knots.

"Yeah…it was," she responded, trying to calm her breathing down. It felt like she had just crossed the finish line of a marathon. Her heart beat so loudly against her chest that she thought it was going to explode.

"What happened this time? Who did you see?" Richard asked, rubbing her back. He could feel the sweat through her PJ top.

Carly looked at Richard, and she did not have to have her reply. He saw it on her written on her face. At first, he drew his hand back and kind of laughed, the way you laugh when something so unbelievable happens that's all you can do. Then the tears came from Carly's eyes, and Richard knew that this was serious.

Richard didn't believe in the occult, parapsychology, spooks, specters, and things that go bump in the night. He just didn't. He believed Carly's stories about her dreams but had just chalked them up to nothing more than mere coincidence. That's all. He never really gave them any credence whatsoever. He believed that his wife believed them, and he supported her. But did Richard believe in that sort of stuff? Not at all. But there was a tiny fraction of him that maybe believed her, just a fraction.

8

In the next few days, Carly had talked Richard into staying at home from work. It was not an easy sell, but Carly was frantic and on the threshold of a nervous breakdown trying to keep him out of a car. At first, Richard said that he was not living his life in fear over a stupid dream. That offended Carly because her dreams were more than just dreams; they were howlers and those howlers, when they came, always meant death to those she loved.

After begging and pleading with her husband, Richard finally relented and called his boss, saying that he was taking the week off: a family emergency, which it was to a degree. Carly hugged him and cried right there in the living room after the call was made.

She was hoping that she could stop the wheels of fate. After all, weren't the howlers a glimpse behind the curtain of the unseen, maybe those who operate the wheels of fate? It appeared that with Richard, there was enough lead time for her to do something about it. Keeping him out of cars was a good start.

"For the whole week, I can't get in a car? At all?" he asked her as she still held onto him while she sobbed. Carly just shook her head against his chest. Richard felt it insane to bend to Carly's demands but yielded because he could see how distraught she was.

"No. At least a week." Carly replied. Richard stood there, holding his crying wife and not knowing what else to say. He just went along with it, like most husbands do to keep their wives happy. He still did not believe that he was going to die. But there was that very small, very tiny fraction of doubt that resided in the back of his mind that did. Just a fraction.

Sometimes that's all it takes to change a life and one's future: just a fraction.

On the first two days of his confinement to the house, Richard was already itching to get out. He saw how his wife was nervous about his probable fate, but Richard? Not so much. He believed that his wife believed, and Richard did not subscribe to the unseen world. So on the third day, Richard decided to get out of the house and just drive down the road. Of course, he was going to have to do this without Carly knowing. That was going to be the hard part.

Before Carly went to school on the morning of day three, she took the keys to his truck with her. She did not ask for them, just took them off the key hook by the front door without him knowing. She had trusted her husband the first couple of days to not go out of the house and down the road for a drive or to the store for a milk run. There was something about the third day that Carly had a gut feeling about.

Richard did not appreciate this gesture because to him it was getting ridiculous. He was a full-grown man of fifty. He could make his own choices and did not need his wife doing it for him. He looked everywhere for his keys that were always on the hook by the front door. He checked drawers, cabinets, Carly's nightstand drawers, and just about every nook and cranny inside their home. Nothing. Fuming at her for taking his truck keys and making him a prisoner in his own home, Richard called his wife later that afternoon to let her know how stupid it was to take his keys away from him.

"It's for your own good, honey. You don't understand," Carly said, trying her best to make him understand.

"I understand plenty," Richard said. "I understand that you're taking this shit to a whole nother level," he ended the call, thinking about throwing his cell across the room in anger.

9

He was supposed to stay inside the house for a week because Carly told him that usually, the howlers came true within approximately a week. It was day three, and Richard had already developed cabin fever. He was downstairs that morning, eating cereal at the kitchen table and reading the newspaper when something smacked his brain with violent force. It was a memory of something: a key.

"That's right!" Richard got up from the table and rushed to his bedroom, to the nightstand in particular, and pulled open the drawer quickly. There were useless bank statement papers, long ago receipts, a box of scattered paper clips, and ink pens but not what he was looking for.

He ran his fingers through the drawer of debris and looked for a key, a spare key to his truck. He remembered that he had put it in the drawer a long time ago just in case something ever happened to his main one. He stood there and wondered for a moment if Carly had swiped it from the drawer.

"She wouldn't have thought about it. I don't even know if she knew about it." Richard said to nobody but himself in the bedroom.

He pulled the drawer out and dumped the contents onto his bed, sending everything in a helter-skelter mess. There it was: a black key, the spare to his truck that sat in the driveway. He laughed wildly as he held the key in his hand in triumph.

Richard had gotten dressed and went outside to his truck. He slid inside and stuck the key into the ignition and turned it. It roared to life and the sound of the engine never made Richard feel more like he was in control of his life. Had Carly had her way, he would not have been allowed to get this far. He had no idea where he was going, but just having the freedom back to drive wherever was intoxicating. He shifted the truck into R and backed out of the driveway. He pulled onto the county road. There he shifted into D and sped away. Where to? He wasn't sure, and it didn't matter.

10

Later that afternoon, Carly called her husband from school. He did not answer. She thought he might be taking a nap or something because that had been the case the first two days of his confinement. She ended the call, and a pang of worry washed over her. She dismissed it.

It's not like he could go for a drive because I took his key, she thought to herself.

Two hours later, right before she left school, Carly called Richard's phone again. Nothing. Now she was getting worried. She hurriedly ran out of the school and across the parking lot to her car. She had a bad feeling in the pit of her stomach that something had happened although she hoped it was just nerves giving her that feeling. Carly got in and took off heading for home. *Probably nothing, but you never know,* she thought.

She turned onto her county road headed for home; and when she came down the hill, Carly was met with a scene of flashing red and blue lights from police cars, an ambulance, and a fire truck.

Black smoke puffed high into the afternoon sky, sending a continuous mushroom-like cloud. Cars that had taken this road were lined up, parked with people who were watching the spectacle. Carly was six cars deep in line from the scene, but the best she could see there had been a horrible accident. What she saw was a tractor-trailer, one of those big rigs that hauled gas, on fire. Not just a simple fire, but a raging inferno– a ring of fire.

Police were keeping the cars back a safe distance in case of another explosion from the tanker. There was so much black smoke and fire that Carly could feel the heat from where she was parked on the road. There was nowhere to turn around and leave the scene so she, along with the cars in front of her and the ones that had started coming from behind, had no choice but to watch the grim reality.

She sat there inside her car, thinking about Richard and why he was not answering his phone– and then it hit her like a ton of falling bricks from the sky. Her heart sank to her feet, and tears came pouring from her eyes. She knew this horrible scene in front of her was Richard. It was the ring of fire that Cash sang about in the truck with her dad.

Carly slung the car in park, jumped out, and briskly walked down toward the scene. The heat from the burning tanker could be felt with each step she took towards the smoke. Something incredible happened on her walk: the winds shifted, and she could see on the other side a truck that was on fire in front of the tanker. Carly just knew that it was Richard's blue truck. Just knew it.

Again the winds shifted and sent the dense black smoke into another direction, making things even more clear for Carly. From behind, she could make out the license plate of the truck that had crashed into the back of the tanker truck on that winding country road.

Although she could only make out the last few letters of the plate on the right side, she knew it was Richard's truck and his plate. Carly fell to her knees screaming, as others in their cars got out to see what the matter was with the woman on the road.

ROOMS OF AN EMPTY HOUSE

HE STOOD there in what used to be a full house: full of memories, full of knick-knacks, full of hope and laughter. Those were the good old days– back when they were young and full of life and forward motion– back when things did not seem as dark and foreboding as they appeared to be now. Now, things seemed desperate, empty, and full of husks of what was and what would never be again.

On the bare walls of the house once hung pictures– family pictures of times past; times that were forever captured to be reminders of what was. In those pictures, they were all happy and in happier times of a bygone era. Those pictures are gone now, and in their wake, nothing but an empty place with a single nail, still protruding from the wall on which those pictures used to hang. That is all that is left behind– a nail. He did not take the time to pull the lonesome nails out, or for that matter, hang anything else. Putting something else in place of where old family pictures used to hang seemed like treason to him.

He had remarked once to a friend that the scariest sound in the house was not from the house settling nor the random pops and cracks when the house changed temperature– but from the silence that swarmed the entire place, especially at night while he lay in bed. Sometimes he could lay there where he and his wife once slept together and hear the doors close to other bedrooms and the footsteps of their children walking to the kitchen for a midnight snack or to the bathroom. Long ago, it seemed the house was alive with sounds. Now, the sounds were gone, echoes of silence.

Most times lying in that bed, he could still feel her beside him. Sometimes he could hear her breathing lightly beside him. He never told anyone about this; just kept it to himself. Who would believe him anyway? To gain fleeting comfort on those empty nights, he would turn over to where she used to sleep on her side of the bed and hold the thick comforter she left behind and hold it. It still had her scent on it, and that brought tears most nights.

The sounds were not the worst part of the empty house for him. It was the imprints, the echoes of ghosts, of times past that he saw from time to time in that big empty house. He saw birthday parties, and family times, like playing board games at the dining room table. He could see over in the family room where they were all huddled watching a movie on TV. And yes, he saw the fights that boiled over hot and burned everyone in the path of destruction.

If the walls could talk, they would have much to say about the eighteen years the family lived in the house. They would reveal the good times, the laughter, and the conversations that inspired; the walls could speak about all the times he and his wife helped heal the broken hearts of their children and dry not only the tears of the kids, but of each other. Those walls would also speak freely about the bad times– the times when glass was broken and strong words of hate thrown about willingly, not caring who they hurt in the process. Times when secrets were spilled out onto the floor. Yes, the walls in the house had a lot to say about the family it protected from the weather outside for eighteen years.

He walked slowly through the empty house, looking at the walls and recalling everything with a flash of imagery that he could never see– even if he sat and meditated on for a spell. He looked across the kitchen from the dining room and out through the window that displayed the backyard. That place had several stories that could rival the walls inside the house.

———

It was out back where he taught his daughter to ride her bike. It was out in the backyard where he, his son, and daughter played Frisbee and created a brand new game out of it. He had even come up with a type of throw with the Frisbee called "Skin The Cat" where the goal was to throw the disc so close to the ground that it made it nearly impossible to catch. If someone caught it that low to the ground, they indeed, "Skinned the Cat."

That backyard hosted many cookouts and many football games between his kids and his nephews. There was such youthful joy when they all got together and played; it was an innocent time– a time where no cares whatsoever invaded their minds as they all played backyard football and laughed. Looking out the window from the kitchen, the backyard sat quietly waiting and wondering if any more kids were coming to play.

There would be no football games or cookouts anymore– at least not with him involved. Those days were all gone, vanished through the sands of time. Everyone, his kids and nephews, were scattered to the four winds. Perhaps a new family with new ideas, new motivations and momentums would take the home and plant their family flag where he once did. Perhaps they would not have an expiration date, like he and his family did.

———

He walked inside his son's bedroom and leaned up against the door facing, taking a look around. It was empty, but in his mind's eye, he could see the bedroom as it once was: full of kid stuff that had evolved into teenager stuff and then into nothing at all. All part of the evolution of life, he surmised.

Over to his left, he saw the drywall patch that was painted over some years ago where his son's fist landed in a fit of rage– over what, he had forgotten now. All he remembered was that he made his son repair it by buying the materials out of his own pocket. You could still see where the hole had been, but it was not terribly noticeable to anyone who didn't know exactly where to look.

His eyes fell over to an empty part of the bedroom where his son's bed used to sit. He recalled with clarity the day he sat down on that bed and told his son that he needed to be very careful about his girlfriend. He knew that they were moving very fast and knew that they were having sex. He advised him about practicing safe sex and to make sure that he always wore a condom because having kids this early in life was not a good choice to make. Turns out his son never listened, not even then, when he advised him on not having a child at nineteen. That was the beginning of the end, and he didn't even know it; was not aware that day in his son's bedroom that the end was at hand. His son had that kid, actually conceived three weeks before he had gone in there to speak to his son about the hardships of having kids at such a young age.

In his daughter's bedroom, it was empty just as his son's. Cleaned out, and nothing stayed behind except a small stack of books that were written for tweeners. She loved those books, and he guessed that carrying them to her new home was not an option. She left them behind because she had outgrown them. Maybe she outgrew everything at seventeen. Who really knew?

He walked into his daughter's old bedroom and looked around– a memory flashed within the walls of his brain. His instant reaction was to smile. It was a memory of him flying his daughter every single night through the house when she was a kid of eight years old like Superman. They would end in her bedroom, him throwing her on her bed and covering her up. She loved it. He did, too. Where did Superman go? Where did she go was a better question.

Every room in the house had a story. The kitchen, the dining room, the bedrooms, the family room– all of them had imprints and echoes of times past. Some of them were great stories, and some were not. Some of them were bad. Some of them hurt, even the good ones. The stories in that house had been written for eighteen years, like in a daily journal. He could not recall all the times, just the highs and lows. He stood there thinking about what was worse: remembering the bad times that hurt or recalling the good times that hurt worse.

It was hard for him to see the house that was once full of life, love, and laughter. He could have stayed if he wanted, and he did for a long time afterwards. The coldness of the place had seeped in, and it slowly, over time, had turned from a warm home to just a cold house. A home is what a family makes it; a house is just a house made of wood, metal, and glass. You cannot make a house a home without a family, and he knew that from experience. His family was gone. So was the home. It was now a place to come home from work, a place to take shelter in from the storms; a place to sleep in.

He stayed for as long as he could, dealing with the ghosts that lived there for two decades gone by. The ghosts were noisy, but they had a certain comfort to them. It was familiar to him, even if he felt like a stranger in his own house. The memories were what kept him there. He could have left a while back, but leaving was difficult. However, something compelled him to stay while everyone else was gone. It was the house, the memories, the good, and the bad that attached him to the place. It was the only thing he had left of them aside from some scant few pictures of times gone by.

He walked slowly into the one place he always had the most emotion: their bedroom. It was in this bedroom where a lot of emotion lingered, more than any room in the house. It was in that bedroom where they had sex so many times, he had lost count. It was in that bedroom where they slept next to each other for eighteen years. It was in that bedroom where she told him that they were expecting their daughter. It was there that they faced the uncertainty of a positive test from her doctor about a spot on her breast during her annual breast exam.

The bedroom also was witness to the end of it all. It was a night in July when, in that bedroom, he and his wife waged their last bitter fight of the marriage. It was the one where the line of demarcation was drawn. His dad had passed away unexpectedly earlier in the year, in January this was. Through the months, he tried to deal with his dad's death and although his wife had been some comfort, she began to pull away and do her own thing which led to the road to ruin.

By the time he could see what it was that she was doing, the marriage was pretty much over. He and his wife were on opposite ends when the line was drawn, separating them forever. Neither was going to relent, not going to consider yielding to the other. The line had been drawn, and that was that. Nothing else could grow between them but hatred and discord.

It all came down to a confluence of emotion and proclamations that night in the bedroom that he was standing in. In fact, he was standing right in the very spot where the fateful words were spoken; words that would never be taken back because they were the truth on both ends. When the fierce argument ensued, the pressure from the year before that hot July night had grown. He remembered it was ten o'clock that night– the time when it really ended. He would never forget looking at the clock on their bedroom wall.

Husband and wife stood nearly eye to eye in that bedroom and yelled over each other, yelling at the tops of their lungs– neither hearing the other– just trying to be louder than the other. Standing in that bedroom looking at the emptiness of it all, he could not recall exactly what the fight started over, just the final words that were never taken back or measured before they were spoken. He was crying, that he remembered.

He had been thinking about his dad and at that point in time, he had no one to lean up against; no one to help him make it through. His wife had pretty much abandoned him, he felt. The stress had withered away his mind, thinning it to the point where any issues or any kind of small stress caused him to fall apart. He needed his wife there to pick him up. Where was she? On her phone on social media talking to another man– that's where.

In that final fight on that hot July night in the bedroom, after all the yelling and screaming, his wife of nearly two decades uttered the infamous words that still ring in his ears. When he shouted in response to her remarks that "he needed her to help him through all this" meaning dealing with his dad's death, she shut up and looked at him dead in the eyes. There was a coldness there. The both of them stood silent for a few moments before she spoke. Those words she spoke– he would never forget. That moment in the fight has been etched into his brain as a painful reminder that the argument was the last they would ever have.

"It's not my job to fix you," she replied coldly.

He stood there mortally wounded by those words, and at first, he did not even think he heard what she actually heard. He looked down at the floor, his breath feeling knocked out of him for a second or two. *Was she serious*, he wondered. He raised his head and looked back up at her, standing there with her arms crossed ready to fight more, if need be. Gathering himself as best he could, he said the only thing that he knew to say; the only thing anyone could say in that moment. His reply was not a booming, vicious retort. Instead, it was a calm statement, a declaration of independence from her. This was where the marriage ended, and it ended right there in that bedroom.

"Maybe you ain't the wife I need." That was it: simple and to the point.

From January to that hot July night, the long-term marriage ended right there in that bedroom.

When he needed her the most, she rebuked him. Why? Over a midlife crisis that she was consumed in at the time. Her words were covered in thorns, and they lashed him and brought about blood. He stood there bleeding from what she had said, and even though he lashed back with his, they paled in comparison to what she had said. For what she said was the truth in its irrevocable state, according to her. She never backed away from that statement even after the fallout weeks and months later. It was how she felt.

He stood in that empty bedroom and wanted to cry because that bedroom represented marriage, the intimate workings of it, through the eighteen years. It was the most painful room in the entire house. And standing there for what was the final time in his physical form, he could see ghostly images of days past: the good and the bad as it was. This was his final visit to the bedroom they shared.

He walked to the front door, grabbed the doorknob, and twisted it like he had millions of times before. It was different now; different because this was the final time that he would feel the cold brass steel in the palm of his hand. He stood there for a second and realized the gravity of the situation. He turned and gave the living room, the walls, the floors, and the interior doors one last look before he left.

It was empty, that house– empty as he felt inside. In his heart, this would always be home. It would always be where his family grew. It would always be where the good memories of their younger days would be forever trapped by those who remembered. And nothing ever dies or fades away really if someone remembers it, right?

He opened the door, closed it behind him, and all that was left was the loud echo of a closing door in an empty house.

A WALK IN THE PARK

1

DOWN AT THE POLICE STATION, Det. White sat across the drifter at a table in the small interrogation room. The disheveled man looked ratty, like he had not been washed in years. He had a smell about him that smacked the detective of dog shit and onions. The man's fingernails were long and dirty– his eyes looked tired– and the hair on his head was stringy and greasy while his bushy beard looked like it could use a shampoo and trim.

The detective had been in the room with the drifter going on an hour with nothing. He avoided the detective's line of questions with silence. Det. White still did not have a name from him and had zero to go on other than his arrest.

"Looks like blood on that jacket. How'd all that get on it? Is it yours?"

The drifter started down at the table and did not utter a word. He had a distant, blank stare and only looked up a few times. Those eyes were dark blue, but Det. White was sure there was nothing behind them...not really. Det. White was not even sure that the man could even comprehend him at this point in the interrogation. How long had he been a transient? There was no way to tell unless the man started talking. *Fat chance of that*, the detective thought to himself.

"Where did you get the three credit cards? They ain't yours unless your name is Martin Yeager. And I know Marty. Have for a long time. You ain't him. Did you know that Marty is missing at the moment? Yup, just went for a walk down at the park and, poof, vanished into thin air." Det. White once again cycled through the questions. "You know anything about that?"

The detective leaned back in his chair watching, waiting for the man to say something, or maybe even shift in his chair. Nothing. He was stone. No emotion at all. He did fight the police officers that had brought him in; but since then, he had been docile and compliant when told to do something...except answer Det. White's questions. It appeared the fight in him was gone.

Det. White got up from his chair, stiff and frustrated, and walked out of the room into the police office pool. He was greeted by Sheriff Amy Hall and a couple of deputies. "Well?"

"Nothing at all. He's a brick wall in there."

The sheriff nodded her head, "Think this is our guy?"

Det. White put his hands on his hips and considered the question, "Looking that way. I don't want to rush to judgment, but look at the facts: Marty goes for a walk, like he always does, around the time of his disappearance; this guy pops up in town and is apprehended with Marty's credit cards and with blood on his jacket. Which I bet is Marty's."

"But we still haven't found Marty," the youngish deputy said.

"We got dogs coming again to search those woods at first light. And that jacket is being processed as we speak...but I got a feeling this is our guy," Sheriff Hall said confidently.

2

It was October 15th, 2021, in the town of Claxton, Tennessee. It was a normal, ho-hum, run-of-the-mill day in town like it always was. There were several exceptions to the boredom of the town over the years. Charlie Chadwick, and the girls he kidnapped and hung upside down in his attic and basement; the three dead boys down at the Kirby Farm back in 1984; the murders in a house that was supposedly cursed by a witch over forty years; the disappearance of that teacher and superintendent; the man that was hit by lightning all those times; the big fire that burned Hudson's Woods down to the ground in 1998; and who could forget Sally Wilder, and what she did to those poor men? Of course, other odd and macabre things happened in Claxton, but those incidents and people were the most infamous.

He was not aware of it– how could he be– but Marty Yeager was about to be logged into Claxton's book of unfortunate events. He was a retired railroad worker, living out his years with his wife after decades of hard work and saving money for his eventual retirement. He had grown up in Claxton, called it home, and would never think about leaving for someplace else. The town, for better or worse, was a part of the fabric of his DNA. He had no idea that today, on a simple and unassuming Tuesday, was going to be the day he was killed…

3

That morning, Marty Yeager: a sixty-four-year-old retiree, husband, father of two daughters, Mandy and Mindy, and three-time grandfather, sat at his kitchen table, reading the local newspaper. The headline on the front page read: Bobcat Sightings Around Town: Beware. Marty skimmed the article and had heard tales about this alleged bobcat going around, killing dogs and cats and even chasing a few people. The police were on the lookout for it as were many of the townspeople. Hunters went everywhere looking for this bobcat and came up with nothing.

"Daddy used to warn me about camping in the woods because of bobcats. But I never saw one, and I camped in every wooded area in Brook County…twice," Marty said absently to his wife.

Mr. Vortman down the block had told Marty that he had seen the bobcat one night while he was taking the trash out; said he saw it prowling in his side yard and when it saw him it growled, and its ears were pinned back like it was about to pounce. He went inside to grab his shotgun, but by the time he got out, the cat was long gone.

"Big son of a bitch," Mr. Vortman had told Marty one evening at the lodge. The bobcat was the most excitement that the town had seen in a while. Since Marty had retired, reading the local news had become a ritual of his and had been every morning for four years.

Marty woke up that morning of his death, stiff and sore, which had been the usual for the past several years. He chalked it up to old age creeping in. When Marty pinned it down, it was all the decades of manual labor from his time on the rail yard that made his bones hurt. Some of it was genetics on how he felt as he aged.

The other part of it was while at the railroad, he was trying to hang with the younger bucks that worked there and prove to them, and mostly to himself, that he could still do what he did when he was twenty-five. It didn't take long after turning fifty that Marty knew his better working days were behind him.

After finally getting out of bed, Marty went to the kitchen and poured himself a tall glass of orange juice. He stood with that glass of juice looking out his kitchen window that hung above the sink and watched as two blue jays sat perched on his back porch railing. There was a beauty that fall morning in his backyard, his last. The rising sun bathed the landscape with a yellow tint that looked warm, but Marty knew better. It was fall and the temps had been falling slowly in the last few days.

4

The morning—it would be Marty's last one—was cool on that Tuesday. Not cold where you could see your breath just yet, but cold enough. The changing of the seasons had begun, and Marty was ready to get summer in the rearview mirror. But that's not to say his bones were. His arthritis was worse when it got colder, causing him more discomfort as the years rolled by.

Putting the glass of orange juice on the kitchen table, Marty went to the back door in the kitchen, slipped his mowing shoes on, and stepped out into the morning. Wearing a pair of shorts and an Auburn Tigers tee shirt, Marty discovered that it was much cooler than mornings past.

He stood there and rubbed his arms with his hands, trying to make them warm with the friction.

Marty walked around his backyard and inspected it, mostly the length of the grass. Since it had not rained in nearly two months, the grass had stopped growing. With the seasons changing, yard work was pretty much done. The last time he cut the lawn, trimmed around the trees, and flowerbeds was back in the first week of August. Since then, the yard had not really grown much at all.

Marty liked working outside and had nearly all his life since the railroad. Being outside, working in some form or fashion, was like second nature to him. But that summer had put an end to his outdoor chores. The drought and now the fall had made it to where Marty had nothing to do outside. His work was done and had been for quite some time. Nevertheless, Marty inspected his yard, hoping that it needed some tending to. It did not. However, leaves were all over the lawn.

Walking around to the front of the house–he saw the newspaper–rolled up with a thick rubber band and laying on the bottom step of his front porch, courtesy of Stevie Riden, the twelve-year-old delivery boy. Marty bent down slowly to pick up his newspaper. He rolled the rubber band up until it popped off, flying somewhere in his yard nearby. Marty opened the newspaper and gave the front page a cursory glance. Nothing thought-provoking or of any interest except another story about a damn bobcat on the prowl in Claxton.

It was a local paper run by local people. The editor was a sixth-generation paperman. And as the internet trampled print, especially newspapers, the Brook County Register prided itself on still being around. Marty thought that it was because the editor kept it afloat due to the fact it was his family's business, and closing shop would signal the end. And what would the man do then? Retire? Marty could relate because when a man's purpose is gone, what's left? Mindless hobbies?

It's not to say that Marty didn't have his hobbies and passions. He had things to take his mind off of life in general—things that he could escape to for a while. He was an avid baseball fan and watched the Atlanta Braves every night they were on TV, even the West Coast games that came on at ten-thirty at night. He'd stay up and watch his favorite team since he was a kid. What else was he going to do? Sleep? If he wasn't careful he would sleep his life away. And Marty hated that idea. He wanted to be up and doing something all the time.

Another hobby that Marty had was tending to his flowers: Double Knock Out roses in particular. His flower garden was full of them: reds, pinks, yellows, and even purples. Those purples were hard to come by because they were hybrids. He had seen them when he and his wife were out for a drive, and he spotted them at this small nursery off the side of the highway, just sitting here being all pretty and whatnot. Marty, stricken by the color of a Knock-Out he'd never seen before, made a U-turn and pulled into the place to ask how that was possible. Suffice it to say, that purple Knock-Out now resides in a flower garden amongst other reds, yellows, and pinks.

Marty cared for his flowers. He would deadhead the plants, ensuring that the next growth cycle would give way to more beautifully colored bulbs. He would constantly feed banana peels into the ultra-rich soil, and he would water them twice a day. Sometimes, not often but sometimes, people would stop by and ask about his flowers as some sat prominently in his front yard in various large beds dotted throughout his lawn.

5

Marty came back into the house with his newspaper and found Clair, his loving wife of forty years, sitting at the kitchen table scrolling through her smartphone. She was the tech-savvy one of the two. It's not that Marty didn't know how to operate devices; he just didn't care to get his news from them. He preferred the standard mode of information from magazines and newspapers. He was old school like that. He did still have his Playstation 4, which he played a lot when his grandchildren came for a visit, and his phone with all his favorite music apps he'd listen to when working out in the yard or on his evening walks. That was about it for tech.

"Sometimes I don't know why I even get this paper anymore," Marty said, unfolding it to give the inside a read.

"It's more of a gossip rag nowadays. Always talking about what's going on at the city council meetings and such. No one cares because some of the issues have been issues for as long as we've been married with no resolutions," Clair said, still scrolling through her phone.

"You're absolutely right on that. So, are the kids coming over this weekend?" Marty asked, slumped in his chair and reading the paper with the headline: Bobcat Sightings Around Town: Beware.

"Yeah, they said they were. What do you want for dinner when they come?"

Marty sat and considered, "I don't know. Maybe grill out some chicken and steaks."

Clair looked up at her husband and wrinkled her nose, "What about pasta? Chicken parm, maybe? Some Alfredo, stuff like that? Do like a whole Olive Garden thing here at home?"

Marty had known through the years of being married that when his wife made a suggestion, it was her subtle way of telling him that's what she wanted. All he had to do was agree. And he did, which he usually did. "Key to a happy marriage", he once told the guys down at the lodge, "is to just agree with them."

"Yeah, we can do that. Sounds good."

6

As Marty and Clair decided what to do about dinner, the weekend, their children, and their families coming over, on the other side of town, a drifter walked about. His hair was long and greasy, unkempt. His face was covered with a beard that had not seen a razor in many years. He dressed in an old, tattered green military jacket and wore a faded pair of blue jeans that had, by the looks of them, seen many miles. His brown boots were just as dirty as the man who wore them. He walked with his head down and with a limp on the highways and byways.

Claxton was such a small community. It didn't have much in the way of sights. The town was pretty much a collection of around twenty- eight hundred people, according to the last census. Most lived out in the county instead of the city limits. The town has a small grocery store owned by Jack Strafford, a place to have your car serviced where Steve Miner owned and operated it, a diner that has been in the Dean family for generations, a drugstore owned by the Wilson family, a barber shop where an old man who folks affectingly called "Whipper" cuts hair and held court on current events.

There is a police station and firehouse, post office, several churches, a high school and elementary school, along with several shops and eateries down main street; that was about it. The town was a Norman Rockwell kind of town you would see in one of his paintings.

The drifter went inside Jack Strafford's grocery store the day Marty went missing. He had a few dollars from panhandling and was hungry. Jack was standing on one side of the counter while Joe Clinger, the retired mailman in Claxton, stood leaning up and talking away to Jack. Both stopped talking and looked at the man who made no eye contact. Both men watched the drifter as he made his way down the bread aisle. Joe looked at Jack and Jack at Joe. This guy was not clearly a regular.

Later, when interviewed by Det. White, Jack said the drifter that had come into his store seemed...off. When Det. White asked how so, Jack could only reply it was just a feeling he had. When Det. White asked what he did in the grocery store, Jack said that he just bought a loaf of bread with some nasty, sweaty dollar bills and went on his way. That was the size of Jack's interaction with him. Det. White asked Jack if the drifter had said anything to him– anything that struck him as odd. Jack stood outside his grocery store when the detective was interviewing him and shook his head, nope.

"He just didn't speak when I gave him his change back. I told him to have a great day. He turned and left, and that was the last time I saw him," Jack said.

"And you didn't see him again? Anywhere here in town later on?" Det. White inquired.

"No, sir. That was it."

From there, based on other eyewitness accounts, the drifter went and sat down with his loaf of bread in the gazebo in the town's square.

"He stayed there for about an hour, I reckon," Wendell McGree, the owner of This N' That said.

"I saw him from my window when I was cleaning it for the day."

"About what time?" Det. White asked.

Wendell rubbed his beard and hoped that the strokes would jog his memory. "It was early. I hadn't opened up the fabric store just yet."

"Did you see him leave?'

"No. He was gone when I went to lunch around noon. I happened to look over that way and didn't see anybody."

7

Around noon on that day, Marty and Clair had returned home from some grocery shopping in the next town over. Jack's grocery store in town was a good place to stop if you needed something like milk, bread, soap, beer, or pizza. But as far as having a large variety, Jack's didn't offer much in the way of that. Especially what Marty and Clair were planning to buy for when their family came for the weekend.

Clair had settled in her seat on the couch and began to play a word search on her phone. Marty said that he was going outside to rake some of the leaves that had fallen. The leaves had begun to turn colors and had fallen from the trees, covering lawns and streets everywhere in town. Marty didn't really see the point of raking leaves into big piles and laboring them into leaf bags. He didn't see the point in raking at all. But he did it that day, the first time for him in decades.

While outside, a fellow retiree, Carl Walker, came strolling down the sidewalk. He stopped and struck up a conversation with Marty as usual when he saw his friend outside.

"You know you're going to have to do that in another day or two, right?" Carl said laughing.

Marty nodded his head and dropped the leaf bag down onto the grass and ambulated over to Carl, rake in hand.

"Yeah...but I thought I'd get out in the nice weather for a bit. I get tired of just sitting in the house. It's bad for you, you know it?"

"Ever since I retired ten years ago, I refuse to sit around. I don't care what I'm doing as long as I'm moving. I think sitting around is what killed Clem Bolinger." Clem was a neighbor of both Marty and Carl. He lived three houses down from Marty and was known throughout the neighborhood as a shut-in.

"It may have, Carl. It may have. What you got going on today?" Marty asked, standing up against his rake.

Carl rubbed his jaw, "Ah, nothing; just decided to take a walk. June is out taking her mother to the doctor, and I got tired of watching sports talk on ESPN. There ain't nothing on TV anymore, you know it? I don't even know why I pay for cable."

"So you can watch the Auburn and Braves games," Marty replied.

"If not for that, I'd cut the damn cord– I tell you that much."

"I remember back when we were young, there was so much to do– it seemed. Didn't have to rely on TV to entertain us, you know?"

Carl stood there and remembered years gone by. "Yeah, it seemed to be. Those were truly the good old days. When you retire, there ain't much at all to do. Nobody really tells you that. You got all this time and nothing to really do. When we were young men, we worked and worked, building and raising a family, never having enough time for anything because we were constantly on the go doing something. Now...now we got time with nothing to do."

Marty and Carl looked off down the street a piece from Marty's front lawn where it stopped growing at the edge of the sidewalk. With what Carl has just said, it spurred Marty to ask a question.

"You miss working, Carl?" Marty thought perhaps he did. Carl wore his emotions on his face, and Marty could tell that retirement didn't wear well on his friend and neighbor.

Carl looked at his neighbor of many decades and considered his question for a moment.

"Sometimes. It's like I don't have a purpose anymore. I get up, I do some things around the house, or I go visit some people. I go to church. Sometimes I play golf. And then I go to bed. And I do it all over again. It's almost like that movie with Bill Murray: Groundhog Day. You miss work?"

"No way. I love being retired. I'm not one of these guys that would druther be working. This is what I worked for, having time to do whatever I want. I rather enjoy it. Sometimes it does get boring though, I'll admit. But why work your life away like we already did? I'll take this any day of the week over punching a time clock, dealing with a terrible boss, and working with people who just show up and don't put in an honest day's work."

"I think retiring is a prelude to death. It's like we're just waiting on it, you know? The days always seem to be...the same. Hell, sometimes I don't even know what day it is. I have to look at the calendar or this damn phone in my pocket just to see."

"Well," Marty said, putting his hand on Carl's shoulder. "I ain't ready to die yet. And I enjoy being home. Listen, I've got to go finish these leaves up."

"Hey, before I go, did you read the paper this morning?"

Marty nodded his head, "I did. Why?"

"Did you read about that bobcat? There was another sighting of it."

"Yeah, I might have skimmed that article."

"Boy," Carl started, "that'd be bad being outside doing something regular like what you're doing right now, and a damn bobcat come up on you."

"It would. But I don't think I got to worry about no bobcat, Carl. Those things don't come out into where people are. My dad used to warn me when I was a kid about camping in the woods, but out here...nah."

"Ain't what I been hearing. Anyways, I'll holler at you later," Carl said as he walked away.

"See you later, Carl." Carl said bye and walked down the sidewalk.

It was the last time he would ever talk to Marty Yeager. He told his wife after the news came that Marty was missing that he'd just talked to him earlier that day on the sidewalk in front of his house.

"I had no idea that would be the last time I'd ever talk to my friend," Carl said to his wife. He was dumbfounded.

8

It was getting close to Marty's evening walk at the park. The park was a five-minute walk down the street, and it always gave Marty a chance to soak in the neighborhood he loved so much, especially in the fall with all the brilliant colors of the changing leaves from greens to bright oranges and vibrant yellows.

On his walks to the park, Marty would wave at oncoming cars that came down the street or throw up his hand in a friendly gesture at the people that were sitting on their front porches, or cutting their grass, or whatever it was that suburbanites did on the daily. Marty loved his neighborhood and felt a sense of belonging when walking down his street. He had no idea this was going to be his final time.

Marty laced up his walking shoes, hunched over in the recliner. Claire came into the living room, "I'm not going to cook anything big tonight. What do you want to do for supper?"

Marty didn't look up from his shoelaces and answered his wife, "Probably just make me a fish sandwich when I get home and showered from my walk. I ain't really hungry. Hadn't been all day."

"You feeling good?" Clair asked.

Marty nodded and said, "Yeah, I'm fine I reckon– just ain't hungry right now. But that might change when I get back."

Marty tied his shoelaces tight, just how he liked them, grabbed his Braves hat off the hook, and put on a jacket. He yelled to Claire that he loved her, and he'd be back in about forty. That was the last time Claire heard Marty's voice. They were the last words he ever spoke to her.

———

On his walk to the park down his street, Marty saw Dale Stripling looking down at his push mower in his front yard. Marty walked over to him because Dale, a young man in his early twenties with a new family, looked perplexed. He was fairly new to the neighborhood and was a good kid. A few years back, he was captain of Central High's football team. God, could he throw a football.

"How's it going, young man?" Marty asked as he approached Dale.

Dale looked up from his mower and saw it was the old man from down the street. "Oh, hey, Mr. Yeager. The thing just quit on me right in the middle of mowing."

Marty walked over to the mower and looked down at it, "Just quit on you, you say?"

"Yeah. I checked the gas and the tank is half full. So...I don't know."

Marty, who was pretty good at fixing things, knelt on the grass and pulled the black rubber sparkplug cord from the spark plug itself, waited a few seconds, and pushed it back on tightly. "Now…give her a pull."

Dale pulled the cord to start the mower; and as if it was a magic spell that Marty had placed upon the mower, it roared to life. Dale looked at Marty as he raised up. "I'll be damned. How did you know?" he asked over the roar of the mower.

Marty leaned to Dale's left ear, speaking to him over the loud roar of the mower, "Son, when you get as many miles as I do, you learn a few things." Marty clapped his back, smiled, and walked back onto the street towards the park.

It was the last time Dale would ever see the old man. When the news came about Marty's disappearance, Dale told his buddies down at the Neon Tiger, "He fixed my mower that day."

9

A little further down Sunset Avenue, Marty saw one of his favorite people in the entire neighborhood: Mrs. Reeves. Gladys had been in that neighborhood since the thing was built. She was ninety-five and still going strong. Chewed tobacco, mowed her small front yard, swept her front porch, and even raked leaves. A lot of times, she was sitting out on her front porch rocking in her rocking chair and talking with someone.

On that day, Marty was walking to the park, like he did every day. Gladys was alone, which was rare. He had not stopped by and talked to Gladys lately. *Probably been a few months*, he thought to himself. He would always wave going to the park and coming back. And always Gladys had someone with her on that porch she was talking to.

"Marty," Gladys called out in a rather strong voice for a woman of her age, "why don't you come up here and tell me a good one."

Marty smiled and walked off the street and across her small front lawn and up her porch.

"Get you a seat right there," she said as spat into her spit cup that was a Green Giant green bean can with a paper towel stuffed inside it.

"How you been?" Marty asked, taking the rocking chair next to her.

"Oh, I've been right good, 'bout you?" she asked.

"Not bad– been waking up a little stiff lately. Must be the colder weather."

"Well, kiddo, wait til you get me age," Gladys laughed. Marty laughed, too, when she referred to him as a kiddo. *I guess to her I am*, he thought. "Off to the park, I reckon?"

"Yeah, get my walking in for the day."

"Keep moving...keep moving...don't you ever get okay with just sitting around like an old tomcat. Get out there and move."

"Where's Alexandria been lately? I ain't seen her car over here much," Marty asked after Gladys' great-granddaughter.

"Something with school– I think she said. She only comes when she can. It's all right. Young'uns got lives to live, too." Gladys said.

She had outlived both her children, her four husbands, and pretty much all her friends. She was alone except for the people in the neighborhood.

"That they do. I think it's going to be a cold winter, don't you?"

Gladys nodded, "Looking that way; been pretty cold for October already. Usually, it's pretty mild but..." Gladys trailed off with that thought. She often did, more so lately.

"Did you see the commotion up the road the other night?"

"No...what happened?" Gladys asked.

"Police had somebody pulled over at the start of the street up there. Must've been pretty bad because they took the fella and his girlfriend, wife, or whatever she was, to jail and towed the car they were in off," Marty reported. He was up around ten that night watching the whole scene from his window. That passed for excitement for the old man.

"Probably dope. Everybody's on dope these days. Times are getting bad, you know it?" Gladys remarked.

"Yeah," Marty said absently, "yeah I do."

"Ruth Baker brought me some canned beans the other day. I bet ten jars worth. You and Clair want any?"

"Yeah, we'll take a couple off your hands."

"Well, good. When you come back up the road, I'll have them waiting on the porch here. Now, I may or may not be sitting out here when you get back, but if I ain't just take the jars."

"I will," Marty said, looking at the sun sinking low. If he was going to make his laps, he had better shake a leg. "Well, Gladys, I better be hopping along."

"All right. Thanks for stopping by. Come back and visit when you can stay longer. And don't forget about those jars I'll put out here."

"I won't," Marty said walking off the front porch, waving her goodbye as he stepped back onto the road. Marty would never make it back to get the canned green beans.

10

On the evening that Marty was on his walk on the park's paved figure eight, he marveled at how soft the pavement felt beneath the soles of his shoes. The walking track oval had been in dire need of a good resurfacing for years. And it happened a week ago. A machine came down and resurfaced the oval with a new black blacktop. The smell hung thick in the air even with the wind blowing a week later. For some reason, Marty liked the smell of blacktop. He didn't know why. One of life's mysteries, he guessed.

The park's walking oval track was deserted around that time every day. It tickled Marty that he was usually the only one that walked the track. It seemed it was his very own. And why not? He was, after all, the park's only visitor as far as he knew, which was a shame because the park had all kinds of things for the townsfolk to enjoy: picnic tables scattered about under trees, nice swing sets, merry-go-rounds, monkey bars, jungle gyms for the kids, two baseball fields, a pavilion where local bands played when the town celebrated the Fourth of July and the Halloween block parties, and of course, the main attraction for Marty, the oval track.

Marty was on three laps of the four– four being a mile on the track– when something from behind him stirred. His back was turned to the chain-linked fence that separated the park and Hudson's Woods. Marty, who was walking up the steep incline, turned to see what was making that noise. In all the times that he had walked the track, nothing had ever caused him panic. He always felt safe. When he stopped to see what it was making that sound, he no longer felt safe. He was afraid for his life...

11

By the time the police made it to the town's park, a large swath of blood that was on the pavement of the walking track had dried a dark color against the black faded hot top. The night was closing in, and it was getting cooler by the minute. The police were called by Clair because Marty had not made it home. She figured that he was taking in some extra laps, which he was prone to do from time to time. But usually, he would text if he was going to be late, so she didn't worry.

On the day of his disappearance, no text. She did not pay any mind to the evening getting later as she went about doing her house chores: sweeping, mopping, and unloading and loading the dishwasher. It wasn't until the streetlights came on, right before darkness, that she called Marty's phone. Nothing. She let ten minutes pass by, not worried really before she called his phone again...nothing; it went to voicemail eventually.

Unbeknownst to her, his cell phone was on the nightstand in their bedroom, on silent. Marty had a habit of putting his phone on silent at night before bed. It all started when he would get spam calls and couldn't figure out a way to program his phone to catch those. Those calls always came right when he fell asleep. And one thing about Marty, he was a bear when he got woke up.

So, he put the phone on silent and left it at that. In the mornings, he would always remember to turn it back up. But on the day of his death, he left the phone on silent and lying on the nightstand. Also, as if it was written in the stars, he forgot his phone on his walk, which he never did. But a phone would not have spared his life on that day– for his life was to end no matter if he had a phone or not.

Now nervous, Clair walked out of their house and got into her SUV. She headed down to the park to see if something happened to her husband. Crazy thoughts raced wildly throughout her mind: could have had a stroke, maybe a heart attack, could have fallen and busted his head open. Those thoughts made her hit the gas a little bit harder while she traveled down Sunset Ave. When she turned into the parking lot of the park, she saw nobody about. She put the SUV in park and scanned the dusky scene, the oval of the walking track in particular. Nothing. That's when she began to panic.

She rushed out of her SUV and started on the walking track to see if he was off in the distance. Maybe he did fall and was lying to the side or something in the grass. As she neared the dog leg curve of the oval track that was closest to the fence and Hudson's Woods, she spotted something on the track.

It was blood: dark, somewhat wet, and a lot of it. She kneeled, hands shaky, stomach in knots. She touched the blood. It was tacky. She looked to her right and saw an opening that had been made in the chain fence by someone, maybe to crawl through at some point. The blood trail had gone from the pavement of the oval walking track, through the grass, and what appeared to be– the best she could tell– through the opening in the fence.

Clair rose up while tears began to stream down her face. She knew the blood belonged to her husband. Just knew. "Marty!" Claire shouted into Hudson's Woods. Nothing. A few seconds longer; she screamed again, "Marty!"

Feeling as if she was going to throw up, she reached into the front pocket of her jeans and found her phone. She pulled it out but dropped it on the pavement in the tacky blood. She thought for sure that she had broken it. It was still intact, thankfully. She bent down to retrieve it. She wiped Marty's blood off of it on her shirt. She hit the green phone icon and called 9-1-1.

12

That fall day in 2021, the only thing police found on the crime scene of the park was blood on the walking track. The blood, a huge swath of it, covered the part of the track that dog-legged next to the edge of the woods, off to the right. Nothing else.

Blood was all over the grass next to the track and on the fence that separated the park from Hudson's Woods. No one had seen anything because the park, though beautiful, especially on fall days, was always vacant– which was sad because it was such a nice park to take a walk in.

Det. White followed the blood trail from the bend of the track across the grass and to the fence. There was a medium-sized hole in that chain-linked fence where perhaps someone had cut it back to gain entry into the park from the woods instead of climbing over. It was, the detective surmised, big enough for a good-sized man to climb through. But was it enough to drag someone through? The blood trail went through the hole in the fence and began to thin substantially as it led to the wooded area from the fence, across the small service road, and then to the woods.

The operating theory there at the park was that the victim, Marty Yeager, was attacked by someone, apparently cut up with a knife, and dragged into the woods through the opening in the fence. Det. White ordered the crime scene to be on lockdown and directed a few officers, rookies, to stay there at the track and "don't allow anyone to even get close to the blood on the track at the bend or at the hole in the chain linked fence". He and another officer, Officer Killerman, would scale the fence a few yards down and go into the woods.

The two officers walked to the other side of the fence and over to where the hole was. The blood trail that came from the other side drew a nasty, faded bloodline across the gravel service road where it led into the woods, and the trail thinned. But there was no mistake; this was where Marty was dragged.

"You think he's in there?" the younger officer by his side asked.

Det. White looked into the woods, his eyes searching for the body of the old man he had known for a long time. "I'd bet my paycheck on it."

Det. White called in a search party, and an hour and a half later, a team of ten officers from the county sheriff's department came to the park to aid in the search for an old man in his sixties who had apparently been cut badly and dragged from the walking track into the woods. The motive was still up in the air, but it was perhaps robbery. That was the working theory of Det. White had in his head; what else could there have been?

13

"Dogs lost the scent halfway through…so we don't know. We can come back at first light and try again." Mark Huslander, the man who ran the canine unit for the Brook County Sheriff's Department said. Det. White didn't say anything, just nodded his head. Marty had to be in the woods. Huslander pulled his dogs away from the track where the crime scene began, leaving the detective staring into the woods and searching for an answer.

As the night got darker and the streetlights kicked on down at the park, the park grew quieter by the minute. Det. White stood looking at the fence with his flashlight and then at the track with the dried blood. His working theory, the only one Det. White had at the moment, was that Marty was stalked and possibly hit from behind and badly beaten—most likely a robbery. And whoever it was that did it had dragged him into the woods through the small opening in the fence and hidden him in the woods. *Why would anyone take the time to drag a full-grown man through an opening like that*, Det. White wondered. "Maybe he panicked. Maybe all he wanted to do was rob the old man. And when things went sideways, he panicked and got scared because a simple robbery had turned into a homicide. Then he had to hide the body."

The next morning, just before sunrise, the drifter had been picked up. Det. White was still going over notes and possible scenarios from the case as the sun rose at the park. He had stayed there all night until the last remaining officer left the scene. The detective sat in his car in the park's parking lot, smoking a cigarette and keeping his tired eyes on the walking track and the spot where Marty was probably assaulted. Nothing stirred. And when the sun began to bathe the landscape with its rays, the park offered no more clues than it had earlier. From his car, Det. White looked down towards the crime scene, which had been decorated with yellow DO NOT CROSS tape, and in his mind's eye, witnessed the entire crime play out.

A man came out from the woods, crawled through the opening in the fence, and ran up to Marty to rob him. Marty fought back maybe the best an old man could. The robber took a knife from his pocket and stabbed him to death. Then, in a moment of panic, because it was supposed to be a robbery and not a murder, he dragged poor Marty Yeager from the walking track, through the opening in the fence, and into the woods. That's how Det. White saw it- what else could there have been?

Det. White was about to get out of his car and walk towards the crime scene when his cell phone chirped: an officer from Claxton Police Department had contacted him to report they just hauled a guy in that he might want to question.

"Really sketchy guy," the officer told him. "Fought us hard, and we like to have never got him under control. He ain't nobody we've seen around here before. And he's got that missing fella's wallet on him. There was blood on the jacket he was wearing, too. But it's got some places on it where it looks like it was shredded."

"Why was he picked up?"

"He had stolen a kid's bike out of a yard, and the mother saw him do it as she was walking to her car earlier this morning. We picked him up out on Highway 411, going out of town. He matched the description and even had the damn bike that matched the one that was reported stolen. This guy might have something to do with your missing person."

"I'll be there right away."

14

The drifter, later identified as Thomas Brady LeGrange, from Columbus, Ohio, was held in the Brook County jailhouse on theft charges until they could tie him to Marty Yeager's disappearance. Det. White was still thinking that it was a robbery turned murder.

"A body would make a stronger case," the District Attorney told Sheriff Hall and Det. White in his office the days after the arrest, "But seeing is how you have his credit cards on this guy, and a jacket that his wife said was her husband's with blood on it...I'm betting that's probably Mr. Yeager's DNA. I think we can get him. I'll make it work. But the jacket has to have the old man's blood on it."

"We don't have a murder weapon yet. We're still walking the woods, trying to find a body. Maybe we'll get lucky, and find both." Sheriff Hall in the DA's office.

"That would be great to have, but we'll take what we can get. I've had to prosecute circumstantial cases in the past. Not easy, but doable. Just keep at those woods."

15

A few days later, several police stations from Ohio, Kentucky, and Indiana contacted the Brook County Sheriff's Office and inquired about Thomas Brady LeGrange. The man who had been held in lockup had been a person of interest in several other murders in those states and counties. Det. White and the detectives from those places exchanged info, and they each felt that Det. White had a traveling serial killer in his possession.

When this got back to the DA, all Allen Cummings wanted was the body of Marty Yeager. He knew that now with the DNA finally coming back that it was Marty's blood on the jacket; he could convict him in trial. The case against him was circumstantial, but it was glaring and hard for a jury to overlook. In talking with Clair, she wanted the body of her husband. The DA went to Thomas' court-appointed attorney and gave an option:

"Tell us where your client put the body, and we'll take the death penalty off the table. We'll just do life with no parole."

After the court-appointed attorney spoke with Thomas in his jail cell about the offer, Thomas laughed, "I don't fucking know where the body is! Like I've told you and those idiot policemen, I just found the body in those woods tore all to shit and took the jacket off him and his wallet. He was laying there when I walked out of the woods."

"You know a jury is not going to believe that, right?" his attorney said, sitting on a chair outside the cell.

"I don't care! I didn't kill that man! Fucking cops!" That was the truth. Thomas Brady LeGrange did not kill Marty. He was a murderer, however. He was a drifter, a transient, who walked and hitchhiked from town to town and had killed over forty people in the last ten years. He had gotten away with every one of them. Sure, he had some close calls in Ohio and Kentucky, but he was able to wriggle out of them and hit the next town– the next victim.

Laying in his cell at night, he knew that he was going to prison; that God had finally balanced the scales for all those people he had murdered for no reason at all. The only reason that he killed was because he liked it. "The one man that I didn't kill, I'm going to prison for," he said to himself in his cell alone; oh, the irony of it all. All he could do was laugh wildly that night in his jail cell.

16

The trial was quick and lasted just a week. The DA's case was strong. They told a story that probably happened: Marty was out walking as usual that day, and a drifter, Thomas Brady LeGrange, had jumped him from behind and incapacitated him with a blunt object or something of that nature. Perhaps killed him with a knife, robbed him, dragged the body into Hudson's Woods, and hid it.

There were crime scene photos entered into Exhibits A-J of the track and the blood; photos of the trail of blood from the track to the fence and across the service road where it ended in the woods; Marty's jacket was on display, as well as the three credit cards.

"Ladies and gentlemen of the jury," Alan Cummings said during his closing argument, "the defendant asserts his innocence in this case. But let's look at the facts here: he was picked up because of a reported bicycle theft and fought the officers tooth and nail when they stopped to question him out on Highway 411 early that morning. Where do you think he was going to? Leaving town– that's where. He knew what he had done, and he was on his way out. Had Mrs. Coffer not seen him lifting her son's bike over their front yard fence, we wouldn't be here today. He would have gotten away with killing Mr. Martin Yeager.

"Another fact is the very jacket that Mrs. Yeager tells the court that belonged to her husband, the defendant was wearing on the morning of his arrest. Another fact is that Mr. Yeager's credit cards were inside a pocket of that jacket with the defendant's fingerprints on them. Ladies and gentlemen, this was a robbery that escalated to murder. The defendant, Thomas Brady LeGrange, saw an older man walking alone on a walking track. With no one around, he decided to pounce on him, hoping he had some cash on him to get him to the next town. Except Mr. Yeager fought back. Then perhaps a knife came into play and before the defendant and Mr. Yeager knew it, blood was being spilled. What does the defendant do? He drags the body into the woods and hides it.

"Now, this is pretty open and shut, I think. I hope in light of the stone-cold facts, ya'll will see that, too. Don't allow this man to walk out of here a free man, and perhaps go to the next town to do the same thing he did to Mr. Martin Yeager."

The defense attorney knew that it was futile trying to get his client out of trouble because even he knew that Thomas Brady LeGrange was guilty. He hated defending people like that. He did defend him to the best of his ability and tried to poke holes in the DA's case. But there was no getting around Marty's blood on his jacket that Thomas was wearing when picked up. He couldn't defend him stealing a kid's bike; he couldn't defend the fight between his client and the police; nor defend the wallet of the dead man in his possession.

And the credit cards were another piece of damning evidence. The defense attorney had used a crazy theory about a bobcat that had been stalking the town and was the one to blame for Marty's disappearance. "Look at the jacket in question, ladies and gentlemen of the jury. That jacket doesn't appear to have been ripped like that in those places with a knife. Looks to me like claws did that."

Earlier, he put an expert on the stand, a zoologist from the University of Tennessee, to back up his claim. People found that outrageous, even if the well-educated man said that the jacket could have been from the claws of a bobcat. People felt that the defense attorney was reaching for something plausible– and he was– but to be honest, that jacket did not look like it was shredded in places from a knife attack. A few jurors had been reading about the bobcat around the county and had it in their minds already that it could have been a bobcat that clawed the jacket. The defense was onto something but couldn't get around some of the more damning evidence.

"The shredding of the material you see here appears, at least in my opinion, to have been made by an animal," the zoologist said on the stand.

"So, it's within the realm of possibility that a bobcat or even another large predatory animal could have caused this damage to the jacket?"

"Yes, sir, that is very possible. We see here that the way the material was shredded is consistent with animal claw marks."

17

Since Thomas balked at giving up the body, because he certainly had no idea where it was, being nowhere around when Marty was dragged into the woods, he was eventually sentenced to death when the jury came back with a guilty verdict in less than thirty minutes. The verdict at the trial, and the sentencing phase did not bother Thomas one bit. He knew that eventually his number was going to come up.

The funny thing was, he never thought he'd go to jail for a murder he did not commit. But that was not the end for Thomas Brady LeGrange. He was put on trial in Indiana and Kentucky for a couple of murders there. And, just like in Brook County, he was convicted for those with much stronger evidence, with his DNA tying him to the dead bodies that were recovered.

Hudson's Woods was searched for days and weeks. No body ever turned up. The only thing that Det. White had was the blood trail leading from the walking track to the hole in the chain-linked fence, across the service road, and into the woods. Where his body went from there, who really knew? Dogs had picked up a scent, and then lost it halfway in the woods where the UFO clearing was. Det. White on his off days with the Yeager family would go there to Hudson's Woods and walk every square inch. Still...there was no sign of Marty.

"What do you think happened, Det. White?" Clair asked one evening while the two sat on her front porch months after Marty's disappearance.

He considered her question for a few seconds because it was the same question that he had over the last several months.

"I think the DA's picture he painted was right. I think it was a robbery, and then Marty might've fought back and got killed. Thomas dragged his body into the woods and where it's at…I'll be damned if I know."

Clair paused, wiping her tears from her eyes, "You think we'll ever find him?"

Det. White turned to look at the widow, "I sure hope so."

18

Marty turned, and there it was; something that he'd never, ever seen around the park before. Hell, not even in town before. But he'd been told as a kid when he used to camp in the woods around town that there had been those kinds of things roaming around by his dad.

"Be careful camping in woods, Son," Elbert Yeager told his young son, "because there're bobcats running around those wooded areas every once in a while."

"I will, Dad," a young Marty replied.

On that walking track, an honest-to-God bobcat was walking, stalker-like, towards Marty. It had come out of the woods, via the opening in the fence and made its way to the man that was walking the oval track alone. Marty was frozen with fear. The bobcat took off running, sprinting toward its prey, and pounced on Marty who tried to run. It was useless. The wild animal jumped on Marty's aging bones with a frightening ferocity and began to tear into the man who screamed for help in the empty park. No one heard Marty's screams that day.

The animal dragged Marty, who was lying on his back, bleeding and dying, down the track, across the grass, and through the opening in the fence. It pulled him across the service road and into the woods where it nibbled on him a bit before leaving him for later. Marty tried to crawl away from the bobcat but he had no strength. What life he was clinging to was fading and fading fast. In ten minutes, Marty Yeager was dead, lying on his back in Hudson's Woods, where he used to camp some as a kid with his friends.

A little later Thomas Brady LeGrange stumbled upon Marty's body. He was in there to find a place to hold up for the night before he blew town. He needed a good place to sleep. When he was walking around in Hudson's Woods to find that peaceful place, he found the dead man.

He cautiously walked over to him and saw that it was, indeed, a man. He was bloody and had been ripped to hell. Thomas kneeled and gave the man a once-over. He was bad. His face was nothing but mangled meat; his throat was nearly gone; his clothes were shredded; his right arm was nearly chewed off; and his chest had deep valleys in it from the animal's claws.

Thomas was not shocked or horrified by this scene at all. He had done much worse himself to people. He did admire the handwork of who or whatever did this. "Probably a mountain lion or some shit," he mumbled as he started to fleece Marty's person. He rolled him over and ran his hand in Marty's back pocket. He extracted the wallet and opened it up: three credit cards and his driver's license. Perfect.

The drifter pulled the jacket off the dead man. It was shredded in some places, but would do the job as he put it on over the one he was wearing: a double layer to protect him from colder temps that were coming. He didn't seem to mind the blood that was all over it. "It's not like I'm going to run into anybody anytime soon."

Thomas got up from his knees and decided that the woods were not a place he needed to spend the night. He would find something else. He gave Marty one last look, "Thanks, Martin, for your wallet and jacket. You're a good man. I hope someone finds you." And that was it. Thomas turned and began to walk out of Hudson's Woods.

About ten minutes after Thomas left the scene, the bobcat returned to its meal. It fed on Marty for a little bit more before pulling him by his foot across the woods, through a wide and knee-deep stream, and into his den that was a good three miles on the other side of Hudson's Woods in another tract of woodland. Nobody ever knew about the bobcat's den; no one had ever gone that far into the woods, to be honest. Marty was a meal for days to come.

19

Eventually, the bobcat met his fate. He was shot and killed by a city worker who was down at the service road, fixing some down power lines from a violent storm that had swept across town the night before. He was standing at his truck that late evening, on his cell talking when the bobcat came out of the woods. It growled and was inching its way closer to the man at the truck.

Stu Baker, a country boy if there ever was one, always carried his gun with him: a Colt .45 laid in the front seat. He turned, saw the animal, quickly dropped his phone, and opened the truck door. He grabbed the gun and shot the bobcat in the face that had already gotten to within feet of him. In the Brook County Register, he was on the front page, kneeling holding his gun next to the dead animal in triumph.

As far as where Marty Yeager ever went? Locals in Claxton, who had seen and heard their share of stories and notorious people over the years, speculated on his whereabouts. Some said he left to go be with a younger woman. A few said that maybe he was beaten and taken to the UFO landing in the middle of Hudson's Woods for aliens to abduct him. People down at his lodge figured that Thomas Brady LeGrange had killed him and buried him somewhere in there.

One thing was for sure...no one thought a bobcat killed Marty Yeager. That's just crazy talk.

THE CREATOR OF WORLDS

NED DARCY SAT in his gloomy apartment looking out his fifth-story window at the world below. This is where he sat most days now, watching the world bustle about their business. He used to be a part of that world; the ant marching with other ants going to and fro. At the time, back when he was younger, he hated fighting the traffic; walking and cutting his way through the sea of people on the sidewalks that were either coming from somewhere or going to somewhere. He felt claustrophobic most times trying to weave through the hustle and bustle of the day in the busy city.

He hated standing on the sidewalks in the rain or shine, in the cold and heat, trying to hail a cab to get to work. Ned hated most of all taking the subway to get to his office. It could be dangerous down there if he was not careful, especially at night. Sitting in his small apartment looking out his window, Ned wished that he could go through all that again. He wished that he was a part of that movement known as the human race. The stuff he hated back then, back when he was trying to just make it here and there, he missed profoundly nowadays. He longed for something to do again, something that would make him relevant like he used to be; something that would get him get back to good and make him feel as if he mattered to someone like he had back in the good days.

At eighteen, Ned went to art school and honed his talent. He was considered one of the best young students at the school. His artwork, he thought as she sat in his recliner looking down at the world below him, still hung in the hallowed halls of his old art school. At least it had as of 1992. But that, like everything else, was a long, long time ago. It had no bearing on his life now as the past was forgotten by most people. What about the new generation of comic book artists? Forget about it, they paid no attention to the ones that had blazed the trail for them. Ned was a relic of days past. He understood that, and accepted that reality, but did not like it.

Ned Darcy was twenty years old in 1967 when he broke into the world of comic books. He could always draw, and always knew the precise colors to use in the right amounts in all his artwork. Like most kids, he was influenced by the comics of Batman and Superman. He loved the Western, horror, and sci-fi ones too—practically anything that Ned could get his hands on at the drugstore. He liked the stories that were written for them, but the artwork is what had lured Ned to becoming an artist. Not just an artist, but a comic book artist.

During the comic book heyday, Ned was a giant in the industry. His work on Powerman was unparalleled. That was his signature superhero. He had brought the image and idea to a fledgling comic book imprint called Destiny Comics in the mid-seventies. The editor at the time, Joe Post, was not completely sold if Powerman would work among all the other, more popular, superheroes.

"But hey, it's worth a shot," he said. "What else do we really got going for us?" That was when Ned made his biggest mistake.

At a young thirty-one, Ned sold all of his rights to Powerman to Destiny Comics. He was still young and needed the money, and besides, Joe told him that he would always receive the credit for coming up with this character, and would have his name affixed to it. It was not much money; a year's salary in return for signing away the character and the world in which the superhero lived and his villains. After all, it's not like this thing is going to be the next Batman comic, Ned thought.

Wrong. Powerman became a smash hit for the small imprint, bringing them to the forefront of the comic book industry. As years rolled by, Ned saw exactly how Powerman took off. The writing of the character was really good because the company could now afford some of the best writers in the industry. Ned was still working for Destiny Comics drawing the *Powerman* books. It did not bother him that the *Powerman* comic book was not his any longer. He was still getting a check every two weeks for doing what he loved. He saw it as a win-win.

Eventually, everywhere you looked you saw Powerman tees, Powerman lunch boxes, Powerman action figures, and as the mid-eighties rolled around—some ten years since he sold his rights to Powerman away for thirty-five grand—there was even a Saturday morning cartoon of the hero. Powerman had gotten much bigger and more popular than Ned first thought. He knew it was a good character when he first created him, but some of the writers that Joe had brought over to write him made Powerman something of a titan that could stand with the popularity of Spiderman or Captain America.

Did Joe Post swindle him? Ned really could never reconcile this question. He had known Joe for a long time and did not think Joe was that type of guy. But this was business, and Destiny Comics was his baby. So, if Joe saw something that could bring his company into the black, why would he not jump on it? And why was Ned so eager to sell Powerman in the first place? Because he needed the money and because he thought that he could always come up with another character like Powerman, maybe even better. It's not like Ned saw Powerman as relevant as Superman or Spiderman. Joe was at first hesitant but took a shot. It proved the best shot he had ever taken.

As the nineties came, Ned had made money with other comic book companies. Destiny Comics had been sold, and all of its acquisitions along with it, when Joe Post passed away. A new editor and owner came in and cleaned house. Ned was a part of that cleansing. It did not matter to Ned; he was the one who created Powerman, and the creator of worlds should not have a difficult time finding work elsewhere. His name alone should get him some work with one of the bigger comic book companies. Leaving the offices of Destiny Comics for the final time, carrying all that he had from his office in a milk crate, Ned Darcy felt that his future was wide open.

Ned was wrong again. Work was difficult to find. Although his name was recognized as one of the best artists in the comic book biz, no one would hire him for too long—maybe six-month stretches at a time. By the late nineties, most comic book companies were floundering. This was before the blockbuster movies based on the books came into the world-view. It turns out that most people would rather watch a movie based on the comic than read the book and look at the artwork. Who knew?

And it was not just Ned who felt the pinch of the comic book recession; others just like him, some exceptionally better, were having a hard time finding places to bring their talents. The ones that were still doing reasonably well during the hard times were those that had kept the rights to their creations. Ned had only been one of a few stupid ones that sold out because he desperately needed the money. If he had negotiated better and taken something like a percentage, he could have made a fortune off of Powerman and retired comfortably.

Looking back on it, ten percent would have been wonderful. Before the bottom fell out from underneath Powerman, it was estimated that the character was worth almost a billion dollars—especially when you accounted for all the extras Powerman had: shirts, action figures, and eventually theatrical movie releases that were tied to summer block-busters. Money was being made by the character that Ned had created but none of it came to him. He had sold Powerman for a measly thirty-five grand.

Like other artists, writers, and inkers in the comic book field who had been left for dead and forgotten, Ned traveled to comic book conventions carrying the portfolio of work that he did in his spare time. He would sit behind tables in these large conventions waiting for people, fans of his and Powerman, to stroll over and get his autograph—ten bucks—or Powerman artwork signed by Ned Darcy—one hundred twenty-five bucks. Sometimes he made out pretty good, good enough to get him through for a few months. Good enough to pay the electric bill in his apartment, cable TV, and Internet.

The older Ned got, the less people came to his table at the conventions. When he first started doing the conventions, people got their picture taken with him, got his autograph, and his artwork. Hell, people even bought the original work he had dreamed up in his apartment. For a while, things were not going too badly. He was still getting paid for doing something that he loved. Of course not a lot, but he managed. Sometimes in the down time when the conventions were not in full swing, Ned would sell his artwork on his eBay store.

That last year at San Diego Comic-Con, Ned noticed things were changing. The industry was changing. The people were changing. With that change came a downturn for Ned. He saw his money cut nearly three-quarters, and he began to struggle mightily. Suddenly, like someone turning a flowing faucet off, people stopped coming over to see the creator of Powerman. Ned Darcy had lost his appeal.

Ned tried a few more conventions, like the ones in NYC and Atlanta, and even smaller ones. But usually, the trips were busts. He would spend more money getting there and paying the set-up fees than he brought in. It was at a convention in Miami that Ned finally saw it was over. He had become a relic, buried within the catacombs of the comic book industry. He was not needed any longer and sat there at the conventions alone at his table with his artwork sprawled out waiting for someone to happen by and start a conversation with him. People walked on by, glancing at his work, smiling at him, saying hi, and then walking away through all the people milling about looking at the hottest and latest thing in pop culture. Ned's days as a cultural figure in the comic book industry had vanished in Miami.

Ned, once a titan among the comic book elite, was now receiving food stamps and other government assistance. It was a stark contrast to where he was long ago. Sometimes Ned would sit in the living room and watch hours of mindless TV, hoping that his ticker would shut off so he could die. And who would notice? He had no family—never married or had any children. Sure there were women, but just like he did with Powerman, he thought someone else would come along once the ladies left him. Ned was wrong again. He had thought of killing himself a few times, but in the end, he was too much of a coward to do it no matter how depressed he was.

The creator of worlds had been reduced to being another guy that's sipping off the government's tit. He hated that, but what else could he do? He was too old to do anything else, and the many years he spent holding a pencil had riddled his hands with arthritis. They were nearly useless. He tried working at a grocery store a few blocks from his apartment building but the rigors of the job, although not very difficult, proved to be too much for his hands. Most days Ned could not hold the remote to change the channel on the TV, twist a door knob, or open a bag of chips.

Sitting in his chair looking down at the world below, the one he used to be a part of, Ned thought of all the bad decisions he had made throughout his life. The worst choice he made, Ned had decided, was wanting to be a comic book artist. Maybe if he never bought that issue of Batman hanging on the spinning rack in the drugstore when he was a kid, this would have never happened. He would not be sitting in his apartment, alone in a yellowed tee shirt and dirty work pants. He would not be living off the federal government, getting handouts from hard-earned taxpayers' dollars.

He could have done something different with his life. Maybe. Maybe, like in comic books, there was a parallel universe somewhere out there and another Ned Darcy was something like a banker, with a wife and kids. Maybe.

FASTER THAN LIGHTNING

"THE LORD IS a jealous and avenging God; the LORD takes vengeance and is fierce in wrath. The LORD takes vengeance against His foes; He is furious with His enemies" (Nah. 1: 2 HCSB)

He thought about it often. At first, it had crossed his mind here and there in the aftermath of each event. Over time, the thought became more than a little bit here and there; it became a lot. It began to fester inside his brain so much so that it caused his recent bout with insomnia. The insomnia, in some regards, was worse than the seven lightning strikes he had sustained throughout his life. Those seven lightning strikes had taken a toll on Guy Faulkenberry.

Suicide seemed to be the only way out if he wanted the strikes to cease. If he told anyone, especially his wife, about what he was planning, she would most definitely talk him out of what he was thinking. She would tell him that he was crazy for thinking that way and that God would not want him to take his own life. But Guy knew something that his wife didn't…that there was something about him that just pissed God off.

Growing up in church like Guy had from the time he could barely remember until the day he just stopped going altogether in his forties, around the fourth lightning strike, Guy was taught several things about God: One, was that he was a loving God; two, God was the creator of time, space, and of worlds; three, and probably the most frightening for Guy because he felt it, was that God was a vengeful God against his enemies. Guy never thought of himself as an enemy of God, but as the lightning kept finding its way to him, he couldn't help but wonder why God was hitting him.

Seven lighting strikes in total. After the third one, Guy was sought after by Tobin's Records and Oddities. They recognized his remarkable feat by entering him into their record books. He was Guy Faulkenberry, the man who held the world record for being hit by lightning. At the time, neither Tobin nor Guy knew that the record would be extended by four.

Guy could have done without being entered into the record books. Being hit by lightning was not something that he looked forward to. In fact, after the third strike, Guy began to display odd behavior, eccentric to most people around the town of Claxton who had its share of odd towns-folk and happenings over its long history.

Guy's decision to commit suicide did not come lightly to him. He figured that eventually the next lightning strike, which was most likely to come and make it number eight, might be the one that takes him out. He didn't want to continue to live like he was; always in fear, always checking the weather reports, always afraid of doing normal things like mowing the yard, fishing, or even driving down the road.

Guy had become a captive by God in some respects. He feared God and his wrath. After the sixth strike, Guy went to his church and spoke to Father Gline. Guy wanted to know how he could make things square with God.

"What do you think it was that has angered God so much against you?" Father Gline asked, sitting on a pew beside Guy in the empty church that afternoon.

He knew of Guy's infamous popularity with the lightning strikes and was quite amazed that the man was still living. He often wondered to himself why God chose to hit the man so many times. Often, Father Gline wondered why he had survived so many of them. What was God's plan for this man? Father Gline would mull over these questions on nights he couldn't sleep.

Guy shook his head and shrugged his shoulders, "I have no idea. I was always a square kind of guy. I've never cheated on my wife, never gambled, never broke any of the Ten Commandments. But for some reason, I have angered him and I have no idea as to why."

"You've tried praying I assume?"

Guy nodded, "I have...every day and every night for him to have mercy on me. But I don't know what I've done to deserve all this."

"Do you remember the story of Job?"

"Of course," Guy replied. "So you're saying that I'm going to be rewarded someday for all of this?"

"Perhaps. Maybe all of this is a test to see how strong your faith is. Maybe you need to start attending church again," Father Gline suggested. "You see, Guy, God corrects us sometimes much like a parent would correct a child. That correction is out of love, not anger. Sometimes God has to balance the scales once again. Maybe you've done something regrettable and never asked forgiveness and he's settling your debt. I don't know."

Guy sat there on the pew and looked around the quiet church and thought about what the priest suggested. He could be right, Guy thought to himself. But it doesn't feel right. "I've not done anything that needs correcting or balanced."

Father Gline sat there and considered Guy's statement, "Well, there's one last thing it could be."

"Which is?" Guy asked.

Father Gline turned to look at his visitor, "Maybe you've just pissed God off somehow."

Guy sat in his recliner in the living room alone in the dark. His wife, Marcy, was visiting her sister out in South Carolina. Was she coming back? He doubted it. Things had finally worn her down. But could he blame her? No.

He looked down at his right hand and saw the cold silver steel of his Colt .45 in his lap. His finger was on the trigger, relaxed, but ready to stiffen and squeeze when necessary. Outside a storm was brewing. The thundered rumbled and the wind blew the curtains through the open living room windows. It was a strong cool breeze that night as the approaching storm was on its way.

Guy knew that he was going to be hit again. He could feel it deep in his bones. His house offered no protection because he had been hit inside the house before when he opened the front door to see if a storm had passed. It seemed as if the lightning had been waiting for Guy to open the front door to zap him; which it did, sending him clear across the living room that night.

Guy sat there in the recliner with his gun ready to put the Colt to his head and say goodnight nurse. He was tired of being fried, cooked, electrocuted, burned, scorched, and every other adjective that he could think of. Guy was tired of riding the lightning. He was tired of feeling that he was losing his grip on reality.

People around town and even his wife started wondering if good old Guy Faulkenberry, the town's mailman for a spell, had finally lost his mind. It's not that people would have blamed him; good Christ the man had been struck by lightning seven times and lived to tell the tale each time. But he, like everyone else, began to wonder if all those volts had finally done something to him; something so profound that there was no repairing the damage.

Guy, after the sixth lightning strike, started to feel better mentally and physically. Why? The doctors had no idea and neither did Guy. He thought for awhile that maybe he had settled with God, and balanced those scales that Father Gline had spoken about. All his memories came back in a slow drip fashion and eventually, he could remember things that were lost again, almost like his mind was put back to factory settings.

He could remember his family back when he was a kid. Guy could not for the longest recall his parents and siblings in old photos when he and his wife would go through them. She hoped that seeing their faces would jumpstart his scrambled brain. Nothing happened with his memory as it pertained to his family growing up until after that sixth strike. It was as if that most recent jolt had brought back the lost memories somehow. But more memories were recovered after that sixth strike...

The birth of his first son, Barney, when he started working for Jack Johnson after he graduated high school came back to him in a flood. He could remember things that were long forgotten now like the day of his marriage and the first night he drank alcohol with his buddies on Big Hill. He could remember what it felt like when he got his first paying job.

He smiled when the memory of how he felt on the day he signed the papers at the bank for the house. There were so many things that came back to Guy that it overwhelmed him at times. Sometimes he would cry with joy and sometimes he would laugh at some of the more funny memories. Not everything was lost during those strikes, but his mind had holes in them.

That sixth strike somehow put back what was stolen. Guy maintained those memories and good feelings for nearly five years until the seventh strike got him while he was walking to his truck from trout fishing in the Rabbit Trail River. Since that strike, everything was once again taken from his mind leaving him broken and scattered. Memories that were returned were now stolen like a thief in the night.

Sitting there in the recliner he could feel the wind coming through the open windows from the approaching storm. Thunder rumbled off in the distance but it was growing louder each time it cracked. Guy managed to retain a memory of a time and thought back to when all this lightning business first started. It was 1946 in Claxton, Tennessee...Guy Faulkenberry was ten.

FIRST STRIKE

Guy was out in a wheat field one day in a pair of overalls that had severe signs of wear and fade when the first bolt of lightning touched his life. He was not out in the field in the middle of a storm. It was a clear and sunny day, temps around seventy-four on October 2nd, 1946.

He had taken his dad's scythe out of the tool shed and went walking out towards the fields. Most of the wheat had already been harvested by his dad and his two older brothers earlier. What was left was scattered about narrow wheat trails where the crop was still standing in the sprawling fields. Guy, just killing time as he often did, went to the field to cut down some wheat that had been missed the week before.

The kid walked and swung the scythe cutting the tops of the wheat; not caring how his brothers and dad did it. Doing it right was not the plan. He was out there just to have something to do before Mom called for supper. Guy would swing and cut the wheat high and then low and several times he would miss the nearly waist-high wheat entirely. The scythe was extremely sharp and when his dad taught him to use it last season, he warned him that he could hurt himself very badly if he was not paying attention.

Guy's mom did not like for her youngest to be using it, but what could she do? Soon, Guy would replace Carter, her oldest son who was getting married and moving by the time the next season rolled around, and Rebecca Faulkenberry would have to get used to the idea of her son, like the other two, using objects that could hurt or kill them.

Although Guy never saw the bolt of lightning and never told anyone that it was a bolt that came from the sky, but that's exactly what it was. On that clear afternoon out in the middle of a wheat field in early October, a blink-and-you-miss-it bolt of lightning came hurling down from the blue sky and struck Guy's raised scythe, knocking him back ten feet from the path he had been cutting.

He found himself on his back after he regained consciousness in the middle of the wheat looking up at the sky. He tried to figure out what happened, why his hands were tingling like he was just stung by a bunch of yellow jackets. *Why do I smell burned hair*, he wondered as sat up, woozy from the jolt he had taken.

When the bolt hit the blade of the scythe, a glob of electricity bounced off of it and landed on the ground in the wheat while Guy was sent flying through the air. The electricity instantly caught the dry wheat on fire and it was not long after that the fire began to spread burning the crop in its crawl of destruction. Guy finally got to his feet from the blast, woozy and touching his burnt hair on top of his head, and saw to his horror the field was on fire.

Leaving the scythe behind, Guy ran through the burning wheat field back home to get his dad on nothing more than fear and adrenaline. The dizziness inside his head was forgotten. By the time the fire department arrived on the scene, nearly five acres of the Faulkenberry fields were already blackened.

When the fire was finally contained and put out, the fire from the bolt of lightning managed to burn a total of fifteen acres of the field. Firemen, along with locals and Claude Faulkenberry, Guy's dad, wondered what could have started the blaze. Carter mused out loud to his dad if the fire might have been started by Guy sneaking smokes out there from their dad's dresser. It was a claim that Guy vehemently denied of course. But when asked what happened, Guy said that he was out in the field when something hit the scythe and he was knocked backward.

"Look at my hair if you don't believe me." Claude and Carter, along with a few firemen, took notice of Guy's head. There was a black spot there all right. Also, a few chunks of his blond hair were missing.

"Lightning?" Claude asked a fireman.

He shook his head, "I'll be damned if I know. If it was, it's the first time I'd ever seen it on a clear blue day." And there it was: the first time that Guy Faulkenberry was ever hit by lightning. Why him? He never knew. Why didn't the strike kill him? Well, Guy didn't know that either. Those two questions would be asked by him throughout his life as lightning seemed to seek him out. Maybe it was God. Maybe there was something that God just didn't like about Guy Faulkenberry.

SECOND STRIKE

The second time that Guy was struck by lightning was ten years later in 1956. He was twenty. Guy was working a job as a fire lookout patrolman in Brook County. His lookout tower stood in the middle of the acreage that was set aside by the state of Tennessee for the forestry service to conduct their work. He was married and had a baby boy, Barney, affectionately called Barn by Faye's parents. Life was rolling by just like it usually does: a job and family, what more was there?

Guy had gotten the job with the forestry service by sheer accident. He was not trying to get a job with the state and honestly did not know about a forestry service being around his area. His friend, Willy Johnson, was the man who had gotten Guy in touch with Big Dale Wannamaker, the supervisor over the forestry service there on the outskirts of Claxton. Guy had just graduated high school and married his high school sweetheart, Faye Dobbs, right after they both graduated Central High School. A year later, Barney arrived.

Before the job with the forestry service, Guy was content working at Jack Johnson's garage working on cars.

"You're learning a trade," Guy's dad had told him. "Pay attention, son, because being able to fix cars is like being a doctor."

Claude Faulkenberry wanted his son to get out of farming. Things had not been good in the industry in a while and he did not think that a young man should tie himself to a sinking ship. He pushed Guy into a new line of work. Claude called in a favor with his good pal Jack Johnson and asked if his son could work there and learn.

"Of course," Jack said. "I can't pay him very much to start out, but if he learns it pretty good then I can maybe up his pay some over time." It was 1953 when Guy started there at the garage. His first partly solo project was Melvin Marshall's 1951 Stuabaker.

Two years had gone by and although he was pretty handy with his hands fixing cars and trucks, it was not what Guy wanted to do with his life. College? Nah, Guy hated school and wanted no more of that. What about the military? Not a fighter. Jack made good on his word and increased Guy's wages especially since Barney was born. Besides, Jack recognized that Guy was really good, efficient, and honest to boot. At one point, Jack pondered a future partnership with Guy. That partnership would never come to pass.

One of Guy's friends from high school, Willie Johnson, came into the garage with a 1949 bluish-gray Ford two-door sedan. "It's making a damn knocking sound when I hit the gas," Willie said to Guy.

"Might be your plugs," Guy said while the two of them looked at the engine with the hood raised.

"Hard to change out?" Willie asked as Guy pulled the hood down closing it.

"Nah, give me a day and I'll have her all changed out."

"That's swell. I knew you'd know what was wrong with it. Hell, I ain't had it long and this knocking stuff is driving me bananas." The two men walked to the office part of the garage for Guy to write Willie a service order and to sign. "So, you like working here?"

Guy opened the small office door and walked in with Willie behind him, "Yeah it's all right, I guess. Money's okay. Jack's a good man to work with."

Guy walked around to his desk and took a pad of paper that was the service order receipt book. He took a pen off the desk and scribbled some stuff that he was going to do to the Ford, who it was for and how much it was going to cost, the parts, and the labor.

"Sign here if you please." Willie signed with Guy's pen and Guy ripped the service order page out of the pad and placed it on his desk on top of a thick green notebook with other orders.

"Just bring it back by tomorrow around ten if you can and I'll change out your bad plugs."

"I'll do it," Willie promised.

Guy and Willie walked out of the office towards Willie's Ford, "What have you been into since high school?" Guy asked passively, making more small talk than anything.

"Well, I got a job with the forestry service."

"Where's that at?" Guy inquired.

"Out on County Road five-fifty. You never been down that way before?"

"I've been down that way, but didn't know that a forestry service was down there."

"Yeah, it's pretty neat. My uncle, he's a supervisor there, he got me a job. It's a state job so you know you'll be took care of. You ort to come down there," Willie suggested, using that country slang "ort" to replace "ought".

Guy stood there and looked around at the garage where a few parked cars sat waiting to be worked on. "Maybe. What's it pay?"

"Dollar thirty-five an hour. Fifty-four bucks a week, a little over two hundred a month. Pretty good considering minimum wage is what, seventy-five cents nowadays?" Willie replied.

"Yeah that ain't too bad at all," Guy said.

"How much you pulling in here?"

"Ninety cents an hour right now," Guy replied.

"Man, if you want, I can get you a job with me in no time flat. I mean, hell, who couldn't use a forty-five cent raise?" Guy nodded and for the first time, he felt that he had a career direction to go towards. He liked working on cars, but he did not want that to be his life.

"Yeah...you think you could get me on?" Guy's mind latching onto the notion of switching jobs at a quick pace.

Willie smiled and nodded, "Sure thing. I can run by there and talk to my uncle after I leave here and have it set up. We need people like mad right now."

Guy stood there and considered it for a few moments. "What would I be doing?"

"Watching for fires up on the lookout tower. You ain't afraid of heights, are you?"

"Nah, they never bothered me much."

"Last fella didn't last five minutes climbing up the stairs. He got halfway up and came back down pouring sweat saying he couldn't do it."

"And all I'd be doing is just watching for fires?"

Willie nodded, "Pretty much. The only thing about the job is that it's cold in the winter and hot as Hell in the summer. It's lonely work though. You're up there by yourself for twelve hours a day. You'll be working the day shift. We got a guy, Elmer Acres, that takes the night shift. He sits up there and drinks and listens to ball games and music all night. Tells me you wouldn't believe all the radio stations he can get on a clear night. We're hiring for all kinds of stuff but if you want the lookout tower that'd be the fastest way to get hired on. Nobody wants to do it."

"That sounds pretty neat-o. Yeah, tell your uncle that I'd like to take a swing at it."

"Will do, my man."

And that was how Guy Faulkenberry got his job at the forestry service. A few days later, after meeting with Big Dale Wannamaker at the forestry service, and given the grand tour of the area and what his job would be, Guy went back to Jack's garage and broke the news to him. Jack was visibly disappointed but he understood. He could not offer Guy as much as the forestry service could. They shook hands and parted ways on good terms,

"You ever need a job if things don't work out over there, you come on back at the same pay, maybe a little more." Guy smiled and nodded his head.

Guy had been on the lookout tower for two years. And Willie was right: it was lonely work high up there all by himself. He never got visitors and the only communication he had was a long-range walkie-talkie to call for medical help if he ever needed it or to call in a fire to the local dispatch. Fortunately, Guy nor Elmer ever had to call for medical help or the fire department for large, out-of-control forest fires. For the most part, things were always calm.

On that fateful day of Guy's second lightning strike, it was August 20th, 1956. The South had been in the grip of a terribly dry summer and an extreme heat wave where high nineties to low one hundreds were common nearly every day that summer. Listening to the old folks around the region they never saw a heat wave like that before and not since. The summer of 1956 was the hottest on record. The forestry service had been placed on high alert because of the dry conditions, but thankfully, nothing in the way of fire ever happened. For two years all was quiet on the lookout tower...until the lightning strike.

On the day of the second strike, Guy started his day like normal. He arrived at work on time as usual and climbed the stairs carrying his two jugs of water in one hand and a cooler that had his ham and cheese sandwich. Also in that cooler, if he got hungry later on, was a peanut butter sandwich and a bag of plain chips.

Elmer was coming down the stairs from his shift.

"Goodnight, Elm," Guy said as the two men turned to the side to allow the other to walk by.

"Have a good'un," Elmer replied. Elmer was not a man who was blessed with the gift of gab. It had taken two years for Guy to get a verbal reply from the old man. Usually, it was just a grunt or nothing at all. Guy reached the covered lookout office and got settled in. He took the binoculars and scanned around the tops of the forest and saw nothing: no smoke, no sign of a fire. He took a seat in the same comfortable chair

Elmer had been resting in throughout the night and turned on the radio.

The station was on country music and Hank Williams sang about a cheating heart. A pack of smokes was sitting on top of yesterday's newspaper. Guy reached for the pack and took one. Elmer wouldn't mind and struck a match on the side of the old wooden desk. He lit the cigarette and blew smoke in the already hot and heavy morning air. Guy snuck a peek at the thermometer and the mercury already showed eighty-two. The sun was in full swing and Guy could see the haze gathering across the tops of the trees. It was going to be a long, hot summer day.

The lookout tower was a lonely business as advertised. Guy did not mind the solitude. He had enough to do up there on high. Sometimes he would play solitaire on the desk with a pack of heavily used cards. Sometimes he would do push-ups. The only time he was permitted to come down from the lookout tower was for ten minutes every three hours. There he would go pee by a nearby tree and use the outhouse that was close by. After that and stretching his legs, up the stairs he went and back into the lookout tower to his post. Nothing ever happened until that day when it did.

It had been ten years since his last lightning strike and that was when he was a little kid. He did not forget that event out in the wheat field, but the memory had waned some over the years. Graduating high school, marriage, and a family had pushed that day out in the field further from his mind. The only time that day when he was ten ever came to the forefront of his mind was when a storm was coming. Otherwise, the strike out in the wheat field was something he never brought up. Even his family stopped talking about it years ago.

It was around four-thirty that afternoon when it happened. The air had gotten hotter and heavier; the kind that made the clothes on your back stick to your skin. The humidity had to be around a hundred percent. Guy told his wife later that night that the air was so moist and hot that you could have reached up and grabbed water out of it. Guy noticed that dark clouds had been forming off from the south for the last couple of hours. Dark and foreboding clouds; grays and blacks covered much of the southern landscape.

Guy had read the weather report in the newspaper the day before and it said nothing of rain coming. The report also said the weather was more of the same: hot, sticky, and dry. He figured the approaching storm was just one of those pop-up thunderstorms that tend to happen during the summer sometimes.

Around three-thirty, the storm clouds of the dangerous kind began to slowly reach past the midway of the sprawling forest on the southern quadrant. The air was still hot and heavy but there was something new; a breeze was blowing from the south, bringing with it the violent storm. Guy took his binoculars and looked towards the direction of the storm clouds. They were coming all right, straight for him and the town of Claxton behind him. And by the look of the clouds, it was going to be a whopper. Guy had been up in the lookout tower before during storms and heavy rains, and even snow last year that netted six inches in accumulation. He was not afraid of storms. That would change after this storm cell crossed over him.

Four o'clock came and the thunder was roaring and the wind had gotten up to forty miles per hour by Guy's guess, but hey, he was not a weatherman. The thunder was so loud that it shook not only his body but the entire roof, half walls, and floor of the lookout tower. At that point, Guy was legitimately scared of being up there. The rain had not yet started, but it would. Off in the distance, he could see streaks of forked lightning shooting down from those dark gray and black clouds. He wondered if he was going to be in the path of a tornado. Then he wondered how in the hell he would survive something like that if he was.

His mind frantically thought about his family and then he thought about giving it up and running down the stairs and across the five hundred yards to the station house where Big Dale Wannamaker posted up. Before he could formulate a plan, it was four-thirty and the ominous clouds were already on top of him.

Rain came down in the heaviest downpour had had ever seen in his life; so hard was the rain it looked like white sheets. Wind was blowing so hard that it was swaying the lookout tower causing Guy to think that the structure was going to topple over. The thunder crashed and rumbled so loudly that his teeth rattled. Lightning flashed all around him in streaks and quick flashes. It was not long at all Guy found himself soaking wet from the rain that was blowing through. There was nowhere to go now. *I should have left when I saw the clouds coming*, he thought to himself.

Standing in the middle of the lookout tower, the once sunny day was now eerily dark. To Guy, it looked like it was ten at night with the way the clouds overtook the sun. He was scared for the first time in his life. He felt like a castaway on a floating board in the middle of the ocean during a hurricane. Guy just stood in the middle of the lookout tower with nowhere else to go.

There was no protection, no getting into a stable shelter. He was out in the storm, out in the elements of Mother Nature's wrath as it was. He looked at the desk and it was flipped over and blown to the other side of the lookout tower's half wall. The pack of smokes had vanished, the newspaper had flown out at some point, and his cooler and chair had been blown across the lookout tower next to the desk. It was just Guy standing there getting pelted with rain and hailstones watching the flashes of lightning and feeling the wind and thunder. Then it happened...

It happened just like it did when he was ten out in the wheat field in 1946. It happened fast. It happened with no warning. It happened in one of those, 'blink and you miss it' occurrences. Standing there in the middle of the lookout tower not knowing much else to do, a bolt of lightning came from the dark sky and ran underneath the lookout tower's roof and struck the man standing in the middle of the room. Guy never saw it coming; did not even feel it hit him.

The electricity zapped him so violently that Guy was knocked clear across the room, sliding against the wooden floor and landing back first against the half wall next to the desk, chair, and cooler.

Guy lay there unconscious for ten minutes. He would never realize it. When he came to the storm, the brunt of it had passed, but it was still churning violently across the region heading north into Claxton. It was still raining hard with now golf ball-sized hail crashing down on the roof and into the lookout tower. Guy got up off the floor and felt so funky like he was not in his own skin. He felt as if he was going to throw up, which he did there on the rain-soaked floor, and fell back down.

His head was swimming and his stomach flip-flopped. He managed to get on all fours there on the floor, trying to get up using the half wall for leverage with his right arm which was ninety percent numb, but good enough for his fingers to at least feel the wet wood of the wall.

Guy managed to get up on his legs of jelly and looked through the wind and rain and saw what his nose couldn't catch; smoke. There was a fire growing through that pouring rain somehow on the far side of the lookout tower, the part facing the southern quadrant. Knowing that he had nothing to put out the fire, Guy did the only thing his scattered mind allowed him; he staggered across the lookout tower's floor, out of the door, and down the stairs using the wooden handrail for stability as the storm started to ease up some.

When Guy reached the last rung of the stairs, he turned and looked back and saw smoke blowing in the wind. He watched as flames danced and whirled. Guy knew that the tower was a lost cause and he had to get as far away from it as he could before it came crashing down in a burning heap; which it did an hour and a half later. Guy staggered, falling a lot, across the five-hundred-yard distance between the lookout tower and the station where Big Dale Wannamaker sat, probably hunkered down from the storm.

About two hundred and fifty yards into his trek through the storm, Guy fell again and passed out. He woke up five minutes later with Big Dale and Willie kneeling beside him trying to wake him up in the rain. Off in the distance, smoke poured from the lookout tower and the smell of wet, burning wood wafted toward their direction.

Big Dale and Willie looked at Guy's shirt which was nearly ripped to shreds from the lightning strike and his green pants where the right pant leg had been burned away.

"What happened?" Guy asked weakly.

"Son," Big Dale started, "I think you got your ass hit by lightning."

THIRD STRIKE

The third strike came twelve years later in 1968. By the time the lightning found Guy again, he was divorced and was remarried to a woman named Marcy Day. He met her on his mail carrier route a year after his divorce was final from Faye and the two seemed perfectly happy together. They would eventually have a child of their own, Wesley. The day of the third strike started innocuous like the other two times that he was hit.

A few months after the events of the lookout tower twelve years prior, Guy quit his job with the forestry service. There was no way that he was going back up on that tower and the forestry service could not offer him another job because all the positions were filled. Elmer, the older man who served on the tower at night, had quit and eventually got a part-time job at a bait and tackle shop that his cousin owned out by the river.

Guy spent some time in the hospital, just a few days worth, recovering from the act of violence that came down that day of the storm. When he got out, he finished his convalescence at home with Faye being the helpful wife playing nurse. When he finally got his strength back, Guy wondered what his future held because getting back up a lookout tower for the forestry service was not going to happen.

Guy toyed with the idea of going into the military briefly but Faye would not hear of it. He went back and worked for a spell with Jack Johnson at his garage in 1957. He stayed there for three years until 1960 when Jack died from what people thought was a heart attack. The day he died, he was working under a car in the garage, lying on his back on a creeper. Guy noticed that Jack had been under the car for a long time and also found it odd that Jack had not rolled out from underneath it nor had he asked for a tool. He went over to Jack and called for him. No response. He took his shoe and tapped Jack's black boot. Nothing. Guy squatted down and grabbed Jack's boots. He pulled him out from underneath the car on the creeper. His eyes were open and he was not breathing. He was deader than a hammer.

Jack was dead and so was the garage shortly after. Guy did not have the money to keep it going six months after Jack's death because other mechanics had moved into the county offering cheaper rates to fix cars. Guy was not much of a numbers kind of fella nor did he have any business acumen.

Plus, he did not desire the headache and stress that came with owning a business. He had seen the stress of the business side of things on how it affected Jack over the time he spent with him. So, after six months of trying to keep the garage going, Guy worked on his last car and closed the doors for good.

In the fall of 1960, a month after he shuttered the doors of Jack's garage, he found his way into the post office delivering mail in Claxton. It was an easy job and one that he liked. What he did not like were the dogs that would bark at him or try to bite when he was on his rounds. He hated dogs and had a deep-seated fear of them; big dogs, the ones that could eat a man, were the ones that Guy feared the most.

He told a lot of the owners that they needed to do something with some of those bigger, vicious dogs; they never did. Out of spite, Guy would delay the delivery of mail to those certain houses that had those mean dogs. In all honesty, he wanted to take a .45 and kill the mutts. Withholding the mail, sometimes important, was all the retaliation that he had.

On the day of the third strike in 1968, twelve years had passed by since the lookout tower. Storms that had not bothered Guy before the tower certainly did now. He became fearful of the weather and during the spring and summer months and even into fall, Guy would catch the weather reports as often as he could. He did not want to be surprised by anything like he was up on that tower. With every storm that came through Claxton over the years, Guy was a nervous wreck.

When he heard thunder or saw the forecast of stormy weather, Guy took heed and kept a watchful eye on the sky above. The day of the third strike was no different. The weather had called for scattered storms and rain off and on all day. Fortunately for Guy, his work day was storm and rain-free. There were clouds here and there that looked dangerous but nothing ever came of them. However, Guy watched them cautiously all the same while out delivering the mail.

The lightning strike did not come during his mail route. It came after his work day was finished when all the letters and packages had been delivered. He was in his old truck driving home; window rolled down, left arm casually hanging out on that early March evening. The wind had been up and the clouds had turned gray and black. He was two miles from his house and would be home soon. He looked through his windows while driving and up at the clouds blotting out the waning sun. He was a little nervous. "I'll be home before it storms," he said to himself.

The rain came quickly smacking against his windshield. He turned the wipers on. Guy was only a mile from his house when the storm caught him with such speed that he didn't think it *could* catch him. He brought in his wet arm from the driver's side window and was cranking the window up when a bolt of lightning hit two trees off to the side of the road and shot a blot through the halfway rolled-up driver's side window hitting Guy with a force he never felt, but only recognized afterward when he came to on the side of the road.

The bolt of lightning hit Guy while he was cranking the window up. Just like the two other times previously, he did not have time to scream or feel the point of impact from the high voltage. He was rendered unconscious and fell over across his bench truck seat and the truck that was doing a cool thirty-five down the country road went off into a ditch and crashed into a thick wooden fence post.

Guy was lying there on the floorboard in his truck for fifteen minutes before he opened his eyes. The hair on top of his head had been singed off and the hairs on his left arm were gone. But that's not what he felt at first. What Guy felt was that maybe his ribs were broken from the crash and falling onto the floor of the truck.

Fifteen minutes later, the storm had rolled on by and was gone by the time a passerby saw Guy's truck in the ditch wedded to the fence post that was askew. The man got out of his car and trotted over to the truck to look inside. Guy got himself slowly up from the floorboard feeling the taste of copper in his mouth and thinking his nose had been broken with perhaps those ribs.

Thin smoke tendrils were coming from his left arm and scalp. "You okay, mister?" the passerby asked through the driver's side window.

Guy got himself onto the bench seat inside his truck, feeling that funky feeling like the last time he was hit in the lookout tower. He turned to look at the man bewildered. Blood had dried around his lips and chin from where his nose bled.

"Do you need a doctor?" the passerby asked. Guy heard the man's voice but it sounded far, far away, like he was on the other side of the world.

A few minutes passed and Guy managed only one question before being taken out of the truck by the passerby and walked drunkenly to his car where he was rushed to the hospital. "Where am I?"

FOURTH STRIKE

After the events of the third strike made the county paper, national wires got it and reprinted it. Soon, Guy Faulkenberry became a local celebrity but in the worst kind of way. He did interviews with the hometown paper of course, along with the *Knoxville News-Sentinel* and other regional papers. His national interview with *The Washington Post* was the interview that got the attention of the record book people.

It was not much longer after that, four months after all those papers and his fifteen minutes of fame tapered off, that the founders of Tobin's Records and Oddities came calling. They came to visit Guy and his family to tell him that he was going to be entered into their record book.

"We've gone all over and you're the only person to have been hit by lightning three times and live," Thomas Tobin, the founder of the record book, told Guy and his wife in their living room.

"Well, I guess I am known for something after all," Guy chuckled.

The following year, Thomas Tobin sent Guy a copy of the new edition of *Tobin's Records and Oddities* record book. Guy and Marcy quickly turned to the index to see where his record was located. It was in the middle under the section on Man vs. Nature.

On the page, there was a picture of Guy standing on the side of the road where the lightning had struck the two trees and then sent a bolt into his truck. The small entry told readers of Guy's first brush with lightning in 1946 when he was ten, the lookout tower in 1956, and the road that he was standing on in 1968.

Guy really did not know exactly what to think about the attention he received from the events in his life. While other people were fascinated with him getting hit three different times in a span of twenty-two years, Guy began to see his misfortune as something other than fascination; he began to see it as a punishment from God. But for what?

He had lived a clean life. Sure, there had been a divorce thrown in the mix, but he was never a cheating spouse to Faye or Marcy. He never hit his wives up to that point nor was he ever mean to them. Guy sat in his chair with that record book in his lap with Marcy leaning over his shoulder from behind reading it again. Reading his misfortune for the first time caused Guy to wonder what he had done to piss God off.

The third strike had done something to Guy's cognitive framework. The other two lightning strikes might have fried the circuits in some way inside his brain, but the third one was what caused Marcy great concern. The townsfolk of Claxton became aware of how eccentric their mailman had become. His brain was scattered, there was no doubt about that and even though Guy was still the same man he had been fundamentally, there were noticeable changes about him that made him become...strange.

Some of those eccentricities started small. Marcy noticed that her husband would forget simple things like her name and would often call her Faye, his first wife. Sometimes at the dinner table, he would call their son, Zane. Who Zane was, Marcy never knew. She wasn't sure that Guy even knew.

He would tell Marcy about The Torbett family, a family on his mail route, and how they threw huge parties out on their front lawn from morning til midnight. None of that ever happened of course and there was no Torbett family anywhere in town.

When Barney, his son from his and Faye's marriage would visit, he would call him Big Dale. Sometimes while sitting in the living room watching TV or reading the newspaper, Marcy would be doing a crossword puzzle sitting on the couch while her husband would be sitting in his recliner.

He would spring up suddenly and look at his wife and ask, "Do you hear barking dogs?"

The first time this happened Marcy tried to listen for the dogs that Guy heard. But there were never any barking dogs. Guy would do this several times a week, different times a week, sometimes right before bed, during dinner, or even on a Sunday drive.

There were other issues where Guy got into the nightly habit of locking the front and back doors six times each, counting out loud every time and making sure Marcy was there watching him as a witness.

He would go through their home and open and close all the windows in the house five times each night.

He would go outside in the driveway and open and close his car doors three times each every night.

Marcy watched all this with tearful eyes and wondered if her husband due to all the lightning strikes was losing his mind. It was a secret that she held inside her home until people in Claxton started seeing Guy acting funny out in town while on the job as a mailman or out doing normal after-work things.

Guy's work began to suffer after that third lightning strike. His memory used to be really sharp. Not so much after the third hit. For months people had been getting the wrong mail stuffed in their boxes, the wrong packages delivered to the wrong houses. There were times when Guy at the end of his day had a truck full of mail that he just plum forgot to deliver.

He would just ride around all day to those on his route and open their mailbox doors, act like he was placing mail inside it, close it, and drive off. The mail that he should have been delivering was sitting in bags and boxes, all sorted by the post office, in the truck. One day, as he was going back home, he looked at his truck and saw all the mailbags and boxes. He was horrified.

He pulled into Wilson's Drugstore parking lot and looked at all the mail. "What's going on here?" he mumbled to himself.

His rational mind was coming back some. Guy realized that he had not delivered the mail that day but had *imagined* that he did. He took some of the envelopes out of the bag and read the addresses. He remembered the houses, remembered putting those pieces of mail in the boxes...or did he?

He leaned back in his truck seat and started to breathe deep breaths. He was having a panic attack. He looked at his watch and it was time for his work day to end but looking over at all the mail, there was at least eight hours worth of stuff to be delivered. So, Guy pulled out of the parking lot and went to deliver the mail, all of it from the past few days he had realized, up until the wee hours of the morning.

Complaints rolled into the post office over time and Guy's supervisor, Mark Millsaps, finally had a talk with Guy. After speaking with him, Guy made a promise to Mark that he would be better. He did not get any better.

Even though he had caught his mistake awhile back there at the Wilson's Drugstore parking lot, Guy's scattered brain went right back to giving him illusions that he was delivering the mail when, in fact, he was not. Eventually, he was let go for performance after nearly nine years with the post office in 1969.

From there, things did not get any better for Guy or his family for a stretch. Without a stable source of income, Marcy took a job with Peter Ritchie, the attorney in town, as his secretary. The money was not great but it was better than no money at all. Guy did odd jobs around the town and was given what most called handout jobs just because he was a good guy who had a run of bad luck.

A lot of people wondered how in the hell a man could be hit by lightning three times and still live. Since most people around the town were God-fearing and church-going folks, they all wondered what it was about Guy Faulkenberry that God did not like. Guy wondered the same thing.

The fourth strike came years later: Nine to be precise. It was 1978 in late May when it happened. Guy had been doing somewhat better than he was years previous. His memory was still not as sharp as it once was but it was somewhat better. He could remember his kids' names and stopped calling Marcy, Faye, all the time. As a bonus, he stopped hearing those phantom barking dogs and locking the doors and windows excessively every night had gone away too.

Guy even got a new job. Well, it was a new/old job. He was hired back at the forestry service by Willie Johnson, who had taken over as supervisor when Big Dale Wannamaker passed. Willie heard about Guy's troubles and offered him a job in 1970. "I don't want back on that lookout tower," Guy said to Willie.

Willie laughed but could not help it. "Lord no! You'll just be riding around the area looking for signs of illegal activity, stuff like clearing trees off back roads, planting trees in bare patches, stuff like that."

The job that was offered to Guy was just really busy work, work that Willie had teenage kids doing for internships to put on their college resumes. But he knew that Guy needed the work and knew the situation he was in. Besides, in some weird way, Willie felt responsible for that incident up at the lookout tower in '56.

The fourth strike did not occur at the forestry service. It was at Guy's house this time. Guy was outside working in his garden, one of his passions that he had gotten a taste for the last few years and never let it go. He loved to cultivate the land and to grow things. After all, farming was in his blood. There was something about eating out of the garden knowing that you planted it and cared for it. As a bonus, it gave Guy something else to do besides being plopped down in his recliner in front of the TV.

It was around six that evening in July, the later part of it when Guy walked outside to check in on his garden. It was not a huge garden there in his backyard by no means, just a thirty by thirty space out back for him to tend to.

Walking in between the rows, he looked at his tomatoes. They were looking good. He had already taken several off the vine and ate tomato sandwiches with them. They were probably the best tomatoes Guy had ever eaten in his life, much better than the ones he planted and raised last summer when he thought those were the best.

The squash was doing good as well although he was not a big squash eater. That was Marcy. She loved cooking fried squash. The watermelons were good and ripe. Most he had given away to the folks in the neighborhood. Only a few were left in the garden. Guy had eaten two watermelons whole by himself in the last few weeks and was completely tired of them. He figured that next week he would give the four that remained away to someone.

The corn that he planted was standing high and swayed in the breeze. Those ears of corn were some of the sweetest ears he had ever eaten. Last year's crop was not as sweet and Guy wondered about that.

In the sky, a storm was coming. He had been watching the weather reports and nothing major coming their way that hot day in late July. Guy did not put much stock in the weathermen anymore. He had been hit three times already and one of those days was on a clear and sunny day out in a wheat field. Off in the west, the clouds were a little dark, and off to his east, north, and south the skies were clear as a bell. Above, a small aircraft was droning towards the county airport.

Standing there looking at the green beans that he had already produced two, five-gallon buckets worth from the garden, the wind picked up all at once blowing his hair back. Guy decided that it was time to get back to the safety of his house. He walked briskly out of the garden and across the backyard he had cut the day before.

Right before he crossed the midway point between the house and the garden, a crack of thunder so loud that it rang in his ears caused Guy to jump with fright. He let out a scream and started to run quickly to the house. A streak of lightning quickly followed that thunder crack and struck the power pole across his yard.

The bolt of lightning hit the transformer, throwing bright white sparks and a boom louder than the thunder clap afterward. Then the lightning bolt jumped from the power pole and transformer and chased across the yard towards Guy who was running for the back door. He did not make it. The bolt flew across the yard hitting Guy in the chest from the front and knocking him in the air and back into his garden laying him out in the corn. Just like the other three times, Guy never felt the strikes, just the aftermaths.

His doctor, Dr. Walker, asked him after his third strike what it felt like this time and Guy replied the simplest way that he knew how, "How the hell should I know?"

FIFTH STRIKE

The fifth lightning strike proved to Guy that nowhere was safe, not even the confines of his home. On December 10th, six years had passed since the last time Guy was jolted. His cognitive abilities which seemed to be getting back slowly from the third strike were right back at zero thanks to the fourth strike out in his backyard. He was doing all the same weird behaviors as before but this time around there were newer ones, strange ones.

One such behavior was that he would go into stores and walk in backward and shop that way.

Another odd behavior was that Guy started mowing at night, like at ten o'clock, much to the consternation of the people in the neighborhood.

This lightning strike had erased the memory of how to tie his shoes and how and when to take a shower. There was a time when he had forgotten how to drink water and had to go into a rehabilitation center where stroke victims had to go to learn basic motor skills all over again. This place was where he learned how to drink and swallow liquid, tie his shoes, and button his shirts.

This time around after the fourth lightning strike, Guy could no longer operate his truck. He got in his truck eight months after being cleared by his doctor to start driving again. He sat there looking at the steering wheel and the dashboard. He had no clue as to how to start the thing and most importantly what to do after he started. "What in the blue hell does P R N D L mean?" Guy thought long and hard about what the letters meant on the steering column.

Sitting in the driver's seat of his truck, Guy began to get mad at the situation he was in. He knew the memory of how to operate a moving vehicle was in his brain somewhere but the question was where? Then tears came. Guy never felt so lost before. Feeling something warm spread across the crotch of his jeans, he looked down and saw a wet spot form-ing. He had pissed himself.

Six years had passed and just like last time, Guy's memory came back slowly on how to do things. He had seen several specialists in the field of neuroscience and cognitive behavior. He was a case study for the doctors and all involved wrote papers about Guy Faulkenberry. Nobody had ever seen anything like him in the medical field and probably would never again.

Guy went through every battery of tests imaginable, every psychological exam, every blood extraction, and every MRI. There were several theories as to why Guy was acting the way he was, and why he had lost pieces of his memory but when the rubber met the road all the doctors had pretty much the same opinion:

"We don't exactly know. There's not been too much in the way of research for people like you," Dr. Mallher told him.

"And there's no explanation as to why my memory starts to come back little by little?"

"Not exactly." Dr. Mallher began to go into a long and complicated doctor explanation and Guy tuned him out completely. That was the last time he ever went to the doctor because they were of no help to him.

Not feeling safe within his own home anymore and once his cognitive behavior began to come back along with some of his memories, Guy began installing tall lightning rods on the outside four corners of his and Marcy's house. His memory had not lost how to build things. That was the frustrating part for Guy: he could forget some things, like everyday things, but things he did not do all the time he could recall in no time flat.

Two summers ago he had torn down and rebuilt the back porch in two days. On the B-side of that, at dinner one night, days after the porch construction was completed, he had forgotten how to eat with a fork and brush his teeth.

Neighbors stood outside watching as he installed those lightning rods one by one. When he was finished he stood there on his front lawn with a few of his neighbors.

"You think that'll work, Guy?" Roy asked, looking at the rods that stood taller than Guy's house.

"I sure as hell hope so. At least these rods will divert the bolt if it ever hits the house."

"But ain't your house already grounded?" Pat quizzed.

"Yeah, Pat…it is," Guy replied, seemingly aggravated by his neighbor's stupid observation.

Aggravation was one of those newer traits that did not dissolve over time. Guy's temper had gotten the better of him several times both verbally and physically when it came to Marcy after the fourth strike. Sometimes Marcy had to cover her black eye with makeup so no one out in town or at work could see that her husband had tuned her up. Marcy planned on leaving Guy but deep down she knew that it was not her actual husband that was calling her names and punching her.

The lightning had done something to him, scrambled his brain. Sometimes Guy was all there and sometimes not. The man Marcy married was only a quarter of the way present those days. He was a good man, but she was unsure if the good man was ever coming back…at least not all the way. A lot of times she wondered through the tears late at night while sitting on the back porch if she could live with the rollercoaster that was her husband. She wanted to leave, but could she?

"As many times as you've been hit, I think I'd move in a fucking cave," Arnie, a burly neighbor that was a retired police officer, said.

Guy shot him a look that told Arnie that he had just better not comment on anything else. "I think I'll be fine in there now hopefully. These rods plus the grounding will do the trick." Guy was wrong.

Four years later after the placement of the lightning rods and seeing many storms, several that were bad to the bone severe, Guy got that false sense of security thinking that as long as he was in the house when a storm came maybe he was out of harm's way.

"I figured that once I placed the lightning rods on the four corners of the house I'd be okay. Looks like I was wrong," Guy was quoted saying to Miles Wayward of the Brook County Register after his fifth strike.

That December 10th, 1984 a cold front had swept across the state of Tennessee spawning several tornadoes and severe storm activity. Claxton was not spared in the paths of destruction that the cold front caused. From the weather reports that he and Marcy had watched, the storm line was going to produce some bad storms. Guy could feel it deep within his bones. But he felt good inside the house, as long as he stayed inside the house. He had seen many storms since the lightning rods were installed and felt comfortable. Never in a million years did he think lightning strike number five would be in his own house.

The storms rolled through the town of Claxton and all of Brook County, hitting everything in their path with fury. There were six tornadoes spotted but only one had formed and touched down just off of County Road 409. That tornado did some damage while spinning on land and claimed three houses and two barns. Luckily, no lives were lost.

Inside the Faulkenberry home, Guy and Marcy stood in the middle of the living room, blinds down and closed and curtains pulled together. They could hear the rain and hail hitting the roof and against the windows and vinyl siding of their home. The wind, which had to be around sixty to seventy miles an hour, rattled their home at times and both wondered if a tornado was close by.

The thunder rolled and cracked loudly above them and the house, along with nearly everyone in town, lost power. Violent flashes of lightning lit up everything for a split second causing Guy to jump and scream. He tried to tell himself that he was safe inside and had been with the other storms in the past. But the storm outside was a howler, a whopper, that he had not seen since, well, the lookout tower. *But this ain't the lookout tower so get a grip*, he thought to himself while Marcy paced about the home visibly nervous, wondering if the weather was going to get any more worse than it already was.

Around five-thirty, the storm began to taper off. The howling winds had finally calmed down. The rain that had been mixed with hailstones had all but turned into a drizzle. The thunder overhead had barreled its way eastward and the lightning, oh the lightning, had finally stopped flashing and streaking. It appeared that things had calmed down considerably. The power, however, was still out and the only thing that lit the living room was a single candle that was placed on an end table.

Thinking that things were finally over, Guy walked across the living room and over to the front door. He wanted to see if things were as calm outside in the darkness as they seemed inside the house. He twisted the doorknob and pulled it open and when he did out of the December night sky just as random as you please, a streak of jagged lightning tore through the darkness of the neighborhood and the sky above and zapped Guy violently, sending him flying across the living room and against the far fall that the kitchen shared with the living room. Marcy screamed.

SIXTH STRIKE

Had Guy contacted Tobin's Records and Oddities to inform them that he had been hit with more lightning, he would hold the record beyond his record of three strikes as they noted back in 1968. He never contacted them. He never did another newspaper interview or magazine piece. He was just tired of it. He was tired of being hit, tired of himself, and tired of being looked at as a freak. Guy was tired of having his brain scrambled, tired of forgetting how to do everyday things. He was tired of his temper and tired of being afraid of storms.

At one point he wondered if there was something to Arnie's observation that day out in the street: something about living in a cave, wasn't it? Guy could not remember. He just remembered some of that interaction but not the particulars. Hell, he was even surprised that he recalled that moment in time.

As for the fifth strike, Guy did not have any memory of that at all. He told Marcy that all he remembered was the candle giving off some low light, the rain and hail hitting the house, and of course the lightning. As far as going over to open the front door? Nothing, he did not remember a thing about doing that.

What about being thrown clear across the living room and crashing against the wall? Nope, not that either. When Marcy rushed over to him, Guy was lying against the wall, slumped on the floor, back to the wall. The drywall had an impression on it where Guy hit it full tilt from the strike. From what she could tell, his hair, what little he had those days, was smoking and his shirt had pretty sizable burn holes.

The right pant leg of his pants looked as if it had gone through a paper shredder. His watch was missing from his wrist. It would later be recovered, blackened, over by the recliner close by the front door. Upon further examination, Marcy saw that Guy's fingers were moving quickly as if they were playing the piano in some concert.

Blood poured from Guy's nose. His lips were pulled back and contracted giving Marcy the thought of someone smiling and frowning in rapid succession. This was a first for her being in the same room and witnessing lightning hitting her husband. Guy had asked her weeks later what it looked like and Marcy really could not say for sure, that it happened so fast that her mind was not able to photograph the precise moment.

All she could recall was that when he opened the front door the lightning, which oddly seemed to be waiting on him, hit him and tossed him like a ragdoll across the living room, fifteen feet away against the far wall of the room.

As the days went on, Guy began to recover some. He did not go to the doctor. "I've survived four of these now so what's the point? I'm tired of being a conversation piece," Guy told Marcy when she nagged him about going to see Dr. Walker. She finally relented after realizing that Guy might be right. What were the doctors going to be able to do at this point? Nothing.

Along with all the usual suspects that befell Guy as his brain tried to reset itself back to factory settings, a new thing began that had not been there in the previous strikes: Guy began to talk backward. He and Marcy or he and any of his neighbors over the months and years would be carrying on a normal conversation and then all of a sudden he would start to speak words backward.

To Arnie, it sounded like a vinyl record being played slowly backward. Guy had no idea that he was even doing it. In his head, he still heard himself talking just as usual, much like when he thought he was delivering the mail but in reality, was not. But to others, it was backward. It only lasted for a few moments and then the moment was gone and Guy was speaking normally again.

Another new odd thing that cropped up after the fifth strike was insomnia. Through every one of the previous strikes Guy had taken, he was always able to sleep. After the fifth one, Guy discovered that he could not sleep and if he did it was only for twenty minutes or so and he woke up feeling like he had been asleep for fifteen hours. He and Marcy would go to bed usually around the same time every night, just a shade before nine o'clock. Guy would wake up in twenty minutes every night, eyes open starting up at the ceiling while Marcy lay beside him softly snoring. Usually, she fell asleep as soon as she hit the pillow. Guy mostly did as well even after the lightning strikes. The fifth strike that reached him inside the safety of his home was different. Sleep was different.

Guy would wake up after a twenty-minute slumber feeling like he could go run a marathon. When it first happened, he would lay there in bed and toss and turn all through the night trying to will himself to sleep. It was no use. Then the alarm clock would go off meaning that the work day was about to get underway for the two of them.

Marcy and Guy would do their normal morning rituals of showering, eating a quick breakfast, and a quick kiss goodbye. Guy was fine throughout the workday on that first day of his insomnia. He felt as if a long day at work with no sleep would be exactly what the doctor ordered. When he and Marcy came home from their work day and decompressed from the day that was, Guy found himself tired, exhausted even, and thought his sleep cycle was within his grasp. Much like the lightning, Guy gravely miscalculated.

Just a shade before nine that night, he and Marcy had gone to bed and she was, per usual, asleep in no time. Guy fell asleep rather quickly. At nine-fifteen, twenty minutes later, Guy's eyes sprang open and he started up at the ceiling just as he had the night before. He felt good, felt rested but how in the world was that possible? Guy played with this question, worked it around and around in his scrambled brain until he got bored with it and decided that there was no answer, at least not for a man of his educational caliber. So, Guy eased himself out of bed to not wake his wife.

He softly walked out of the bedroom, down the hall, and into the living room. He turned on the TV set, sat down in his recliner, and watched whatever cable TV had to offer at that time of night. "So, this is what I've been missing?" Guy said to himself flipping channels aimlessly with the remote in his right hand. "The better question is, why are we paying for this?"

The insomnia went on for the better part of a year before it finally disappeared just as mysteriously as it appeared. In the time during his lack of sleep, that twenty minutes a day rest, which should have been impossible by any medical standard, Guy started to lose weight, not that he had much to lose to begin with. Marcy at first noticed it and remarked that Guy looked sick, but she said it in the nicest way she could. Guy agreed.

He showed her his belt which he had already started using the last hole. He had lost two pants sizes in the last few months. "I just ain't been hungry is all," Guy told her. He was right. His appetite was nonexistent. He only ate because he had to; just to keep his body going. He knew that if he stopped he would waste away into nothing and nothing was not too far away.

In that year trapped in the clutches of insomnia which led him into the darkness of depression, Guy sat alone in the house, alone in the stillness pondering his life, and what he could remember. The lightning had stolen some of the memories he knew. Which ones? He did not remember but he felt empty when he tried to remember simple things about the past: things like what his mother looked like or what his dad's name was.

Guy thought that he had two brothers but was not sure if they were both living or for what matter where they lived. Guy sat in that recliner in the living room, the TV turned off because there was never anything good on anyway, trying to remember things from back when he was a kid. He remembered a bicycle wreck on the country road by his house where he skinned his knees and hands up pretty good.

He knew that he had to have been married once but for the life of him, he could not remember her name. He knew that they had a son together. He remembered Barney, his son by her, but her name? Guy cussed himself and cussed God for stealing her name from his mind and stealing all those memories, the good and the bad, out of his brain with those lightning bolts. Why did God hate him so much? What had he ever done?

Sitting in his recliner on one of those sleepless nights, Guy for the first time talked to God about the lightning strikes. He had prayed like Father Gline had suggested earlier on when he went to consult him about his condition. The priest had nothing to offer but prayer. Guy prayed but he still got his ass hit by lightning. That night in his recliner, sitting there in the darkness and quietness of the living room, Guy started a long-awaited one-sided conversation.

"God, it's Guy Faulkenberry here. But you probably already know that. So, you know why I'm coming to you tonight. I just...what is it about me that you hate?" Guy asked as tears welled up in his eyes. Guy sat there as if he was waiting for God to speak to him like he was across the room.

"I mean what is it? I know that I'm not the best man alive or the holiest. I know that I've done things bad to my wife. But let's be honest here: I didn't do any of that before I was hit by lightning. I was a kid when you hit me out in a field the first time and what does a kid do to make you angry?

"God...so much has changed since all of this lightning business. And I don't know what I've done to make you so angry. But whatever it was...I'm sorry. I wished that I knew what I did so I could atone for it. Don't you think five strikes are enough? Because I do. I mean, look at me. I'm a shell of a man now. I'm barely hanging on. I sometimes think about killing myself just to end the pain and escape the fear. It's like I have nowhere to go to be safe. So, I'm asking you, God, please just don't light me up no more. I don't think I can handle another one. I just don't."

———

On July 5th, 1987, three years after his fifth strike, Guy was jolted once again. Guy had just turned fifty-one days before his sixth strike. There was a birthday party that Marcy and the boys and their families had put on for the "old man". A great time was had by all and not one time did the word lightning ever get mentioned. Guy was all smiles and played with his grandkids, trying to recall their names was a chore, but it did not matter.

His family was there and the cake was delicious and the time seemed to stand still. It was the first time that Barney, Wesley, and their families were in the same place at the same time. Work and other obligations had them all separated through all the holidays and such over the years. It was the happiest time Guy could recall.

Since the last time he was hit by lightning, storms had come and gone through Claxton without incident to Guy. In a naïve sort of way, Guy thought that maybe his talk with God that night in his living room might have done some good. He was not sure about it but was hoping that God might see fit to just leave him alone and stop with the lightning.

What point God was trying to make with Guy, he was getting it. Although he had no clue as to what his point was or what he was doing. Maybe it was not God doing the lightning, Guy sometimes thought. Maybe there was just something about me, maybe inside me, that attracts lightning. Maybe I've got too much iron in my blood or something stupid like that. It was the first time that Guy thought about the lightning being something other than God's punishment or correction or whatever Father Gline would call it.

Not letting go of this iron notion, and not even knowing that could be a factor, Guy went to see Dr. Walker and asked for a blood panel to be conducted to see if his body did indeed have too much iron in it. If it did, maybe that was a reason.

"I don't know if that's how it works, Guy. There's a bunch of people walking around with more iron in their bodies than needs to be. The last time that we did blood work on you all your levels were fine. I've got the paperwork in your file if you want to see it for yourself. There was nothing whatsoever in your blood that would cause you to get hit by lightning."

Guy sat there across from the doctor's desk feeling defeated once again.

"I just wish I knew what caused me to get hit so I could avoid it."

"Well, on the bright side, you've not been hit in a while. What, three times now?"

Guy shook his head and held up all four fingers and thumb, "Five, doc. I didn't tell anyone about strikes four and five."

Dr. Walker's eyes grew large and was astounded by Guy's admission, "Interesting. When was the last one?"

Guy kind of chuckled at the question, "In my house during that big storm that rolled through a few years ago in December. Remember? The tornado that came down over on 409?"

"Yeah, I do remember that. That twister was about two miles from my house. Too close for me, I can tell you that."

"Well, I was inside my house right in the middle of the living room for the whole thing and when the storm finally passed, I went over to open the front door to see if it was as calm as it sounded and when I opened it, I got hit."

"Sounds like the lightning was waiting for you to open that door," Dr. Walker said.

"Kind of does, doesn't it?" Guy replied.

Dr. Walker took his glasses from his face and rubbed his eyes, placing them back on and looking at his patient, "You're a mystery, Mr. Faulkenberry."

"Hell, don't I know it."

Strike six came out of nowhere as a pop-up thunderstorm formed over the town of Claxton and the rest of Brook County coming down from the north. Storms usually never came from that direction but hey, Guy was no weatherman and guessed that storms could go wherever they wanted, right? He was in his truck hauling some two-by-fours in the bed for a project he wanted to work on in his spare time.

He would build Marcy some flower boxes to affix to the house under the windows so she could put whatever flower arrangements in them she wanted. She was going to buy the boxes premade but Guy told her that he would build them. "It'll give me something to do next weekend," he told her.

On an idle Saturday afternoon, Guy went to Kirk's Lumber Yard and picked up the materials that he needed for the flower boxes. He planned on building seven in all for the seven windows. Guy loaded up the eight, two-by-fours into the bed of his truck. They hung over the closed tailgate by two feet but it was okay, they weren't going anywhere. He had hauled stuff much longer than the wood before without incident. Guy did not think this time would be any different.

On July 5th, 1987, Guy Faulkenberry was struck by lightning yet again on his way home from the lumber yard. He was driving home, nearly there, past the spot on the county road where the site of the third strike happened. He had gone by this site before, millions of times, on his way home and always cringed when he drove by. It was as if he was waiting for lightning to come down and hit him again on the very spot in the road. It never did. The lightning waited until Guy got a little further down the road this time.

A half mile from his house something strange happened. A gust of wind caught one of the two-by-fours that were hanging over the closed tailgate. It flipped it up from the bed and flew it out of the truck. Guy heard the commotion and looked in his rearview mirror and saw the board turning over and over in the road behind him. *Thank God there wasn't a car behind me*, Guy thought to himself as he stopped in the middle of the road.

Guy stopped his truck and put it in park. He got out and looked up at the sky. Black and gray clouds had been forming from the north and the wind was blowing much harder than it was when he left the lumber yard; had to be at least forty from Guy's crude wind estimation. He walked towards the two-by-four in the road and a clap of thunder came so loud that it caused birds to fly out from their nests in the trees around him.

Guy jumped nearly a foot high from the thunderclap. He rushed over to the wood, bent down, picked it up, and ran back to his truck. He slung the board back into the bed and was about to make it to the driver's side door when lightning struck him knocking Guy fifteen feet across the road and into a ditch. Guy's shoes were left on the road smoking.

SEVENTH STRIKE

April 17th, 1992. The seventh lightning strike came while Guy was trout fishing in the Rabbit Trail River at just around five in the morning. It had been nearly five years since the last hit and each time, sunny skies or dark skies, Guy worried himself nearly sick with fear. And then one day, out of nowhere, he just stopped being worried at all. For no reason, Guy woke up and did not think ever again about being hit by lightning. It was as if he had forgotten every time that he was hit. Was it possible?

Marcy thought so because in the years between the sixth strike and seventh Guy was rolled back to factory settings and was the man she married many years ago. Even Barney and Wesley could see a difference in their dad. Gone were the odd things he did.

His memory, which had been Swiss cheese at that point, seemed to be whole again. It was strange and some would even call it a miracle that he appeared to be back…all the way back.

Guy Faulkenberry was mentally back to the way he was. How, Marcy did not know but she did not mind it at all. That was a good thing. Very mysterious, but why question it?

Guy's old personality came back little by little at first and then in waves. He was smiling a lot more, laughing more merrily, calling his kids by the right names. He was no longer walking backward into stores to shop. He could remember phone numbers and particular times in pictures when looking at family photos with Marcy on the couch. He even recalled Faye, his first wife's name. His temper had cooled to what it used to be back when he was a mailman when he and Marcy first met. For the first time since the '60s, she and Guy were both happy and very much in love.

On the day of what would be the final lightning strike, Guy was standing in the middle of Rabbit Trail River, waders on with the water near his waist. He had been trout fishing that river for years but not since the 1950s when he was much younger. The lightning strikes had erased his memory completely taking the joy and love that he had of being out there in the streams and rivers fishing for trout.

Memories of trout fishing had been taken away from him from those lightning strikes but Guy did not know which bolt was the actual one that robbed him. Much like everything else lately, all his memories came back in a slow drip and eventually his memory on most things that were forgotten were back like they were, coming in those waves. Trout fishing was one of those things.

Being out there in the Rabbit Trail River, Guy remembered exactly how to cast, what flies to use, and where to look for deep pools and shady spots where trout liked to gather. To his glee, he remembered everything that his father had taught him about fishing. Guy even remembered his dad's name and what he looked like when the memories were restored. That put a smile on his face standing out there in the river fishing, thinking about his dad. Life was back to normal. Or so it seemed.

An hour and a half passed by and the clouds above were gathering dark and ominous. Guy reeled in his line, nothing on the end of it but the red and yellow fly that he had tied to it the night before, and began to walk towards the bank. The last thing he wanted was to be standing out in the water when bad weather came.

The weather report said scattered storms were in the forecast for later on in the afternoon, but it was only eleven o'clock. *Weathermen are never right*, Guy thought to himself as he was wading through the current sideways to reach the bank.

Thunder lowly rumbled overhead as the winds picked up and the sun was taken hostage by the low-hanging black clouds. Guy was somewhat nervous about making it out of the water but laughed to himself about why he was so nervous. He had been told and even read about his lightning strikes in a record book a while back, but Guy had forgotten all about the strikes thanks to the sixth hit of electricity. To him, they never really happened because he did not remember them the least little bit.

Guy calmed his nerves down and took his time managing his footing on the slippery riverbed rocks beneath his boots. One bad boot placement on the slippery rocks and he could fall and float down the river or worse, drown. That'd be something, wouldn't it? Survive all those lightning strikes and end up dying from falling into the river and drowning.

Eventually, Guy made it out of the river and onto the bank where his boots sunk in several inches in the mud. His truck was up the hill a piece. Guy was out of breath and feeling his age of fifty-six. He stood there on the muddy bank of the river for a moment catching his breath.

Getting out of the river had taken some of the wind out of his sails and climbing up that steep hill before him was going to take a lot more energy. "Getting old sucks," Guy said out loud to nobody. The wind blew a little harder, the trees began to sway back and forth more violently. A storm was coming and by the looks of the clouds, it was going to be very soon.

Several minutes passed by and the clouds were nearly over his head. He looked up at the bank and clearly, he was not ready for the climb back up the hill, but he needed to get going. So, Guy walked to where the hill began to rise and up Guy went, grabbing onto a low tree branch to pull himself up a piece. Then, he grabbed another branch and then another and another as he made his way up the hill.

It was not as bad as he thought it was going to be and the hill was not as steep as it looked. In the sky, thunder loudly rumbled and the wind blew all the trees that he was now in the middle of and rain began to fall. The lightning was low, and low lightning Guy did not like. It was too close for comfort.

Guy had finally made it to the top of the hill and his truck was in sight across the old country road. Guy emerged out of the thicket of trees and walked towards his truck at a medium pace. The storm was in full swing by then. Carrying his fishing rod, Guy happened to look down at his fishing vest. Inside it were extra flies, a spool of line in one pocket, a knife in the other, and a pair of pliers. He briefly wondered if the metal in that vest was enough to bring any unwanted attention to him. As he walked, Guy looked up at the dark clouds moving on, rain hitting his face like tiny pieces of broken glass, and said, "Nah."

Guy was about three feet away from his truck, arm extended ready to open the truck's driver's side door when from the clouds a bolt of jagged electricity shot down and zapped Guy sending him sprawling across the country road and into the thicket of woods where he just came from.

Guy lay there for nearly thirty minutes before he came to as the April sun shone brightly and birds chirped in the trees. The storm had passed and the remains of the violence were nowhere to be seen. It was just a perfect-looking spring afternoon when Guy woke from his unconsciousness. He remembered all the lightning strikes now...all of them.

THE END

It was June 1st, 1997, five years after the final strike out at Rabbit Trail River. Guy was sitting in his recliner recalling all the lightning strikes he had endured over the decades, seven in all.

Outside, a storm was knocking on his front door. The windows in his house were raised letting in the wind and rain. Guy had the hammer on his Colt .45 cocked and ready. Marcy had gone and visited her sister in South Carolina and Guy, maybe it was husbandly intuition, felt that she was not coming back. Guy had reverted to his old ways of hitting her and losing his temper. He had even lost it a few months ago when he broke his grandson's arm when he grabbed him by the said arm to turn him around to swat his ass for messing with the stove.

Guy did it so violently that Barney said that they would never come back. Guy was profoundly sorry for what he had done, but could not control himself. The same went for when he would hit Marcy for saying something that he deemed out of line or for dinner not being ready at a certain time. The seventh strike took away most of Guy's memories yet again, and it also created a more violent man at home.

Guy had enough goodness inside of him still to know that what he had become from the seventh strike was not what he was. The lightning, for whatever reason, had created him into a monster of violence. He was not a violent man by no means. But there he was, hurting the people he loved for no reason.

Guy knew that he could no longer go on the way he was. The years after the sixth strike were great, perhaps the greatest he ever had, but those days were gone thanks to the jolt he had taken at the river that day in April. He had gone trout fishing a happy-go-lucky man in his fifties and came back a sour, mean, and violent man. That seventh strike was the final strike that Guy Faulkenberry was ever going to take.

Guy sat in the recliner as the storm outside grew louder. Lighting flashed brilliant silver and white all over. His hand tightened on the grip of the gun, his index finger on the trigger. With every flash he saw the gun in his hand, shiny and ready to go. The hairs on his arms began to bristle and somehow that was an indication that the lightning was coming to him.

Guy knew that the bolt was coming through the house to fry him in his recliner. Guy raised the gun, put it to his right temple, and steadied his hand. He was not nervous, and never had any second thoughts. He had to end it because the lightning had changed the man into something he hated. It had robbed him of his life, taken away all his joy, and stripped him of living a good and fulfilling life. He was going to take control and end things on his terms. No more living in fear of storms.

A crack of thunder roared loudly shaking the living room walls. Guy knew that this was it, now or never. He squeezed the trigger, the gun went off and a bolt of lightning came through the window and zapped Guy as brain matter blew to the other side of the dark living room against the far wall and into the floor. The bullet had shot through his head a fraction of a second before the lightning had hit him. He had beaten the lightning.

In the subsequent flashes of lightning, Guy lay slumped to the side, bleeding profusely out of the side of his head. His shirt had been burned as smoke steamed off of it. The recliner was catching on fire, and the arm that was holding the gun had been turned black.

The gun had fallen to the floor and his eyes were staring wide into the direction of nothing but the darkness of the room. The lightning flashed, brightening up the inside of the living room in split-second allotments, but Guy was not worried about the lightning anymore.

For the first time, he was faster than the lightning.

AUTHOR'S NOTES

This collection is the final batch that came from my archives from 1995-2021. Some people have asked me already if this collection of shorts and long fiction is as good as the last one, *Scarecrows and Shadows*. My answer is no. Since all the stories came from the same file, all I did was literally make a line right down the middle for two collections, with my previous editor. I didn't go into any detail on what story went where. I look at these two collections as one large volume.

So what makes a good story? Geez, that's a great question, right? I get asked that a lot. Sometimes people think that being a writer means you have all the answers. I can assure you– I don't. I am just as confused as everyone else out there. In fact, I'm still learning how to write, and I've been at this for decades now. I honestly don't think a writer masters the art. If a writer is any kind of writer at all, they grow and get better as their works go by. This applies to me. My hope is that I have gotten better as time has gone by. But have I mastered it? No, not even close.

But what makes a good story? Sorry– I got off point– which writers are prone to do. Too many rabbit holes in our minds. I think what makes a good story depends on the type of person that is asking. A good story is not a one-size-fits-all. It's not how that works. A good story is all about preferences, much like everything else in life. However, with that being said, there're some things that a good story has to have in order for anyone to call it a "good story".

A good story's first ingredient is that it has to have a good plot, something that is very engaging for the reader. Now, this can vary depending on a reader's preference. Some writers have cultivated a following over the years on the type of material they write, and those readers will read everything the author produces. However, not everything an author writes is good. All authors, even yours truly, have and will continue, to produce some clunkers here and there. It's all part of the process of being a writer. A good plot is essential for a good story. Sometimes, a writer can have a good plot, and the entire book can just misfire.

The second ingredient for a good story is how the author writes. Some authors, indie and mainstream, will do one of two things: fall in love with their power of description and bore their readers to tears, making them put their book down; OR they don't paint enough of a picture in their reader's mind, losing and confusing their audience, making them put the book down. The balance, that highwire act a writer must successfully do, is describing enough but still allowing the reader's mind to fill in the blanks. That's the hardest part of being a writer, at least to me. Sometimes I worry that I didn't write enough description or if it was complete overkill. My rule of thumb is: if it bores me, then it will bore the reader.

The third ingredient to a good story is all about being entertained. That's what a good story does– it takes you away and entertains you for as long as you read it. A lot of writers sometimes forget that. Not me. I'm very self-aware that a good story must, above all else, entertain you. If I'm not entertained writing the story, then rest assured that the reader won't find it that way either.

The last important ingredient of a good story are the characters. Without them, the story is not a story at all. The plot is a driver, but the characters within the plot make the story go. A writer has to form these characters to act a certain way in the story. And the reader has to buy what the character is doing, saying, and feeling. If a reader can't relate to, hate, or love at least one of the characters, then that character(s) becomes hollow, and a piece of the story is gone.

A good story, at the end of the day, is up to the reader to decide. I've had people not like what I felt was my best writing and choose something that I thought wasn't as good. Sometimes a writer doesn't know what story will connect with people. It's a literal roll of the dice. In this collection, what will you like?

Will you think *Halloween Night* is better than *Faster Than Lightning,* or vice-versa? I don't know. You could pick another short that you connected with much better. It's totally up to you and the good part is: you won't be wrong.

I want to also say a big THANK YOU to my new editor, Rebeka Arms, before I go. Rebeka took on this book last minute and really brought it to where it is now. Behind every good writer is an exceptional editor. This writer is no different. Having Rebeka on this project put my mind at ease, and I look forward to working with them in the years to come.

I want to close by saying how nice it is for us to be here again. We still have a long way to go, you and I. Four books in now, and it feels that we're getting to know one another, don't you think?

See you in time!

-Matthew McConkey, September 23rd, 2023

EXPECTATIONS AND PREDICTIONS

In 2000, I wrote a story about this group of guys that were talking about the future. I based this story on a similar discussion that me and my three friends had under an oak tree in my backyard one night. We each talked about our futures and where we saw ourselves when we reached thirty. How much would change? Where would we be? Would we have kids, be married, have a nice house and a good job? We were just sixteen at the time, but man did those questions weigh heavy. The point is, that most people don't meet their expectations.

SLUMBER PARTY

I had read a news article about this guy who killed his wife one night. He stabbed her dozens of times. When he was arrested, he claimed that he had no knowledge of doing it, and that he must have done it in his sleep. I wondered about that: could a person do something so terrible in their sleep and not know it? I remember when I was a kid, I used to have a bad habit of sleepwalking. One time, I was trying to put myself in the oven before my dad woke up and stopped me. So is it possible to do something crazy in your sleep? I explored this question in 2003.

DEATH ON A PARK BENCH

I remember writing this in 2005 after thinking one day, "What if Death just stopped and took a few minutes off?" What if Death itself had gotten tired of being death? This story has deeper meanings about life I think: the state of our lives, the constant day-to-day stuff we have to do, the feeling that we need a change but sometimes don't know what that change is, and having to go to a job that we hate. What if Death itself had all these feelings? I think this story speaks to all of us in some way or another, and we can relate to how Death is feeling on the park bench in this story.

HISTORY OF BIRCH

This story is a personal one for me. Back in 2003, my wife at the time had brought home a small birch tree that looked to me to be dead. She got it for $5 at Wal-Mart because they were about to trash it. So, she took a chance on it, and we planted it in our backyard, which had no trees or flowers in it at the time. Over the years and to my surprise, the tree came back to life and has now stood in my backyard since 2003, some nineteen years. It stands as a reminder to me to never give up, that even when something looks to be dead and gone, there might be life left to keep going. I remember writing this in 2012 when the tree was big enough to produce a nice shady spot in the summer.

THE CREATOR OF WORLDS

I wrote this short in 1997 when I read an article about a comic book artist who had sold his creation to one of the big comic book companies back in the day. That character had become somewhat famous and had a long run in comic book history. It even had some appearances in some blockbuster movies along the way. I always thought that this guy made a fortune off this creation. I was wrong. He said that he needed the money and sold the rights to his character and had no idea that the superhero would take off like it did. The company that now owned the character made a boatload of cash off of it, but the man that created it got zero because he sold his rights long ago. When I started doing research for the story, I discovered that writers, inkers, and artists within the comic book industry did not have much to fall financially back on. This was sad to me. This short is for all those creators of worlds out there who are still working those comic-cons.

ALL THAT WAS LEFT BEHIND

This story was written in about a few hours. It's a simple story, but a story that is pretty common. When people die, especially when they've lived a long life, the question comes up about what to do about all their belongings. That stuff that was bought and collected over the years had special meanings for the people who bought it. I call it junk, but some people call it treasure. To each their own, I guess. At any rate, somebody has to make a call on where all the stuff goes once the owners pass on if there's no will. Does it all get tossed into the trash? Does it get donated? Does it get sold at estate sales? Written in 2009, I explore two siblings having to deal with all this stuff in an attic that was amassed over the years by their parents.

EVENING DRIVE

In 2014, I wrote this short story in like an hour. It just seemed to pour out of me. It was based on a drive that me and my family made one night during a snow, and I wanted to get out in it in my truck and drive around my small town. We came down a hill on this back road, and my truck started to sway left to right from the snow and ice on the road. That was the first time I had ever been scared driving on snow. Then I was thinking, I'd hate to die just a mile from my house.

ROOMS OF AN EMPTY HOUSE

Written in late 2021, this short was the last story that I worked on that year. I had been dealing with the emotional toll that my divorce had taken on me and the changes that I was going through from when I filed to when things were officially over. It was a very tough and trying time. Writing was one of my outlets to work things out. This story is one of the products of my "working things out." It's about the end: looking back, surveying the land, looking at what was and what will never be. It's about the good and the bad that we all have in every relationship. This story is about looking at what life was like and trying to figure out what life is going to be.

THE HOWLERS

I tend to have very vivid nightmares and dreams from time to time. I guess it comes with the territory of being a writer. When your mind is constantly making stuff up, creating worlds, people, and places out of thin air, the brain doesn't know when to shut off. I remember some really scary dreams over the years that when I woke from them, they felt real and took hours to burn away in reality. Those particular nightmares and dreams feel real to me. I call them howlers. This was written in 2018.

HUSH

The influence for this story came from none other than my fanboy infatuation of *Tales from the Crypt*, both the show and comic book. I wanted to sit down and write a really good short that had a turn of events much like those stories from TFTC usually had. So, in 2002, I wrote an homage to TFTC.

JIMBO

Written in 2011 initially, this was just a goofy story to pass the time away. I had no idea where it was going until I had written three-quarters of it. I didn't plan it out, didn't really think about it much. I just wrote, what was to me, a funny short about a country farmer and an alien. There's not much to it. It was probably the most fun writing I've ever had.

WHAT EVER HAPPENED TO EDDIE MILLER?

I remember writing this in the summer of 1998, a year removed from high school. It was violent, and it was unlike anything that I had ever written before. There were several drafts and versions of this story over the years, but the mainstays that were written in '98 were never taken out. I personally think that every kid who has been bullied and pushed to the brink has given thought to doing something to their tormenter(s). It was originally collected in, *Toe Tags and Body Bags,* and I remember when it came out that it was pretty controversial at the time. I had people ask me if I was "right in the head" or did "I advocate violence" or the staple, "how could you think up something like this?" I had to remind people that it was a story, and nothing more. The act itself wasn't real life…but maybe the thoughts were.

FASTER THAN LIGHTNING

This story was inspired by the real man who was hit by lightning a record seven times, Roy Cleveland Sullivan. I read his story and was astonished that someone had been hit that many times. My astonishment then turned to a question: Why? What was it that attracted lightning to this one fella? To figure this out in my head, I started writing a story in 2008 about an unfortunate man from the first time he was hit by lightning to the last. Even in my own fictitious world, I couldn't figure out what it really was about him and the lightning. Some things I guess we'll never know.

A WALK IN THE PARK

I wrote this short many moons ago in 2008 and never liked it. Not that it wasn't a good story, it just never really flowed right. For some reason, I could never get this story the way I wanted it. I tried three or four different versions before this one. It's not my favorite short. I honestly thought about just shelving it. But I wanted to see if I could do something with it. The story came about while I was on my daily walk down at the town's park on the walking track. With my back turned to the woods, which are the very woods that are the inspiration for Hudson's Woods throughout my work, I heard what I thought was a bobcat. Then my mind wondered, *what if a bobcat comes from those woods and eats me? Who would know if it dragged me back into the woods and ate me down to the bones? People would think that I was just missing. My family would be frantic trying to find me. It would be the biggest mystery in my small town.* All these thoughts ran through my head in a matter of a few seconds. Needless to say, I finished up my walk and left.

HALLOWEEN NIGHT

This is another one of those shorts that was collected in, *Toe Tags and Body Bags*, that was controversial. It was originally called, "Clippers." I ended up changing the name and a lot of the story, most of all how it was told. "Halloween Night" is a violent telling of a man who murderers his entire family with a pair of oversized hedge clippers. How I got the idea for the story was one day, I was in my grandmother's tool shed, and I spied this huge pair of oversized hedge clippers hanging on the far wall. For some reason, that image of them hanging on the wall stuck with me over the years. Eventually, in 2002, I came up with a short about a man who got violent when drinking and took those clippers to his family.

BOOKS BY MATTHEW MCCONKEY

Home Again
Scarecrows and Shadows
Maple Lane
Everything Fades in Time
Summerland

www.ingramcontent.com/pod-product-compliance
Lightning Source LLC
Chambersburg PA
CBHW020745310726
48969CB00002B/431